D0774116

Some Kind of Wonderful

Sarah Webb was a children's bookseller for twelve years and now writes full time. She lives in Dublin with her partner and young family. She also reviews children's books for many Irish newspapers and magazines, and has written many of her own, including the popular *Kids Can Cook* series. She appears regularly on Irish television's *The Den*. Her previous novels *Always the Bridesmaid* and *Something to Talk About* were number-one bestsellers in Ireland and her next book *It Had to Be You* is being published later this year. She is currently working on her sixth novel, *Take a Chance*.

Find out more on her website www.sarahwebb.info.

'With two bestsellers already under her belt, Webb's talent to tap into the popular vein is undisputed' *Irish Independent*

'A modern-day fairy tale with the frogs (and even the odd Prince Charming) included!' *U Magazine*

Also by Sarah Webb

Always the Bridesmaid
Something to Talk About

Kids Can Cook
Kids Can Cook Around the World
Children's Parties
The Eason Guide to Children's Books

SARAH WEBB

Some Kind
of
Wonderful

PAN BOOKS

First published in Great Britain 2003 by Macmillan

This edition published 2004 by Pan Books
an imprint of Pan Macmillan Ltd
Pan Macmillan, 20 New Wharf Road, London N1 9RR
Basingstoke and Oxford
Associated companies throughout the world
www.panmacmillan.com

ISBN 0 330 41215 9

Copyright © Sarah Webb 2003

The right of Sarah Webb to be identified as the
author of this work has been asserted by her in accordance
with the Copyright, Designs and Patents Act 1988.

All rights reserved. No part of this publication may be
reproduced, stored in or introduced into a retrieval system, or
transmitted, in any form, or by any means (electronic, mechanical,
photocopying, recording or otherwise) without the prior written
permission of the publisher. Any person who does any unauthorized
act in relation to this publication may be liable to criminal
prosecution and civil claims for damages.

1 3 5 7 9 8 6 4 2

A CIP catalogue record for this book is available from
the British Library.

Typeset by IntypeLibra, London
Printed and bound in Great Britain by
Mackays of Chatham plc, Chatham, Kent

This book is sold subject to the condition that it shall not,
by way of trade or otherwise, be lent, re-sold, hired out,
or otherwise circulated without the publisher's prior consent
in any form of binding or cover other than that in which
it is published and without a similar condition including this
condition being imposed on the subsequent purchaser.

This one's for Ben with much love

Thanks

As always, to my wonderful family – Mum, Dad, Kate, Emma, Peter, Luan, Charlie and Richard. And to Ben and Sam – my favourite boys who keep me sane(ish!).

To Andrew Algeo for all the boozy and ambitious dinners, to Tanya Delargy and Nicky Cullen for being your wonderful, mighty selves and for putting up with me.

To all the community midwives at Holles Street Hospital, Dublin, for their support and care.

To Ali Gunn, my agent, for all her enthusiasm and sound advice. And to Jack – welcome to the world, baby boy.

To all the booksellers who have supported my books from the very beginning – especially Tom Owens, Alan Johnson, Eoin McHugh and David O'Callaghan in Eason. And good luck to Adrian White in all his future endeavours. To Maria Dickenson, Cathal Elliot and all the reps. Also Hilary Hamilton in Bridge Street Books, Michael Simmonds in The Exchange, Tony

Hayes and the gang in Bookstop, Dun Laoghaire, and last but not least, Bernie King and Christian Bradley, Bert Wright and Caron Butler for always making me feel so welcome in their shops. And a special thank you to Norman Brunker for the most enjoyable tour.

To Patricia Byrne and all the staff in Dalkey library for all their help with the research.

To all at Macmillan – especially Imogen Taylor, my editor, David North, David Adamson, Emma Bravo, Talya Baker and Trisha Jackson. And not forgetting Cormac Kinsella in Repforce.

To Lizzie Dunne and the staff at Dalkey Arts, for introducing me to the fascinating world of art galleries and letting me 'work' there.

To all at Louise Kennedy, including the good lady herself, for keeping me dressed in style and to Kate for all the fascinating clothes and fashion information and the dinky illustrations.

To Professor David McConnell for his time. And to Gerry Creighton Senior, Senior Animal Curator at Dublin Zoo – a man of great wisdom and generosity of spirit. I look forward to reading your autobiography some day!

To Nena Bhandari for letting me, Sam, and baby Charlie 'research' her wonderful Powerscourt wedding.

To Gus Nichols, for information on Hindu funerals in Ireland.

And, as always, to you, the reader. I hope you enjoy reading this book as much as I enjoyed writing it.

The following books were most useful and I would like to acknowledge them:
The Great Safari: The Lives of George and Joy Adamson, by Adrian House, Harvill, 1993
Last Animals at the Zoo, by Colin Tudge, Radius, 1991
Born Free, by Joy Adamson, Macmillan, 2000 (originally published in 1966 as *The Story of Elsa*)
Zoos and Animal Rights, by Stephen Bostock, Routledge, 1993
Some of My Best Friends are Animals, by Terry Murphy, Paddington Press, 1971

If you would like to help wildlife conservation by adopting an animal in Fota Wildlife Park, Cork, contact Fota on 021 4812678 or email *info@fotawildlife.ie*
If you would like to become a friend of Dublin Zoo or adopt an animal there, contact the zoo on 01 4748900 or check out their website – *www.dublinzoo.ie*

Sarah loves hearing from her readers. If you would like to contact her please write c/o Pan Macmillan.

'People travel to wonder at the height of mountains, at the huge waves of the sea, at the long courses of rivers, at the vast compass of the ocean, at the circular motion of the stars; and they pass by themselves without wondering.'

St Augustine

Rosie

'I'll be late home this evening,' Darren said, standing up. 'I'm showing a house.' He pushed the kitchen chair out with the back of his calves, making the legs screech loudly against the ceramic floor tiles.

Rosie winced. She hated when he did that but said nothing.

He leant down and kissed their four-year-old daughter, Cass, on the cheek. 'See you, poppet.'

'How late?' Rosie asked absently. She was watching Cass spoon more and more sugar onto her already sugar-saturated Frosties but she didn't have the energy to stop her.

'After nine, I'd say. Don't cook for me, I'll grab a sandwich or something in the office.'

'Fine.' She sighed. 'You're never home these days. If I didn't know better I'd think you were having an affair.'

'Listen, I have to go,' he said quickly. 'Will you be in later?'

'What are you talking about? Of course I'll be in. Where else would I be? Out clubbing in Lillie's with Cass? On a hot date with Brad Pitt?' She tried to catch his eye but he was staring at the door. 'Darren, what's wrong?'

'Nothing.' His hand was on the door handle. 'I just need to talk to you, that's all.'

She followed him into the hall. He opened the front door without looking back.

'Darren?' she said to his disappearing back. 'Darren?'

He turned around and gave her a lopsided smile. 'Everything's fine. I'll see you later.' He opened the door of the jeep and stepped inside. She was still standing on the doorstep in her stockinged feet, her arms folded around her body against the biting late-September wind.

Darren lowered his window and blew her a kiss.

'Are you sure you're OK?' she asked.

'Yes, stop fretting. Work's getting to me, you know how it is. Have a good day.'

'I'll try.'

She watched as he pulled out of the drive, gravel crunching under the chunky tyres, and drove down the avenue. There was definitely something up, but she couldn't quite put her finger on it. He wasn't himself at the moment and she was worried about him. Maybe he should go to the doctor for a check-up. It could be something quite simple – like his blood pressure for instance.

Cass looked up as Rosie walked back into the kitchen.

'Why are you shivering, Mummy?'

'I'm just cold.' She shouldn't have stood on the doorstep in her shirtsleeves. She sat down.

'I'm not cold,' said Cass.

'Good. Now eat up your Frosties.' Rosie leant over, removed the sugar bowl from the table and put it on top of the fridge.

'Mummy! I need that.'

'You also need your teeth,' she said firmly.

A short while later Rosie had managed to get Cass into the car.

'Mummy, Alex Hargreaves said I was a baby. I'm not a baby, am I?'

'No, love.' Rosie grabbed the seat belt and pulled it across her daughter's chest. 'Sit still, please, I can't buckle you in otherwise.'

Cass stopped wriggling. 'Can I have a treat?'

'You're not even in playschool yet. No.'

'Please?'

'No.'

Cass began to cry.

'Please stop crying, Cass. You can have something on the way home, OK?'

'Can I have some sweets?'

'No.'

She began to cry again.

Rosie gripped the steering wheel tightly. 'You can have a mini-Mars, OK?'

'Can I have two?'

3

'Yes, whatever.' She started up the engine and pulled out. It was nearly half nine and she'd never get into town by ten at this rate. At least the school was only down the road.

'Sorry we're late.' She smiled half-heartedly at Miss Morris, her daughter's teacher. The young blonde woman nodded curtly and finished reciting the days of the week in Irish. As Rosie walked quickly down the corridor she could hear the children chanting the months of the year after their teacher like a mantra. 'Wee Things' was a highly regarded playschool and day-care centre but sometimes she wished the teachers would lighten up a bit.

'Sorry I'm late.' Rosie pushed open the door of the meeting room. Emily Hayes, the managing director of Frames R Us and her boss looked up over the top of her half-moon reading glasses.

'What's new?' Emily smiled. It wasn't a pleasant smile. Rosie felt decidedly awkward.

'Don't worry.' Ruth, Rosie's assistant came to the rescue. 'We're flying along with the suggestions for the next season's prints, aren't we Emily?'

'Yes. Ruth even came in early to prepare the presentation. And I'm impressed, most impressed.'

Ruth beamed.

'Great.' Rosie took off her black suit jacket, hung it on the back of a chair and sat down. Bloody Ruth. Far too young and enthusiastic for her own good. Straight out of Rathmines College with a diploma in business after obtaining a first in history of art at Trinity College, Dublin, no less. Your average nightmare.

The way things were at the moment – juggling work, Cass and Darren – Rosie felt she was hanging onto her job by her fingernails. And being regularly late and having an angelically punctual assistant didn't help.

Emily pushed a sheet of paper towards her. 'Here are Ruth's ideas for the new range of motivational prints and art prints.'

Rosie scanned the sheet in front of her. '*Our* ideas,' she said after a moment. Mostly my ideas, she thought to herself.

Ruth smiled sweetly. 'Rosie did a lot of the work. I just added my creative input.'

Typing up the document and adding some graphics was hardly adding much creative input, Rosie thought to herself. But she hadn't had the time to do it and Ruth had offered to come in over the weekend, so she couldn't really complain.

'Let's get on, shall we?' Emily snapped. 'Rosie would you like to continue? Ruth and I were having a little informal chat about the proposals –' Emily looked at her pointedly – 'While we were waiting for you.'

Rosie cleared her throat. 'Good.' She tried not to be put off by her boss who was staring at her unnervingly. 'Well, for next season I've been looking at the market for new art prints and motivational prints. Motivational prints is an area that we've been extremely successful in over the past three years and one that can be expanded.' She pointed at a graph on the second sheet of the document. 'The sales figures are very strong, as you can see from the graph.'

'Yes, indeed.' Emily nodded.

'I was also looking at increasing the range of Irish art prints – including some more contemporary artists such as Alan de Markham, Graham Knuttel and—'

'Who?' Emily interrupted.

'Alan de Markham used to be a model and he's now one of Dublin's up-and-coming artists. If you turn to the back page, you'll see some of his work.'

Emily flicked through the pages in the folder. 'Is that his?' She pointed at a brightly coloured image of a group of women.

'No, that's a Graham Knuttel. Great, isn't it? I think the more contemporary offices would really—'

'Too modern.' Emily glanced at the remainder of the colour images, her nose wrinkling unbecomingly. 'All too modern. Not what our customers want.'

'But I think you'll find—'

'What are these?' Emily held up another page.

Ruth jumped in. 'I took the liberty of including some of my own ideas.' Rosie tried not to glare at her. 'They're Impressionist artists – lots of nice, gentle colours and tranquil scenes.'

'I like them,' said Emily. 'Much more suitable.'

'We've done them before!' Rosie protested. 'In fact, the majority of our back catalogue is made up of Impressionists. I thought it would be good to try something different, something new.'

'We haven't done these particular images before,' said Ruth. 'I checked.'

'Good, great,' Emily said firmly, closing the folder in front of her abruptly. 'We'll go with those. And the new motivational prints. Anything else?'

Rosie and Ruth both shook their heads.

'Excellent.' Emily stood up and left the room without a backward glance.

Rosie sighed inwardly while tidying up the meeting table. Ever since she'd been made creative director and marketing manager three years ago she'd been trying to change Emily's mind about art, but she had almost given up. Emily, as she was always telling anyone who'd listen, knew nothing about art but knew what she liked and she refused to allow Frames R Us to move forward.

'That went well, don't you think?' Ruth asked, a nervous edge on her voice.

'Ruth, please tell me if you've added anything to a presentation. It was a little embarrassing. And I wanted Emily to look at the Irish artists' work.'

Ruth looked at Rosie. There was a slight smile lingering on Ruth's lips.

'What?' Rosie demanded.

'You didn't honestly think she'd go for the Graham Knuttels did you?'

'Why not?'

'Her taste is stuck in the Dark Ages, that's why. You know that. I don't know why you bother.'

'Because I think we should be supporting our Irish artists, that's why,' Rosie said a little more strongly than she'd intended.

'This is a business, Rosie, not an art gallery.'

'I know. More's the pity. Anyway, we'd better get on with finding the copyrights on the Impressionist images.'

'Most of them are out of copyright,' said Ruth smugly.

'Are you sure?'

She nodded.

'Good. Well done.' It meant that no fees had to be paid for reproducing the images on posters. Smart girl, Rosie thought to herself.

'What are you doing for lunch?' asked Kim.

'Sorry,' said Rosie. 'I'm up to my tonsils here, maybe tomorrow.'

'No problem. How are things anyway?'

'The usual. Just about keeping it together.'

'You do too much. I'm always telling you to go part-time.'

'I know, I know. Listen, I'll talk to you later.'

'Too busy for your own sister, I don't know.' Kim laughed.

'It's not that . . .'

'I'm only joking. I know what it's like in there, I'll ring you this evening.'

Rosie rubbed her temples with her knuckles. She could feel a headache coming on. Maybe it was only dehydration – the office was really hot and muggy. She took a slug of water from the bottle of Ballygowan on her desk. She was trying to come up with a marketing plan for a new shop which was opening in Dun Laoire.

So far she'd jotted down 'grand opening – local cel-ebrity/politician'. Her heart just wasn't in it today. In fact, it hadn't been for a long time.

When she left college with a degree in history of art (with a second, unlike Ruth) she started working in Frames R Us on Wicklow Street. She'd had her heart set on working in an art gallery, and a print and framing shop, she thought at the time, was a step in the right direction. It was her first 'proper' job and she loved it. She had a real flair for choosing the right frame to suit every baby, christening, wedding and graduation photograph and she loved talking to the customers about the fine-art prints. She worked hard and in less than a year she was the manager of the shop and had made such a success of it that the owners, Emily's parents, asked her to help set up a new shop in Black-rock. Within three years Frames R Us had five shops and Rosie had been moved to the new 'head office' over the Wicklow Street shop.

But these days she was becoming more and more disillusioned with the work. Her priorities had shifted when she'd had Cass. Darren had encouraged her to keep working, but now she wasn't sure she was doing the right thing by any of them. She was so damn tired all the time and she never really got to see Cass at all. The weekends were spent trying to catch up on 'house' things – trying to stop the garden from becoming a complete wilderness, washing clothes, walls, hoover-ing, shopping – the list was endless.

Rosie's phone rang. She picked it up.

'Do you have the projected marketing plan for the Dun Laoire shop finished?' asked Emily curtly.

'Nearly. I'm working on it now.'

'I need it before the end of today. Maybe Ruth could help you.'

'Yes, thanks.' Rosie put down the receiver. She held her head in her hands and stared at the wall. Someone had replaced the dramatic bright red Georgia O'Keeffe poppies picture with a chocolate-box Renoir. Emily, she presumed. It was shaping up to be one of those days.

'Rosie?'

Darren walked into their bedroom that evening and flicked on the light. It was only just after nine but she was already fast asleep, her face buried in the pillow, breathing deeply.

He switched off the light and hesitated, then went back down the stairs, into the living room and took out his mobile. It was answered immediately.

'Hi, love. I'm just ringing to say goodnight.'

'Have you talked to her yet?'

'What? No, she's asleep.'

'Darren!'

'I know, but I don't have the heart to wake her. I'll talk to her tomorrow, I promise.'

'Do you mean it?'

'Of course I mean it.'

'I love you.'

'I know. Me too. Bye.'

He sat back on the sofa and stared straight ahead of him. His eyes were accosted by one of Rosie's new acquisitions – a huge original oil painting of some sort of white lily-type flower. It was much too in your face for his liking. Rosie said it reminded her of Georgia O'Keeffe, whoever that was. He had a good mind to take it down, put it the garage and replace it with his new framed poster of Tiger Woods. Soon, he promised himself, just bide your time.

'I'm not a bloody mind-reader,' said Rosie, banging the milk carton down on the kitchen table the following morning and sloshing milk all over the white ash surface. 'How was I supposed to know you needed your blue shirt today?'

Darren sighed and ran his fingers through his damp hair. He was standing in front of her, naked from the waist up. She noticed in passing that he'd lost some weight.

'You knew I had an auction today,' he said huffily. 'I presumed you'd realize . . .'

'Well, you shouldn't presume anything,' she said shortly, spooning the last of the Frosties into Cass's mouth. 'Run downstairs, there's a good girl and clean your teeth.' Cass jumped up. 'And don't forget to wash around your mouth,' she added to her daughter's disappearing back.

'You should go with her,' Darren said mildly. 'She never does her teeth properly.'

She glared at him. 'You go with her, then.'

'I'm sure she'll be fine.'

'Listen, I'm sorry your shirt isn't ready, OK?' She stood up and began to clear the breakfast bowls and plates into the dishwasher.

'I'll get the ironing board out. It's almost dry and if you give it an iron—'

'If *I* give it an iron.' She laughed maniacally. 'Cass is already late for school, I've no make-up on and I have to fix her school lunch. I don't think so.'

'It's an important auction. You know how bad I am at ironing. Please? Just this once.'

She sighed. It wasn't worth arguing with him. 'Give it to me. Go and check Cass is ready.'

Ten minutes later Darren had left in his precious blue shirt and Rosie was hurrying Cass out the front door. She strapped her into the car, threw the pink Barbie school bag onto the floor under the pink runnered feet, ran back to the hall, grabbed her make-up bag, work bag and coat and pulled the front door behind her with her foot, nearly straining a calf muscle in the process. Flinging everything onto the front passenger seat she smiled at Cass.

'Are you OK, love?'

'Fine, Mummy.'

'Good girl. Where's your coat? Did you take it off?'

Cass shrugged her shoulders.

'Damn!' Rosie jumped out of the car, opened the front door, dashed up the stairs and grabbed the small pink coat from the back of the bedroom door.

Reaching the car again she took a deep breath before

turning the key in the ignition. She was running twenty minutes late. If Dublin Corporation hadn't decided to install some new roadworks this morning she might just get into town on time, fingers crossed.

Rosie

'Hi, Rosie.' Darren walked into the living room that evening and collapsed beside her on the sofa. 'I have something to tell you. It's important.'

She peeled her eyes off the screen where Paul and Niamh, her favourite *Fair City* characters were having a blazing row. You could always rely on the Dublin soap for a good fight. She hadn't expected Darren until later and she was already in her pyjamas with a rug pulled over her legs and cuddled around her feet which always felt the cold – bad circulation, her mother always said.

'Um?' she murmured, her eyes sneaking back to the television after a few seconds.

'I'm having an affair.'

'An affair? Who's having an affair?' She began to pay attention.

'I am,' he said nervously.

She looked at him incredulously and began to laugh. 'Good one!'

14

'I really am.'

She looked at him again, more carefully this time. His face was pale and he was picking at the skin around his nails. He always did this when he was anxious.

'You're serious?'

He nodded.

Rosie felt the blood drain from her face. She could hear blood rushing past her ears and her heart beating faster and faster.

'Are you all right?' he asked.

'No,' she whispered. 'No.'

She began to watch the telly screen again. Niamh and Paul had stopped arguing and were now passionately embracing. How ironic, she thought to herself.

'Rosie? Rosie?'

She looked over at him. She felt as if she was underwater. Everything was happening in strange slow motion, dragging along. 'Yes?'

'I think we should talk about this.'

'OK. I presume you're not going to see her again.'

'I don't think you understand. I've decided—'

'These things happen,' she interrupted. 'I'm sure it was just a drunken fling with a girl in the office, wasn't it? Some floozy. Darren?'

He was staring at the floor and shaking his head.

'Stop! I'm leaving you. It's over.'

'What? I don't understand.'

'I'm in love with her. I don't want to be with you any more.'

Rosie felt like she wanted to cry. She had a huge lump in her throat and her eyes prickled but no tears seemed to come out, but inside she was crying her heart out.

'Who? Who is she?'

'I don't think—'

'Tell me! I have a right to know.'

Darren shrugged. He'd have to tell her sooner or later so he figured he might as well tell her now and get it over with. 'Tracy.'

'Tracy who?'

'Tracy Mullen.'

'Not the receptionist!' Rosie snorted. 'The blonde one?'

'She's not the receptionist any more. She's a trainee estate agent now in Ryan's.'

'But she's only nineteen.'

'She's twenty-two.'

'She probably still lives at home.' She looked at him and he looked away. 'She does, doesn't she?'

'So what if she does? Her parents are really nice—'

'You've met her parents? How long has this been going on?'

'Fifteen months.'

Fifteen days, Rosie said to herself. Just over two weeks. He's been lying to me for two weeks.

'Since the Milan trip,' he added.

'The Milan trip? That was last year.' Then the penny dropped. He'd said fifteen *months*.

'We really hit it off. Neither of us meant it to happen, it just did. And then at last year's Christmas party—'

'I was at the Christmas party,' she murmured.

16

'We want to get our own place,' he said, ignoring her. 'In town maybe.'

'You could always move in with her parents,' Rosie said sarcastically. 'That would be fun.'

'Stop it! She's a nice girl.'

'Nice girl, my ass! Nice girls don't go around stealing other people's husbands and breaking up families.'

'It was wasn't her fault.' Darren unfastened his watch and rubbed his wrist. 'Our marriage isn't exactly great, is it?'

'What are you talking about?'

He waved his hands in the air. 'All this. The arguments, snapping at each other, the boredom. We haven't had sex for weeks.'

'It's called real life. I didn't realize that you were so unhappy. You should have told me.'

'What was there to say? That I was sick of you? That I couldn't stand living with you? That you'd turned into your mother?'

'That's not fair! I'm nothing like my mother. And yes, if you were so bloody unhappy you *should* have told me. At least then we could have tried to do something about it. Talked about it, gone to counselling. Instead you've just taken the easy way out.'

'Meaning?'

'It's much easier to leave than to stay and work things out, isn't it? Trade me in for a new model who isn't tired all the time from running a house and looking after Cass, not to mention working full-time.'

'You don't look after Cass. The crèche does. And it was your choice to work, not mine. It's not my fault that you're tired all the time. Or that you feel guilty about working and not seeing Cass all day.'

She felt like she'd been slapped in the face. 'How dare you!' Rosie said, her body finally allowing itself to cry. 'I *do* look after Cass. And it *was* you who encouraged me to work so hard. How do you think we can afford this house? My bloody wages, that's how.' She wiped her eyes on the back of her hand and stood up. 'I'm going upstairs. If you're thinking of staying, you can sleep on the sofa.'

'Rosie!' he called after her. 'Rosie!'

She ran up the stairs, into the en-suite bathroom and closed the door. Tears were running down her face and she was finding it hard to catch her breath. She sat on the cold tiled floor, put her head in her hands and rocked backwards and forwards.

After a few minutes she heard a gentle knock on the door.

'Rosie? Are you OK?'

She ignored him.

When her breath had become less laboured and she'd splashed some cold water on her red puffy eyes, she decided to go back downstairs and face him. As she walked slowly towards the top of the stairs she could hear him talking to someone in a low voice on his mobile. She heard him say 'Yes, love, I've done it' and her heart sank. Bastard! She stood perfectly still before taking a deep breath and walking back to the bedroom. She took two sleeping pills and fell into a deep, dreamless sleep.

*

My head, Rosie thought as she woke up. She glanced over at the alarm clock on the bedside table. It was just after six in the morning. Where was Darren? Realization shot through her like a poison dart. She lay in bed, thoughts racing through her mind faster and faster, making her heart pound. How was she going to get through today? Maybe it would be best to go into work, at least she wouldn't have time to think about things. But she wasn't sure if she could face Emily today – if her boss gave her a hard time she knew she'd start crying or something and she couldn't bear that. No, she'd call in sick and stay at home. And she'd keep Cass with her. God knows she needed some distraction. And what Darren had said last night about Cass had really hit a raw nerve. Maybe she wasn't a good mother. Maybe he was right.

She picked up the phone and dialled her boss's direct line. 'Emily, this is Rosie. I just wanted to let you know that I have a really bad stomach bug and I'll be off for a few days. I'll ring tomorrow and give you an update. Bye.' She put down the receiver feeling decidedly guilty. She knew it was cowardly, leaving a message at this early hour when there was no hope of even workaholic Emily being in the office, but she felt relieved that she wouldn't have to deal with it later.

A striking image came floating into her head – Tracy's mane of blonde curls brushing Darren's naked chest. She gasped as a dagger of pure anguish shot through her heart. Only a few weeks ago, when Tracy had still been the receptionist in Diffney's Estate Agents, she'd had a perfectly pleasant conversation with the girl about the terrible weather they'd been having.

Rosie began to wonder where Darren and Tracy met. They could hardly carry on when the parents were in the same house, could they? All those evenings he said he was working late and showing houses they must have been meeting up. And maybe his 'business trips' weren't business trips at all. She sat up suddenly. She had to know. She pulled on her white towelling dressing gown and went downstairs. Darren was on the couch, snoring gently. She watched his chest move up and down with his breath and for a split second thought of grabbing a cushion and pressing it against his lying face.

'Darren?' She knelt on the floor beside him and shook him.

He grunted.

'I want to talk to you.'

He opened his eyes slowly. 'What time is it?' he asked sleepily. His watch was on the coffee table.

'Nearly seven.'

Darren stretched his arms above his head and groaned. She watched this familiar morning ritual. He still seemed like the same old Darren, nothing had changed. Maybe this would all blow away. If he'd promise never to see her again and attend counselling everything might be all right again. It would take time but . . .

'What is it?' he asked, sitting up. He rubbed his eyes and pulled the blanket up over his chest.

'When do you see her? I need to know.'

'Do we have to go into this now?'

She nodded firmly.

'OK then.' He sighed. 'After work and sometimes at the weekends.'

'Where?'

'Hotels mainly. And houses.'

'Houses?'

He had the good grace to blush slightly. 'Only the ones they've moved out of already.'

'You mean the houses you were selling?' she asked incredulously. 'Clients' houses?' If it weren't so close to home she'd laugh. It was like something from a *Carry On* film.

'The odd time. Listen, do you really have to know all this?'

'Will you stop seeing her?'

Darren stared at her. 'What do you mean?'

'What I said.'

'Why would I stop seeing her?'

'I think you should get some perspective on all of this. Talk to someone, a counsellor or something. We've been married for five years, for goodness sake. You can't just throw it all away. There's Cass to consider, too.'

'You'd have me back?'

'I'd consider it.'

'And you're not angry with me?'

'Of course I am. But it's our marriage we're talking about, not some sort of stupid tiff. I haven't given up on it, you have.'

Darren looked at her carefully. 'Actually, I haven't completely made up my mind what I'm going to do.'

She felt a faint glimmer of hope.

'You'll have to give me some time,' he said, 'to think things over.'

'I'm not waiting months for a decision. And while you're thinking about it, I want you to promise that you won't see her.'

'It's not that simple,' he protested.

'It's that simple to me. Stop seeing her and move out.'

'Where to?'

'To your brother's I suppose, or a B & B.'

'I suppose Jeff might let me stay for a bit.' Jeff was Darren's younger brother. 'But what would I tell him?'

'You could try the truth.' She stopped herself adding 'for a change'.

'Mummy. What time is it?'

Rosie was sitting at the kitchen table later the same morning flicking through a copy of *Cosmopolitan* which she'd bought last week but hadn't found the time to read yet. She'd bought it for the sex tips – '101 Ways to Spice up Your Love Life' – but this morning she had skipped that section and gone straight to the agony aunt instead. Maybe someone else's problems would take her mind off things. She was still in her pyjamas and dressing gown, which she was finding most liberating. If the whole business with Darren wasn't dancing around in her brain, she'd be feeling quite chirpy. She'd

gone back to bed when Darren had gone to work and
he'd promised to call in that evening to collect some
clothes and to see Cass.

She looked at her daughter. Her Barbie pyjamas
were ruffled and her curly brown hair hung in messy
clumps around her face. Cass had inherited her father's
great skin and bright blue eyes and she was a stunning child. At times she couldn't believe she and her
daughter were related. 'It's nearly ten. Would you like
some Frosties?'

Cass smiled, her little white teeth visible. 'Yes,
please, Mummy. Is it Saturday? Is Daddy away?'

'No love, it's Tuesday. But we're both having a day
off today. I thought we might go to the cinema and to
Burger King later. Would you like that? We might even
go to Dun Laoire and get a treat.'

'Yes! Is it my birthday?'

'No.' She smiled. 'We're having a special day
together. Just you and me.'

'I love you, Mummy!' She threw her little arms
around Rosie's waist and gave her a big hug. 'Big hug
for Mummy.'

Rosie took a deep breath. Tears began to seep into
her eyes and she willed them back. She patted Cass on
the top of her head. 'Sit up at the table and I'll pour
you some Frosties.'

'That was brilliant!' Cass beamed. 'I love Tigger.
Bouncy, bouncy, bouncy.' She jumped up and down,
pulling out of Rosie's arm in the process.

Rosie laughed. 'You're my own little Tigger, love.' She winced as Cass pulled a little too hard on her arm. 'Would you like a burger now?'

'Burger, yum yum.'

As they walked down the main street towards McDonald's, Cass swung her arm animatedly. She was in flying form. She hadn't had her mummy all to herself for a long time.

Rosie couldn't remember the last time she'd taken Cass to the cinema. She and Darren used to take her together sometimes as a treat but they'd got out of the habit recently, which was a shame. She'd forgotten how much fun it was. And she'd enjoyed *The Tigger Movie* almost as much as her daughter had. She'd always liked Winnie the Pooh as a child. I should buy the book and read it to Cass, Rosie mused as they passed an Eason Bookshop.

'We'll just pop in here for a second,' she told Cass.

'I'm hungry, Mummy,' Cass complained.

'Let's find a Tigger book, shall we?'

In the children's department Cass immediately spotted a movie tie-in Tigger book and Rosie found a copy of A. A. Milne's *The House at Pooh Corner* just beside it. Passing the popular psychology department on the way to the till Rosie noticed a whole shelf of divorce and separation books.

Typical, she thought to herself. When you're pregnant you see pregnant women everywhere, when you're buying a house 'For Sale' signs jump out at you, now it's divorce books. She toyed with the idea of buying one, just in case, then decided that would be bad karma.

'Thanks, Mummy,' Cass smiled as they left the shop. 'It has stickers, you know.'

'What has stickers, love?' Rosie was miles away.

'My book.'

'That's nice,' she said, hoping that the stickers would stay in the book this time and not be plastered across Cass's bedroom walls and heater, like last time. 'Look, Cass, they have Tigger toys with the kid's meals.' She pointed at a poster in the window of McDonald's.

'This is the best day ever,' Cass beamed as they walked into the burger joint, 'isn't it?'

'Yes,' Rosie lied. 'The best.'

By six o'clock Rosie was exhausted. Cass had gone to bed blissfully early and Rosie was now collapsed on the sofa, her eyes closed. Her body had wiped out but her mind was still racing. Images of Darren and Tracy were swimming before her eyes so she snapped them open. She toyed with the idea of ringing Kim. But until things were clearer she didn't want to tell anyone, her sister included. After all, it might just be a blip in their otherwise unsullied marital record. Darren had said that he hadn't made his final decision. Maybe there was still hope.

She wondered how things would be if they got over this. Would life get back to normal? Would she ever be able to trust him again? If Darren said he was working late, would she believe him? If he said he was going to

London on business, would she follow him over and check on him? Or hire a private investigator . . .

Stop it! she told herself. She heard a key turn in the door and she sat up. Darren.

She heard him drop his briefcase at the door and walk upstairs. She sat and listened. Nothing. She thought she heard the faint thud of a drawer being pushed in and the click of a wardrobe door.

'Darren?' she called a few minutes later as she walked up the stairs.

He came to the bedroom door. 'You gave me a fright.' He looked at her carefully. 'You're home early. You don't usually get in till well after six.'

'Can I come in?' she asked. He was blocking the doorway of the bedroom. He hesitated, then stood aside.

The bed was littered with piles of clothes – work shirts still on their hangers, his dark grey 'good suit', T-shirts, jeans, trousers, boxer shorts and balls and balls of black or white socks. He didn't buy any other kinds of socks – just black and white. So he didn't have to worry about matching pairs, he always said. Black went with black, white with white – it kept things simple. Was that what he was doing now, she wondered, keeping his life simple? No wife, no daughter, no fuss.

'What are you doing?' she asked quietly.

'What does it look like? I'm packing. Have you seen the large suitcase? Is it still in the attic?'

She stood and stared at him. 'Where are you going?'

'To Jeff's. I thought you said . . .'

'I didn't think you'd go today, that's all. I thought we'd talk about it more.'

'I think it's for the best. I'll come and see Cass at the weekend, if that's OK.'

'The weekend?'

'Have you something planned?'

'No, it's just . . .' She tried not to cry but tears were stinging the back of her eyes.

'What?' he asked gently.

'She'll miss you. She's used to seeing you every day. What will I tell her?'

'That I'm working. Don't worry, it'll be fine. She won't even notice, you'll see.'

Rosie looked at him in amazement. He had no idea. Was he really that naive? 'I'll get the suitcase for you. It's in the garage.' As she turned away tears spilled from her eyes, down her cheeks and onto the carpet. *Their* carpet.

She walked down the stairs clutching the balustrade. In the garage she leant against the cool concrete wall and took several deep breaths. Somehow she had to get through this. For everyone's sake.

'Here you are.' She leant the suitcase against the end of the bed. 'Do you really need so many clothes? You can always call back for things.'

Darren gave her a half smile. 'I think it's best if I don't.' He started layering his clothes into the suitcase. 'What time on Saturday suits? I thought I'd take her swimming.'

'Swimming?' Rosie was confused. He'd never taken Cass swimming before. That was always her job – when

27

he was playing golf. If that was what he'd really been doing on Sunday afternoons – she just wasn't sure any more.

'In the sports centre,' he continued. 'May as well use it, the membership's enough. Cass likes swimming, doesn't she?'

'Yes. She loves it.'

'Well?'

'Well what?'

'What time suits on Saturday? I'll call in to collect her. Are you all right?'

'Of course I'm not bloody all right. What do you expect?' She sat down on the bed, the hook of a wire coat hanger digging into the flesh of her bottom. She started crying again. 'Don't go! We'll work this out, you'll see. It'll be fine . . .'

'Rosie, things haven't been fine for a long time. You know that.'

'I don't know that. I thought everything was normal. I thought we were just getting on with life, the same as everyone else.'

'I wasn't happy.'

'So you keep saying. But no one said marriage was going to be easy. I don't understand why you are throwing everything away for a fling.'

'It's not a fling.'

'What then? An affair?' she snorted. 'You hardly think it's going to last, do you?'

He was silent for a few seconds. Then he said, 'Excuse me.'

She looked at him.

'You're sitting on my shirts.'

She sat up and he pulled them out from under her. She hoped they were well and truly creased.

'Do you still love me?' she asked, staring at her hands.

'I don't know.'

'Do you love her?'

'Yes,' he said quietly. 'I think so.'

She stood up. She felt faint and a little nauseous. 'Two o'clock on Saturday. I'm going to check on Cass.'

'Rosie . . .'

'Stop! I'm tired. Just leave me alone.'

'Charming,' he muttered as she left the room.

She sat on the edge of Cass's bed. Tiny stars of light flickered around the room from the night light. Darren had bought it for her in New York when he'd been at a conference and she loved it. And now her beloved Daddy was going to break her tiny little heart. It was too much to bear. Tears spilled down Rosie's face again. She sat and watched her daughter breathing until she heard the front door bang several minutes later. Then she slowly got up and went back into the bedroom. A ball of black socks sat forlornly on the white duvet cover, forgotten by their owner. She picked them up, opened the window and threw them out angrily.

It was only seven o'clock but she felt like death. She got undressed, removed the make-up from her blotchy red face and popped two sleeping pills. As she began to feel woozy she realized that she'd forgotten to brush her teeth. But that, she decided, was the least of her worries.

Rosie

'It's a bright and dry morning. Everybody up! And now it's our old mates U2 with "Beautiful Day".'

Rosie leant over and hit the alarm clock-radio with her hand. Most mornings she enjoyed *The Ian Dempsey Breakfast Show*, he had a lively yet easy-going manner, but this morning wasn't most mornings. She groaned and opened her eyes. She'd forgotten to draw the curtains fully last night and she could see grey sky outside which definitely threatened rain. Wherever Ian Dempsey was, he wasn't in Glenageary!

She pushed herself up with her arms. She felt terrible. Her eyes hurt, her head hurt and she felt nauseous again. Wouldn't it be ironic if I had morning sickness, she thought. Although she realized it wasn't possible as she'd had her period two weeks ago and herself and Darren hadn't had sex since. In fact, carnal knowledge had been decidedly thin on the ground recently. She'd put it down to both of them being exhausted most of the time. At weekends they usually managed it, unless Darren had been overindulging at the golf club and had fallen sound asleep as soon as his head had hit the pillow. And on bank holidays and when they were away. So much for their trying for a second baby.

As far as she could tell from magazines and from friends, their sex life was pretty normal. Or so she'd thought. She hadn't realized that there'd been other reasons for his sexual apathy. Or, to be correct, another reason – Tracy Mullen.

Now will I go into work or not? she pondered. She was tempted to lie back down again, pull the covers over her head and never surface, but she knew this wasn't realistic. I may as well go in, she decided. It will keep my mind off Darren.

'Are you feeling better?' asked Ruth. 'You look a little pale.'

'I'm fine, thank you,' said Rosie. 'Just a touch of food poisoning, nothing serious.'

'I finished the marketing plan for Dun Laoire. I wasn't sure if you'd be in today and Emily wanted it finished. Here, have a look.'

Rosie bit her lip. She'd wanted to complete it herself. She read through the impeccably laid-out pages. It was good, very good. She couldn't have done better herself. 'Thank you,' she said, handing her back the sheets. 'This is excellent. You can give it to Emily.'

'You don't want to change anything? Or add anything?'

'No, it's perfect.'

Ruth beamed. 'I was up till all hours last night getting it finished. I'm glad you like it.'

For a split second Rosie was reminded of herself – before she'd got married and had Cass. Where had all her old enthusiasm gone? 'You're doing really well. Keep it up.'

'Thanks.' Ruth smiled.

'Hi, Rosie, what's up?' Kim said. 'You were supposed to ring me. Remember?'

Rosie wedged the receiver between her right shoulder and her right ear, leaving her hands free to rummage through her in tray. 'Sorry, I've been really busy.' She found a handwritten letter and opened it with a biro.

'What have you been doing?'

'Nothing much. This and that.'

'Are you reading something while you're talking to me?'

She put down the letter. 'No, of course not. What were you saying?'

Kim laughed. 'I'm calling over for dinner tonight. Greg's working late. I'll cook. You just buy some wine, OK?'

'But Darren—'

'Is meeting his mates from the golf club as it's Wednesday night. Creatures of habit, the pair of you. So stop trying to wriggle out of it. I'll see you at seven.'

'But—' Her sister put down the phone on her.

*

'How's my favourite god-daughter?' Kim kissed the top of Cass's head.

Cass looked at her aunt beseechingly. 'Anything for me?'

'Cass!' Rosie scolded. 'That's rude.'

Kim laughed. 'It's all right. I might just have a little something. But only if you help me cook, Cass. You don't want to end up like your mother, do you? A disaster in the kitchen?'

Cass shook her head gravely. 'I'll help you, Kim. I'll put on my apron. Where is it, Mummy?'

'On the back of the kitchen door. I'll get it for you.'

Kim dumped the plastic shopping bags on the granite kitchen counter. 'I always mean to use my "green bags",' she said as she unpacked the groceries. 'I have them in the car and now and again they look at me accusingly. But I never remember to bring them into the supermarket with me.'

'I'm the same,' Rosie admitted.

'Our teacher says we should always recycle everything,' said Cass. 'Jam jars, I think. And we always use toilet rolls for making things in school, don't we, Mummy?'

'Yes, love.'

Kim looked at her sister. She was very pale and she had dark circles under her eyes. She also seemed edgy.

'Why don't you go into the playroom and watch your video of the Muppets?' Kim suggested to Cass. 'Call me when Miss Piggy's on.'

'OK.' Cass skipped off, thoughts of helping cook forgotten.

33

Rosie hung the tiny Beatrix Potter apron back on the hook.

'What's up, sis?' Kim asked gently. 'You're not yourself.'

'I'm just tired. I haven't been sleeping very well.'

'Have you been taking the sleeping tablets?' Kim knew all about Rosie's recurring insomnia. It was she who'd persuaded her sister to see Dr Donald about it a couple of years ago. He'd said it was caused by stress.

'Sometimes.'

'You should. Everyone needs a decent night's sleep. Especially someone as busy as you are.'

'What are you cooking?' asked Rosie.

'Are you trying to change the subject?'

'No. I'm just hungry.'

'Chicken fajitas. You can cut the chicken up, I'll do the onions and peppers. If you use the scissors it'll be easier.'

'Deal.' She opened a drawer and pulled out the new kitchen scissors that Kim had given her for Christmas.

'Have you never used them?' Kim laughed as Rosie took the cardboard and plastic wrapping off.

'No. I've been too busy to cook.'

Kim smiled. 'That's why I'm here.'

'How's Greg?' Rosie asked as she cut the chicken into strips. Greg was Kim's boyfriend. He worked in the Bank of Ireland with her and they'd been together for three years. To Rosie it seemed that Kim and Greg lived very independent lives – too independent for her taste – they did an awful lot of things without each other – but it seemed to suit them both.

'The usual.' Kim pulled the skin off the onions and began to chop them. 'We're thinking of going away to Wexford for the October bank holiday. You and Darren should come. There's this nice hotel there with a kids' club and a swimming pool. Cass would love it.'

'That sounds lovely, but Mum won't be too pleased. It's Dad's birthday, remember. She'll want us all over for dinner as usual.' She ignored the fact that Darren was unlikely to be going on holidays with herself and Cass ever again.

'She can go take a flying jump. I need a break and Greg's been working far too hard for his own good.'

'You can tell her, then. How is she, anyway?'

'Has she not rung you this week?' Kim smiled. 'She must be busy with her new antiques course. Has she told you about it?'

Rosie groaned. 'Not another course. She was bad enough after the wine one. Now she'll think she's an expert in antiques too.'

Kim laughed. 'I know.'

'What does Dad think of it?'

'You know Dad. He's keeping a low profile as usual.'

'As long as she doesn't try to value all our furniture.'

'No doubt she will.'

'Anyway, at least we know it's only a passing fad. Her Italian for art lovers phase was over almost as soon as it began. Now, what do I do with the chicken?'

'Heat some oil in a frying pan,' Kim said patiently – she was well used to her sister's ineptitude in the kitchen – 'and drop the chicken in gently. And stir.

I'll put the onions and peppers in when I've finished chopping them.'

'OK.' While the pan was heating on the ring Rosie pulled a bottle of white wine out of the fridge. 'Would you like a glass?'

'Is the Pope a Catholic?' Kim smiled. Rosie poured her a glass and they leaned against the kitchen counter and sipped amicably.

'Will I put the chicken in now?'

Kim looked at the pan on the hob. It wasn't hot enough. 'I'll do it. You go and check on Cass.'

'Are you sure?'

She nodded, turned up the heat and began to drop the ingredients into the sizzling pan. As she stirred she surveyed the room. The smart, top-of-the-range kitchen with its American-style larder fridge and chunky, stainless-steel Smeg cooker was wasted on her sister. What she wouldn't give to have a kitchen like this. Although if it meant being married to Darren, she wasn't sure it was worth it. She'd never trusted Darren – he was too good-looking. Too good-looking and far too charming. But he treated Rosie well and he doted on Cass. There was just something about him that she didn't like – she couldn't quite put her finger on it.

Darren couldn't understand why she and Rosie had to talk to each other nearly every day. If he only knew – it was actually more like several times a day some weeks. She had stopped calling around in the evenings so much as Darren was never exactly thrilled to see her. Not that he'd said anything, of course. He was always more than polite. 'It's Kim, again' he'd say, or 'Kim's dropped in, isn't that a nice surprise?'

Rosie came back into the kitchen. 'Cass says you've missed Miss Piggy but she'll rewind it for you later.'

Kim smiled. 'Little sweetie.' She poured Tex-Mex sauce into the frying pan and stirred.

'Sauce from a bottle,' Rosie teased. 'I'm shocked.'

'I'm starving. I don't have the energy to make a proper sauce. Here.' She handed Rosie a packet of tortillas. 'Wrap these in tin foil and put them in the oven on a low heat.' She watched her sister for a minute. 'Rosie, you need to take the plastic off them first,' she said, trying not to smile.

'Sorry. I was miles away.'

'Are you sure there's nothing wrong?'

'No, honestly. Work's getting to me a bit, that's all.'

'Emily being a bitch?'

'Something like that. I'm a bit premenstrual too. Now is there anything else I can do?'

'You could cut the lettuce up. And then we're pretty much set.'

They chatted easily over dinner, Rosie fielding any questions about Darren with aplomb. She was proud of herself but exhausted with the strain of not letting anything slip.

'You have sauce all around your mouth.' Kim smiled.

'So do you.' She tore off two sheets of Winnie the

Pooh kitchen roll, handed one over and wiped her own mouth with the other.

'I presume Cass chose this.' Kim looked at the pictures on the paper.

'Who else?'

'What time's Darren back?'

She could feel her body stiffen. 'Late. There's something on this evening – a prize giving I think.'

Kim looked at her watch. 'I'd better get going soon enough. Jump on Greg before he falls asleep on me.'

She laughed. 'I know the feeling. I'll give you a ring at the weekend.'

'Make sure you do.' Kim stood up.

'Thanks for bringing dinner,' Rosie said, showing her to the door.

'My pleasure.' Kim gave her a kiss on the cheek. 'Take care of yourself.'

'I will.' She closed the door behind her sister and leant against it. She was wiped out. She went back into the kitchen and tidied up a little before flicking off the lights.

Rosie

'Where's Daddy?' Cass asked on Saturday morning as she had on Wednesday, Thursday and Friday mornings.

'Away working, love,' said Rosie, trying to sound normal. 'He'll be here later to take you swimming.'

'Swimming! Yippee!'

'Eat your Special K.'

'Don't like it.' Cass poked the soggy brown flakes with her spoon despondently.

'I'm sorry. But I don't have anything else. I haven't been shopping yet. I could make you some toast.'

Cass wrinkled her nose. 'Maybe Daddy will get me a treat.'

'I'm sure he will. But you still have to eat some breakfast.'

'Mummy,' Cass moaned.

The doorbell rang. She glanced at her watch. It was only half ten and she wasn't expecting anyone. She pulled her towelling dressing gown around herself and answered the door.

'Hi, Rosie,' said Darren. 'I know I'm early but I didn't think you'd mind. Can I take Cass now?'

She stared at him and cursed inwardly. Twelve o'clock, he'd said. She'd had the whole morning planned carefully – shower, wash and blow-dry her hair, put on a little make-up and her favourite pair of lycra-mix black trousers and a white shirt, and be calm and composed when he called. Instead here she was – a sleepy bag lady. Typical! Things were just getting better and better.

'I suppose so. You'd better come in.'

'Daddy!' Cass flew into his arms. 'Where have you been? I've missed you.'

He swooped her up and tossed her over his shoulder. 'How's my favourite sack of potatoes?'

She giggled and kicked her feet in the air. 'Put me down, Daddy,' she admonished.

He dropped her gently to the floor and patted her nappied bottom. 'Go on upstairs and wash your teeth. I'll be up in a minute.'

They both watched her little padded bottom waddle up the stairs.

'I thought she was out of nappies,' said Darren.

'She was. She's been wetting the bed the last few nights.'

He raised his eyebrows. 'Is that normal?'

She stared at him. 'She's missing you. She doesn't understand. I'll go up and get her dressed.'

'I'll go.'

'No. You stay here.' She was damned if he was going to flounce around the house as if nothing had changed.

When she came back down with Cass, Darren was sitting in front of the television in the living room watching an old black-and-white John Wayne Western. She coughed.

He looked around. 'All ready, Cass?'

'What about Mummy?'

'Mummy's staying here. She's got things to do, don't you, Rosie?'

She was tempted to say no but she decided to play along – for Cass's sake.

'Yes, I have to tidy the house. Daddy will drop you back later.'

Cass looked at Rosie and Darren. 'And stay?'

'Let's go swimming,' he said quickly. 'Are you ready? And maybe we'll get some sweets on the way back.'

Cass's eyes lit up. 'Mummy never lets me have sweets. Can I have jelly tots and some baby marsh-mallows?'

'You can have whatever you like.'

Rosie sighed. 'Please don't let her have too many sweets. You know they're bad for her teeth.'

He looked at her with a strained expression on his face. 'Whatever. See you later.'

'What time?' she asked.

'About one or two.'

'Well, which is it – one or two?'

He looked at her strangely. 'You're not doing anything else are you? Does it matter?'

'I might go out for lunch with Kim or something.'

'Two then.'

She handed him Cass's swimming things. 'I'll see you both at two, so.'

At two o'clock Rosie was sitting on the sofa flicking through a magazine. At twenty past two she stood up and started pacing the room. At half past three she heard a car pull up outside.

'Sorry we're late,' Darren said as she opened the front door. Cass ran in clutching a bright yellow plastic bag. 'We stopped off in Toymaster in Dun Laoire Shopping Centre and lost track of the time.'

'We went to Burger King, Mummy. And Daddy bought me loads of sweets.'

Darren had the good grace to look a little sheepish.

Rosie glared at him but bit her tongue. 'What's happening next week? When are you calling in?'

'Does Tuesday suit?'

She nodded.

'What time?'

'Six. We won't be home till then. But Cass will have to go to bed at seven, so just for an hour. I don't want you disrupting her routine.'

'Rosie. We need to talk.'

'About what?' She looked over at Cass who was sitting on the stairs trying a wedding dress on her new Barbie. 'Cass, can you go into the playroom? Put your *Little Mermaid* video on.'

Cass toddled off, holding her new Barbie by the sleek blonde hair.

'Well?' she said. 'What about?'

'Money, I guess. And Cass.'

Rosie suddenly felt hot. Her pulse was racing and she could feel her heart thumping in her chest. 'We don't have to talk about that now. You haven't even made a decision yet, have you?'

He shifted uncomfortably. 'Not really. But it's better to get things out in the open, you know – child access, planning a budget . . .'

'A budget? Darren . . .'

'Listen, I have to go. I'm late. I'll talk to you on Tuesday. Bye.' He let himself out the door, leaving her staring after him. A budget, she whispered to herself. Access. Suddenly the rug had been pulled from under her feet. He really was leaving her. And what was even more scary – he seemed to have it all planned. How long had he been thinking about this? Rosie ran upstairs, threw herself on her bed and began to sob in great, heaving gulps.

'Mummy?' Cass was standing in the doorway. 'Are you OK?'

How long had she been there? Rosie wondered. How long had her little daughter been listening to her crying? 'Hi, love. I have a really bad tummy ache. But it's fine now, don't worry.'

'I'll make you better. Will I get my doctor's kit?'

'Good idea.' Rosie brushed away the tears. If only life were that simple.

On Sunday morning Rosie heard the doorbell ring and dragged herself off the sofa. She'd been gazing at the

TV but as soon as her eyes left the screen she couldn't for the life of her remember what she'd been watching.

She opened the door cautiously.

'Hi.' Kim smiled.

'Kim, I wasn't expecting you.'

'Have I caught you at a bad time? I have something for Cass and I just thought I'd drop by.' She was holding a large Mothercare carrier bag.

Rosie tried to smile. 'No, sorry. Come in. I'm not really doing anything.'

'Where's Darren? I didn't see his car outside.'

She shrugged her shoulders. 'At the golf club, I think.'

Kim looked at her carefully. 'What do you mean "I think"?'

She sighed. 'Sorry, I'm not really myself today. He's playing golf with some guys from work.` I wasn't paying much attention this morning. Would you like a cup of tea?'

'Love one. Where's Cass?'

'In her room playing Barbies.'

'Can I go up?'

'Of course. I'll just put the kettle on.'

Kim walked up the stairs and pushed open Cass's bedroom door. 'Hi, Cass.'

Cass jumped up and gave her a hug. Then she stood back and stared at the Mothercare bag. 'What's in the bag? Is it a present?'

'It might be. Will we look and see?'

She handed the bag to Cass whose eyes opened wide as she looked in.

'Barbie clothes,' Cass squealed. She pulled out a denim pinafore dress with large pink Barbie lettering, matching denim jacket and a pink top with white glitter stripes and a picture of the blonde doll. 'You're the best.' She threw her arms around her aunt. 'I'm going to put them on right now and show Mummy.'

'What about Daddy?' Kim would have liked to think it was an innocent question but something was niggling at the back of her mind. She knew Darren played a lot of golf but rarely on a Sunday morning. Maybe she was being overly suspicious but Rosie just wasn't herself these days. Perhaps she and Darren had had a fight.

'Daddy's away at work today.' Cass pulled her little pink corduroy skirt down over her legs and stepped out of it.

'At work?'

'He took me swimming yesterday and bought me sweets,' Cass continued innocently, 'but he didn't stay the night. He had to go back to work.'

'Kim!' Rosie yelled up the stairs. 'Your tea's here when you want it.'

'Thanks. I'll be down in a second. Quick, we'll get you dressed and show your mum.'

Rosie laughed as Kim and Cass walked into the kitchen. 'You shouldn't have,' she said, smiling as Cass twirled to show off her new outfit.

'I saw it yesterday when I was shopping in town and I knew she'd love it. I couldn't help myself.' Rosie handed her a large mug of tea. 'Thanks.' They sat down at the kitchen table and Cass pottered back upstairs to her Barbies.

'What a miserable day,' Rosie said, staring out the window. The sky was dark and it threatened to rain at any moment.

'Not great weather for golf,' Kim said watching her. 'Darren will get drenched.'

'Um,' Rosie murmured noncommittally.

'Did you go out last night?'

'No. We had an early night. We were both tired.'

'How's Darren's work?' Kim asked 'There seems to be a bit of a lull in the housing market, according to the papers.'

'I guess so. He's still busy though.'

'Is he away a lot at the moment?' Kim tried to sound casual.

'Away?'

'You know, on conferences and things.'

'Oh, right,' Rosie said carefully. 'No, not really. Just busy. And how's work for you?'

'Fine. The usual. Before I forget, Mum called in yesterday and I told her about the bank holiday weekend.'

'What did she say?'

'She wasn't too impressed. You were right – she had everything planned. But she made a suggestion.'

'What?'

'That she and Dad come with us to Wexford.'

'Are you serious?'

'Unfortunately. But listen, it might not be that bad. It's a big hotel and we could do our own thing most of the time. What do you think?'

'I'm not sure.'

'It'll be fun,' Kim cajoled. 'No cooking for four days – think of it. And there's a kids' club, so you and Darren can spend some time on your own.'

'I'll think about it.'

A little later Kim kissed Rosie and Cass goodbye and stepped into her car. As she pulled away she wondered if she should have asked Rosie about Darren straight out. It was crystal clear that there was something seriously wrong. Where was he? She intended to find out. Rosie was quite obviously as miserable as hell and she was damned if she was going to sit idly by if there was something she could do about it. She drove down Avondale Road and took a right to Killiney Golf Club.

'Where have you been all morning?' Greg asked, rolling over.

'Greg! It's lunchtime, what are you doing still in bed?'

'Sleeping.' He grinned lazily. 'And waiting for you. Come here.'

She sat down on the edge of the bed, leant over and kissed him firmly on the lips. Greg's hands snaked under her shirt and up her back. 'There's something I want you to do for me.'

'Later, love.' He smiled.

'Promise?'

'Yes.'

She squealed as he pulled her horizontal on the bed,

jumped on her and pinned her arms back with his hands.

'Get off me, you big ape! You're heavy.'

'I might. Then again, I might not.'

On Tuesday morning Rosie woke up with knots of stress in her stomach. Sitting in work after the usual dash to Cass's crèche and negotiating the ulcer-inducing Dublin city traffic, she rubbed her temples and stared out of the window. Yesterday she'd dropped into the Dublin Bookshop on her lunch break and purchased a book on divorce and separation – *Teach Yourself Divorce.* The last teach-yourself book I bought, she thought as she handed over her euros, was *Teach Yourself French*, before a romantic week in Paris with Darren. How ironic.

She'd read the book in one sitting, trying to come to terms with the financial and legal implications of a separation. She wanted to be prepared for this evening's meeting with Darren. But the book hadn't exactly been ideal bedtime reading – she'd had no idea how complicated and drawn-out things could be. But, she had reasoned, Darren and I are grown-ups and we can sort this whole thing out in a civilized manner – can't we?

The day dragged by. Emily had approved the marketing plan for the new Dun Laoire shop and Rosie was trying to find a suitable 'personality' to open it. So far she'd had a no from almost everyone, except a conditional yes from Alison Brothers, the RTE newsreader who'd demanded an extortionate appearance fee, and a maybe from a local politician, depending on her work schedule. It wasn't exactly looking good. Ruth was trying some of her media friends to see if she could come up with anything.

In fact, Ruth was being brilliant. Rosie had begun to rely on her more and more over the last few days. Emily seemed more than happy to deal with her, leaving Rosie to get on with her work. Meetings were never her forte.

After lunch Ruth came bustling into her office. 'Good news!' she announced.

Rosie looked up. She was poring over designs for the launch invitation, trying to get the look and the wording exactly right.

'Well?' she raised her eyebrows.

'I talked to my friend, Isolde, in TV, and she said that Lorraine Keane from TV3 might be available.'

'Really?' She smiled for the first time that day.

'Isolde gave me Lorraine's number and I tried it. I hope that was OK, I just thought—'

'Of course. Did you speak to her?'

'Yes. She was dead nice. I told her about the launch and guess what?'

'What?'

'Her mum and Emily's mum are old friends. So she said she'd do it.'

'Let me get this right. Lorraine Keane said she'd launch the new shop.'

Ruth grinned again. 'Correct.'

She stood up and before she could stop herself gave

Ruth a hug. 'You're a genius. She'll be perfect. Well done. I think you should tell Emily yourself.'

'Are you sure?'

'Go on. I insist.'

After Ruth had left, she sat back down. Ruth was destined for great things, she could feel it in her bones.

She picked up the phone and dialled Alison Brother's number. At least she'd have the pleasure of telling the egotistical newsreader the news.

'Rosie, are you there?'

She jumped. She was upstairs in the bathroom, rinsing the bubble suds from Cass's plastic bath toys when she heard Darren's voice behind her.

'Sorry, I didn't mean to startle you. I did ring the doorbell. I thought it would be OK to let myself in.'

She stood up slowly and stared at him. He was an hour late. 'I'd prefer it if you didn't in future.'

'Fine. What are you doing?'

'What does it look like? I'm tidying up.' She dried her hands on a towel and looked at him. He was standing in the doorway. 'Are you going to move?'

'Right, sorry.' He stepped into the hall. 'Can I go and say goodnight to Cass?'

'She's asleep. It's after eight.'

'Sorry. I got held up in work, you know how it is.'

'You'll see her at the weekend. I'd prefer if you didn't wake her up.'

'I'll just give her a kiss,' he said, opening Cass's door before Rosie could protest.

She went downstairs. Her heart was pounding and she felt sick. He looked the same, he sounded the same. But something about Darren had changed. His eyes seemed colder, almost flinty. And he couldn't look her in the eye for long before looking away.

'You should have rung to say you'd be late,' she said after they'd sat down in the kitchen. She switched the kettle on and sat down.

'I didn't think you'd mind. It's no big deal, is it?'

'No. Not to me. But Cass was upset – she was looking forward to seeing you. It's not fair on her.' Rosie stopped. There was no point in continuing, she could see that he wasn't even listening. 'Do you want a cup of tea?'

'Please.'

She waited by the kettle until it had boiled. He sat silently staring out the window.

He looked up as she placed a mug in front of him. 'Thanks.'

She sat down. She wanted to ask him all kinds of questions – but she stopped herself.

'I just thought we should sort out a few things,' he said eventually. 'I talked to a solicitor and he went through some of the basics with me.'

So he has seen someone already, she thought. 'Who?'

'One of the guys at work. You don't know him.'

'Does he play golf?'

He gave her a funny look. 'What's that got to do with anything?'

'Nothing,' she admitted.

'I think you should see someone. Just so you know where you stand. Do you know anyone?'

'No.' This was moving much too quickly for her. 'I thought you said you weren't sure.'

'About what?'

'About me. About us – the marriage, everything.'

'I never said I wasn't sure.'

'You did!' she protested. 'You said you'd think about it and you promised not to see her and—'

'Tracy?'

Rosie nodded.

'I never promised not to see Tracy. You know that. You're imagining things.'

'I'm not! You'd said you hadn't make up your mind yet and—'

'Rosie, I love Tracy. I'm leaving you. I'm going to live with her.'

She felt as if someone had punched her in the stomach.

'Live with her? But—'

'That's why we need to sort out a budget. We want to buy a house. Here are the figures I worked out.' He handed her a sheet of paper. It was a spreadsheet. At the top of the sheet was 'Suggested Budget – Monthly', as if it was just another business plan.

She scanned the sheet. 'This doesn't look right. You've left off the mortgage, Cass's crèche fees and the long-term savings plans.'

'You'll have to cover those yourself. You're working, so it shouldn't be a problem.'

'But what if something happens? What if I need to

leave work for some reason. I'd never survive on this. I can't believe you haven't even included the mortgage.'

'We need to talk about the house. We're not going to be able to keep it.'

She stared at him. 'What? I don't understand.'

'Myself and Tracy want to buy an apartment. We'll need a deposit. I'm sorry.'

'What do you mean you're sorry? I'm not moving. This is my home, Cass's home.' She felt her heart pounding again and she was on the verge of tears. How the hell could he be so casual about all this? Her life had just been turned upside down.

'Let's talk about Cass.' He could see that Rosie was upset and he wanted to keep things on an even keel – it would be easier that way.

'What?'

'Cass. I'd like to see her at the weekends and maybe one evening a week.'

'I can't do this. I need you to leave. Right now.'

'Don't be so melodramatic. We just need to decide access days and times—'

She stood up. 'I'm serious. Get out of this house right now. I'll ring you when I'm ready to talk.' Tears began to run down her cheeks. 'This is all too sudden – budgets and access and everything. And you can't tell me you want to sell the house and expect me to be OK about it. Please, just go.'

'Fine. But I'd like to see Cass on Saturday though. Maybe you could ring me to arrange a time.'

She put her hand over her eyes. Tears were spilling

from her eyes and she was embarrassed that he could see her crying.

'I'm sorry. I didn't mean to upset you,' he said.

'Just get out.'

As soon as he'd left Rosie picked up the phone.

'Can you come over? I need you.'

Rosie

Kim knocked on Rosie's front door. It was opened almost immediately. She saw that Rosie's eyes were bloodshot and her face was red and puffy.

'What is it, love?' Kim asked as she walked into the hall.

Rosie began to cry. 'Darren's gone. He's left me.'

Kim put her arms around Rosie and held her tightly. 'Oh, love,' she whispered. 'I'm so sorry.'

They stood like this in the hall for a few minutes until Rosie pulled away.

'I'm sorry.' She wiped the tears from her eyes with the back of her sleeve. 'It's late, I shouldn't have rung you.'

'Don't be silly. I'm glad you did. Let's go into the kitchen. I'll get you a drink'.

Kim took two wine glasses out of one of the kitchen cabinets. She had a look in the wine rack and pulled out a bottle of Merlot. It was an expensive bottle but she didn't care.

'I'm not sure I want a drink. And that's Darren's best—' Rosie began as she watched Kim take the corkscrew out of one of the kitchen drawers.

But it was too late. Her sister had already punctured the metal seal at the top of the bottle and was twisting the corkscrew into the cork, ignoring the protest.

'Here you go.' Kim smiled as she placed a large glass of red wine in front of Rosie. She sat down beside her with another glass in her hand. 'I knew there was something up with you and Darren but I didn't realize how serious it was. I don't know what to say. I'm so, so sorry.'

'How did you know?' She had stopped crying now but her breath was still raspy and uneven.

'Cass let it slip on Sunday that Darren had been staying somewhere else the previous night. She said he was "at work". And then I drove up to the golf course and—'

'You what!'

'I know, I know,' Kim said feeling more than a little guilty. 'I just wanted to see if he was really there.'

'And he wasn't, of course.'

'No. And then I got Greg to ring Jeff's house and pretend he was a friend from work.'

'Kim!'

'Well, I figured he might be there.'

'And was he?'

'No.'

'Where was he?'

Kim paused for a moment and then sighed. Rosie

needed to hear the truth. There'd obviously been some serious lying going on and she was damned if she was going to lie to her too. 'Jeff said he'd gone to Paris with someone called Tracy and wouldn't be back till Tuesday evening.'

Rosie stared at the table in front of her. Tears spilled from her eyes again. She felt so damn stupid. Darren had no intention of coming back to her – that was blatantly obvious. And he'd taken that stupid bitch to Paris – their special place. The place they'd spent their honeymoon, for heaven's sake. What a bastard!

'Rosie. Are you all right?'

'No, I don't think I am.'

Kim put her arm around her again. 'I'm here now,' she said gently. 'Everything's going to be fine.'

'Hi, Greg?'

'Kim, thank goodness, I was worried about you. Is everything OK? Where are you?'

'I'm still at Rosie's. I'm going to stay the night.'

'What's happened? Is Rosie all right?' It was after eleven and he'd been sitting up waiting for Kim.

'Not really. Darren's left her.'

'What? Are you serious?'

'Yes. He's been having an affair with some young one from work for the past year.'

'The girl he went to Paris with?'

'Yes. Tracy something or other. And he wants to sell the house and buy an apartment with her.'

'Poor Rosie. How's she taking it?'

'Not very well. I think she's in shock. She can't quite believe it.'

'And Cass?'

'She doesn't know. She thinks her daddy's been working a lot, that's all.'

Greg sighed. 'Poor little mite. Is there anything I can do?'

'Not tonight. But maybe tomorrow you could contact your lawyer friend, Brian O'Mara. Would you mind?'

'I'd be happy to. I'm not sure if he does family law, but I can ring him anyway.'

'And one other thing. Do you know any locksmiths?'

'Not really. But there's a company in Dun Laoire that the bank have used before, they seemed good. But why do you need a locksmith?'

'To stop that bastard letting himself into my sister's house unannounced. He's upset her enough.'

'Is she allowed to change the locks? Legally, I mean.'

'I don't know. But maybe that's something Brian can tell us tomorrow. Are you sure you don't mind me staying over?'

'Of course not. Sleep well and give Rosie my love. And if she needs anything tell her she only has to ask.'

'Thanks, pet. Goodnight.'

''Night, try to get some sleep. I love you.'

'Love you too.' As she put down the phone she realized how much she loved and trusted Greg. What would she do if he ever betrayed her the way Darren had betrayed Rosie? It didn't bear thinking about.

*

'Are you *sure* you want to go to work?' Kim asked Rosie at seven the following morning. They were sitting at the kitchen table, drinking coffee and trying to wake up. They'd been talking well into the early hours, Rosie trying to make sense of what had happened and Kim listening and calling Darren every bad name under the sun.

She nodded. 'I'd only sit here and think about things if I don't.'

'I could ring Emily for you.'

'Honestly, I'll be fine.'

'I'm staying the night again.'

'You don't have to do that.'

'I know. But I want to. I'll pick up some food on my way home and cook for you.'

'I'm not that hungry at the moment.'

'You have to eat. You'll get sick otherwise and you need your strength. Anyway, it'll probably be easier to eat if I'm here watching you.'

'Spooning it into me, more like. You're as bad as Mum.'

'Speaking of Mum, have you told her yet?'

'No. No one knows except you. Please don't tell her. I don't think I could cope with her "I told you sos". She's never liked Darren.'

'No,' Kim said thoughtfully. 'She took a bit of an instant dislike to him, didn't she? It was something to do with his closely set eyes and thin lips, wasn't it?'

'Mum was right though, that's the worst thing.' Rosie sighed.

'You'll have to tell her eventually.'

'I know. But not just yet.'

'What are you doing here?' Darren asked Kim on Saturday as she unlocked the Chubb lock and answered the door. She'd stayed all week in the end – she couldn't bear to leave Rosie on her own at the moment. 'And where did that bloody lock come from? I couldn't open the door.'

She glared at him. That's the idea, asshole, she thought, but she didn't answer his question. She didn't like his aggressive tone of voice one little bit. 'I have every right to be here.'

'That's not what I meant. I was expecting Rosie, that's all.'

'She's out,' Kim lied. Rosie was actually upstairs in her bedroom.

'Out where?'

'I don't think that's any of your business. Cass is ready, I'll just run up and get her coat.'

'I'll get it,' he said, stepping into the hall.

'No. Stay here. Cass!' she said loudly. 'Your daddy's here.'

She came running out of the playroom. 'Daddy!' she yelled, throwing herself at him and clinging onto his legs.

Kim went upstairs to fetch Cass's coat.

'What time will you be back at?' She asked Darren as she handed him the small pink jacket.

He glared at her. She was as bad as her sister. 'I don't know, five or six.'

'Let's say half five then. Cass usually has her tea around six, doesn't she?'

He shrugged. 'Fine, whatever.' He glared at her one more time before letting himself out.

'Bloody women,' Darren muttered as he put Cass into the car. 'What would you like to do today, princess?' he asked her as they drove away.

'Can we stop at the shop and get some sweets, Daddy?'

'Of course. As many as you want. And would you like to meet a friend of mine?'

'OK, Daddy.'

'I'll murder him,' Rosie said that evening. 'What the hell is he playing at? How dare he let that bitch near my child.'

Kim sighed. 'I don't think he realized. Maybe he just didn't think.'

'Of course he realized. He's not bloody stupid. Cass is really confused now.'

Cass didn't seem all that bothered, Kim thought, but she held her tongue. She seemed to have quite enjoyed playing Barbies with Daddy's 'friend' Tracy, to be honest. This had more to do with Darren respecting Rosie. Introducing Cass to his new 'friend' wasn't exactly a smart move.

*

'This all seems to be moving way too fast,' Greg had said earlier when Kim had rung him. 'Darren seems to have his new life all planned.'

'I know. And I have a feeling it's all going to get nasty where money is concerned. He's already told Rosie he wants to sell the house as soon as possible.'

Greg whistled. 'Can he do that?'

'Apparently he can. Brian said it's worth so much that the court will probably instruct for it to be sold and the proceeds to be split so they can both buy new places.'

'That's tough on Rosie. And Cass.'

'They'll have to find somewhere else. But who knows how long all this legal stuff will drag on.'

'When is she seeing Brian again?' Kim and Rosie had gone to see the lawyer the previous Thursday afternoon.

'She has to wait until the end of the month. Darren may change the standing orders or stop his wages going through. If he does, Brian will send him a threatening letter. Apparently Darren can't change anything until all the financial claims have been settled. Until then, she has to sit tight.'

'It all sounds complicated.'

'It is. And then there's Cass's custody to consider.'

'Of course. Poor little mite.'

'The bank holiday's only two weeks away,' Kim said to Rosie that evening. 'Why don't I go ahead and book the hotel in Wexford?'

'I'm not sure . . .'

'Please, Mummy,' said Cass. 'Kim says it has a cool swimming pool and a kids' club. And Granny and Grampa will be going.' Cass's eyes lit up. Her grandparents spoilt her rotten.

'It'll be fun,' Kim promised. 'Go on.'

'OK,' Rosie said finally. She didn't exactly have any other plans and it was much better than spending the long weekend alone, even if her mother would be there.

'Yippee!' Cass shouted.

She smiled. Maybe a few days away was just what herself and Cass needed.

Cass toddled back into the playroom to play swimming and kids' club with her Barbies.

'You're going to have to tell Mum and Dad about Darren,' said Kim.

'I know. Just give me a little more time.'

Rosie

'I love this place.' Rosie smiled. Herself and Kim were sitting in the jacuzzi in the Ferrycarrig Hotel in Wexford. Adjacent to them was the swimming pool, and in front of them, through huge plate-glass windows, was the river Slaney estuary.

Rosie pressed the button at the side of the jacuzzi and the warm water began to bubble furiously once more, sending vanilla scented white foam to the surface.

Kim rolled her neck a few times. 'I can feel the tension just melting away. Can we stay here all day?'

Rosie laughed. 'We might turn into prunes. I'm already feeling a little wrinkly.' She poked her left foot out of the water. It was bright pink. 'See?'

'Nice nail polish.'

Rosie's toenails were a vibrant, sock-it-to-me red. 'Darren hates bright nail polish.'

'Old fart!' Kim snorted.

Rosie smiled. She hadn't been on holiday with her

sister for a long time. She'd forgotten how easy it was. 'Greg's playing a blinder. Do you think he's OK?' He had taken charge of Cass in the pool while they were being bubbled alive.

'Absolutely. He loves kids.'

Rosie raised her eyebrows.

'Stop that!' Kim laughed. 'Other people's kids, I should have said.'

'Have you ever talked about it?' She flicked the bubbles in front of her with her hand.

'What?'

'Having kids.'

'Not really. We'd both like them so there's nothing really to talk about.'

'We were trying for another,' Rosie said quietly. 'Me and Darren. I came off the pill months ago but nothing was happening.'

Kim looked at her sister. 'I didn't realize. I'm sorry.'

'Nothing to be sorry about. It would have happened in time, I guess. The doctor said not to worry. He thought my body just needed time to readjust.' She gazed out of the window. There were two crows sitting on an old, dead tree which hung over the side of the river. 'He suggested a holiday. But Darren kept saying he was too busy at work.' Rosie's eyes began to blur. She blinked back the tears.

Kim reached out and put her hand on Rosie's. She could kill Darren. Stupid prick!

'I don't think he really wanted another baby,' said Rosie. 'Not with me, anyway.' She brushed back a tear.

'Try not to think about him,' Kim said gently. 'I

know it's hard but . . . I'm useless at this, I don't know what to say. I'm sorry.'

Rosie squeezed her hand. 'You're great. I don't know what I'd do without you.' She smiled warmly at her sister. 'Let's go for a swim.'

'OK.'

They climbed out of the jacuzzi and stood at the edge of the pool. In the smaller children's pool Greg was playing with Cass, throwing her into the air and laughing as she splashed him and cried 'Again, again!'

'Race you to the other end and back.' Kim grinned.

'You're on.' Rosie jumped in. 'It's bloody freezing!' she squealed as she kicked off from the end of the pool.

Kim jumped in and began to overtake Rosie, her smooth, clean breaststroke much more practised than her sister's. 'Come on, slowcoach.' she laughed as she passed Rosie.

Rosie made more effort, quickening her strokes and putting more energy into it. She'd forgotten how much she liked to swim. She was used to splashing about in the shallow end with Cass, not swimming proper lengths like this. She drew level to Kim as they reached the back wall of the pool. 'Slowcoach,' she said as she passed her.

'Come back here.' Kim grabbed the back of Rosie's swimsuit.

'Cheat,' Rosie spluttered. She put her feet on the bottom and turned around. Kim was still holding her swimsuit and laughing. Rosie splashed her.

'Rosie!' Kim splashed her back.

'Ladies!' they heard a voice from the side of the

pool. The young female lifeguard was staring at them. 'No splashing, please. It's usually the kids I have to tell.'

Rosie and Kim stifled their laughter. The lifeguard was all of seventeen, if she was a day.

'Sorry,' said Kim. 'Just got a bit carried away. It won't happen again.'

'No problem.' The girl smiled. To be honest, it was the most excitement she'd had all morning. That, and watching the rather cute dark-haired father who was playing with his daughter in the children's pool. Now he was a bit of all right.

Rosie towel dried Cass's hair. There were hairdryers at a large mirror, but Cass hated them. Once when Rosie was drying her fine light brown hair she'd accidentally burnt Cass's scalp with the hot air. Her daughter had never let her forget it and had refused to go near a hairdryer since. Kim was sitting on a white plastic chair in front of the mirror putting on her make-up. Beside her was a buxom blonde who was blow-drying her hair completely naked.

Kim looked over at Rosie and rolled her eyes to heaven, surreptitiously nodding her head slightly towards the naked woman. Rosie tried not to giggle.

'Did you see your one?' Kim asked as they walked along the corridor towards the hotel bar.

'The nudey lady?' Cass said.

'Cass!' Kim exclaimed.

'Well, she was. Totally nudey.'

Kim laughed. 'I can never understand people who do that – would they not get a bit dressed first. Put their underwear on at least.' She leant over towards Rosie. 'Do you think she was a dyke?'

'Kim! Of course not. And anyway, I'm not sure that's a very politically correct word to use.'

'What's a dyke?' Cass asked wide-eyed.

Kim tried not to laugh. 'Something they have in the Netherlands.' She whispered to Rosie, 'She doesn't miss a thing, does she?'

'No,' Rosie agreed.

'I see Granny and Grampa,' Cass said as they walked into the bar. She let go of Rosie's hand and dashed over, nearly sending a young waitress carrying a heavy tray of food flying.

'Sorry about that,' Rosie apologized to the waitress.

'No problem.' The girl smiled. 'We're used to kids in here.'

'If this was Dublin she'd bawl you out for it,' Kim said nodding at the waitress who was delivering the food to a nearby table.

'Too right,' said Rosie. 'They're so un-child friendly it's unreal. It drives me mad. I don't know what the tourists must make of it.'

'Over here, girls,' Julia called. She waved at her daughters. Rex was sitting beside her, his head buried in the business section of the *Irish Times*. Greg was staring out the window at the estuary, his dark hair still damp. Rex put the paper down as soon as his daughters joined the table.

Julia stood up and flamboyantly kissed Kim and

Rosie on the cheeks. She sat back down and pulled Cass onto her knee.

'I wonder what Granny has for you in her bag.' She pulled her red leather Orla Kiely bag onto the seat beside her. 'Let me see.' She handed Cass a bright red packet of sweets.

'Skittles!' Cass giggled. 'Mummy doesn't let me have these.'

Rosie tried not to frown. 'They're full of sugar and E-numbers,' she said looking at her mother pointedly. 'And anyway, she won't eat her lunch now.'

'Live a little,' said Julia. 'You're on your holidays. Cass can brush her teeth after lunch. Can't you, munchkin?'

Cass nodded. Her little mouth was already crammed full of sweets.

'How was your swim?' Rex asked, trying to diffuse the situation. 'Greg was telling us about the pool. It sounds wonderful. May have to have a dip myself later. Sit down here, Rosie.' He patted the seat beside him. 'I haven't seen you for ages.'

Rosie sat down, leant over and gave him a kiss on the cheek. 'I know, Dad. I'm sorry. It's just been so busy, what with work and everything—'

'You girls do too much,' Julia interrupted. 'In my day mothers stayed at home and looked after their own children. They didn't farm them out—'

'Mum,' Kim said quickly, 'things have changed, you know that. And we're not having this discussion again, please. We're on holiday.'

Sarah Webb

'Too right,' Rex said. 'Now what's everyone having to drink?'

'But I still think—' Julia continued.

'White wine for you, Julia?' Rex asked. He handed her the wine list. 'Why don't you choose.' That would keep her happy for a few minutes, he thought to himself. Julia liked to think of herself as a bit of a wine connoisseur. He wasn't sure where she'd got this idea from as, up until a few years ago, she'd been quite happy with a bottle of Blue Nun or Black Tower. He blamed her women's 'cultural club' – a gang of old friends who met up, ostensibly to attend 'cultural' events like the theatre or wine tastings – a lot of wine tastings, which they called their 'wine appreciation course'. Although Julia came home in such a giggling heap that she was most certainly doing more than just tasting.

'Let me see,' Julia pondered. 'They have a rather nice Hamilton Russell Chardonnay.'

Rex looked over her shoulder, checked the price and tried not to wince. 'Fine. Sounds lovely. Is white OK for you, girls? Greg?'

Rosie and Greg nodded.

'Perfect.' Kim smiled broadly. 'This is the life. What looks good on the menu, Dad?'

'I'm having the swordfish steak,' Julia said.

Kim wrinkled her nose.

'Is there something wrong, Kim?' she asked.

'Sorry, Mum. It's just a nervous reaction, pay no attention.'

'To swordfish?' Rosie asked with interest.

Kim sighed. 'I knew I shouldn't have read that book. You can blame Greg.'

Greg smiled. 'You're far too sensitive, my sweet. I might have the swordfish myself.'

'Greg!' said Kim.

'What,' Julia demanded, 'is wrong with ordering swordfish?'

Greg looked at Kim and frowned. She shrugged her shoulders.

'I'm waiting.' Julia tapped her nails impatiently on the table.

'What would you like, Cass?' Rex asked. 'Chicken nuggets or fish sticks?'

Julia was still drumming the table with her long, perfectly manicured nails and staring at Kim.

Kim sighed inwardly. 'OK, Mum, if you really want to know I'll tell you. I was reading this book Greg gave me called *Kitchen Confidential*. It's by this chef from New York and, well, basically he won't eat swordfish because he says it's usually riddled with parasites and worms. That's all.'

Julia sniffed. 'New York. Hardly Wexford. New York isn't on the sea, is it?'

'Well, actually . . .' Greg began. Kim kicked him under the table.

'Quite right, Mum. Let's all have fish. Lovely fresh Wexford fish. Cass, you'd love the fish sticks, wouldn't you?'

Cass smiled. 'OK, Kim.'

'Good girl.' Kim smiled. 'Let's get a waitress over and order.'

'I think I'll have the lemon sole,' Julia said.

Rosie glanced over at Kim and smiled. She could see that her sister was trying not to laugh. Rosie felt decidedly giddy. She wasn't thinking about Darren all the time – she was having far too much fun. Maybe this break was just what she needed. There was only one thing hanging over her like a black rain cloud – she would have to tell her parents about Darren. They thought that he was at a European estate agents' conference until Monday. She knew Julia was going to go ballistic and she just couldn't face it.

'How's your walk so far?' asked Kim. They'd snuck off after lunch on the pretext of having a 'walk'.

'Not energetic enough.' Greg grinned. 'Come here.' He was lying on the bed in his boxer shorts, his arms behind his head.

Kim kicked her runners off, took the clip out of her long dark blonde hair and shook her head. 'What did you have in mind?'

'Oh, I don't know. What do you think?'

Kim locked her eyes on his, unbuttoned her white shirt and threw it behind her. She then undid her jeans and shimmied out of them. She stood in front of him in her Victoria's Secrets underwear – white lacy bra, matching thong and lace-topped stockings. She didn't normally wear stockings under her jeans but she knew Greg would love them. She stretched her arms over her head. 'I'm feeling very sleepy,' she purred.

'Why don't you lie down, then?'

'I just might. Stay exactly where you are,' she commanded. She knelt down on the end of the bed and crawled her way towards him.

'Close your eyes.' She removed the stockings and ran them over his face, tickling him with the silky sensation. 'Keep them closed.' She sat back on her hunkers, lowering herself until she could feel his hardness against her body. She toyed with the idea of tying his hands together with the stockings but decided it might give him a fright. Maybe next time, she thought as she leant forward and kissed him firmly on the lips.

He reached up, put his strong arms around her upper waist and tried to pull her forwards. 'I've got you now.'

'Oh really?' She put her arms on his chest and gripped him with her thighs.

Greg gasped. 'Strong legs.' He tickled her under her arms, forcing her to collapse on top of him.

'Cheat!'

'And what are these?' he asked as he gently pulled the lacy ribbons tied in a bow on her hips. The lace thong fell off his hands. He undid the ribbon on the back of her bra and smiled broadly. 'Kim,' he said, smiling as he moved his hands deliciously over her breasts.

'Yes?' she whispered.

'Great underwear.'

'I'm taking Cass shopping,' Julia said after she'd finished her coffee.

'You don't have to do that,' Rosie protested, but Julia had already stood up.

'I'm going to buy her some books and a toy. And she needs a new jacket, that pink fleece is far too small on her.'

'Yippee!' Cass said. 'Can I get a new Barbie, Granny?'

Rosie looked at her mother. The fleece was fine – she'd only had it a few months. And Cass didn't need any more Barbie dolls – the house was full of them. She already had six or seven, most of them courtesy of Julia. Books she didn't mind so much, at least they didn't take up so much space. But there was no arguing with her mother. 'Fine,' Rosie said. 'Whatever.'

'We'll stay here, if you don't mind,' Rex said. 'I don't fancy shopping today.'

'Good,' Julia said holding out her hand. 'You'd only slow us down. Come along, Cass.'

'Bye, Mum.' Cass kissed Rosie on the cheek.

'Be good,' Rosie said. 'See you later, alligator.'

Cass smiled. 'In a while, crocodile.'

Rex looked at his eldest daughter when Julia and Cass had gone.

'Are you all right, Rosie? You look tired, if you don't mind me saying.'

'I am a bit tired, Dad. I'm fine though, thanks for asking.'

'Don't take it too much to heart, love.'

'What?'

'Your mother. She doesn't think before she speaks most of the time.'

Rosie patted Rex on the arm. 'Don't worry. I'm used to it by now.'

He looked at her carefully. 'Where's Darren's conference?'

'In Paris,' she said quickly. It was the only place she could think of.

'Pity he couldn't make it.'

'Yes, I know.'

'And how is Darren?'

'Fine,' Rosie said looking down at her hands. 'He's fine.'

'What is it, pet? You don't have to tell me if you don't want to, but I'd like to help. Is it money? You know if you ever need—'

'No, Dad. It's not money. There's nothing wrong, honestly.'

He sighed. He knew there was something up. 'If you want someone to talk to, I'll always be there for you.'

Not again, Rosie thought to herself as she felt tears prick the back of her eyes. 'Thanks, Dad.'

He looked at her carefully, noticing her blurry eyes. 'It's you and Darren, isn't it?'

'Yes. How did you know?'

'I'm your dad,' he said, holding her hand. 'I notice these things. Your mother may not, but I do.' He handed her a napkin. 'Let's go for a walk.'

Rosie nodded. 'I'll go upstairs and get a jacket.'

*

They walked along the estuary in silence for a few minutes, Rex's arm draped protectively around his daughter's back. They stood and watched some seabirds landing on the water, the light splashes of their bodies interrupting the silence of the still October afternoon.

'Darren's left me,' she said finally. 'He's in love with someone else.'

'I see. Foolish man.'

Rosie and Rex had found a small, quiet pub along the estuary and had talked earnestly and openly over coffee. Rex listened as his daughter told him everything – Darren's initial confession, the awkward access visits, and Darren wanting to sell the house. He was amazed. They had seemed so happy together. They had everything a young couple could wish for – a nice house, cars, holidays, a beautiful daughter – but it obviously wasn't enough for Darren.

'I don't know what to say,' Rex said finally. 'I'm so, so sorry. If there's anything you and Cass need, anything, please ask. Promise me.'

'Thanks, I will.'

'Would you like me to tell your mother?' he asked after a long pause. 'I'm not sure how she'll react. Maybe we should wait until we get back to Dublin.'

'I can't ask you to do that . . .'

'You've had enough trauma in the last few weeks. I insist.'

'Thanks,' she said again.

'Have you seen a lawyer yet? You should, you know.'

'Yes. Brian O'Mara, he's a friend of Greg's. He's nice.'

'Good. These things can get nasty, unfortunately.'

Rosie sighed. 'I know.'

He looked at her. 'Sometimes things happen for a reason, love. It's difficult for you now, but you will get through this.'

'I know you're right. It's just so damned hard.'

'It could change your life for the better. You never know.'

'Let's hope so. It certainly can't get any worse.'

'I can't believe it's Sunday already.' Kim yawned and stretched her arms over her head.

'I know,' Greg said, sitting up. 'It's flown by. And I haven't even slapped your mother yet.'

'Greg! She's not that bad.'

'She is too. All that stuff about Rosie's hair at dinner last night and your clothes. She's so bloody rude. She asked me how much I earned and got really annoyed when I wouldn't tell her. You and Rosie are used to her, that's all. I don't know how your dad puts up with it.'

She shrugged. 'They love each other, I guess. I've never understood it either, to tell the truth. Although she was pretty stunning-looking in her day. Anyway, it's our last morning. Forget about Mum. Let's make the most of it.' She kissed him firmly on the lips and pushed him back against the mattress.

'How are you both this morning?' Rosie asked.

'Great.' Kim smiled. 'We had a lovely lie-in, didn't we, Greg?'

Greg squeezed her hand and nodded. 'Lovely.'

Rosie felt almost jealous. She wished she could turn back the clock. Darren would have adored this hotel. But it was pointless looking backwards. She looked at her watch. 'You're just in time for breakfast. Mum and Dad have taken Cass to see the swans on the estuary. They won't be back for a while.'

'Great!' Greg said smiling.

Kim scowled at him.

'It's nice for Cass to see the swans. That's all I meant.'

'I know what you meant, Greg Kinnear.' Kim laughed.

'Finding Mum a little full-on, are you?' Rosie smiled.

Kim kicked him under the table.

'A little,' he said honestly.

'Don't worry,' Rosie said. 'She has that effect on most people.'

'What would you recommend?' Kim said, looking at the menu.

'I had cheese and fruit, and a full Irish,' Rosie admitted. 'Oh, and a croissant.'

'Go, girl!' Kim laughed.

'The cooked breakfast wasn't that big.'

Kim put the menu down. 'I'll just have to order one and see.'

They ordered their food and helped themselves to the breakfast buffet.

'Will you eat all that and a fry?' Rosie asked Greg as he put his heaped plate on the table.

'Too right.' He tucked into a generously buttered croissant enthusiastically.

'He's a total pig,' said Kim.

Rosie looked at her sister's plate which was piled nearly as high and snorted.

'Don't say anything.' Kim smiled. 'So, what's the plan for lunch? Are we giving Dad his presents then?'

'Yes,' Rosie nodded. 'Mum suggested we met in the dining room just before one. We have a table booked.'

'Listen, we were thinking of using the sauna and steam room this morning. Are you on?' she asked Rosie.

'Sure. I'll give Dad a ring and ask him to pop Cass into the kids' club until lunchtime. I could do with some time out.'

A waitress delivered two breakfasts – plates heaving with bacon, eggs, sausages, mushrooms, beans, tomatoes and fried potatoes.

'Tiny breakfasts.' Kim winked at Rosie.

'Here's my favourite grandchild.' Julia kissed Cass, leaving a prominent coral stain on her cheek. 'And doesn't she look pretty?'

'Thanks for the dress, Mum,' said Rosie. It was dark red velvet with a delicate white lace collar. Dry clean only, the washing instructions commanded. Julia had left the price tag intact and it had been eye-wincingly expensive.

Kim smiled at her sister. She knew it was exactly the sort of dress that Rosie hated – fussy and impractical.

'Please, sit down,' said Julia with authority.

Rosie looked at the table. She recognized her mother's spindly handwriting on the place cards. Luckily she was sitting between Kim and her father. She didn't know if she could cope with any more of her mother's criticisms. She'd nearly been at breaking point last night when Julia had likened her hair to a bird's nest. 'Your hair's a state, darling. For heaven's sake, get it cut. I can't believe Darren hasn't said anything.'

Greg had interrupted, asking Julia about the wine they were drinking, which was just as well. Rosie had been about to say something about her mother's wig-like sheet of white-blonde hair, a style which, at hitting on fifty-five, was much too young for Julia. She looked like Donatella Versace without the tan.

Greg didn't look too pleased. He'd been seated between Julia and Cass.

'Look what Granny has for you, my little darling,' Julia cooed as she handed Cass a long, rectangular box. 'I'm sorry,' she said to the table. ' I couldn't wait.'

Typical, Rosie thought to herself. They'd only just sat down and already her mother was hogging the limelight.

Cass tore the gold wrapping paper off with abandon and opened the top of the red Thornton's box. 'Thanks,

Granny,' she beamed as she pulled out the chocolate bunny. She immediately took a bite out of one of its ears.

'Cass!' Rosie scolded.

Julia flicked her hand at Rosie. 'Leave the child alone, dear. She's enjoying herself.'

Cass bit the rabbit's other ear and Rosie flinched.

'That's enough till after lunch, I think,' Rex said gently, prising the rabbit out of Cass's hands. He put it back in its box and hid it under the table.

Cass scowled.

Julia glared at him. 'But Rex . . .' she began.

'And this is a little something from me,' he said, ignoring his wife and handing Cass a green shoebox.

'Rex, did you not wrap it?' Julia tut-tutted.

Cass pulled the lid off the box and grinned. 'Cool! Thanks, Grampa.' She pulled out a tiny yo-yo, a small wooden man attached to two sticks, a packet of jacks and a little bouncy ball, and several jokes and magic tricks, including a bloody finger and a packet of chewing gum that snapped your fingers if you tried to remove a stick.

'Where did you get all of this?' Rosie smiled as she helped Cass arrange her new 'treasures' on the table in front of her. 'You're a genius. It'll keep her occupied for hours.'

'In Nimble Fingers in Stillorgan mainly. And a joke shop in town.'

'You still should have wrapped the box.' Julia sniffed.

Cass occupied, Rosie began to relax. 'What's on the menu?'

'The lamb looks good,' Greg said. 'Or the pork.'

'If no one objects, I'll choose the wine,' Julia said, the list already open in her hands.

Greg looked at Rosie and raised his eyebrows. Rosie stifled a laugh.

'No,' Rosie said. 'Go ahead, Mum.'

'Tell you what, Mum, you choose the white and I'll choose the red with Dad,' Kim suggested.

Julia glared at her. 'But the wines must complement each other—'

'Hello, Mr White, you look very handsome today,' Kim joked. 'How's that, Mum?'

Rosie and Greg laughed.

Julia sniffed. 'You know very well what I mean, Kimberly.'

'Of course I do. Lighten up. I was only joking. I'll get another wine list.' She was determined not to let her mother get her own way all the time.

Julia's mouth twitched but she decided to keep quiet. Rex should have backed her up – he always let her choose all the wine when they were out together. She glanced at him but he was showing Cass how to set up the chewing-gum trick.

'Would you like some chewing gum, Granny?' Cass asked her as if butter wouldn't melt in her mouth.

'No, thank you, darling. I don't touch the stuff. Try your mother. I'm sure she likes *gum*.'

Rosie was sure there was some sort of implied criticism here but she decided to overlook it. 'It's not real gum, Mum,' Rosie whispered to Julia over the table. 'It's a trick. Go on.'

'No,' Julia said firmly. She didn't like tricks – they were undignified.

'I'd love some gum,' Greg said. 'May I?'

Cass smiled broadly at him and nodded.

He pulled out a stick and was rewarded with a sharp rap on the knuckle of his finger.

'Ow! Cass, you're terrible.'

Cass giggled. 'It worked, Grampa. It worked.'

Rex ruffled her hair affectionately. 'It sure did. Now I'll show you how to do the disappearing coin trick.'

'Yippee!'

Kim had attracted a waiter's attention and had been furnished with another wine list. 'The Benchmark Syrah sounds nice,' she mused. ' "Full of berry fruit and subtle spice",' she read. 'Or there's a nice Shiraz Sauvignon. What do you think, Dad?'

He looked over her shoulder. 'I've had the Shiraz before, it's very good.'

'We'll go with that, then.' She closed the list and put it down on the table.

Julia was still reading hers with her half-moon reading glasses. She peered up at Kim. 'You should take your time choosing wine.'

Kim smiled. 'I'm like Dad. I know what I like and I like what I know.'

'That's all very well—'

'Granny, would you like to see a coin disappear?' Cass asked, thrusting a red rectangle in Julia's face.

'Not right now, darling,' Julia said. 'Granny's busy.'

'Show me instead,' Kim said kindly. 'Here, I'll even give you a coin.' She handed Cass a euro across the table.

'Thanks, Kim.' Cass took the coin from her. 'Now you see it.' Cass held up the coin. She put it in the container and tapped it twice, her small fingers deftly manipulating the secret compartment into which the coin 'disappeared'. 'Now you don't.' Cass opened the container and the coin had 'vanished'.

'That's amazing.' Kim laughed. 'How did you do that?'

'It's a secret. Isn't it, Grampa?'

Rex nodded. 'That's right.'

'Can I keep the coin, Kim?' Cass whispered behind her hand.

Everyone stifled their laughs.

'Of course, pet. Anyway, it's disappeared, hasn't it?'

Soon everyone was tucking into their starters – a creamy vegetable soup for Julia, Rosie and Cass, and seafood chowder for the others. Julia had eventually chosen a Chablis, but it wasn't a patch on the Shiraz. Greg was drinking white, to keep her company, but everyone else had opted for the red, much to her chagrin.

Rosie's mind drifted as they waited for their main courses. Greg, Kim and Julia were talking animatedly about holiday destinations in Italy. Julia swore by the northern lakes, Kim liked the cities and Greg was undecided – he liked them both.

'Are you all right?' Rex asked her quietly.

'Sure. Just thinking about the future.'

Rex put his hand on hers. 'Better than thinking about the past.'

'Scary, though.'

'Yes. I suppose it is. But talking of the past, do you remember Rory Dunlop from school?' he asked, changing the subject. Julia was notorious for eaves-dropping.

'Yes, I do. Nice guy. Left in the third year to go to some posh boarding school in Surrey.'

'I bumped into his father, Conor, in the club. We had lunch together. Interesting man. They've almost finished renovating a stately home in Wicklow called Redwood House – they got some sort of grant from the EU and the Irish government. Rory is running the commercial side of things – the shops, wildlife park . . .'

'Did you say wildlife park?'

'Yes. Like Fota Island I guess, or the African Plains in Dublin Zoo.'

'In Wicklow?'

'I know. Sounds mad, doesn't it?'

'A little. But Cass would love it.'

'You should give Rory a ring. I'm sure he'd be pleased to hear from an old school friend. He came home last year – almost got married to an English girl apparently but she jilted him. Dreadful business. Poor boy was quite cut up.'

She looked at her father carefully. What was going on here? Was her father trying to set her up? Her marriage was only over a wet weekend, for heaven's sake. 'I don't think so, Dad.'

'It was only a thought.' He seemed a little hurt.

She realized he hadn't meant anything by it at all. 'Sorry. But right now I've got enough on my plate.'

'I know, love. I should have thought. I'm meeting Conor for lunch again soon. I'll tell him you said hello to Rory.'

'Please. Send him my best wishes.'

'What are you two talking about?' Julia asked. It sounded interesting and she didn't want to be left out. She could have sworn she'd heard 'Redwood' and the Dunlops mentioned.

'Tennis, Mum,' Rosie said, saying the first thing that had come into her head.

'Tennis?' Julia said incredulously. Neither of them had, as far as she knew, any interest in tennis.

'And this is our food, I think,' Greg said, interrupting her. Two waiters were walking towards the table brandishing large white plates. He was starving. Must be all the 'walks'. He smiled to himself.

The starters and main courses all went down a treat and they tucked in with relish. Rex ordered more wine, and some milk for Cass. She'd asked for Coke but he knew how Rosie felt about fizzy drinks. After dessert they gave Rex his presents – a voucher for Bray Gardening Heaven from Rosie (and Darren in absentia), a framed crayon picture of a dustbin lorry from Cass, and a blue and white checked brushed-cotton shirt from Kim and Greg.

By the end of lunch Rosie was exhausted and completely drained. She'd had about all she could take of her mother and Cass had started to act up, which wasn't surprising considering the amount of chocolate bunny and other junk she'd eaten.

'I'm going to take Cass upstairs for a rest now,' she said standing up. 'Happy birthday, Dad.' She kissed him on the cheek. 'See you all later.'

'Will I come up with you?' asked Kim.

'No, it's fine, honestly.'

As soon as Cass was settled on the bed watching *Powerpuff Girls*, Rosie went into the bathroom and turned on both the taps in the sink. She sat down on the closed toilet seat, held her head in her hands and began to cry.

Rosie
Seven months later

Rosie heard the doorbell ring. It was only nine and Darren wasn't due until ten. She'd been snuggled up in bed with Cass, dozing while her daughter watched *102 Dalmatians*.

Damn, Rosie muttered as she dragged herself out of bed, flicked back the curtains and stared out of the window. Her dad was on the doorstep. Her curiosity was immediately aroused – Rex hadn't called at this hour on a Saturday for as long as she could remember. She grabbed her towelling robe and made her way downstairs, all the time wondering what was up. Maybe there was something wrong with her mum.

'Hi, Dad,' she said as she opened the door. 'Come in.'

'Sorry to call so early.' He stepped into the hall. 'Your mother thinks I'm at the library. If I'd told her I was calling over she would have insisted on coming too.' He noticed Rosie's robe. 'Did I wake you, love?'

'No. It's fine. I was in bed all right but I wasn't

really asleep. Cass has been up since half six. It's time I got up anyway.'

Rex grimaced. 'Does she always wake up that early?'

'No. She's been a little unsettled lately. She still misses Darren.'

'Of course.'

'Would you like some coffee? I could use some.'

'Thanks, I'd love a cup.' He followed her into the kitchen and he sat down at the table while she put the kettle on and prepared the cafetière.

'How did the child psychologist go?' Rosie had decided to take Cass to see someone in a family-therapy practice on Kim's advice.

'It was good. The psychologist was really nice and she put my mind at rest about a lot of things, like Cass's sleeping and her bed-wetting. Apparently children react to divorce quite physically and it's all relatively normal, if you can call any of this normal.'

'And is that what you and Darren both want? Divorce?'

'Yes, I suppose. It's what Darren wants, anyway. I don't have much say in the matter. It'll take a few years, of course. We have to be separated and living apart for at least four years before we get one.'

'I'm sorry. It all sounds very final. I hadn't realized . . .' He was lost for words.

'It's OK, Dad.' She poured the boiling water into the cafetière, waited, then pushed down the plunger. The kitchen was filled with the heady aroma of fresh coffee. 'It still seems like it's not really happening to me. Like it's all one big nightmare and I'll wake up any time now. But Darren has made his mind up and there's no stopping him. He's just moved in with Tracy and—'

'Moved in with her? That's all a bit quick, isn't it?'

'It's been months now, but I know what you mean.' Rosie handed him a steaming mug of coffee. 'It came as a bit of a shock to me too.'

'Where is he living now? So I can avoid the place. I don't know what I'd do if I bumped into him.'

Rosie glanced at the clock on the wall. She wondered if she should tell him that bumping into Darren might happen sooner than he thought. She decided against it. He might insist on staying to have words with him. Hopefully Darren would be late and her dad would have left by then.

'Sandycove. They're renting a house on the seafront until our place goes up for sale, then they're buying somewhere. Darren found it through work, apparently. I went to see it last week. It's nice. Big, with a garden. They wanted to get an apartment but I didn't think that would be suitable for Cass.'

'Sandycove? But that's only down the road from here.'

'I know. Tell me about it. He's taking Cass there for the first time today. I hope he's childproofed the place like I asked him to.'

Rex raised his eyebrows. 'How do you feel about Cass being there? Is she staying the night?'

'Not tonight. But once we have access sorted out she may be staying every second weekend or so. And, to be honest, I feel terrible about it. Confused, upset, the works.'

'I'm sorry,' Rex said putting his hand on his daughter's. 'Listen, what are you doing today?'

She thought for a second – she didn't want her dad to know Darren would be calling in at any minute. 'Once I've got dressed and dropped Cass to Darren's I'll probably go shopping, clean the house . . .'

'In that case, I'll pick you up at eleven. I want to show you something.' He smiled, his eyes twinkling. 'It's why I called in really.'

'But as I said, I have to go shopping—'

'Shopping!' he snorted. 'This is far more interesting.'

'Will Mum be coming?'

'No. Leave your mother to me.' He stood up. 'I'll go now so you can get ready. See you later.'

She closed the door behind her dad in relief. As she made her way upstairs to drag Cass away from the video she smiled to herself. Her dad was full of surprises, and he was right – anything was better than cleaning the house and shopping!

'What time will I see you?' Rosie asked Darren as she tried to manipulate Cass's arms into her fleece jacket. 'Stop wriggling,' she told Cass firmly. 'Stay still or I'll tickle you.' Cass giggled.

'What time suits?'

'Can you give her tea and drop her back at sevenish? I'll be out until then.' She knew she wouldn't, but she could do with a rest. And anyway, it was the least he could do – he hadn't seen Cass all week.

'Fine. See you then.' He took Cass's hand and walked out of the door.

That didn't really suit at all, he thought to himself as he strapped Cass into her car seat. He and Tracy were going to a twenty-first birthday party near the Four Courts and they were meeting her friends in the Morrison at half seven for a drink. But he'd managed to bite his tongue. His lawyer, Noelle Thomas, had told him to be as accommodating as possible until his access had been agreed with Rosie's lawyer. In retrospect he wished he'd chosen a male lawyer but Tracy had advised him to go with a woman. 'It'll look better,' she'd insisted. 'More compassionate, more open to your female side.' He'd thought Tracy was going mad, but surprisingly Jeff had agreed with her.

'She's right,' he'd said. 'It does look better, mate.' So he'd gone with the general consensus. More fool him.

Noelle had told him in no uncertain terms not to antagonize 'the other party' in any way. Antagonize, indeed. It was Rosie and that bloody lawyer of hers, Brian O'Mara, who'd been antagonizing him. They'd stopped him taking anything from the house, even his own things, until a settlement was agreed. Thankfully it looked like that might not be too long now.

To be fair, Rosie was being pretty decent when it came to money. But access, that was another thing altogether. She'd dug her heels in about him seeing Cass in the evenings during the week – she said that it had made Cass too tired, and it had unsettled her when they'd tried it for a few weeks. She'd said something about some child psychologist and her theory about Cass's sleeping patterns too. Load of old cobblers, Darren thought. Rosie just wanted to get at him and to stop him seeing his daughter.

And how was he supposed to furnish his new place if she wouldn't let him take any of his furniture? He'd paid for most of it. Hell, his granny had left some of it to him when she'd died – he was at least entitled to that. Rosie had screamed at him when he'd called round to take the television and the DVD player. He didn't see what the problem was – she had another set in the bedroom with a video player and most of Cass's films were on video. He'd got a strong letter from her lawyer about that all right and a sharp verbal rap on the knuckles from Noelle to boot.

In the end he and Tracy bought some cheap furniture from Woodie's, borrowed the rest from her parents and hired a television and video to tide them over until he got his own back. He wouldn't have signed the lease for the house in Sandycove if he'd known they couldn't furnish the place. There were plenty of other places around that came fully furnished. But Sandycove was handy for the Dart and it was also near Cass, which would make visits easier. Anyway, he liked Sandycove. Still, they were only there until the settlement was sorted out and he had his share of the proceeds of the house. And as far as he was concerned, the sooner the better.

Tracy had originally agreed to an apartment in town but was now edging towards a 'family home' in South County Dublin. Tracy insisted it was because of Cass, but it was making Darren very nervous. He wasn't sure if he wanted another roaring baby in the house – Cass had been bad enough. Still, he considered, Tracy was only twenty-two after all. She had loads of time for all that.

Rosie had visited the house last week to check if it was 'suitable' for Cass. She'd been really anal – going on about covers for the plug sockets and childproof latches on the fridge and the cupboards in the kitchen. Tracy had left her make-up case on the window ledge in the bathroom and Rosie had gone on and on about leaving medicine within Cass's reach. There were only a few Panadol in it, for heaven's sake, nothing to worry about.

Rosie hadn't approved of the furniture in Cass's room either – this really cool unit from Argos that he'd spent a whole day putting together himself from the flat-pack. The bed was perched on top of a wooden platform and there was a ladder up to it. Underneath the platform were a small desk, a chest of drawers and a pretend house in Barbie pink for Cass to play in. She was going to love it. It was a pity her mother didn't feel the same way.

'Darren!' Rosie had said when she'd seen the unit. 'That's so dangerous. Cass could fall out of bed and split her head open. She can't sleep up there, no way.'

'Myself and Jeff had bunk beds when we were her age,' Darren had protested. 'They're perfectly safe. Don't be such a kill-joy.'

'She's not sleeping up there and that's final. You can take the mattress down and put it on the floor, there's plenty of room.'

'Right, fine,' he'd said just to pacify her. He had no intention of doing any such thing.

'How's the dragon?' Tracy asked as she opened the front door to Darren and Cass.

He gestured towards Cass and frowned.

'Sorry.' Tracy bent down and kissed Cass on the cheek. 'And how's my little princess. Ready to play Barbies?'

Cass nodded eagerly.

'And guess what I found in SuperValu?'

Cass looked up at her, eyes wide with curiosity.

'Barbie pasta! Have you ever had Barbie pasta?'

Cass shook her head.

'Would you like some for lunch?'

'Yes, please.'

'I thought we could show Cass her new room,' Darren said. He helped Cass remove her coat and smiled at her broadly. 'You're going to love it, Cass. It's just like me and Uncle Jeff had when we were your age.' He held out his hand and led Cass towards the stairs.

'Would you like a drink, Cass?' Tracy asked. 'I have baby cans of Coke in the fridge.'

Cass's eyes lit up. 'Yes, please!' This was just getting better and better.

'Where are we going, Dad?' asked Rosie. 'Brittas Bay?'

'No.'

'Powerscourt?'

'No.'

'The waterfall?'

'I'm not going to tell you, so stop asking. You're as bad as Cass.'

'OK, OK.' She smiled and looked out of the window of Rex's car. It was a glorious May afternoon, sunny enough to wear shades and warm enough to leave her jacket at home. They drove a little further in companionable silence before Rosie said, 'Wicklow. That's it. Why are we going to Wicklow?'

He laughed. 'You'll see when we get there.'

'Ah, so it is Wicklow.' Rosie smiled.

Rex turned left off the main road and up a freshly tarmacadamed drive. The impressive black and gold wrought-iron gates glistened in the sun. There was a small white gatehouse tucked in behind the walls. Huge dark green conifers stood like sentries on either side of the drive and in the far distance to the right Rosie could see the dark grey slates of a roof peeping through the treetops. The grass was freshly mown and she could make out ornamental shapes cut into the tops of some of the hedges.

'I have no idea where you're bringing me,' she said, 'but I'm impressed.'

They drove on a little way and when they turned right, up a smaller drive, Rosie gasped. She couldn't believe her eyes. There in front of her was a magnificent white cut-stone house – if you could call such an imposing building a house. It was four storeys high, with huge sash windows. There were double-storeyed wings to the left and right and semicircular colonnades joined the wings to the main block. An old bottle-green Range Rover was parked beside the entrance stairway and a black Labrador lay sleeping against one of the tyres, enjoying the sun. To the left and right of the Range Rover there were several cars and vans, and men and women were bustling in and out of doors in the front of the wings. Some looked like electricians and builders, carrying ladders and canvas tool bags. Rosie was intrigued.

'What's going on here, Dad? Why all the people?'

'They're putting in a coffee shop and fixing up some of the other space too for . . . um . . . another retail unit.'

'Brilliant idea! I'd come here to see the house alone. It's amazing – like something out of *Brideshead Revisited*. Who owns it?'

Rex smiled. 'This, my dear, is where Rory and Conor Dunlop live. Welcome to Redwood House.'

Rosie spotted a figure waving at the entrance. 'And who's that?'

'Conor. He's expecting us.'

'Good morning, Rex,' Conor boomed as he strode down the steps to meet them. 'So glad you could come. And you must be Rosie.' He shook her hand firmly, looking her unflinchingly in the eye.

'Hello,' she said a little nervously. Conor Dunlop was a striking man. Tall and muscular, with a full head of dark brown hair peppered with grey, a handsome tanned face and intoxicating navy-blue eyes. He was wearing a white shirt and well-worn Levis and his rich, plummy voice lingered in the air like a musical note.

'Please come in. Rory may be along presently. He's helping move one of the lions.'

She couldn't contain her interest. 'You have lions?'

'Yes, my dear. Did your father not tell you? There's a wildlife park at Redwood. It's behind the house.'

'He did. But I must admit I didn't really believe him at the time.'

'Oh, ye of little faith.' He smiled broadly. 'Rory might introduce you to King or Elsa later. Elsa's his favourite. Leo brought her with him from Dublin Zoo. She pined after him so much when he left that they had to agree.'

'Is Leo another lion?' She asked innocently.

He laughed. 'Good heavens, no. Leo's the head keeper.'

'Is that his real name?'

'I don't know, to be honest. You'll have to ask him yourself. He doesn't talk much though – keeps to himself.'

She was fascinated – lions, silent lion keepers and this overwhelming house. It was turning out to be quite a day.

'Would you like some tea, my dear, before we look at the space? Or will we go straight ahead?'

'Tea would be lovely,' Rex said quickly. 'And maybe you can tell us some of your plans for Redwood. I'm sure Rosie would be interested.'

'Yes, very.' She nodded. She was intrigued. What space was Conor talking about and what had it got to do with her?

They followed Conor through the rich lacquer-red

hall with its sweeping iron and mahogany staircase and dramatic black and white tiled floor and turned left into another room, where a full tray was sitting on an ornate gold and white coffee table.

'How old is Redwood?' she asked eagerly. 'Eighteenth century?'

'Please do sit down. To answer your question, Rosie,' Conor said as he poured the tea from the antique silver teapot, 'Redwood was built between 1730 and 1740 by an Italian architect from Florence called Alessandro Galilei. He also built Castletown House in Kildare.'

'I've been there. It is quite similar in style. Palladian, isn't it?'

'Yes. Exactly. You know your architecture, my dear. It's been in our family ever since. Most of the furniture and interiors were commissioned by Lady Charlotte Dunlop in the second half of the eighteenth century. Sadly we had to sell most of the paintings to pay for the roof a few years ago. But we managed to make good photographic copies of most of them.' He waved his hands at the walls. 'That's what you see here.'

She looked around. The large-scale portraits and landscapes certainly were very good copies; unless you scrutinized them they appeared genuine. They were sitting in the 'gallery' or drawing room and it was quite a room – the epitome of elegance. It was one of the longest rooms Rosie had ever seen – at least eighty or ninety feet, with tall columns at regular intervals holding up the ceiling. There were eight large sash windows along the wall and light flooded into the room, bouncing off the white decorative plasterwork and the off-white walls. The furniture was a heady mishmash of antiques – delicate and spindly French-looking chairs and dark mahogany sideboards and tables. It was unlike anything Rosie had ever seen before.

'It's quite a room,' Rex said.

'Yes.' Conor smiled. 'But a devil to heat in the winter. We tend to decamp to the family room beside the kitchen when it gets cold.'

'I can imagine,' Rosie said.

'We've just had the hall and some of the reception rooms repainted. And by next year we hope to have most of the house open to the public. The west wing, which used to be the old kitchen and servants' quarters, will be the coffee shop and food hall,' he continued. 'The builders should be ready in a few days, fingers crossed. And the east wing, which housed the stables, will hold the clothes shop and the—'

'Gallery,' Rex interjected, looking pointedly at Rosie.

Rosie looked back at her dad. 'Gallery? What type of gallery?'

'I haven't told her yet,' Rex explained to Conor.

'I see. Well then, let's visit the east wing immediately.' He put down his cup and stood up. 'Shall we?'

'Tell me what?' she whispered to her dad as they walked through a curved corridor towards the east wing, past electricians on ladders who were fitting spotlights in what must be the clothes shop. There were already rails of brightly coloured clothes in place under heavy transparent plastic dust covers. He just smiled.

They walked to the end of the clothes shop, outside again and through a high wooden-framed door further down the building.

'Wow!' she exclaimed as she surveyed the rectangular white room. There were large windows running double storey along one wall, and the floor was covered in old, timber boards, the pungent smell of fresh varnish still lingering in the air. 'What a room. The natural light is amazing.'

'But would it make a good gallery, Rosie, that's the question?' asked Conor.

'Fantastic! Especially for large modern pieces. It would be perfect. Who's running the gallery?'

Conor looked at Rex. 'I think you should put her out of her misery.'

Rex cleared his throat. 'You are. That is, if you're interested. I've decided to invest in the retail side of Conor's business and I thought you might like the chance to . . .'

'Me?' she asked incredulously. 'Run a gallery. Are you joking?'

'No, love.' Rex smiled.

'But what about my job? And anyway, I can't run a real gallery, I wouldn't know where to start.'

'You'd start at the beginning. And I'd help you all the way.'

She shook her head. 'It's ridiculous. I couldn't do it.'

Conor looked her in the eye. 'My dear, you can do anything you want to do. I've built a wildlife park in the middle of Wicklow, for heaven's sake.'

'But it's different for me. I can't change my life so

dramatically. I have a hus—' She stopped suddenly. 'A daughter, I mean. And a large mortgage to pay. How would I support her?'

'Don't worry about that,' Conor said. 'Something could be sorted out, I'm sure. Think of the bigger picture.' He looked at Rex pointedly.

'Rosie,' said Rex, 'you've always dreamed of opening your own gallery, haven't you?'

'Yes.'

'This is your dream. "The Redwood Gallery".'

She took a deep breath, looked around and slowly began to smile. 'Maybe you're right. I'll think about it.' She had a strong feeling her life was about to change dramatically. 'The Redwood Gallery' – it did have a nice ring to it.

Martina
Back in March

Martina sat on the lime-green sofa, cursing her Marc Jacobs shoes. She'd worn them to look smart and fashionable – this was London Fashion Week after all – but they weren't doing her any favours. She'd been traipsing around the fair endlessly, from appointment to appointment, and now her feet were aching and she was exhausted. Still, she thought as she flicked through the large notebook perched on her knee, she shouldn't complain, as she'd had a very successful day. To think that a few weeks ago she was still working in the designer room in Brown Thomas. And now she was buying the new autumn/winter collection for her very own exclusive clothes shop, Designs on Red. It was like a dream come true. She was early for her appointment and was grateful for the time out from the noise and bustle surrounding her. The booth she was sitting in belonging to the Norwegian label Sami was blissfully spacious and peaceful.

'Martina Storey?'

Martina looked up. A tall, elegantly dressed blonde woman was smiling at her. She nodded, stood up and proffered her hand. The woman shook it warmly.

'I'm Helena Williams. I'm the Sami sales director for the UK and Ireland. I understand you're interested in stocking our label in your new shop.'

'That's right.'

'Please, follow me.' Helena smiled, leading the way towards a small red velvet-covered table. They both sat down. 'Can I get you a coffee?'

'I'd love one.'

Helena murmured to a young man standing at the back of the booth and seconds later he placed two generously sized mugs on the table.

'That's better.' Helena smiled again, taking a sip. 'I find Fashion Week exhausting, don't you?'

Martina grinned. 'No kidding.' It was her first time there, but she didn't want to appear green.

'We'd better get started. I've a lot to show you. I presume you're interested in autumn/winter primarily?'

'Yes.'

'And it's a new shop?'

Martina nodded. 'It's in Wicklow, just outside Dublin. In a stately home called Redwood House, no less.'

'Really? Tell me more.'

'The owner, Conor Dunlop, sold his computer company, Aran Industries, a few years ago and bought the house and the land surrounding it. The buildings were in a bit of a state but he's put a huge amount of money into renovating them and setting up a wildlife park in the grounds. And he's also renovating the wings of the house and turning them into retail units – they're nearly finished. There'll be a gallery and a coffee shop as well as my clothes shop. The whole lot opens to the public in June.'

Helena whistled. 'Very ambitious. And how exciting. And you're buying for the clothes shop?'

'That's right – Designs on Red. I'll be the manager and buyer. And that's where you come in. I saw some of your clothes when I was in Norway on holiday last year and I loved them – they're so different and so feminine. Just what I'm looking for. I'd like Designs on Red to be the first shop in Ireland to stock the Sami label.'

Helena smiled broadly. 'Sounds great! Let's talk clothes.'

Two hours later Martina had bought her favourite pieces from the Sami range – long, bias-cut velvet skirts in dark silver and dark red; flattering striped dark pink and cream polo-necked jumpers; versatile floaty chiffon shirts in floral patterns; and a range of red, pink and cream velvet wraps and beaded evening scarves. She'd deliberately shied away from anything in black, as one of the labels she'd bought earlier – Ellison from Denmark – concentrated on black pieces.

As she walked slowly back to the hotel she mentally ticked off her new labels – Sami, Ellison, Luna from London and Kati G from Dublin. Martina smiled to herself. Kati Gallagher. If only her boyfriend, Rory, knew. Maybe she'd come clean after the opening in June. Maybe not.

Once in her hotel room she picked up the phone and dialled nine to get an outside line. Her mobile had run out of juice earlier that afternoon and she was dying to ring Rory and tell him about her day.

'Hi, love.'

'Martina, how are you? Spent all the bank's money yet?'

She laughed. 'And more! But I don't even want to think about it at the moment. Don't tell your dad. It was really good of him to guarantee the loan and I wouldn't like him to think I was taking advantage.'

'Speaking of which, when are you back? I'm dying to take advantage of you.'

'Tomorrow morning. I'm on the red-eye,' she groaned. 'I left it so late to book that all the evening flights were gone. Still, it means I can have an early night and get some of the paperwork out of the way. Account-opening forms, that kind of thing. I have to get a letter from the bank, pronto, saying I'm good for the money or I won't get any clothes in time for the opening.'

'You don't have to pay for them all up front, do you?'

'No, thank goodness. I managed to wangle forty days' credit from most of them. And sixty from Sami, the Norwegian label. But it's still going to be a bit of a juggling act for the first year or so until we get established.' She sighed deeply. 'I've so much to do still –

interview staff, book ads in the magazines, talk to the shopfitters—'

'Hold it right there. It's March. You're not opening till June – that gives you three months. And as I keep telling you – I'll help, you just have to ask, OK? You need to take it easy – it'll all get done.'

'I know. Sorry, ignore me, I'm just overtired. Listen, I'm going to have a bath now and try to relax. I'll see you tomorrow.'

'Martina?'

'Yes?'

'I love you.'

'Back at you.'

She put down the phone and lay back on the bed, her head propped up on the pillows. The sound of traffic seeped in the slightly open window. She gazed at the bland watercolour print which was screwed firmly to the wall in front of her. She had no idea what to do about Rory Dunlop. She loved him, she was sure of that. They were very happy together and she didn't want things to change, but she knew they would – it was only a matter of time. She let out a deep breath and rubbed her weary eyes, no doubt smearing her mascara. Life was so unfair sometimes.

They'd first met over a year ago at a 'White Ball' in aid of the Irish Children's Fund, held in the lofty environs of Powerscourt House in Enniskerry. Martina had borrowed an incredible full-length white Dolce & Gabbana ball dress from the designer room at Brown Thomas and spent most of the evening trying to avoid anyone holding a glass of red wine. The frothy white creation was worth well over three thousand euros and there was no way in high heaven she could afford to buy it if something happened to it.

She'd spotted Rory early on in the evening – he was the only person wearing a white velvet suit with a dark pink shirt, so he was hard to miss. She'd admired the suit, not to mention the rather tasty dark-haired man wearing it. Martina in turn had caught Rory's eye, but he wasn't sure how to approach the tall elegant woman without making a fool of himself. He'd never been very good at chat-up lines.

Towards the end of the evening, bored with facile, empty conversations about clothes with the rest of the fashion set, and tired of fending off drunken lurches from boorish men who thought that she should be grateful for their attention, Martina made her way outside. There, sitting under one of the outdoor burners, was Rory.

'Hello,' she said. 'Do you mind if I join you?'

'Um, no,' Rory stammered. 'Of course not.'

'Lovely evening,' Martina remarked as an opener. She hoped this man wouldn't bore her like all the ones inside had. Somehow he looked different, but maybe she was wrong.

'Yes, isn't it? You can see most of the constellations. I was following the Lux satellite. It's so clear tonight it's easy to see. It's usually hidden by cloud cover.'

'Satellite? Can you show me? I've never seen one before.'

'Really? They look a little like shooting stars but

they move in a slower, smoother manner.' He pointed at the sky. 'Fix your eyes at the top of the fountain.'

'I don't see anything.'

'Wait for a few seconds. Now! See the bright light moving in the sky?'

'Yes! You're right – it does look like a shooting star. And that's the satellite?'

'That's Lux. It's a French telecommunications one.'

Martina looked at him with interest. Finally, an interesting man. 'I'm Martina, by the way.'

'And I'm Rory. Rory Dunlop. Nice to meet you.'

She looked at him and smiled. 'Well, Mr Dunlop, tell me more about the stars.'

Martina felt reasonably alive on the flight the following morning, despite the uncivilized hour. Waiting for take-off, she watched the raindrops fall down the small plastic window. It was grey and dull outside, but she didn't care. She'd had a very productive few days indeed. The engines revved and the plane taxied towards the end of the runway. She gripped the arm-rests on either side of her. She wasn't a great flyer and missed Rory's reassurances that they weren't going to fall out of the sky.

'Are you all right?' the man beside her asked kindly.

She looked at him – a smartly turned out middle-aged man in a dark navy suit. 'Yes, thank you,' she replied shortly. She didn't really want to get into a conversation.

To Martina's relief he got the message and put his head back in his paper.

Halfway across the Irish Sea, half-finished paperwork on the tray in front of her, she dozed off, lulled to sleep by the drone of the engines. As she slept she dreamed about Designs on Red. It was opening day and the clothes hadn't arrived yet. She was running around the shop in a demented state screaming 'my life . . . my life'. Customers were staring in the windows and laughing at her. In her dream she looked down and found that she had nothing on except her raggy old grey tracksuit bottoms.

Martina woke up suddenly, her heart racing. She rang the bell on the ceiling and asked the hostess for some water. As she sipped the cool liquid, her heart slowly began to return to its normal rhythm. She stared at the paperwork in front of her, her eyes swimming with the figures. Rory was right – she'd have to take some time out and stop obsessing about the shop. But it was hard when so much of her future depended on its success. Because success, after all, was the most important thing in the world. Perhaps the only important thing in the world.

'What are you doing on Saturday?' Rory asked. They were sitting in the kitchen at Redwood the following day, discussing the lighting for the shop.

Martina cocked her head to one side. 'That depends.'

'How about a walk up the mountains? I could do with some fresh air after the week I've had.'

'Would you mind if we left it till Sunday? I'll have more time free then and we can make a day of it. Bring a picnic or something.'

'A picnic?' He laughed. 'It's the middle of winter, woman. Are you completely mad?'

'I think you'll find it's spring, not that you'd know it from the weather. But it'll be fine. We'll find somewhere sheltered and I'll make a flask of soup to warm us up.'

'OK, then.' He grinned. 'Sunday it is. I'll collect you at eleven. But I'll bring the food, including the soup. One less thing for you to worry about. Now back to business. Do you want halogen spots over the desk as well as the central aisle?'

She smiled at him. 'Whatever you think. I want to make the shop look as bright and airy as possible. I'll leave the technicalities up to you, if you don't mind.'

'What about the flooring?'

'Something natural – coir perhaps or antique floorboards.'

'The gallery will have floorboards, Dad's already ordered them from an architectural salvage place in Dublin. I'm sure we can source some more. How about floorboards with rugs? It would be a way of introducing some colour without going overboard. And that way, you could update the look quite easily by changing them if you wanted to.'

'Great idea! You're really good at this. They have some amazing brown and pink rugs in Habitat. They would look great with natural coloured floorboards and walls. A couple of brown leather sofas and I think we're almost there.'

Sarah Webb

'Can you afford sofas?' he asked, a little concerned. 'I don't remember seeing them in your budget.'

'Kind of.' She leant over and kissed him on the cheek. 'You're such a worrywart. It'll be fine, you'll see.'

'What's my son worrying about now?' Conor asked, striding into the kitchen, Cleo, his black Labrador, following closely behind him.

'Designs on Red,' said Martina.

'Is that the name you've decided on for the clothes shop?'

'What do you think?' she asked. 'Do you like it?'

Conor thought for a moment. 'Designs on Red. Yes. Yes, I do.'

'Good,' she said, throwing a look at Rory. 'I knew you would. Rory wasn't so sure.'

Rory said nothing.

'Have you seen Anna?' Conor asked her. He clicked the kettle on. Anna was Conor's housekeeper, and a completely indispensable part of Redwood House. She and Martina were close friends.

'She's gone to Wicklow,' she said. 'She said something about looking at some furniture. She'll be back soon.'

'I see. Now, who wants some tea?'

'We're fine thanks, Dad,' Rory said. 'We've just had some.'

'I hear your snow leopards arrived from Finland yesterday,' Martina said. 'Do you think I could see them?'

'You'll have to ask Leo,' Conor replied. 'I think Rory has a meeting with him later, actually.'

'Would you mind asking him for me?' she asked Rory. 'He scares me a little.'

'Not at all. I'll give it a go. You know what Leo's like though. He's very protective of his animals, especially the new ones. I think it's unlikely.'

'I know. But you could always try. Maybe he'll be in good form today.'

'Unlikely again,' Conor observed. 'I don't think the man's smiled once since he's been here.'

'He smiles when he's with Elsa and some of the other animals,' said Rory. 'It's just *people* he's not mad about.'

'Who's Elsa?' asked Martina.

'A lioness,' Rory explained. 'She came with him from Dublin Zoo. Her mother died when she was a cub and Leo reared her. They're inseparable now.'

'Named after the lion in *Born Free*,' Conor added, pouring the now boiled water into his mug.

'I knew I recognized the name.' She smiled.

'Leo's a damn fine keeper,' said Conor. 'Had to offer him a really good deal to leave the zoo – they were desperate to keep him. The zoo headhunted some hotshot from Boston Zoo to replace him, I believe. Leo's people skills leave a lot to be desired though.'

'Phew,' she said. 'I thought it was me he didn't like. I've said "hello" to him several times and he's ignored me.'

'It's just his way,' said Rory. 'Once he gets to know you he's not so bad.'

*

'How much further?' Martina complained. Rory had taken her into the depths of the Wicklow Mountains and they were now squelching through some spectacular mud. She'd agreed to a picnic and a walk, not a bloody ten-mile hike. Luckily she'd worn her Timberland boots, although she was going to have a devil of a time scrubbing the mud off them later.

'Another few minutes. And then we'll stop, I promise.' He powered on ahead of her.

She scowled at his back. Her hands were cold, and from the look of the dark, heavy clouds on the horizon, she was sure it was going to rain.

'Look!' said Rory. 'Over there.' He pointed to his right. Looming huge and grey was a rocky hill. They tramped on, the hundreds of years of pine needles making the ground spongy beneath their feet.

Martina winced as a large raindrop splashed onto her nose. It was followed by another and another until she could barely see in front of her. She pulled up the hood on her jacket.

She stood under the nearest tree to take shelter. 'Rory!' she yelled at his back. He turned around. 'We'll get soaked.'

Rory joined her under the tree. 'It's only a bit of rain. It's not going to kill us.'

She glared at him. 'I don't want to catch pneumonia, thank you very much. I'm too busy.'

'Why don't we stop and eat now? We can sit on that tree trunk over there.'

'OK,' she said grudgingly.

He took the small rucksack off his back and pulled

out two black plastic bin bags which he spread on the tree trunk. 'To keep our bums dry,' he said, smiling.

She sat down. It was a waste of time being in a bad mood with Rory. It was hardly his fault it had started to rain, after all. 'What's for lunch?'

'Vegetable soup, smoked salmon and brown bread,' he said pulling out a large tin-foil package and a flask. 'And bananas and Flake bars. I was going to wrap the bananas in tin-foil and bake them in a fire with the chocolate in the middle.'

She laughed. 'You're such a Boy Scout. Why don't we just eat them uncooked? It's a bit damp for a fire.'

'OK. And here.' He handed her a small bottle of red wine. 'Might help warm you up.' He also pulled out plastic plates and two cups for the soup.

Martina was impressed. 'This is great. Sorry if I'm moaning a bit. I'm not really used to hiking, that's all.'

'No problem. We have walked about five miles I guess. But it'll be worth it, I promise.'

'Where are you taking me?'

'It's a secret. Now take some salmon before I eat it all.'

After they'd finished and packed away, he offered Martina his hand.

'Come on. The rain's let up, we should get moving.'

They reached the foot of the hill after a few minutes. She looked up. There were clouds scurrying quickly past the top of it, giving the impression that the hill itself was moving. Rory started scrambling up the rocky path.

'No way,' she grumbled half-heartedly. 'I'm not

mountain climbing today, Rory. I might break my ankle or something.'

'It's only a hill. It won't kill you. Just follow me. I'll go nice and slowly, I promise.'

She sighed. She didn't have much choice. They were silent as they climbed, each concentrating on where to put their feet next. The wind was blowing strongly, catching in her hood and whipping around her already cold ears. By the time they reached the top she was out of breath. She staggered up to Rory who was looking down at the scenery beneath them.

'There's Redwood,' he said loudly against the roar of the wind. 'See?' he pointed.

'It looks so tiny,' she shouted back. 'Like a Monopoly house.'

Rory put his arm around her. 'Fantastic view, isn't it?'

Martina looked around. To the left was the sea, a violent, choppy dark green. To the right and behind them lay pine and deciduous forests as far as the eye could see. And in front of them was Redwood – the house and lands. It was truly spectacular.

'You're right, it's amazing!' She smiled.

He fumbled in his coat pocket. He turned towards her, his back against the wind. 'I wanted to give you this.' He handed her a small black box.

She opened it. A diamond ring was nestled in the black velvet. Even in the dull March light the single stone sparkled. 'Oh, Rory.' She looked up at him, a strange expression on her face.

'Well? What's your answer?'

Anna

Anna rubbed Redwood House's brass letter box with fixed concentration. She was trying to keep her mind off what she knew was going to be a difficult conversation with Conor Dunlop. Because today, she'd decided, was the day she'd finally hand in her notice. She'd been putting it off for weeks now, but she couldn't procrastinate any longer. Conor had been so good to her over the past two years, since her marriage to Simon, a London-born-and-bred stockbroker, had broken up and she and her son, Ollie, had moved back to Wicklow to live with her mum. He'd become a good friend in the process and they'd spent many happy afternoons in the garden together – sharing a passion for the outdoors and for rose bushes in particular.

She heard the gravel crunch on the drive and looked up. It was Conor. She watched as he flung open the door of his jeep and jumped down, followed by Cleo. He waved up at her.

'Hi, Anna.' He grinned. He loped up the steps. 'I was looking for you earlier.'

'I was in Wicklow,' she explained, 'looking at some Montessori furniture.'

He stared at her with a strange expression on his face, his eyebrows raised.

'I've been meaning to talk to you for weeks now,' Anna said, 'but it's been so busy around here I haven't had the chance.' She took a deep breath. 'I'm setting up my own Montessori school and crèche.'

'Will you have time?' Conor asked.

'Sorry?'

'With working here as well – will you have time?'

'I won't be working here any more, Conor,' she said gently. 'I'm handing in my notice. I'm sorry.'

'You can't leave me. What will I do without you?'

'You'll manage,' she insisted. 'And you knew it wasn't for ever, I told you that in the beginning. You even lent me the money for the Montessori course.'

'I know,' he sighed. 'I just didn't realize it would happen so soon. You've been here such a short time.'

She smiled gently. 'I've been here nearly two years, ever since I came back from London.'

'But things are running so smoothly. I'll miss you.'

'And I'll miss you too, Conor, but I have to do this. I really want to work for myself.'

'What if you went part-time?' he pleaded. 'Come and cook for me in the evenings. Please.'

'I don't think that would work. It's time for me to move on. I'm sorry.'

The phone rang in Conor's office. 'Don't move. I think that's Nixon. I'll be right back.'

She went back to polishing the door brasses, rubbing the lion's head doorknocker with renewed vigour. Conor didn't seem to be taking this too well. She'd enjoyed working as his housekeeper but it wasn't what she wanted to do with her life. And besides, things with him had become a little strained lately. Ever since she'd refused his third dinner invitation in a row.

Conor Dunlop's wife Agnes had left him over a year ago – jetting off to Portugal out of the blue one day with Donall Mahon of Mahon's Hotels and never coming back. Donall had been one of Conor's closest friends and he had been understandably cut up about it. Anna had never taken to Agnes. All fur coat and no knickers, as her mother would say. She wasn't in the least bit perturbed to see the back of her. A stunner in her day, Agnes Dunlop was very fond of the good life. She'd been less than delighted at moving out of Dublin's fashionable Ballsbridge to 'the sticks'. Agnes loathed animals and was horrified when Conor had adopted Cleo from the dogs' home. And as for the wildlife park. It was a wonder Agnes had lasted a whole year in Redwood before escaping. Apparently Agnes and Donall were living the tax-exiles' life of Reilly in Portugal, giving lavish parties for all the ex-pats there and yachting and playing golf to their hearts' content.

The only thing Conor had left to remind him of his wife was a fifty-foot yacht called *Angie*. It used to be called *Agnes*, but he'd changed it for obvious reasons.

As it was bad luck to change the name, he thought that if he only changed one letter – replacing the 's' for an 'i' – and rearranged the others, he might minimize the bad luck. So far it seemed to have worked. Since his wife's departure, things had been going very well indeed for Conor. Redwood was coming together and Rory was back to help him run it. Maybe losing his wife was a blessing in disguise. He'd been able to concentrate on running Redwood, not pandering to his wife's every whim.

Anna had been sailing on *Angie* with Conor, Rory and their crew several times last summer. Growing up in Wicklow Town, home of the famous Round Ireland Yacht Race, she'd spent her childhood summers in the dinghy club. Living in London, she'd missed the sea and sailing like nothing else. On coming home, she'd been delighted to join the crew of Conor's boat, which was an amazing machine – bought almost brand new and immaculately kept by the boat hand, a local lad called Nixon.

Anna rubbed the large door handle till it gleamed. There was something very soothing about brass cleaning. She always left it till last, after the dreaded bathrooms and the hoovering.

'Any news on *Angie*?' she asked as Conor walked back into the hall. The boat had been taken out of the water for the winter and was being stored in a large barn on a local dairy farm a few miles away.

'Not really. Nixon's still waiting for one more replacement part for the engine. But he says she'll be ready within the next two weeks.'

She smiled. 'You promised you'd take myself and Ollie out cruising as soon as she was in the water. Remember?'

'Yes. And you promised you'd go out to dinner with me as soon as I stopped being your boss,' he countered slyly.

Touché, Anna thought to herself. When had she said *that*? She really couldn't recall. She poured some more Brasso onto her cloth and began to rub the letter box with renewed vigour. 'We'll see.' She suppressed a smile. 'Now I have to get back to work. Buzz off, you're distracting me.'

Conor muttered something under his breath and walked away before thinking better of it and coming back. 'When will you be leaving exactly? I'll need to find someone new.'

'In two weeks.'

'Two weeks! I'll never get someone that quickly.'

Anna smiled. 'How about Pat Liddy's wife, Celine? Pat says she's looking for a new job.' Pat was currently putting lights into Martina's shop and loved to chat.

'Really? I've met Celine, nice woman. Do you think she might be interested?'

'I'll ring her for you this morning.'

'Thanks. I'll be in the office if you need me.'

As Conor walked away Anna smiled to herself. Little did he know that on a tip-off from Martina she'd already talked to Celine, who had practically accepted the job on the spot. After six months' housekeeping for the Shine-Thompsons she said she'd had a bellyfull of them, especially that Philly one who seemed to do nothing except eat and shop.

'The chairs and tables arrived today,' Moyra said to Anna as soon as she walked in the door the following Tuesday. 'And the shelves. I unpacked them and put them all in the Montessori room. I hope you don't mind – they were blocking up the hallway.'

'Of course I don't mind, Mum.' Anna smiled. 'I wondered what all the boxes and newspaper by the bin outside were from. I'm just sorry I wasn't here to help you. Let's have a look.'

Anna and Moyra stepped into Montessori room. It still had a faint smell of paint and floor varnish.

Anna clapped her hands together. 'It's perfect! The furniture looks almost new.'

They had found the child-sized furniture in *Buy and Sell* magazine for a snip. The owner, a bubbly Scottish woman called Shona Rose was shutting down her school and moving back to Glasgow with her husband and family.

'What's in those boxes?' Anna asked, nodding at several large cardboard boxes which were sitting on some of the table tops.

'Shona included some of her equipment. I'm not quite sure what they are, but I'm sure you'll be able to enlighten me.'

Anna reached into the box and unwrapped some pink blocks from the crinkly white tissue paper. 'A Pink Tower!' She unwrapped several more pieces. 'A Broad

Stair and a Sound Box. This is amazing, she's included all her Sensorial and Maths equipment.'

'There was a note in the box,' said Moyra. 'Here.'

She unfolded the sheet of handwritten paper. *'Thought these might find a good home at "Little Daisies". Best of luck, Shona Rose.'* What a sweetie! I'll have to ring her and thank her.'

Moyra smiled. 'I already sent her some flowers from us both to say thanks and bon voyage.'

Anna laughed. 'Great minds think alike.' She looked around the room. The large pinboards on the eggshell blue walls were ready for the children's artwork. The shelves would soon be filled with brightly coloured Montessori equipment courtesy of Shona and the nature table was ready and waiting for pine cones, frogspawn, pebbles, flowers and any other found objects the children wanted to bring in.

Moyra smiled at her daughter. 'Happy?'

'Very.' She gave her a hug. 'And thanks for all the help.'

'Not at all. This old house could do with some livening up. I'm looking forward to it.'

A series of loud thumps echoed from the ceiling above them and the light fitting began to sway slightly.

'Ollie!' she shouted. 'Stop jumping on your bed and come down here.'

Seconds later a whirlwind of blond hair clattered into the room and flung itself at her. 'Hi, Mum. You look lovely.'

'I'm glad you think so.' She laughed, prising the

123

little charmer's arms from around her waist. 'Have you done your homework?'

'Um, kind of. I was helping Granny with the tables and chairs so I didn't really have time to finish it.'

'Have you done your writing?'

'No.'

'Your reading?'

'No.'

'Irish reading?'

'No.'

Anna sighed. 'What exactly have you done then?'

'Spelling.'

'Into the kitchen with you,' she said firmly, patting him gently on the behind. 'You can finish it while I make your dinner. Now go and get your school bag.'

'I'm sorry,' said Moyra as soon as he'd left the room. 'He promised me he'd do it before you came home.'

'Not to worry. You've had a busy day. I'll make dinner, you go and have a rest.'

'Are you sure?'

'Positive.'

After finishing Ollie's homework with him, feeding him and sending him into the living room to watch *The Simpsons*, Anna popped a pizza in the oven and began to prepare a salad. She didn't have the energy to cook anything from scratch. Her mobile rang in her pocket and she wiped her hands on her jeans before fishing it out.

'Anna, it's Simon.'

'Yes?' She tried not to sound irritated. Her ex-husband always made her irritated these days.

'We need to talk about summer hols.'

'Simon, it's March. Can't it wait?'

He ignored her. 'Myself and Chrissie were thinking British Virgin Islands. Cruising. Sun. Sea. Get the picture?'

'Um,' she grunted. It was well for some. Last summer she'd just about managed Benidorm with Martina for a week.

'Ollie on for it, d'you think? Summer hols, all that.'

I wish he'd form proper sentences, she thought to herself.

'Anna?'

'I'm thinking.'

'Ten minutes. Ring back, ya? Catch you.' He cut her off.

She stared at the phone murderously. God, she hated that man. Why the hell had she married him? She tried to think of a good reason to scupper Ollie joining him and Chrissie cruising. Jellyfish allergy? Sun intolerance? Blonde bimbo intolerance? She sighed. Who was she kidding? Ollie would love it. She rang the familiar number back.

'Simon.'

'Well?'

'Sounds fine. Give me the dates and I'll put them in my diary. How long will you be going for?'

'Two weeks, max,' he assured her. 'Work, you know. I'll text dates later, OK?'

Sarah Webb

'Fine.' She put her phone back in her pocket and stared out the kitchen window. It was nearly dark outside. It had been grey and dreary all day. She closed her eyes and imagined bright blue sky, a large yacht and shimmering sea.

Martina

Martina stretched her hands out on the table in front of her and stared at her ring finger. The diamond solitaire glinted at her accusingly. She lowered her head towards the table and rested her forehead on the cool wood surface. After a few minutes she raised her head, wiggled the ring off her finger and slipped it back into the black velvet of the box's interior. She'd have to give it back to him today, it was only fair. Rory had told her to keep it for a few days to think about it but she didn't need any more time. She'd made up her mind. She didn't have any choice. She would love to be able to say yes, but she couldn't, not at the moment, and it wasn't fair to keep him hanging on indefinitely. Once she'd explained the whole situation to him she was sure he'd understand. She'd ask him to keep the ring safe for her until a later date.

The intercom buzzed and Martina lifted the receiver on the wall.

'Hi, it's me,' Rory said.

Martina held down the button for a few seconds and waited anxiously in the hall. She could hear Rory bounding up the stairs and she opened the front door before he had a chance to knock.

'Hi,' he said, grinning, 'how's my favourite girl?' He leant over and kissed her cheek.

'Fine.' She attempted a smile and then walked into the kitchen. He followed her and sat down at the table.

'Coffee?' she asked.

Rory looked at her carefully. 'Are you OK? Your eyes look a little red.'

'I'm grand. Just a bit of a cold.' She switched on the kettle and stood propped up against the kitchen counter.

'You're not wearing your ring,' he observed.

'No.'

Rory sat back in the chair and stared out the window. 'I see,' he said finally. 'Would you like to explain?'

'I can't accept it. Not at the moment. I'm sorry but—'

Rory stood up abruptly, sending his chair clattering to the floor. 'I knew this was going to happen. I've felt it all week – you don't love me any more, do you?'

'Rory, that's not it. There are some things going on, family things. I should have told you about it all a long time ago but—'

He stared at her, his eyes flashing with anger. 'Spare me the excuses. I don't want to hear them.'

'But that's not fair, they're not excuses. If you'll just let me explain.'

'I thought you loved me the same way that I love

you,' he said, his eyes damp with tears. 'I thought you were the one. But I was wrong. I can't believe I've let this happen to me again. You're as bad as Cat.'

'That's not fair. If you'd just listen to me.'

He stood up abruptly. 'Not any more. You've already made a complete fool of me. I'm leaving.'

'Rory!' Martina called after his disappearing back. 'Rory! Listen to me.' But it was too late – he'd gone. She wanted to run after him, to tell him that of course she loved him, but there would be no talking to him when he was in this kind of irrational mood. He had a terrible temper but he usually calmed down after a few hours, although she'd never seen him quite so angry before. And saying she was as bad as Cat, his ex-girlfriend who'd left him at the altar, just wasn't fair. She knew he'd been hurt before, badly hurt, and she understood how things must look. But if he'd only let her explain.

She was distraught. This couldn't be happening. She wouldn't let it get any worse – she'd ring him later. Once they'd had a chance to talk everything would be all right. Or so she hoped.

She picked the kitchen chair up and replaced it at the table. She tried to blink back the tears but it was no use, they came pouring out of her eyes, spilling onto the linoleum.

A couple of hours later Martina was at her parents' house. They had very kindly allowed her to use the attic as her 'office' until she could afford one for herself.

The daylight was good, as huge dormer windows had been put in several years previously. The space had never been used for anything other than storage though, and piled and stacked around her were visual reminders of her childhood – an old tin dolls' pram, 'Ted', Jemima and Tess – her favourite dolls – all looking a bit bedraggled, and cardboard boxes of dressing-up clothes, roller skates and all kinds of other things. The boxes of Christmas decorations nestled against a broken rocking horse. Martina's mum, Nita, was a determined hoarder and nothing was ever thrown away, even if it was broken beyond repair.

Martina dropped her cutting scissors onto the large table and they landed with a sharp clunk. Her eyes felt gritty and tender. She rubbed them gently with her knuckles. It was late – past ten o'clock – and she had to be in the shop early the following morning to open the door for the carpenters. Rory had offered to do it but she wasn't sure he still would, not with the way they'd left things earlier. She couldn't take the risk.

Her stomach was in knots. She couldn't stop thinking about him. She'd tried ringing him several times, but his mobile was turned off. She'd thought about calling in but had decided against it. She'd wait until the morning – maybe he'd have cooled off by then. Being emotionally involved with him was one thing – if they still were after this evening – but she also depended on him and his father business-wise. And Martina didn't like being dependent on anyone for anything, especially not a man. If Rory got it into his head to make things difficult for her . . . she sighed.

It wasn't worth even contemplating. No Designs on Red would mean no Kati G. The one thing she'd been working towards ever since she was a girl. And losing her dream was something she didn't even want to think about.

At least working kept her mind off things. Her family knew nothing about Rory and that was the way she wanted it to stay. That way she didn't have to deal with any of their questions. And boy, did her mother like to ask questions! Martina was a very private person and had always kept her love life to herself. She could never understand people who divulged every little detail to their mothers, not to mention their families. Apart from Anna, no one knew how serious things with Rory were. As far as her parents were concerned, she dated when she felt like it but there was no one 'special' on the scene. As she kept telling them, she was only twenty-six and there was plenty of time for men once she'd got her career on track. But at the moment, with her granny's illness and the unsettled atmosphere that it had brought to the house, her love life was the last thing on even her mother's mind, thank goodness.

Martina held up the toile and studied it carefully. It looked good. Now for the test.

'Mum, are you ready?' she shouted down.

'Give me one second.'

A few minutes later Nita Storey's silky black hair appeared through the opening in the floor.

'I hate this stepladder,' her mother complained. 'I never feel safe on it. I don't know how you zip up it like some sort of mountain goat.'

'Here.' Martina put out her hand to help her.

'Thanks.' As soon as she was on solid ground Nita looked around. 'You've been busy.' She walked towards the clothes rail beside the table and fingered one of the jumpers carefully. 'Can I have a look?'

'Sure.'

Nita took the jumper off the rail and examined it closely. It was ruby red with a purple ribbon trim around the edges of the sleeves and around the collar. 'What are these?' she asked pointing at the carefully stitched symbols on the left sleeve.

'Mountains,' Martina explained. 'It's the Kati G logo.'

Nita nodded. 'It's cashmere, right?'

Martina smiled broadly. 'You'd think so, wouldn't you?'

Nita felt the delicate woollen material again. 'It *is* cashmere.'

'Honestly, it's not, Mum,' Martina laughed. 'It's a synthetic fabric from Italy called "Spun Air". It looks and feels like cashmere but it's a quarter of the price.'

'I've never heard of it,' Nita said suspiciously. She'd been in the rag trade for over thirty years, in India and in Dublin, and there wasn't much she didn't know.

'It's brand new. It was launched at the last fabric fair in Paris.'

'Where did you find it?'

'One of the London wholesalers I deal with had some in stock. They gave me some sample lengths to make up and test for them. It's been fully tested in Italy but the guys in London are still a little unsure of its durability. They've had a few problems with synthetic cashmere over the years. But I've put several of the jumpers through the wash and I've given one to Anna to wear and there have been no glitches at all. So fingers crossed I can use it in my first collection.'

'And as it's such a new material, no one else will have discovered it yet,' said Nita.

'Bingo!'

'Clever girl. You always have to be at least one step in front of the competition.'

'You and Dad taught me well.'

'Now, where's this toile you want me to try on? Your dad's out at some charity meeting or other and Granny will be fretting about her hot milk soon. You know how she is.'

Martina sure did. Her maternal grandmother had been living in Wicklow with the Storey family for the last seven years, ever since Grandpa Patel had passed away. She was a formidable woman – dressed from head to toe in the finest Indian silks with a booming voice that could be heard in both English and Hindi all over the house. She'd been heartbroken when her only daughter, Nita, had married an Irishman, and a Catholic to boot.

Thomas Storey, Martina's father, had moved to England at sixteen. Work was scarce in Dublin at that time and his father's small drapery in Wicklow Town could barely support the family as it was. Thomas's uncle owned a clothes shop in Birmingham and had agreed to take on Thomas as an apprentice buyer. Here he showed an aptitude for numbers and a voracious appetite to learn, and within four years he was buying for this shop and another two that his uncle had opened in the meantime. Every few months Thomas travelled to India to buy high-quality silk shirts and scarves for the shops. And it was on one of these buying trips that he had met Nita, who worked as a designer and pattern cutter in one of the biggest factories in Bombay. It had been love at first sight for both of them – Thomas was spellbound by Nita's long black hair which hung in a thick snake-like plait down her back, her expressive eyes and most of all her warm and easy manner. Nita adored the Irishman's wide, infectious smile – no matter how bad her day had been he always managed to make her smile. They began to look forward to their monthly meetings and Thomas bought rather more silk shirts than were strictly necessary for his uncle's shop. But his uncle didn't mind – since Thomas's arrival business had been booming, as the young man had a good head for business and was quick to pick up on trends. When other shops played safe, Thomas took well-calculated chances and more often than not they paid off.

Three years after meeting Nita for the first time, Thomas asked her father for her hand in marriage. A modern and liberal man, Mr Patel realized that Nita loved and respected Thomas Storey, who was a kind, hardworking and ambitious young man, even if he was fifteen years her junior. Nita was nearly thirty-five and Mr Patel had almost given up hope that she would ever meet anyone. His own marriage had been arranged and although he loved his wife very much, he often wondered what life would have been like if he'd been allowed choose his partner for himself.

After thinking it over for several weeks, Mr Patel had decided to accept Thomas's proposal on behalf of his daughter. Mrs Patel was another matter. Nita was her only daughter and she'd expected her to marry a respectable Indian businessman, not a pale-faced Irishman. She should never have allowed Nita to attend fashion college – Nita should have been married and settled at seventeen as she had been. They were Hindus for heaven's sake! Nita could certainly not marry a Christian – what would everyone say?

In the end there was nothing she could do about it – Nita's mind was made up and her father was supporting her. Mrs Patel refused to attend the registry-office wedding in Bombay and it was only when Martina was born that she spoke to her daughter again. By that time Thomas and Nita were living outside Wicklow, Thomas running his own highly successful wholesale business with his wife by his side, importing Indian clothes and accessories and supplying hundreds of shops all over Ireland.

Martina and Granny Patel had always got on like a house on fire, much to everyone's amazement. From a young age Martina was strong and confident and well able to cope with her granny's demanding personality.

'I'll go down and talk to Granny before I go,' Martina promised. 'How is she, anyway?'

Nita sighed. 'Let me see: cataracts – good, swollen ankles – bad, irritable bowel – fair to middling.' She made no reference to the real problem – her mother's heart. Mrs Patel's heart was slowly wearing out. The family tried not to think about it too much, but according to the doctors it was only a matter of time.

'Not too bad today, then?' Martina smiled. She handed her mother the toile – the cheesecloth test version of a pair of trousers.

Nita removed her own trousers and carefully pulled the toile onto her legs. 'The things I do for you,' she smiled as she held the cheesecloth waistband up with one hand.

'I know, Mum. And I really appreciate it. But I don't think Granny would fit into them.'

'Probably not.' Nita laughed. 'What material are you making these up in?'

'The Spun Air.'

'What colours?'

'The red and a New York grey with blue trim to start with.'

Nita nodded. 'They'll look good. And the accessories?'

'If I have the time.' Martina sighed. She'd designed a darling range of tote bags, evening bags, hats and scarves, each trimmed with contrasting ribbons and sequins and embroidery detail. She really wanted to include them in the Kati G autumn/winter collection but time was running out. She'd be lucky if she got the jumpers and trousers ready at this rate.

'I could help you. I'm a dab hand on the old sewing machine, remember?'

'I couldn't ask you to—' Martina began.

'Yes, you could. Now show me your designs again and we'll see what we can do.'

'But what about Granny?'

'She'll be fine. She can ring her bell if she needs me. Now let's get going. I don't have all night, girl.' Nita sat down at the table.

'Haven't you forgotten something, Mum?'

'What?'

'You're still wearing the toile.'

'Pah! No matter.' Nita swatted the air with her hand. 'Now show me those designs.'

Martina smiled to herself. Her mother was almost as impatient as she was.

Anna
Three weeks later

'What are you up to this weekend?' asked Martina. 'I thought we might go to the cinema on Saturday night. What do you think?'

'I'm not sure,' Anna replied. 'I might have something on.'

'What?'

'Just something.'

'Why are you being so evasive? What are you trying to hide?' She stared intently at Anna who began to blush under her gaze.

'Stop! It's nothing.'

'It's obviously something –' Martina smiled – 'or you wouldn't be so uncomfortable.'

Anna stood up. 'Ollie,' she shouted out the window, 'leave the tree alone.' She turned towards Martina. 'He's pulling off the bark.'

'And you're trying to change the subject.'

'I'm not. I'm just trying to save the poor old tree.'

'Forget about the tree and tell me about Saturday

night. You're going out with Conor Dunlop, aren't you?'

'How do you know? Did Rory tell you?'

'The guy's had the hots for you for ages.' She grinned. 'Everyone knows *that*. You've already told me you're going sailing with him on Saturday. And now that you're no longer working for him . . .' She shrugged her shoulders. 'Doesn't take a genius to work it out.'

'Please don't tell anyone. And don't say anything in front of Ollie. It might upset him.'

'Ollie's nearly eight,' Martina pointed out. 'Surely he'll understand. Talk to him about it. You have to live your own life. It's about time you started getting out there again.' She stopped for a second. 'Although I might have to question your taste in men.'

'Ollie's still upset about the divorce. He may not say anything about it but I know him. He's always asking when we're going back to live with Simon in London. Anyway, what's wrong with Conor Dunlop? You don't seem to have a problem with the rest of the Dunlop clan.'

Martina sighed. 'I haven't spoken to Rory for days.'

'Why? What happened?'

'We had an argument, that's all. And now he won't talk to me.'

'But you'll work it out?'

'I hope so.'

'You're good together. He's a nice guy, you'd be mad to let him go.'

'I'm sure it'll be fine.' Martina attempted a smile.

She'd been trying to block the whole situation out of her mind all day, and talking about it with Anna would only make it worse. Rory was behaving completely erratically – not answering his mobile, refusing to take her calls to Redwood, and when she'd called to the house to see him refusing to come out of his office. Conor, who'd gone to fetch him, had been mortified on that particular occasion and had been most apologetic on behalf of his son. She didn't know what to do. She prayed he'd snap out of it in a few days, but things weren't looking good. 'It's just a silly mis-understanding,' she continued. 'Nothing to worry about. So you and Conor, eh? You know he's twice your age?'

'Hardly. I'm no spring chicken myself, remember? Do you not think Conor's good-looking?'

'I've never really thought about it. I suppose he is – if you like that sort of thing.'

'What sort of thing?'

'Ah, listen, I'm not getting drawn into this . . .'

'Go on. I swear I'll keep it to myself.'

'You'd better. OK? I guess he looks a bit like an Irish Robert Redford, especially when he wears those faded denims.'

'You think?'

'Yes. And he has great teeth.'

'Teeth?'

Martina smiled. 'Teeth are very important in a man. Nice teeth and a great ass.'

'I'd agree there. So basically you approve?'

'Now, I never said that.'

Anna laughed. 'You're a hard woman to please.'
'That's what they all say.' Martina grinned.

Anna woke up at seven on Saturday morning. It was already bright outside. She sat up, brushed back one of the curtains with her hand and looked out. The early spring leaves were moving gently on their branches. Excellent, she thought to herself.

'Mummy, are you awake?' Ollie came bounding in the door and threw himself onto her bed.

'I am now.' She ruffled his hair. 'And how are you this morning?'

'Fine. When are we going sailing?'

'At eleven. Not for ages. Why don't you go and watch some television and I'll be down to you in a few minutes? And be quiet, you don't want to wake your granny.'

'OK.' He jumped down onto the floor.

'Shush!'

'Sorry,' he whispered, leaving the room.

Anna lay back down on the bed. She should never have agreed to go on a date with Conor – she was really regretting it now. But Ollie was so looking forward to sailing that she couldn't cancel it on him, he'd be so disappointed. He'd told all his friends in school about it already. She'd talk to Conor while they were out sailing and cancel dinner. That was the sensible solution.

'What time will you be going out at this evening?' Moyra asked a little later.

Anna was sitting at the kitchen table, reading yesterday's *Irish Times*.

'I don't think I'll go actually, Mum. Thanks anyway.' Moyra had offered to babysit.

Moyra looked at Anna carefully. Her daughter was still staring at the newspaper.

Anna felt her gaze and lifted her head. 'What?'

'You should go, he seems like a nice man. It's only dinner, Anna.'

'I know. It doesn't seem right, that's all.'

'Is it because of Ollie?'

'Maybe.'

'He'll be fine about it, you'll see. Children adapt a lot quicker to things than adults do.'

'I just worry about him, Mum. He's had a lot to deal with in the last couple of years and I don't want to rock his boat again, you know.'

Moyra smiled. 'You used to love that song when you were a child – do you remember? "Sit Down You're Rocking the Boat". Your dad used to sing it to you and rock you on his knee.'

Anna laughed. 'You're right, so he did. Do you miss him?'

Moyra nodded. 'Every day. He was a good man.'

'I miss Simon too. I know things didn't exactly work out between us, but I still miss him.'

Moyra put her hand on Anna's. 'Go out this evening. It will do you good. Ollie will be fine with me.'

'I'll see.'

*

'There's Conor,' Anna said to Ollie. *Angie* was moored alongside the Wicklow dock and Conor was loading boxes and bags onto the boat. Anna parked the car and pulled their large black Musto sailing bag out of the boot. Ollie stuck closely by her side. He looked a little anxious.

'What's up, pet?'

'Do you think Conor will let me steer like Daddy does?'

'I'm sure he will.'

'He won't think I'm a big baby?'

'Of course not.' Anna looked at Ollie. 'Who says you're a big baby?'

'Boys at school. The ones who play soccer at break time. They won't let me play with them 'cause they say I'm only a big baby.'

'I bet they've never helmed a great big boat like *Angie*, have they?'

'No.'

'Well then. We'll show them, won't we?'

She took Ollie's hand firmly and crossed the road.

'Hi, Conor,' she said loudly as they approached him.

He put his hand over his eyes to shield the surprisingly strong sun. 'Hi, crew. You brought the good weather with you.'

'Of course. And you seem to have to have brought everything else with you.' She nodded at the boxes.

'Restocking the drinks cabinet, you know how it is.'

She raised her eyebrows.

'I'm only joking.' He laughed. 'It's mainly lunch and

some bits and pieces for the boat – charts, maps, racing rules, that kind of thing.'

'I brought some wine –' she patted the bag over her shoulder – 'so we should be well prepared.'

'This isn't some sort of gin palace,' Rory said, his head popping up from the cabin. 'This is a serious racing machine which is going to win the Wicklow Cruisers One Series this season, I'll have you know. Booze cruises are off limits. Except at weekends.'

'And on sunny evenings?' asked Anna.

He nodded. 'But of course.'

'And am I allowed join the *Angie* racing crew this season, Rory?' asked Anna. 'It all sounds like it's getting a bit serious for me.'

'We're counting on it. Who else would we get to skipper? What do you think, Dad?'

'Definitely. We need you. Dessie's just bought his own boat, so we need a new skipper.'

Anna was thrilled. She'd been doing the pit last year and this was a huge promotion. 'If you're sure, I'd love to.'

'Excellent!' said Conor. 'That's settled. Now let's stow the bags and get under way. Young Ollie, can you untie the wheel and help me steer her out of the harbour?'

'Yes, Mr Dunlop!' Ollie jumped up excitedly.

Conor smiled. 'You can call me Conor.'

Anna began to untie the mooring buoys from the side of the boat. As she worked, she bit her lip. Conor was the tactician on the boat – this meant that he'd be telling her, the skipper, where to sail to and when to tack. She hoped to goodness that they didn't have a falling out before racing started – that would make things really awkward.

'Need some help?' Anna asked Rory. He was taking the sail cover off the mainsail.

'Sure.'

Anna helped him untie the cords that held the cover in place. 'Nixon's done a great job. The boat looks immaculate.'

'The engine's still not firing properly, but apart from that everything is perfect. He's a good little worker.'

'What age is he? He looks so young.'

'I'm not sure. Dad, what age is Nixon?'

'Twenty, I think. Maybe a bit older. He left school at sixteen to do a boat-building course and he also worked in the Eastern Sailing Company for a while fixing marine engines.'

'I'd like to do that,' said Ollie. 'Fix boats and engines and stuff.'

Conor patted his head. 'I'm sure you would. Better finish primary school first though. Now, have you finished untying the steering wheel?'

He nodded.

'Then we'll start the engine. I'll show you but you need to watch carefully, OK?'

He nodded again.

Anna smiled to herself. Conor was good with him. And it was healthy for Ollie to be around some grown men for a change. All the teachers in his school were female and he didn't see Simon all that often, although he talked to him the odd time on the phone. She still tried to play rough-and-tumble games with Ollie, but he was getting so big. Last week they'd been wrestling on the floor and he'd really hurt her elbow when he was pinning her down. He hadn't meant to of course, but it was still bruised and tender. He sometimes had friends over from school to play and he seemed happy enough, but other times it was difficult to tell. Her mum and Martina were always telling her to stop worrying about him, but it was hard not to. She wanted to protect him from everyone and everything – she knew this wasn't practical, but it didn't stop her from trying.

While Conor and Ollie started up the engine, Rory and Anna untied the boat from the dock.

'Everyone ready?' Conor asked.

'Yes!' came the chorus back.

'Then we're off.'

Outside the harbour Rory pulled the genny and the mainsail up, Anna tailing him on the winch. Conor kept the boat head to wind with the engine still running, with Ollie by his side 'helping him'. As soon as the sails were up, Conor killed the engine and turned the wheel. The sails flapped and began to fill with the gentle breeze. Within seconds they were under way.

'Would you like to helm on your own, Ollie?' Conor asked.

'Yes, please!'

'We're on a reach, OK. So you need to keep the wind filling the sails. If they start flapping, pull the wheel a little this way.' Conor showed him. 'Try steering towards that mark ahead of us. Do you see it?'

'The big red one?'

'Exactly.' Conor took his hands off the wheel. 'You're on your own now. Keep it nice and smooth.'

Ollie's face was scrunched up with concentration. He was determined to get this right. He'd done lots of helming with his dad on their boat in London, but it was a dinghy, not a big boat like this. He gripped his little hands on the wheel and stared at the red mark intently.

Conor sat down beside Anna.

'Thanks,' she whispered.

'No problem. He's a natural, look at him. He's a credit to you. I'm going down to make some tea, would you like a cup?'

'That would be nice, thanks.'

'Tea, Rory?'

'Thanks.'

'Martina was saying that you'd had an argument,' Anna said to Rory as soon as Conor had climbed down the steps into the cabin. She couldn't help herself, she had to say something.

'Really?' Rory said curtly. 'An argument?'

'Um, sorry. Maybe I shouldn't have said anything. But you two seemed really good together.'

Rory stared at her. Anna felt decidedly uncomfortable.

'I shouldn't have brought it up. I'm sorry,' she said.

Rory softened. He knew she was only trying to help. She didn't have a bad bone in her body. 'No, I'm sorry. I didn't mean to snap at you. I asked her to marry me and she said no. I'm . . . I'm just not taking it that well,

147

that's all. After Cat and everything.' Anna knew all about Cat, as she was one of the few people, apart from Martina and his dad, Rory felt comfortable confiding in.

'I had no idea! I'm so sorry. Martina never said.'

'You know what she's like. She likes to keep things to herself.'

'I know, but this . . .' Anna was in complete shock. 'Did she give you any reasons?'

'No. Not really. But I didn't exactly give her a chance to.'

Anna sighed. 'I don't know what to say. Is there anything I can do? Would you like me to talk to her for you?'

'No. Please don't say anything about this. I'm sure she'll tell you in her own good time. I just need some space to get my head together, that's all. Away from her.'

Anna nodded. 'I understand.' She had no idea what Martina was playing at and she was upset that she hadn't told her the truth about their 'argument'. They were supposed to be close friends after all, the kind of friends that told each other everything.

'Tea's up,' Conor said, balancing two cups on the top of the cabin steps. Anna and Rory picked up their cups quickly, both grateful for the distraction. Conor climbed up with his own cup and stood beside Ollie.

'I've reached the mark,' Ollie said. 'Where to now, Conor?'

'I though we'd put the spinnaker up after we've had our tea. Why don't you head towards that yellow and black mark, do you see it?'

'Yes. Will that be a broad reach?'

Conor smiled. 'It will, good lad.'

As they sat sipping their tea Anna's mind was racing. Why hadn't Martina told her about Rory's proposal? Did she not trust her? And why had Martina said no? Nothing seemed to make sense. She glanced over at Rory, who was discussing a new compass for the boat with Conor. She knew she shouldn't get involved, but Martina was so damn proud and stubborn she made mules look easy. If this 'argument' wasn't dealt with properly and soon, Martina was quite capable of never speaking to Rory again. You never quite knew with Martina.

Martina

Martina dropped the last heavy cardboard box on the floorboards with a bang. She blew her hair back off her face, the breath hitting her hot and sticky skin like a cool breeze. She'd been lugging boxes around all morning and she was exhausted. She was holding the interviews for shop assistants today, thank goodness. The sooner she had some help the better. She slit open the box with her Stanley knife and smiled. It was another box of Designs on Red bags, specially made for her in Wicklow Town by a small local company. They were matt brown stiff paper with red velvet ribbon handles. The ribbon had been expensive but it gave just the right touch – classic yet funky. Martina had also invested in matching red tissue paper to wrap the purchases in and large red stickers with the shop's name printed in gold to seal the tops of the bags with. It was just as well Rory wasn't in the picture and breathing down her neck about budgeting – he would have had a fit – the stickers cost a fortune. Still, Martina reasoned, it was definitely worth it. The type of clients she was hoping to attract to her shop would definitely be impressed.

Martina pushed the box of bags behind the till with the other boxes, making a mental note to store them all somewhere sensible later. She glanced at her watch. Damn! She swore under her breath. The first interviewee was due in less than twenty minutes and her black trousers seemed to have picked up all kinds of dust and flecks of paper from the boxes. A thought went through her head. She walked over to one of the rails against the wall and whisked a pair of size-ten Ellison trousers into her arms before she had a chance to change her mind. She knew it was a bad habit to get into – borrowing clothes from the shop's collection – she was sure Rory wouldn't approve, but she didn't have time to go home and change. Feck it. She smiled to herself as she also helped herself to a Sami top – a dark pink, black and cream striped long-sleeved chiffon shirt. She pulled off her own black trousers and had just slid one slim leg into the new ones when she heard a discreet cough behind her. She jumped, unbalancing herself and landing awkwardly on the ground in a heap. She looked up.

'Rory! What the hell are you doing here? I nearly killed myself.' She stood up, whipped the offending trousers off her leg and left them dangling in her hand. She was sure she'd bruised her hip but she was damned if she was going to rub it in front of him. 'Well?'

He couldn't help himself. She was standing in front of him in a creased white shirt and tiny leopard-skin pants. He started to laugh. 'What am I doing here? What are *you* doing?'

'None of your business,' she snapped. 'Now if you don't mind I'm very busy – what do you want?' Her chin was jutting out provocatively and her eyes were cold and hard. It was the first time she'd seen him all week – he hadn't bothered answering any of her calls and she hadn't slept in days with worrying.

'I'll call back later,' he said evenly. He was in no humour to argue with her. It was best to leave her alone until she was in a better mood. She was obviously busy and stressed. 'It's nothing really.'

Martina watched him as he walked out the door. She considered going after him, but she wasn't exactly dressed for it. Damn, she muttered to herself. Too late. A sharp dart of regret pierced her heart as she realized how much she missed him. Why had she snapped at him like that? She regretted it already. She looked at her watch – she didn't have time to analyse it right at this moment, she had work to do. She pulled on the trousers and top and opened the drawer under the till where she'd stashed her bag earlier. She glooped some sticky neutral-coloured lipgloss onto her lips, smacked them together to spread it and ran a brush through her hair. That would have to do.

Then she settled down on the shop's brown leather sofa to read through the shortlisted CVs. 'Concentrate,' she muttered. 'Hattie Caulfield,' she read. 'Born 6 July 1949 . . .' Martina sighed. Too old. She picked up the next one. It was printed on bright pink paper and smelt of roses. 'Cindy Roche. Born 14 September 1985 . . .'

she sighed again. A grandmother and a schoolgirl. She should have looked at their details more closely. But they both had experience in clothes shops – Hattie in London and Cindy in Dublin. The other two women she was interviewing – Maureen Hayes and Fiona Quinn – seemed better bets. Both local Wicklow women in their late twenties, Fiona also seemed to have some retail experience. Martina took a swig of the bottle of mineral water that was sitting on the floor by her feet and waited for Maureen.

An hour later Martina was nearly at her wit's end. Maureen had turned out to be a nightmare – a rich Wicklow socialite who made silk cushions, 'darling', in her spare time and thought that Designs on Red would be a good place to flog her wares. She had no interest in clothes whatsoever. She did, as she kept stressing to Martina, have a lot of very rich friends who she was sure would love to visit the shop if *she* was working there. Martina doubted that the woman knew the meaning of the word 'work' as she had never actually had a real job. She had a nanny for her young son, Herbie, and a housekeeper. Seeing as it took her two weeks to 'create' one cushion, Martina doubted that unpacking and labelling the stock would be quite Maureen's thing.

Fiona seemed a better bet. Originally from Boston and now living locally, she'd worked in Vogue, a designer shop in Wicklow Town, and seemed a practical and sensible woman. Dressed in a natty black suit with a sharply pressed white shirt underneath, she looked the epitome of the successful businesswoman. But she hadn't smiled once during the whole interview and when Martina had cracked a joke about the Wicklow jet set Fiona hadn't found it funny. Martina was damned if she was going to spend her working day with someone so serious unless she had to.

But beggars can't be choosers, Martina thought to herself as she waited for Cindy Roche. Maybe Fiona would do. She didn't relish the thought of working with the dour woman though.

Martina was taken aback when a tall, elegant brunette walked into the shop.

'Cindy?' she asked uncertainly.

The girl smiled. 'That's right. And you must be Martina.' Cindy looked around. 'What a lovely shop.'

'Thanks.' Martina stood up. Cindy towered over her, which was no mean feat as Martina was five foot eight herself. Dressed in smart grey pin-striped trousers with a simple white shirt, Cindy had the sharp, poised look of a professional model. 'Please sit down.' Martina gestured at the sofa.

'Thanks.'

She studied the CV which was sitting in her lap. 'So you're seventeen, Cindy, is that right?'

'Eighteen next month.'

'Did you do your Leaving Cert?' Martina asked looking at the CV again. 'I don't see the results here.'

'No, I didn't do it. Is that a problem?'

The girl seemed uncomfortable and Martina regretted asking the question. 'No, not at all. I see you've worked in Marks & Spencer and in Pia Bang's. Tell me about that.'

'I started as a part-timer in Marks & Spencer and then moved to a full time position in Pia Bang's. I was in charge of the shoe department, the evening wear and accessories – bags, scarves, jewellery and hats – that sort of thing.'

'And you liked it?'

'Very much. Marks & Spencer was OK, but I really wanted to work in a smaller, more personal shop. Pia Bang's was great! It sounds like a cliché, but I love helping customers find something that really suits them. We used to get a lot of different age groups in the shop – from teenagers looking for debs' dresses to older ladies looking for dramatic evening dresses, something a little different. It was great.' She told Martina all about the exclusive designer shop and about some of her experiences there.

'And why did you leave?' Martina asked gently. She needed to know if Cindy was trustworthy. She'd already rung the manager of Pia Bang's who'd given Cindy a glowing report and expressed regret that the girl was no longer with them.

Cindy blushed. 'Personal reasons.'

Martina wasn't sure what to make of this. Cindy seemed ideal – well groomed, interested and bright. But she was definitely holding something back and Martina above all wanted someone she could trust. After all, there would be times when she was at trade fairs or out on business, and she needed to know that Designs on Red was in good hands.

'How would you describe yourself? In one sentence.' She'd been reading a book called *Perfect Interview Questions* the previous evening and thought she'd put some of the suggestions into practice.

Cindy thought for a second. 'Enthusiastic, hardworking, ambitious, um . . . punctual and honest.'

'Good.' Martina smiled. 'And why do you want to work in Designs on Red?'

'I'd like to open my own shop one day. But I know I need to learn a lot about the business side of things and I thought this might be a good place to start. I've read all about Conor Dunlop in the business sections of the papers and in *Business and Finance* magazine and I think Redwood is a great idea. This shop would be a good opportunity for me.' She stopped and looked Martina in the eye. 'I'd work really hard, Martina. I'd really, really like this job. And I think I'd like working for you.'

Martina was torn. Cindy seemed perfect – just what she was looking for. She took a deep breath. 'Cindy, you have good, solid experience and I'm sure you'd work hard. But I get the feeling there's something you're not telling me. Is there?'

The girl stared at her hands. After a few seconds she lifted her head. 'No.'

'Well, OK then,' Martina said standing up. 'I'll be in touch.'

'Wait. Please.'

She sat back down again. 'Yes?'

'I have a baby, he's called Ryan, and that's why I left Pia Bang's – I was pregnant.'

Martina was dumbfounded. She hadn't expected this. 'I'm sorry, I didn't mean to pry. I just . . .'

'I understand. You need to know you can trust me. I didn't put it on my CV because I thought I wouldn't get an interview. A lot of people . . . I'm young, you know.' She started to cry. 'I'm sorry, it's just so hard.' She brushed the tears away from her eyes with her hand. 'Sorry.'

'I understand, really. My friend Anna brings her little fellow up on her own. He's a bit older but he's still a handful.'

'Thanks.' Cindy stood up quickly. 'And thanks for giving me an interview. I know I'm probably not what you're looking for. I won't waste any more of your time.'

'Hang on a second. Who'll look after Ryan when you're working?'

'My mum. She's been brilliant. My brother's only eight and he loves Ryan.'

'And the dad?'

'My dad?'

'No, the baby's dad.'

Cindy smiled. 'Actually he works here.'

'Really?'

Cindy nodded. 'He's Leo's assistant. Do you know him – Makedde?'

'The refugee guy?' Martina asked before thinking.

'He's not a refugee any more. He's been given Irish citizenship.'

'Sorry, I didn't mean—'

'It's all right. He doesn't mind. He's just delighted

157

to be here. He loves working with animals – he wants to be a vet. He's doing his Leaving Cert in Wicklow Community College at the moment and I'm sure he'll get the points – he's really clever.'

'That's great. I hope he does well.'

'Fingers crossed. Anyway, as I said, thanks for giving me an interview. I'd better be going now.'

Martina put her hand on Cindy's arm. 'I'd like to give you the job.'

Cindy looked at her in amazement. 'Are you sure?'

'Yes. Absolutely.'

'Excellent! When can I start?'

Martina laughed. 'You're keen. How about to-morrow if that suits. I could certainly do with some help. The rest of the Sami order is arriving in the morning.'

'Nine o'clock? Or earlier if you like.'

'Nine is fine.' Martina smiled. 'And bring your P45, OK?'

'Sure.'

'And Cindy?'

'Yes?'

'Do you not want to hear about the wages?'

'Oh, yes.'

'Twenty thousand euro a year, paid monthly into your bank account. I'm sorry it's not more . . .'

Cindy's eyes lit up. 'Twenty thousand euro. Twenty? Are you sure?'

Martina nodded.

She threw her arms around Martina. 'Thank you so

much! We'll be able to rent a house now and be a proper family – me and Makedde and Ryan.'

Martina laughed. 'I hope you're ready to work hard. We have a lot to do before opening.'

'I'll work my fingers to the bone,' Cindy promised. 'Designs on Red is going to be the best shop in Wicklow. No, in the whole country!'

Martina smiled. She was going to like working with Cindy.

The following morning Martina reached the shop at eight thirty. She'd been up until eleven the previous night finishing some bags for the Kati G range and she was exhausted. Still, she thought to herself as she turned the key in the glass door and punched the code into the alarm panel, now I have two employees.

She'd been completely wrong about Hattie, who'd turned out to be delightful. An older woman whose children had all left 'the nest', she reminded Martina of Anna – calm, practical and elegant. With cropped grey hair and a classic understated style, she would be the perfect foil to Cindy's youthful enthusiasm.

Martina flicked on the lights and surveyed the shop. The rails were nearly full now – the Ellison black essentials had all arrived, the Sami range was building up nicely with one more delivery due that morning. The Luna dresses and separates had been in the shop for a few days now and already Martina had dressed some of the mannequins in the flowing, colourful skirts. She intended to change the mannequins several times a day to showcase as many of the different clothes as possible and it was one task she was looking forward to with relish. Only the Kati G rails remained empty.

She leaned against the ash pine cash desk and smiled. It was all coming together very nicely indeed. Through the large plate-glass shopfront she spotted a lone figure. It was Rory. She watched as he strode past. He didn't turn his head to look in and she found herself disappointed when he'd gone. She thought about running out after him but decided against it.

If that's how he wants to play it, she thought, that's fine by me. He hadn't called in to the shop again the previous day, as promised, and still hadn't returned any of her calls. She was past upset at this stage, her heart gradually hardening and becoming colder towards him each day as he put her through yet another twenty-four hours of Coventry. She was sick of doing all the running – it was time for him to contact her and stop all this childishness.

Anna

'How did the big date go?' Martina was scooping the froth of her cappuccino onto her saucer. They had just finished an excellent lunch in the Bayside Coffee Shop in Wicklow Town. Moyra had taken Ollie to the cinema and Anna was enjoying a completely child-free day.

'What are you doing? That's the best bit. Are you mad?'

Martina sighed. 'I know, I know, I should have ordered normal coffee. I wasn't thinking.' She wasn't in the mood to be scolded, not today. 'Anyway, answer my question.'

'I didn't go in the end. Ollie was tired after sailing and—'

'Don't use Ollie as an excuse. You chickened out, didn't you?'

'I guess so. I'm just happy the way things are at the moment. I'm not sure if I'm ready to see anyone again.'

'It's just a date,' Martina said evenly. 'No big deal. It's not as if you're going to marry the guy.' She took a sip of her frothless cappuccino. 'Anyway you're probably better off. Things are easier on your own.'

'What's up? You seem a little out of sorts.'

Martina sighed and stared at her hands. 'Nothing. Everything. Oh, I don't know.' She looked up. 'I could just do with some time out, I guess. What with the shop opening in a few weeks, it's all a bit hectic, that's all.'

'Do you feel stressed?'

She shrugged her shoulders. 'I suppose.'

'Are you sleeping properly?'

'Kind of.'

'Truthfully?'

'Well, no, I'm not. I keep waking up in the early hours of the morning and worrying about things.'

'Eating?'

'Yes, when I remember to.'

'Are you getting any exercise?'

'Anna, you're worse than my mother. No, I'm not getting any exercise. Unless lifting boxes and working the sewing machine counts.'

'You definitely need a good break. You sound very stressed, Martina. You need to take care of yourself. Maybe you and Rory could go walking tomorrow. Get away from it all.'

Martina said nothing.

'Is everything OK with Rory? Have you talked to him?' From the way Martina was behaving, she had a strong feeling that she hadn't.

'No. It's over, there's no point.'

'Over?' Anna said, genuinely shocked. 'What do you mean – over?'

'There's no point going backwards. We both have to get on with our own lives now. Rory doesn't seem too bothered—'

'He's in bits!' Anna exclaimed before she could stop herself.

Martina stared at her. 'What are you talking about? Have you seen him?'

Anna blushed. 'I saw him last Saturday, on *Angie*. He came sailing with Conor and Ollie and myself.'

'And you were both discussing me?'

'No, not really. Only a bit.'

'What did he tell you?' Martina said sharply. 'He told you that I'd refused to marry him, didn't he?'

Anna lowered her eyes and said nothing.

'He did, didn't he? I'll kill him. Stupid prick.' She stood up, sending her chair flying. 'I won't have you both talking about me behind my back. It's none of your business.'

'Martina, sit down. Let's talk about this. I'm really sorry . . .'

'So you should be. I bet you told him you'd talk to me about it, didn't you? Go on, admit it.'

'Actually I did offer but he asked me not to, if you must know.'

'I see,' Martina said coolly. She was exhausted, upset and sick with worry and the last thing she needed was Anna getting involved, however well-intentioned she was. She could cope with this on her own, like she always had.

Sarah Webb

'Why didn't you say yes, Martina? I know how you feel about him.'

Martina put her hands on the table and leant towards her. She'd had enough. 'Don't interfere in my life.'

'I was only trying to help . . .' But it was no use. Martina had already walked out the door. Anna's words lingered in the air like a bad smell. Her eyes began to water. She only wanted Martina to be happy. Surely Martina could see that.

'I know it's short notice but I was wondering if you were free this evening,' Conor said.

Anna hesitated. She'd been sitting at her kitchen table all afternoon waiting for Martina to ring. She'd called into Martina's apartment and into her parents' house and she'd rung her several times on her mobile, but she obviously didn't want to be found. When the phone rang Anna had picked it up immediately, hoping it was Martina.

They'd only ever fallen out once, when Anna had organized a weekend away in the Delphi Lodge in Galway. Martina had presumed they'd be going on the spa weekend to be pampered from head to toe with all the latest health and beauty therapies. Anna had however booked the activity weekend – walking, horse riding, yoga, cycling. Martina had brought all the wrong clothes and hadn't stopped complaining all weekend about ruining her new DKNY runners and cashmere jumpers. Eventually Anna had had enough

164

and had told Martina to cop onto herself and Martina hadn't liked this one little bit. They'd made up in the end – when Anna had apologized of course. Martina suffered from what Anna called 'only-child syndrome' – she liked having things her own way. As Rory was an only child too, it made for quite a tempestuous relationship at the best of times. Which was making itself more than apparent in light of recent events.

'Hi, Conor. I'm sorry, I don't think so. I'm kind of tired, to tell the truth.'

'Oh.' He sounded disappointed. 'Listen, Anna, this is the last time I'm going to ask you. Nothing personal but I can't take all the knock-backs. I hope you understand.'

'Sure, I understand. Sorry.'

'That's OK. I'll see you around.'

'Yes,' she whispered.

She clicked her mobile off and sat staring at it. Her eyes began to water again. Great, she thought to herself. Now Conor's annoyed with me too.

'What's wrong, Mummy?' Ollie asked, coming in from the garden. His runners were covered with mud. When he saw Anna staring at his feet he sat down on the kitchen floor and pulled them off.

'You should untie the laces.' She wiped away a lone tear from her cheek and sniffed discreetly. 'And I'm fine, just something in my eye.'

'When are we going sailing again with Conor and Rory? That was fun.'

She took a deep breath. Shit, she thought to herself.

Conor was hardly going to want her on the boat now. 'I'm not sure, pet.'

'Conor is nice. He let me helm, didn't he, Mum?' She nodded.

'And he had some good jokes.'

'Did he?' she raised his eyebrows.

'Yes.' He grinned. 'He told me not to tell them to you as they're kind of rude. Boy's jokes, he said.'

'I can imagine.' Ollie was at the age when anything to do with bums or farts was hysterical.

'Can I watch telly now, Mum?'

'For a little while.'

'Yippee!' He ran out of the room and she winced as he slammed the living-room door behind him.

Anna stared at her phone. She tried Martina's number again. It connected immediately to the answering service. 'Hi, Martina, it's Anna. Please ring me. I know you're annoyed with me and I'm sorry. I didn't mean to hurt you. That's all. Bye.'

She dialled another number. 'Hi, Conor, it's Anna. Actually I am free this evening. What would you like to do?'

'What made you change your mind?' Conor asked after he'd handed the menus back to the waiter.

'About what?'

'About this evening.'

Anna shrugged her shoulders. 'I needed to get out.' She looked around. 'Nice place.' Davey's Boathouse Restaurant was perched on the Wicklow cliffs overlooking the sea. Decorated in an eclectic style, it managed to look both modern and homely at the same time. Large driftwood and blue glass ceiling-to-floor mobiles separated the open space in a very unusual way and tall, chrome gas braziers heated the glassed outside area where they were sitting.

'Great, isn't it? I read about it in the *Irish Times Magazine*. They were reviewing the building rather than the food, but the menu looked good too so I wanted to try it. It's my first time here. Anyway, you didn't answer my question.'

Anna blushed. 'I was hoping you wouldn't pursue that line of enquiry, your honour.'

'Sorry. Was I being too personal again?'

Anna laughed. 'Not really. I'm just in a funny mood, sorry.'

'Funny haha, or funny peculiar?'

She laughed again. 'Both, I guess. It's been a strange sort of day really.' Anna took another sip of her wine. It was already going to her head, but for once she didn't care.

'I'm delighted that you're finally here, whatever the reason,' Conor said graciously. 'And how is Little Daisies working out?'

'Really well. I have eight children now and mum's helping out in the mornings. A couple of the children stay on in the afternoons and Ollie likes that – it means he has friends on tap to play with.'

'Does he ever get jealous of the other kids?' Conor asked astutely.

'Yes. Now and again. But he's old enough to under-stand that Little Daisies is my job and he's my life.'

'Incidentally, would you have space for one more child?'

'Who?'

'There's a woman called Rosie O'Grady who's going to be running the gallery in Redwood. Her daughter, Cass, is three or four. I think Rosie was hoping to send her to Redwood National School in September if she can get a place. I told her about Little Daisies and she sounded keen.'

Anna thought for a second. 'I could just about manage one more, I suppose. Ask her to give me a ring. I'll hold a place for Cass, but I'll need confirmation within a week or two.'

'Great. She's a really nice woman. I know her father from years back. She's moving to Wicklow on her own so she needs all the help she can get.'

'On her own? How do you mean?'

'Her husband ran off with some girl from the office, apparently. All a bit messy.' He looked at her. 'Gosh, I'm so sorry, I didn't mean to . . . did that happen to you? You've never gone into details.'

'No, thank goodness. Our break up was fairly mutual. But that poor woman. Life's hard sometimes, isn't it?'

He nodded. 'I was devastated when Agnes left me. But you get over it.' The waiter walked towards them. 'Our food, I believe.'

*

After dinner Conor dropped Anna home. It was after twelve and the house was in darkness except for a light on in the hall. Anna felt decidedly light-headed. She rarely drank these days and even a few glasses of wine had a strong effect on her. And the Irish coffee after dinner hadn't exactly helped.

'Would you like to come in for coffee?' she asked as they pulled up outside her house.

'Sure. If that's OK.'

'Of course it is.'

As she unlocked the door she felt momentarily awkward. She hoped he wasn't expecting anything other than actual coffee. She felt suddenly all at sea. She hadn't so much as kissed another man apart from Simon since her early twenties and she had no idea how to behave.

'Um, I'll just put the kettle on,' she said as soon as they stepped into the hall. 'Or would you like something stronger?'

'I'd love a brandy. If you have one.'

'Should do. Mum loves the stuff. Follow me.' She led him into the sitting room. K'nex building parts were still scattered over the floor. Ollie had almost finished a large helicopter model and Anna hadn't the heart to move his work.

'Sorry about the mess. Ollie . . .'

Conor put his hand up in a 'stop' gesture. 'No need to explain. Rory was just the same at that age, always making something. Although it was Meccano in his day.'

She smiled. Up until now she'd forgotten how much

older Conor was. Not quite her mother's age but not far off it.

'Showing my age, aren't I?' He laughed, reading her mind. He sat down on the sofa as Anna poured brandy into two heavy Waterford crystal tumblers.

She handed him a glass and sat down beside him. 'Yes.' She smiled.

'Does it bother you? My age, I mean.'

Anna stared at her glass. 'You're very direct, Conor.'

'Sorry. I suppose I am. Do you hate it?'

'I haven't decided,' she said honestly. 'It's a little disconcerting sometimes, I suppose.'

'Disconcerting. Good word. Let's talk about something else then. How about sailing? How did Ollie enjoy his jaunt on *Angie*?'

'He loved it,' she said, relieved that the conversation had taken a safer turn. 'He's already asking when we're going out again. You have him hooked.'

'I'd say he has you to blame for that. How could he not like sailing with a national champion as his mother?'

'That was a long time ago. In another lifetime.'

'Perhaps. But you should give it one more shot. You'd be in the Masters League now, being over thirty-five—'

'How do you know what age I am?'

'Your CV. It's all there in black and white. Leaving Cert results too.'

'I'd forgotten about that. But seriously, I'd never be fit enough to sail a Laser again. Big boats maybe . . .'

'I'm sure you could do it. You have winning genes

– they don't go away, you know. Your father was an Olympian, you can't forget that.'

'I know. Back in the days when they wore big yellow oilskins, shorts and wellies to go sailing in. It's all changed now.'

'It's still the same sport, even if money has taken a bit of a hold of things. The skills needed are still the same. And the boats themselves haven't changed all that much.' They talked about sailing for a little longer, comparing different boats and how they'd been adapted over the years.

Anna smiled. She was really enjoying this evening. It was just what she needed. A bit of ego boosting and some conversation that didn't centre around three-year-olds.

'Why are you smiling?' he asked.

'No reason. I'm just happy.'

'Good.' He took her glass out of her hand and placed it beside his on the floor. He leant over and kissed her lightly on the forehead. 'So am I.' He cupped her chin in his warm hand and drew her face close to his. She could feel his warm breath on her mouth and she closed her eyes in anticipation. She allowed herself to be kissed gently on the lips and after a few seconds she responded. Conor's hands caressed her back through her shirt, moving in deliciously smooth and sensual circles. Soon her whole body began to fill with a warm glow.

I've missed this, she thought to herself as she ran her hands through his hair while kissing him passionately. God, how I've missed this.

Rosie

'What's this I hear about you moving to Wicklow?'
Julia shrieked down the phone. 'You can't be serious!'

Rosie held her mobile phone away from her head.
'Can I ring you later? I'm in the supermarket.'

'I suppose so. Ring me as soon as you get home,'
Julia muttered before hanging up abruptly.

Rosie sighed. She should have told her mum about
Darren leaving herself. Things had been decidedly
chilly between them ever since her dad had broken the
news to Julia a little while ago. And now this.

But she was damned if she was going to let anything
or anyone stand in her way. Her dad was quite right,
she needed to start standing on her own two feet and
making her own decisions, no matter how much it
displeased other people – even her mother.

On the way home from Redwood, Rosie and her dad
had talked non-stop about the gallery.

'Rosie,' he'd said. 'If you don't change your life now, you may never do it.'

'But the commute,' she'd argued. 'It's bad enough now. If something happened and I needed to collect Cass from school it would take me forever to drive to Glenageary from Wicklow. I'd spend my life in the car.'

'Maybe you shouldn't commute then. Think about it. It might be nice to get out of Dublin, put Cass in a small, local school. Take someone on to help you in the gallery and work part-time. Spend some more time with her.'

'Live in Wicklow? Are you mad?'

'Why? It's a lovely place to live and you wouldn't be that far from us or from Kim.' He and Julia lived in Delgany, and Kim and Greg in Bray. 'And it's on the train, so if you needed to go into town you could travel that way.'

She stared out the window. She couldn't move to Wicklow, could she? It would be crazy. And Darren would go mad – he'd say she was making his access impossible. She smiled to herself. Although that might not be such a bad thing – pissing Darren off. And she knew in her heart that she should be spending more time with Cass. Her little daughter was growing up so fast. One day she'd blink and she'd be all grown up.

'And Conor said you could rent the old game-keeper's cottage at a very reasonable rate,' Rex continued. 'Incidentally, it's called Rose Cottage – apt, don't you think?'

'Dad! You have this all thought out, don't you? You're incorrigible.'

'Actually the cottage was your sister's idea,' Rex said sheepishly.

'Kim's in on this too? And who else knows? Mum? Greg?'

'Just Kim. And maybe Greg, I guess, if she told him. I don't know.'

She sat back against her seat smouldering. So much for taking control of her own life – it seemed like her whole family had done that for her. She wasn't a child, she could make up her own mind about things. There was no way she was moving now, no way, Rose Cottage or no Rose Cottage. They could all take a flying jump.

'Don't be like that.' Rex could sense his daughter's irritation. 'We all want to see you happy—'

'I'm perfectly happy, thank you very much,' she snapped. 'Everything's just great. My husband's gone off with some floozy with legs up to her armpits, my dad and my sister have been conspiring behind my back, I hate my job, I never see my daughter and I'm so bloody tired all the time.' She shut her eyes tightly. She was damned if she was going to cry. 'Everything's just rosy.'

She stared out the window again, still trying to hold back the tears. But it was no use – they began to spill out of her eyes and down her face in hot streams.

Rex pulled the car over and turned towards his daughter. He put his arms around her and held her tightly.

'Oh, Dad. What am I going to do?'

'Paint the cottage. It needs it. We'll all help. Hand

in your notice and set up the gallery.' He handed her a large white cotton handkerchief.

'You make it all sound so simple, but I can't.' She wiped away her tears and blew her nose. 'I'm not strong enough. And I don't have the energy.'

'Yes, you do,' he said gently, stroking her hair. 'I know you do.'

'Mum,' Rosie said nervously into the receiver when she'd got home from the supermarket, plonked Cass down in front of Cartoon Network and put the shopping away. 'It's me. I'm at home now, but I only have a few minutes. Darren's calling round.'

'What is going on? Your father said that you're taking Cass out of that wonderful Montessori and moving to Wicklow. Is it true? And that you're selling the house and living in some little cottage thing. And selling paintings. Paintings, I ask you. You're a manager in a wonderful company, with a good salary. And what are Emily's parents going to say?'

'Mum,' Rosie said, trying not to laugh. 'Please don't make it all sound so dramatic.' Emily's parents had actually been very nice about Rosie's announcement – they'd given her a very generous gift voucher for Brown Thomas department store and had apologized for Emily's behaviour. To their mortification, on hearing the news their daughter had asked Rosie to leave immediately in case she stole any ideas for her 'little shop', as Emily had so succinctly put it. Emily had immediately promoted Ruth and had instructed her to watch Rosie clear her desk 'just in case'. Ruth had been extremely embarrassed but Rosie had laughed it off. If Emily was going to be such a petty bitch then good riddance to her. Rosie was only too delighted to be leaving without working her notice – it gave her more time to sort out her future.

'Well,' demanded Julia. 'Is it true?'

'If you'd let me get a word in edgeways—'

'You're making a big mistake, my girl. Mark my words. Jobs like yours don't come along every day or people of Emily's calibre . . .'

Thank God, Rosie thought to herself.

'I think you're being rash, very rash indeed. You should be thinking of Cass. What will living in the middle of the country do to her? Taking her away from her friends and family? And when you and Darren are back together . . .'

'That's enough! As I keep telling you, myself and Darren will not be getting back together, ever. And that's final. I don't want to hear any more on the subject. And for your information, Cass doesn't have any friends.'

She could hear Julia catch her breath.

'That's right, Mum. Cass doesn't have any friends and I don't have any friends. Not one! If it wasn't for Kim I'd lose my mind. And I'll tell you why I have no friends – because I spend my whole goddam life working. I don't have time for friends. I don't know any of the mothers from Cass's school and I don't know anyone else with children. I'm totally and completely isolated. And do you know the worst thing, Mother? I don't know Cass.'

'But darling—'

'Let me finish. I've been working so hard I've lost sight of what matters. I want my life back. I want time to play with Cass, to read to her, hell, to do nothing with her. I thought you'd understand. You're always going on at me to stop work and look after her myself.'

'But things are different now. You don't have a husband to support you.'

'I don't need any bloody husband to support me! I can't win with you! I'm going to do this on my own. And you're not helping. You never help. You're a selfish, meddling old cow and you can just feck off and leave me alone.' She slammed down the phone and immediately began to cry.

She hadn't meant to say such awful things to her mother, but she couldn't help it. Why couldn't the woman just be supportive for once in her life? Why did she always have to criticize everything she and Kim did? Why?

Rosie heard the doorbell ring. It was probably Darren. Brilliant timing. She grabbed some kitchen roll and dabbed at her eyes. 'Just a minute.'

She opened the door and found Kim on the doorstep.

'Kim,' she said, a wave of relief sweeping over her. 'I'm so glad to see you. I've just said the most terrible things to Mum.'

'Come here.' Kim put her arms around her sister. 'I'm glad one of us did. She's gone bats. Take no notice.'

She drew back and smiled. 'Let's have some coffee. You can tell me all about it.'

'Darren's on his way over. I have to tell him about Wicklow.'

'Should be interesting. Can I stay and watch the fireworks?'

She thought for a second. 'You know, yes, you can. Cass is here. If it starts getting too heated maybe you could take her out for a drive or something.' Rosie frowned. 'But I hope it doesn't come to that.'

'I'd be happy to stay, as long as you stand your ground. Don't let him bully you, love. You've made your decision, stick to it.'

'It may not be that simple. But you're right, I won't let him push me around.'

'Good woman. Now where's Cass? I have something for her.'

'Kim! You spoil her.'

'And why not? She is my god-daughter after all.'

'She's in the playroom.'

The doorbell rang. Rosie sighed. She was tired to the bone and Darren was the last person she wanted to see today. But she figured she might as well get it over with.

She opened the door. Darren gave her a smile but she could see it was forced.

'Hi, come on in. Kim's in the playroom with Cass.'

He frowned. 'I was hoping to see Cass . . .'

'That's not why I asked you over.' She walked into the kitchen and he followed her. 'Coffee?'

'Sure.' He sat down in his usual place at the head

of the kitchen table. 'So why am I here? I thought you didn't want to talk about money or access. I thought you wanted to leave that to the solicitors.'

'You're right. I don't.' She took two mugs out of the cupboard and put a spoon of instant coffee in each. She wasn't going to waste any good coffee on the likes of him.

'Well,' he said impatiently, 'what is it then?'

Rosie turned and looked at him. 'I thought I should tell you – Cass and I are moving to Wicklow.'

'What? You can't be serious. What the hell is in Wicklow?'

'My new job.'

'What new job?'

'I'm going to be running the Redwood Gallery.'

'I've never heard of it,' he said scornfully.

'You wouldn't have. It's new.'

'You're not moving Cass to Wicklow. I'm sorry, it's out of the question.'

Rosie took a deep breath. 'I'm not asking you, Darren, I'm telling you.'

Darren's face began to redden. 'And I'm telling *you*. You can't move Cass to some godforsaken place and expect me to agree to it. I'm entitled to see my daughter and you're out of order. You can't do this.'

'Yes, I can. It's Wicklow, Darren, not Outer Mongolia. It's in Cass's best interest and she's my responsibility. And would you please lower your voice, Cass and Kim are in the next room.'

He stood up and put his hands on the table. 'You're not moving to Wicklow,' he barked, ignoring her request. 'She can come and live with me and Tracy. She's staying in Dublin and that's final.'

She could feel the blood pumping through her veins. 'I'm sorry, Darren, I'm not going to argue about this. It won't affect your access in any way, I promise. But there's no question of Cass living with you, we both know that. You made your decision when you left us.'

He glared at her. 'I don't want to hear it. You're just doing this to get back at me. You know your problem, you're jealous. You can't stand the fact that I'm with Tracy now. It's eating you up.'

'I'd like you to leave now. I really have less than no interest in what you think. I thought we could discuss this like adults, but I was wrong. I'll be civil to you for Cass's sake, but otherwise I don't want anything else to do with you. You're a nasty man and I'm well rid of you. Tracy's welcome to you.'

He walked out of the kitchen and into the hall. 'You'll be hearing from my solicitor in the morning.'

'Fine.'

She shut the door behind him and leant against it. She felt completely and utterly drained. Her hands were shaking and the blood was thumping in her temples. How could he be so unreasonable?

Darren sat in his car, gripping the steering wheel as if his life depended on it. How dare she talk to him like that? Who did she think she was? Making decisions without consulting him, she was completely out of order. He'd talk to Noelle first thing in the morning – maybe his solicitor could put some manners on her.

'How did it go?' Kim asked gently. She'd heard

the front door shut and had found Rosie sitting on the bottom stair, her eyes fixed on the hall floor.

She looked up and started to cry. 'It was terrible. I don't really want to talk about it.'

'OK. Listen, I'll put Cass to bed. You go and watch some crap TV or something, try to take your mind off it.'

She stood up slowly. 'I'll start to pack. I have so much to do before next week. I should really make a start.'

'Pack? Are you sure?' Kim asked with concern.

'Yes. The sooner we're out of here and away from *him* the better. You're still all right for house painting on Saturday?'

'Of course. Greg too. And Dad.'

'I wouldn't say Mum's too happy about that.'

'No. Not exactly. She's decided to go into town with her cronies. There's some sort of antique fair on or something.'

'Sounds thrilling. As long as she's out of my hair.' Rosie sighed. 'It's been quite a day, I'm exhausted. Roll on Wicklow. I'm looking forward to the peace and quiet.'

'I don't know. Redwood might be a hotbed of passion, deception and intrigue – and that Conor Dunlop sounds a bit of all right.'

'Kim! He's Rory's father. And anyway, I'm sure there's a Mrs Dunlop somewhere. And Redwood is just an old country house. I'm sure it'll all be quiet and sedate.'

'That's what you think. I bet you're wrong.'

'Go and put Cass to bed before your imagination runs away with you. I'm going upstairs.'

'I still think you should be resting.'

'Yeah, yeah.' Rosie walked up the stairs. 'Stop fussing.'

Rosie

'Are you sure about this colour?' asked Greg, staring at the wall he'd just painted. 'It looks a little . . .'

'A little what?' Rosie cut in with a smile on her face.

'Pink.'

'It certainly is. I've always wanted a pink bathroom. Anyway, it's not so much pink as raspberry.'

'I see,' he murmured doubtfully. It was a peculiar colour for a bathroom, raspberry or no raspberry. 'I'll go ahead, so.'

'Great. I'll be in the bedroom if you need me.'

'That's what I like to hear.' He grinned.

'Greg! You're practically my brother-in-law.'

'Keep it in the family. That's what I always say.'

'Is my boyfriend behaving himself?' Kim asked as Rosie rejoined her in the bedroom.

'No!'

She smiled. 'Why am I not surprised?'

'This looks amazing,' Rosie said looking around.

The small room had been transformed from a gloomy light brown to a bright, fresh primrose yellow.

'Doesn't it? The white undercoat made all the difference. Good old Dad. I'm nearly finished. How's Cass's room coming along?'

'Great. The clouds on the ceiling were a little more difficult than I'd envisioned. My hair is full of paint. Dad's just finishing up the skirting boards for me.'

'He's been great, hasn't he? He's enjoyed having a new project to work on. Since he took early retirement I think he's been a little bored, to tell the truth.'

'I don't know what I'd have done without him. He's even hired a van to help me move on Monday.'

'Are you bringing much with you? You already have most of the furniture you need here.'

'I know. It makes life much easier. I've two new beds being delivered on Monday – one for the spare room and one for Cass – then we're just about set. Everything in Glenageary is much too big for this house and anyway, I've never liked a lot of it.' She wrinkled her nose. 'Especially the white leather suite. That was Darren's choice. To be honest, my clothes and Cass's toys are the worst part. I've taken so many black sacks down to the St Vincent de Paul that I've lost count!'

'I can imagine.' Kim laughed. 'You always were a bit of a hoarder. But you're nearly there now.'

'Yes. And on Tuesday I'll get stuck into the gallery.'

'Are you nervous? About setting up on your own.'

'A little.' Understatement of the year. She been

trying not to think about it too much, but there was so much work to be done it was frightening.

On Tuesday morning Rosie dropped Cass to her new crèche – Little Daisies. She'd been bloody lucky to find somewhere good at such short notice. Conor had kindly asked a friend of his – Anna Wilson – to hold a place for Cass. Anna ran a small Montessori and crèche within walking distance from Redwood and she'd talked to her several times on the phone. Anna seemed really nice and Rosie was quietly confident that Cass would be happy there.

Rosie had already enrolled Cass into the local national school for the following September, despite her mother's objections. Not to mention Darren's. He'd had his heart set on Cherry Farm, an exclusive private school in Dalkey.

Contrary to Darren's threats, she hadn't heard a peep from his solicitor or her own, which was a relief. His solicitor had obviously talked some sense into him. The sooner the separation order was finalized the better, as far as she was concerned. She wondered when he'd get in contact. He'd been seeing Cass every weekend for months now and they'd talked about Cass staying overnight in the near future, but that was before their Wicklow argument.

Anna smiled widely as she greeted Cass and Rosie at the door of her house. Little Daisies was at the end of a terrace of semi-detached small Victorian redbricks. Anna's long, blonde hair hung down her back in a thick, rope-like plait and her cornflower blue eyes crinkled attractively at the edges as she bent down to say hi to Cass. 'You must be Cass. You're very welcome to Little Daisies. Would you like to come in?'

Cass nodded shyly, holding her mother's hand with a firm grip.

As they walked inside a white cat brushed past Anna's legs and out into the garden. 'That's Casper.' She looked up at Rosie. 'Cass isn't allergic to cats, is she?'

She shook her head. 'No, thankfully.'

'Good. Casper sometimes helps in the classroom. He's a very good teacher.'

Rosie laughed.

'This is the cloakroom, Cass.' She opened a door tucked in under the stairs. 'You can hang your coat here. There's also a toilet and a basin for washing your hands.' Rosie smiled at the pint-sized toilet and wash-hand basin.

Cass took off her coat and looked up at Anna.

'I've made a special hook for you with your name on it, see?' She pointed to a large cardboard heart, which read 'CASS' in large capital letters. It had been decorated with pink ribbon and sequins.

Cass hung her coat on the hook carefully.

'Good girl. Now, would you like to meet the rest of your class?'

She nodded.

Anna took her by the hand and led her into a large room towards the back of the house. Sitting at child-sized desks were several children – three boys and five girls. A blonde woman who looked remarkably like Anna was reading a story about a farmer and a duck to them, making animated duck 'quacks' as she went along. As Anna walked in she looked up.

'Hi, Mum. This is our new pupil: Cass.'

'Hello, Cass. I'm Moyra, Anna's mum. I help out in the mornings. Would you like to sit down?'

She nodded again and was shown to a seat beside a red-haired girl.

'I'm Rita,' the little girl said. 'Would you like to smell my strawberry pencil?'

Anna led Rosie out the door.

'She seems OK,' Rosie said, relieved. 'You'll ring me if there are any problems?'

'Of course. But I'm sure she'll be fine.'

'She does talk,' Rosie said a little anxiously. 'She's not always so quiet.'

'They're all a little shy on their first day, it's perfectly normal. Please, try not to worry. Conor was saying that you're setting up a gallery at Redwood.'

'That's right. I'm going there to meet with the electrician now. We hope to have everything ready by the opening, fingers crossed.'

'It sounds wonderful. A friend of mine, Martina, will be running the clothes shop. You might bump into her.'

'The gallery's just beside the clothes shop, so I'm sure I will. I'd better get on. Thanks for everything. I'll collect her around five, if that's all right.'

'Perfect. We're open till six. Maybe you'd like to stay

for a coffee later if you have time. I could tell you all about Redwood village.'

'I'd like that. Thanks.'

Rosie smiled to herself as she walked up the drive past her new cottage, towards Redwood House. It was lovely to be able to walk to work. No more wasting time in the car, grinding her teeth while held up by yet more roadworks or bumper-to-bumper rush-hour traffic. It was raining softly, a gentle mist of water settling on her hair and face, but she didn't mind.

As she approached the gallery there was a white van pulled up outside with Pat Kiely Electrician on the side in large black lettering. She quickened her step.

'Hi,' she said, walking into the gallery. A stocky, dark-haired man was surveying the ceiling. 'Hope I haven't kept you waiting.'

'Not at all. I'm early – I only live down the road. Mr Dunlop let me in, I hope you don't mind.'

'Of course not. In Dublin you can't get a good electrician for love nor money so I'm delighted you're here,' she said sincerely. 'Conor recommended you highly.'

'So,' Pat said looking around. 'Great space. What did you have in mind?'

'I guess we should start with the basics. I'll need some new sockets put in for the cash register and the computer sitting over there on the desk.' She gestured towards the new cherry-wood desk, which had arrived the previous day, efficiently found, ordered and paid for by Rex. Her father had also ordered off-white canvas blinds for the large windows, a new computer from Dell, complete with a top-of-the-range colour printer, scanner and all the latest desktop publishing and spreadsheet packages. He obviously has no idea how computer illiterate I am, Rosie had thought to herself as he'd waxed lyrical about using the computer to design and maintain a Redwood Gallery website, produce catalogues and invitations and keep an inventory of the paintings.

'Light switches behind the desk,' Rosie continued. 'And the most important thing, halogen spotlights on a suspended rail. From here to here.' She swept her arms along the whole length of the rectangular room.

Pat looked up and whistled. 'High ceiling. Very high. Might take me some time, I'm afraid.'

'How long?' she asked anxiously. She'd hoped to have the gallery ready within two weeks. It was going to be a challenge but she was determined to try. The clothes shop, coffee shop and the gardens would be opening to the public on Saturday 14 June, launched by popular RTE personality Geri Maye, and Conor had arranged for the press to visit the whole complex. It would be a shame to miss out on such a great marketing opportunity.

'I won't have it finished until the end of the week,' Pat said. 'I'll have to drive up to Dublin to get the spots and the rail. I've cleared some of my other work but I'm afraid there are one or two other jobs that I'll have to fit around yours.'

'The end of *this* week?' she asked, smiling broadly.

'Yes. But hopefully earlier. I'll do my best.'

She'd been expecting the worst. 'Fantastic! That's brilliant. I hope to have paintings arriving from

Saturday on and it would be so much easier if the lighting was in place by then so that I could start hanging them.' She clapped her hands together. 'Thank you, I'm so grateful.'

Pat smiled. 'You're a resident now, love. Have to take care of our own.'

She felt like hugging him, but she refrained.

The rest of the morning was spent ordering supplies. Jones's Art Suppliers in London had promised to ship over urgently four large wooden 'browsers', or print racks. Haley's Framing Specialists, also in London, were supplying the professional hanging system – a clever system of rails, wires and hooks which would make hanging the paintings child's play, and she had also ordered packing and stationery essentials from Viking Direct – bubble wrap, tape and tape gun, plastic bags, a large red desk diary and a stock book.

At lunchtime, she walked down the drive towards Rose Cottage with a large smile on her face. She'd achieved a huge amount already and it wasn't even one o'clock yet. As she popped some bread into the toaster, Rosie realized that she hadn't thought about Darren all morning. In fact, she hadn't thought about him much all weekend – she'd been far too busy. As she munched on a piece of toast, the sticky, hot butter ran down her chin and she laughed to herself as she wiped it away with the back of her hand. She couldn't remember feeling so good – so alive and light. It was as if someone had attached a thin silken thread to her solar plexus and given it a good hard tug upwards. 'Thank you,' she said out loud to the empty kitchen.

She stood up and plonked the crumby plate in the sink, then settled herself on the living-room sofa and picked up the phone.

'Hi, Alan, it's Rosie.'

'Rosie, how the hell are you? Rumour has it you've upped it to the sticks.'

She laughed. 'Wicklow, Alan – hardly the sticks. I'm opening a gallery in Redwood House.'

'Darling!' Alan shrieked. 'You're never! A little birdie told me you were going to be working in a shop. I had no idea.'

Rosie knew exactly who 'the little birdie' was – Emily. Stupid cow. She was well rid of her. 'And guess why I'm ringing?'

'I'd be honoured, Rosebud. I have a couple of new pieces that are going to blow your mind. My *October Red* series. Wow! Double wow!'

'How big, Alan?'

'Big.' He giggled. 'You know me.'

'Come on,' she cajoled. 'How big?'

There was a brief pause on the phone. 'The colours, Rosebud. They'll blow your mind. All different shades of red – from deep blood red to terracotta red to—'

'The size,' she interrupted, trying not to laugh. Alan de Markham, originally plain old Alan Marks, was one of the most exciting new artists in Dublin. His huge oil-on-canvas paintings were at the cutting edge of Irish art – an explosion of colour and movement – and Rosie loved them. She'd first met Alan when he'd brought some of his drawings into Frames R Us to be framed and they'd been friends ever since. He was one of the

191

most flamboyant, vibrant people she had ever met and Rosie wanted to give him a chance to show his work in Redwood. There was only one problem – some of his paintings would cover a whole wall and she couldn't afford to lose too much space.

He mumbled some figures down the phone.

'Alan!'

'OK, OK.' She could almost hear his hands flapping in the air and his long dark brown hair swishing. '*Study One* is six foot by eight foot, *Study Two* is eight foot by ten foot and some of the others are ten by twelve.' He let out a deep sigh. 'They're too big, aren't they?'

'No,' she said calmly.

Silence.

'Alan? Are you still there?'

'I've fainted, darling.'

'I've so much space here it's unreal,' she said, enjoying herself immensely. 'I can show three, maybe four.'

'Rosebud! I could kiss you.'

Rosie could hear some strange sucking noises down the receiver.

'I'm kissing the phone, darling. When do you want the paintings? They're all ready for you.'

As she put down the phone Rosie smiled broadly. Even if she never made a cent from his work, it was worth having Alan on board for sheer entertainment value alone. And the press loved him. He wore the strangest of clothes and had a knack of saying the most outrageous things at the most inappropriate times.

Now Olivia Miller was a whole different kettle of fish.

'Hello, this is Olivia. I can't possibly take your call right now – I'm frightfully busy. Please leave a detailed message after the beep.'

'Um, hi, Olivia, this is Rosie O'Grady from Frames R Us. Well, actually I'm no longer with them, I'm setting up a gallery in—'

'Did you say gallery?' Olivia said curtly, whipping up the phone.

'Olivia, I didn't know you were in.'

'Of course you didn't, silly girl! That's why my answering machine is on. I'm screening my calls.'

'I see. Sorry to bother you. Will I ring back later?'

'What were you saying about a gallery?' Olivia asked, ignoring Rosie's question.

'I'm setting up a gallery in Redwood House in Wicklow.'

'That old dump. I hope they've done some work on it.'

'Yes, they have,' Rosie said, trying not to get cross. Olivia really could be most unpleasant when she wanted to be.

'What sort of gallery? Not a small, piddly one, I hope?'

'No, Olivia, Redwood Gallery is a good size.'

'Well, go on, girl, get on with it. Tell me about the gallery. I don't have all day. You'll be wanting some pictures, I expect.'

Rosie smiled to herself. She knew Olivia liked her. The reclusive artist didn't even talk to people she didn't like. They'd first met at one of Olivia's shows in the Solomon Gallery in Dublin and had hit it off in a strange sort of way. Olivia had spent all evening talking about her one real passion in life – her cats.

Rosie couldn't but admire the old bird, who was eighty-one and still painting. And what paintings they were – atmospheric watercolours of the sea, and stunning Irish landscapes, which captured all the lush misty greenness like no photographic image could. She was one of Ireland's most accomplished living artists and Rosie admired her greatly. Her paintings were in demand all over the country, as well as internationally, and having some of her work in the gallery would be a major coup.

By the end of the afternoon Rosie was exhausted. She'd ordered some prints online from Roman Designs, a company in Birmingham who supplied high-quality art prints to the trade, and she'd rung Eve Marley, a silk-screen printer who taught in the National College of Art and Design. Eve had promised to drop in some new prints of Wicklow landscapes, which she'd just finished, once they'd been framed.

She'd left a message for Ray Davy, another artist who used Frames R Us, and had started to plan an ad for the *Wicklow Times*. All in all it had been a very satisfying day, but she was exhausted.

Cass was full of beans when Rosie collected her. She flung her arms around Rosie's neck as she bent down to kiss her, almost knocking her backwards.

'I made a worm farm, Mummy. And Anna helped me draw a picture for you – you can put it in the gallery.' Cass held up a square piece of black cardboard. Rosie could make out a house and four figures, all drawn in white crayon on the dark background. 'It's lovely, pet. Who are all the people?'

'That's me.' Cass pointed to the smallest figure in the centre. 'And that's you, Mummy, and that's Daddy. And that's my friend Tracy who kisses Daddy. And soon we'll be all living together in one big house. I'll get my worm farm.' She pottered off through the French doors into the garden.

'OK, love,' Rosie said to her daughter's back. She looked up at Anna in embarrassment. 'I should have explained. We're separated – me and Darren, my husband. Ex-husband.'

'I'm separated too,' Anna said kindly. 'Is it recent?' Rosie nodded.

'Cass said something about it earlier. It's good she's talking about it, but she seems a little confused about the details.'

'I think she is confused, to tell the truth. She's been wetting the bed and waking up with nightmares. It's difficult.'

'It'll get easier. You just have to be straight with children and tell them the truth. It's better in the long run. I've been on my own for three years now. Ollie was five when we left London. His dad is still there.'

'Ollie?'

'My son.' Anna smiled. 'The blonde boy playing with Cass. He's eight.'

Rosie looked outside. A small boy was showing Cass how to hold a worm. There was mud on his rosy red cheeks and his cream trousers were also covered in mud.

'He's a state, isn't he? It's impossible to keep him clean. But I think it's good for the children to be outdoors as much as possible.'

'Yes. You're right.'

'Maybe you should try talking to Cass again,' Anna said gently. 'Tell her the truth. Or are you all going to be living together in "one big house"?'

Rosie laughed. 'No, definitely not.'

'It'll take a little time, but Cass will be OK. You will be too. Wait and see. Now, would you like some coffee? Rita's mum will be here any minute and I'm off duty then.'

'Thanks. That would be nice.'

Rosie

'How was your first day in the gallery?' Kim asked that evening.

'Great!' said Rosie. 'I got so much done it was unbelievable. Most of the supplies are ordered and the first paintings will start to arrive the day after tomorrow. The electrician's a lovely man and—'

'Really? Is he nice-looking?'

'He's older than Dad. And happily married.'

'Pity. Tell me more. Did you ring Olivia Miller?'

Rosie told her all about her phone calls with Olivia, Alan and Eve. And about her coffee with Anna.

'Anna sounds really nice,' Kim said. 'You were lucky to find her.'

'Very lucky.'

Putting down the phone, Kim thought how well Rosie sounded. She hadn't mentioned Darren once and she'd sounded more animated and alive than she'd been for a long, long time. Maybe the old Rosie was finally on the way back.

*

'Show me that again, Dad,' said Rosie. They were crouched over her new computer, putting the first seven paintings onto the Excel spreadsheet. Olivia had come up trumps, sending a selection of her latest work over in a taxi that very morning, each painting freshly framed and ready to sell. For all her eccentricities, Olivia was a practical and organized woman with a keen business sense. She was also a prolific worker, which was an unusual and useful attribute in a much-in-demand artist.

She sighed. 'I'm just not really a spreadsheet kind of person. I think I'll use the stock book and let you transfer everything onto the computer. If you don't mind, that is.'

'Of course not. You know me, computer-mad. The stereotypical silver surfer.'

She smiled.

He cleared his throat nervously. 'Actually, I was wondering if you could do with some help in here, maybe a few afternoons a week. But if you'd rather not have me under your feet I'd quite understand.'

'Dad, there's nothing I'd like better. I'd pay you of course . . .'

He put his hands up. 'I'm an investor, Rosie, not an employee. Once the gallery is màking a profit I'm happy.'

'If you're sure . . .'

'Yes.'

'But what about Mum?' Rosie hadn't spoken to Julia since *that* phone call and she was starting to feel more than a little guilty.

'Leave your mother to me. Now where were we? Ah, yes, inventory. And then I'll ring the bank about the credit-card machine and the insurance company.'

She smiled to herself. It would be great having him on board.

On the day before the opening Rosie was running around like a headless chicken trying to get all the last-minute preparations in place. All the paintings had been hung by now – Alan had arrived unannounced late the previous afternoon to give her a hand, having spent the whole afternoon lying on the sofa watching and singing along to *Moulin Rouge* in preparation. At five, when Rosie was almost in despair, paintings still propped up against the walls and her neck and back exhausted from hanging all day, he'd arrived at the gallery in a pair of skimpy cut-off denim shorts and a ripped and paint-splattered white T-shirt.

'The cavalry's here, darling. Shoo, leave all the rest to me.'

He'd pushed her out the door and got stuck into the remainder of the hanging. When she and Cass called back later that evening he was sitting in the middle of the gallery smoking what she hoped was a hand-rolled cigarette. Alan being Alan, she wasn't so sure.

'Alan!' she'd exclaimed. 'Thank you so much. It's practically finished.'

Alan blew on his hand and pretended to shine his

halo. 'Aren't I the angel? And this must be the lovely Cass. Looking good, girl. I love the threads.'

Cass beamed as he examined the embroidery that adorned the end of her white trousers. Rosie was delighted to see her so happy. Darren still hadn't rung and she was damned if she was going to ring him. It was his loss. She'd explained to Cass that Darren had his own house now with Tracy.

'Like Ollie?' Cass had asked. 'Ollie's dad lives in London with Chrissie.'

'Like Ollie,' she'd said with relief. Anna had been very helpful – over coffee she'd explained to Rosie why children needed to be told the truth. As long as they knew both their mum and dad still loved them, Anna had explained, they seemed to accept things and adapt reasonably well. Cass was still wetting the bed and waking up several times at night, but it did seem to be getting better, thank goodness. Rosie presumed it would just take time. Moving to Wicklow may have taken her own mind off things, but to Cass it was a big change.

'I met the most charming man earlier,' Alan said as Rosie locked up the gallery and put on the alarm. 'Tall and muscular, yum. Dinky voice. Said he was working in the shop I think, Rory something or other.'

She smiled. 'Rory Dunlop. He owns the place, well his dad does. He runs the retail end of things.'

Alan whistled. 'Rich too. My kind of guy.' He tilted his head to one side. 'Single, perchance?'

'I've no idea. I've only spoken to him briefly myself. But you never know.'

'Come along, poppet,' he said, linking her arm. 'Daddy's hungry.'

Rosie glared at him. Sometimes he said the most inappropriate things. Luckily Cass seemed to be miles away. Still, Alan meant no harm and it wasn't as if he was the only one who said inappropriate things.

She grimaced as she remembered her conversation with Rory and the 'delightful' Martina earlier that week.

'Rosie, Rosie, wait up!' someone had shouted down the drive on Tuesday as Rosie was heading home for lunch.

She had turned around and stopped. Rory Dunlop was waving at her from outside Redwood House. He ran down the drive towards her. She couldn't but notice that he was in good shape. She herself wouldn't consider running any distance at all and especially not if she wanted to have any breath left to talk to someone.

He came to a halt in front of her and brushed his light brown hair out of his eyes. 'I thought it was you. You look great. Haven't changed a bit. Sorry I haven't called in or anything, I've been up to my tonsils sourcing products for the food hall. But that's not an excuse.'

'That's OK. I've been busy too.' She smiled.

'The gallery's looking superb. I hope you don't mind but I stuck my head around the door early this morning. I love the big red paintings. Expensive, are they?'

'Yes. A bit.' She couldn't remember Rory talking so much in school – she was finding it difficult to get a word in edgeways.

'Isn't it funny that we're working together after all these years. Who would have thought? What are you doing for lunch? We should catch up. Go to the village and—'

'Leave the poor woman alone, Rory!' Rosie looked towards the owner of the strong, cutting voice. A striking, sallow, dark-haired woman was staring at them with interest. Wearing a brown leather skirt, a black fitted T-shirt and high-heeled black boots she made Rosie feel frumpy in her own jeans and T-shirt. Rosie recognized her from the clothes shop. 'Have you nothing better to do than chat the new girl up?' the woman continued. 'Go and harass the coffee-shop staff or something.'

'I'm not chatting her up. We were in school together. Rosie's an old friend.'

'And I'm the Queen of Sheba! Grow up, Rory.'

'Maybe I'd better . . .' Rosie began. She had no idea what this woman's problem was, but there was no way she wanted to get involved.

'No, do stay,' Rory said. 'Please. Martina was just leaving.'

Martina, Rosie thought to herself. This couldn't be Anna's friend. What a dragon.

'Was I?' asked Martina, arching her eyebrows dramatically. 'Don't tell me what I can or can't do, Rory Dunlop.'

'No, really,' Rosie said quickly. 'I have to get on. Thanks anyway.' She looked at the woman pointedly. 'Nice to meet you, Martina. I'm Rosie O'Grady, from the gallery. Anna's told me all about you. I have meant to pop in and say hello but with the opening and everything it's been a bit hectic – you understand. I'm sure you're mad busy setting up your own shop. But we'll bump into each other again at the opening.'

'I'm sure we will.' Martina was sorry she'd been so rude now. Rosie seemed nice. This must be the Dublin woman who had a child in Anna's place. She suddenly remembered that Anna had asked her to call into the gallery and make Rosie feel welcome. But there wasn't much she could do about that now. How was she to know that the attractive brunette wasn't flirting with Rory? 'Your child's in Anna's playschool, isn't she?' she said, trying to make amends for her rudeness.

'That's right.'

'Good luck with the gallery.' Martina gave a nod of her head and walked away, her heels sending the fine gravel flying behind her.

'Sorry about that,' said Rory. 'There's a bit of history there.'

'No need to explain.' She understood all about 'history'. 'I'll see you tomorrow at the opening.'

'Yes. But what about lunch?'

'I don't think so. Maybe some other time.'

Rory watched her back as she walked down the drive. Damn, he thought to himself. He could kill Martina – she was so bloody rude sometimes. Things had been decidedly chilly in the last few days – they still hadn't talked and now Martina didn't seem to want anything to do with him.

As she stood on the doorstep of Rose Cottage, Rosie waved at the keeper who was driving past her towards the wildlife park. He either ignored her or didn't see her. Some of the people here are downright odd, she thought to herself as she walked inside.

At 3 a.m. on Saturday morning Rosie felt a sharp kick to her kidneys and woke up with a start. Cass was spooned around her body, her little feet just reaching her mother's lower back. She grabbed a spare pillow and lodged it between herself and her sleeping daughter. She hadn't the energy to lift her back into her own bed. Today's the big day, Rosie thought as she drifted back to sleep.

'Where are your red shoes?' Rosie asked Cass. 'Kim will be here any second.'

Cass pointed under the bed.

Rosie looked under the bed, stuck out her arm and pulled out one. The other shoe was against the wall. 'You'll have to crawl under and get it. I don't think I'll fit.'

'Can't we move the bed, Mummy?'

She smiled. Of course they could. Her mind was all over the place this morning.

'Kim's here,' Alan called up the stairs. He'd stayed the night on the sofa, in preparation for the 'grand opening' as he was calling it. She didn't mind, it was nice to have the company. She wondered what Kim would make of him, let alone her mother. Julia was coming to the opening and Rosie was dreading it.

'Hi, Rosie,' Kim shouted. 'Can I come up?'

'Yes! Please do. I'm just getting Cass dressed.'

Kim walked into Cass's room. 'And don't you look lovely, Cass.' Cass was wearing a white dress with a large red poppy embroidered on the skirt. There was a red hairband peeking out of her curly hair. 'Go on down and wait for us in the living room, pet.' Kim lowered her voice. 'Who's your man downstairs?'

'That's Alan. One of my artists.'

'That explains why he's wearing a sarong.'

'I wouldn't expect anything less. I presume it's red.'

Kim laughed. 'How did you know?'

'Woman's intuition.'

Rosie's mobile began to ring and she whipped it out of her pocket.

'Hello?'

'Rosie, it's Darren. I want to collect Cass this afternoon. I need your new address.'

She took a deep breath. His timing was unbelievably bad. She put her hand over the mouthpiece. 'It's Darren,' she whispered to Kim. 'He wants to collect Cass this afternoon.'

'You can't be serious. Tell him she's busy. She has a date with Geri Maye, her hero.'

'Hello, hello? Rosie?'

'I'm still here. Do you have to shout?'

'Sorry, I thought I'd lost the connection. Well – can I have your address?'

'I'm sorry. But Cass is busy this afternoon. You hadn't rung for weeks so I'd presumed . . .'

'What? I'm collecting her at three o'clock and that's

205

that,' he said forcefully. 'My lawyer says you have to let me see her. You'd better have her ready. Now give me the address.'

She clicked off her phone. It began to ring almost immediately.

'Did you cut him off?' Kim asked.

Rosie nodded, biting her lip.

'Good woman.'

The phone beeped loudly.

'A text message?' Kim asked.

She nodded. 'U will b hearin from solicitor tom,' she read aloud.

'Hardly,' Kim said dryly. 'It's Sunday tomorrow. Now let's get going.' She looked at Rosie. 'Are you OK?'

'Sure.' Rosie blinked back tears. 'Better by the day.'

Kim squeezed Rosie's shoulder gently. 'Good.'

As they walked up the drive towards the house Rosie saw the keeper again halfway up the drive, this time chasing what looked like a giant rabbit which had been nibbling the freshly planted flowers. The 'rabbit' disappeared into the shrubbery and the man stood watching him, hands on hips.

She walked over to him, her heels digging into the grass. He wasn't going to ignore her this time.

'Hello, I'm Rosie. I don't think we've met.' She held out her hand politely. 'You work in the wildlife park, I presume.' He was wearing a T-shirt saying 'Redwood Wildlife Park' with a lion's face on the back.

The man turned around with a start. He had a small scar on his top lip and his hair hung over his face, almost hiding his shockingly blue eyes. He said nothing.

'Um, we're going up to the opening,' she continued, more than a little embarrassed. 'Will you be going?'

The man snorted and brushed his hands on his dark blue workman's combats. 'Not really my thing. I have work to do. Bloody maras keep getting out.'

'Was the giant rabbit a mara?'

He nodded. 'Breed like rabbits too. I wish Conor hadn't bought the bloody things. Still, they're an endangered species in Argentina, I suppose.'

'I'm dying to see the wildlife park. I love animals, especially cats. And I believe you have some new lion cubs.'

'Three,' he said.

'And my daughter, Cass, is so excited about seeing the wildlife park today.'

'Rosie,' Kim called over. 'We'll walk on slowly. Cass is dying to see Geri Maye.'

'OK. Be right there.' She looked at the man again. 'Bye, then.'

'I'm Leo,' he said, just as she was turning to walk away.

Rosie smiled. 'Nice to meet you, Leo.'

He nodded at her, the hint of a smile on his lips. Rosie's heart leapt. He was incredibly attractive when he wasn't scowling.

'Who was that?' Kim asked as she rejoined the group.

'No one really. One of the guys from the wildlife park.'

'I see. Nice-looking guy.'

'Hadn't noticed.'

'Yeah, right! He's staring at you too.'

'He is not,' Rosie protested, secretly flattered.

As they approached Redwood House, Cass's eyes lit up with excitement.

'There's a bouncy castle, Mummy!'

Rosie laughed. 'I guess I'll know where to look for you if you go missing.' There were already several children on it. The official opening wasn't until twelve but things were already looking lively. Conor was standing on the steps, surveying the scene. Although he'd banished cars and vans outside from ten o'clock on, there were still some stragglers. Rosie waved up at him.

'Hi, Conor. It all looks brilliant.'

'Thanks, Rosie,' he said, before yelling blue murder at a van that had pulled up at the end of the steps.

She turned towards Kim. 'Are you all right to keep an eye on Cass for a while? I just want to check on everything in the gallery.'

'Sure.' Kim held out her hand to Cass. 'Come on, Cass. Bouncy castle time.'

'This is all so exciting,' Alan said as she opened up the gallery. He was practically jumping up and down on the spot. 'I hear Thelma Riesdale from the *Irish Times* is coming.'

'I knew there was a reason you were here.' She grinned. Thelma was the premier art critic in Ireland

and Alan was no fool. One good review from her and his career would be practically made.

He swatted her playfully on the arm. 'Darling, how could you say such a thing?' He flicked back his hair, which he'd given a copper rinse for the occasion. 'But a bit of publicity never hurt anyone. Bring it on!'

Martina

Martina looked up from the stock book. Someone was rapping on the window with a coin. For a split second she thought it was Rory – he often did that to catch her attention when she was in the shop. But it wasn't a coin, it was a key and the hand attached to the key was black not white. She jumped up and opened the door for Makedde and the large off-road buggy he was pushing.

'Hi, Makedde.' She bent down over the buggy, sat on her hunkers and smiled at the occupant. 'And this must be Ryan.'

'That's right. We are looking for Cindy. Is she here?'

Martina stood up again. 'She ran over to the coffee shop to grab some coffee. She'll be back in a few minutes, you're welcome to wait.' She gestured at the sofa. 'Please, sit down.'

'Thanks.'

'How are things in the wildlife park?' she asked, sitting down beside him. She could do with a break –

she'd been on her feet since six that morning and they were starting to throb. The opening was in exactly one week's time and she wanted everything to be just perfect. Luckily Cindy had offered to come in at seven and work for the whole day, even though it was Saturday, so they were ahead of schedule. And Hattie was coming in at twelve. It looked at this stage as if Martina might even have a whole day free tomorrow to devote to putting the final touches to the first Kati G range, if all went to plan.

'Good. Except for one of the cubs. She's not feeding properly. Leo's taken her home to bottle-feed.' He smiled. 'One baby each: Ryan for me, and one for Leo. '

She laughed. 'Sounds fair to me. And have any more of the maras escaped?'

'No, not this week, but I'm sure at least one will.' The guards had been called out twice already the previous week – once looking for 'an infestation of giant rats' (Mrs O'Brien in the local shop) and the second time for 'dangerous-looking giant mice' (Mr Higgins, a local farmer).

'Most of the time when I'm in here I forget that there are wild animals all around us,' said Martina. 'It's strange really, kind of surreal.'

'Surreal? I guess so. But in my country it is normal, so it seems normal to me. I worked as a vet's assistant and we saw many, many different kinds of animals, including wild animals that people kept as pets.'

'Where in Kenya are you from?'

'Mombasa, but I will not go back. Ireland is my home now.'

'And Cindy was telling me that you're hoping to train as a vet.'

'Yes, I've just finished my Leaving Cert and I hope to get the grades for UCD. Say a prayer for me.'

'I certainly will.'

'Hi, folks.' Cindy walked in the door. She handed a coffee to Martina. 'Would you like a coffee, Makedde? You can have mine if you like. I can always nip over and get another one.'

'Not at all. I'm fine. You have it. You've been working hard.'

'So have you.' She leant over and kissed him on the cheek. 'Looking after this little fellow. And how's my darling baby?' She leant down, unclicked Ryan from his buggy and lifted him out. 'Has he been good?'

'Yes. I took him to see the monkeys' new home and he loved it. The lemurs were flying around over his head in the trees.'

'And how are all the monkeys settling in? He and Leo have been working flat out on the new monkey area,' she told Martina. 'I haven't seen him all week.'

'I'm sorry,' said Makedde. 'I know you must have missed me. You cannot live without me.' He grinned widely, his smile lighting up his face.

'I know.' Cindy laughed. 'Terrible, isn't it?' She winked at him.

Martina smiled. They seemed so happy together – it made her think about Rory. Maybe she'd give him a ring and see if they could meet up this evening. He must have calmed down by now. She missed having him in her life and longed to talk to him.

'Martina?' Cindy asked again. 'Would that be all right?'

'Sorry? I was miles away. What did you say?'

'I was wondering if I could go for a short walk with Makedde and Ryan.'

'Of course. Why don't you take an hour? Hattie is due any minute.'

'Are you sure?'

'Go on before I change my mind.'

That evening Martina faced the shower head and allowed jets of water to cascade down her face. It had been a long day and she was looking forward to collapsing on the sofa in front of the television. She'd rung Rory but he hadn't answered, so she'd left a message to say she was in and would like to see him if he was free. But she didn't expect to hear from him until the following day – he was a devil for leaving his mobile at home when he went out.

Wrapped in her oversized towelling bathrobe she padded barefoot over to the kitchen area of her open-plan living room, opened a bottle of red wine and poured herself a generous glass. Taking the bottle with her, she sat down on the sofa and fished out the remote control from its usual hiding place behind the cushions. She flicked on the television and settled back to watch it.

An hour later she had finished the wine and was sleeping soundly on the sofa, the television still on in the background.

She awoke with a start. Her intercom was buzzing incessantly as if someone was leaning against it. It wouldn't be the first time – young courting couples often used the apartment's porch as a refuge, much to the disgust of the inhabitants.

She sat up and stretched her arms over her head. Her body felt stiff and her neck ached from sleeping at an awkward angle against the side of the sofa. She pressed the intercom.

'Yes?' she said sleepily.

''S me,' came a less than sober voice. 'Rory.'

'Rory? What are you doing down there.'

'I've come to see you, stupid. What do you think?'

She looked at her watch. 'It's very late. Could you come back in the morning?'

'Want to see you now. Please. Go on, Martina, let me in. I'll stay here until you do.'

She sighed. She didn't really have much choice.

He grinned as she opened the door. 'Knew you'd let me in, you big softie.' He leant over to kiss her but she moved her head away and he ended up kissing the air.

'Where were you?' she asked. 'You stink of booze.'

'Don't be like that.' He sat down on the sofa. 'I was at the yacht club with Dad and some of the *Angie* gang. We had dinner after sailing.'

Martina said nothing.

'I got your message when I got home and I thought I'd call over.'

'Rory, it's two in the morning.' She was losing her patience. 'Couldn't it have waited?'

'Thought it might have been important,' he said, looking slightly embarrassed. He hadn't realized quite how late it was. 'Sit down, you're making me nervous.'

'I wanted to talk to you, but not when you're drunk.'

'I'm not that drunk,' he insisted. 'Honestly.' He reached over and began to knead one of her shoulders with his hand. 'You're really tense, turn around.'

'No,' she said, pulling away. 'I really think you should go now.'

'Come here. Let me rub your shoulders and then I'll go. I promise.'

'Well, OK.' She was really stiff and it couldn't do any harm. Besides, Rory gave killer shoulder rubs.

He lowered her robe off her shoulders.

'Rory!'

'Calm it, woman.' He began to roll her knots expertly between his fingers; easing out all the stress and making her roll her head luxuriously in response.

'I've missed this,' she admitted.

He stroked the back of her neck with his hands, slowly moving them across her shoulders and upper back. He leaned forward and kissed her gently on the nape of her neck.

'Don't!'

He ignored her.

She sat glued to the spot as he smoothly pushed her robe down to her waist, exposing her upper body. She felt powerless, out of control. She wanted to tell him to stop but something was holding her back. Maybe it was the bottle of wine – making her drowsy and dulling her senses.

'Don't say anything,' he said. 'Keep still and listen to me. I love you, Martina. Let's stop all this, OK? Just say you'll marry me.'

'But—'

He put his hand gently over her mouth. 'No buts. Do you love me?'

She nodded silently and turned around. His gaze lingered on her breasts and he reached out and caressed them, licking his finger and running it teasingly over her nipples, making her weak with pleasure.

He reached forward and kissed her, deep and full. She could feel her body responding. She kissed him back, her arms around his shoulders pulling his body towards hers.

'God, I've missed you.' He pulled away and shrugged his wide shoulders out of his jacket. Martina helped him unbutton his white shirt and he gasped as she put her hands on his bare chest. 'Cold hands.' He gathered them in his own and blew on them. She looked at him.

'Warm heart,' she said quietly.

He put his arms around her and lifted her carefully onto the floor in front of the fireplace. She winced as her feet grazed the icy-cold marble hearthstone. He lay down beside her, his head and shoulders propped up on his arm.

'Close your eyes,' he whispered.

She did as he requested. She could feel his fingertips caressing her skin, moving down her body from her breasts, to her stomach and finally to her inner thighs.

She gasped as his fingers grazed her clitoris and she

arched her back in response, longing for more. Feeling his warm breath on her stomach she opened her eyes. His head was moving down her torso, his tongue making silky laps of her skin. She closed her eyes again and surrendered to the waves of ecstasy as he caressed her with his mouth and lapped her pleasure zone expertly. Just before she reached the point of no return he stopped, leaving her hungry for more.

He kicked his shoes off, removed his socks and eased his trousers and his boxer shorts down his legs. She pulled him towards her. 'Come here,' she said her voice husky. He lowered his body over hers and entered her smoothly. She lodged her feet against the hearth for leverage and pushed back against his body. Again and again they moved together, Rory holding her wrists above her head with his hands, Martina surrendering to him. She felt waves of release as she came, coloured lights dancing in front of her eyes. Seconds later he joined her in a loud vocal 'Yes!' and collapsed on top of her.

'Rory. Get off me, I can't breathe.'

'Sorry.' He rolled to one side. 'God, that was good.'

She lay on the floor for a few minutes staring at the ceiling before sitting up and gathering her robe around her. This was all wrong. It wasn't supposed to be like this. She wanted to talk to him, not make love to him. This solved nothing. Their sex life wasn't the problem. 'We shouldn't have done that,' she whispered.

'What? But I thought that was a yes,' he said sheepishly.

'You thought wrong. This doesn't change anything.

It was a mistake. I still can't marry you just now. I really need to talk to you about everything, but not when you're drunk. Maybe you should sleep it off and we can talk in the morning. Please, Rory, I have a lot to tell you.'

He glared at her. What kind of woman was she? Using him like that. 'You're some piece of work, do you know that?'

'What are you talking about?'

He glared at her but said nothing.

She took a deep breath. This had to stop – it was tearing them apart and she didn't want to lose him. 'OK, we'll talk now. You see, there are a few things about my family I haven't told you – I didn't feel ready and I see now that that was a mistake. I should have put all my cards on the table from the start. You see I made a promise to my granny when I was a little girl, an innocent promise but now she's—'

'I don't want to hear your excuses!' He jumped up. 'I've had quite enough of you, Martina. If you don't want to marry me, then I'm not forcing you to. It's your decision. I'm going now – I don't want to hear any more of this.' He stormed out of the apartment, slamming the door behind him.

Martina stared after him in disbelief. This was all her fault – she should have been straight with Rory from the very beginning. But how was she to know that she would fall so deeply in love with him. And now because of her own stubborn stupidity she'd lost him forever. In his eyes – after Cat – it was just history repeating itself. Tears pricked her eyes. She leaned back against the sofa and cried her heart out.

Light was shining in through the slatted wooden blinds. Martina winced. Her eyes hurt and her head was throbbing. Her legs and feet were freezing; the duvet had slipped sideways in the night, leaving them exposed. As she sat up she remembered what had happened with Rory. She tried to block it out of her mind but it kept sneaking back. It was all her fault – she should have trusted him from the beginning. As she stood in the shower, she remembered how his hands had felt caressing her skin. She grabbed a loofah and began to scrub her body systematically from head to toe.

Driving past Redwood on the way to her parents' house, her resolve weakened. Maybe he'd had a change of heart this morning.

She pulled up outside the gates and switched off the engine – she needed time to think. She put her head on the steering wheel and stayed like that for several minutes. Eventually she turned the key in the ignition and drove back onto the main road. If he was tired and hungover, talking to him now might only make things worse.

'Are you OK, love?' her mother asked as she walked in the front door. 'You look a little peaky.'

'Sure. I've just been working hard, Mum, you know how it is. Less than a week till the opening and all that.'

'I know.' Nita gently stroked her daughter's silky

black hair. 'But I'm here all day, so if you need any help just ask.'

Martina could feel a lump in her throat. Her mother was so sweet. She didn't deserve her.

Nita looked at her daughter. Martina looked as if she was about to cry. She put her arms around her and held her tightly. 'I know you're working hard, love. But is there anything else bothering you? You can tell me.'

Martina pulled away. 'No, Mum. Like I said, it's just work. Honestly.'

'OK. But if you want to talk about it . . .'

'Talk about what?' a voice boomed from the sitting room.

'Nothing, Gran.'

'Come in here and give your old granny a hug,' Mrs Patel commanded.

'I'll go and put the kettle on,' said Nita.

Martina walked into the sitting room. She almost gasped as she saw how frail her granny looked. Mrs Patel's face was grey and listless, her eyes were rheumy and her mouth flabby.

'Granny?'

'I know, I know. I look awful, you don't have to say it. I feel bloody awful too. The doctor says my heart is getting worse – he's pumping me full of pills, but they don't seem to be doing any good. Doctors – pah! They don't know what they're doing if you ask me.'

'You look all right, Gran.'

'No I don't. But thanks all the same.'

'I'll go and get you a cup of tea.'

'Thanks, I'd like that.'

'Mum –' she closed the door behind her – 'is Gran OK? She looks terrible.'

Nita sighed. 'Not really, to be honest. She had a mini stroke during the week and—'

'A stroke? You never told me!'

'We didn't want to bother you. You've been so busy.'

'What are you talking about?' Her hands gripped the kitchen table. 'Granny practically died and you didn't bother to tell me!'

'Now, Martina. She didn't practically die. She was quite sick one evening and the doctor came, checked her out and gave her pills. He sent her into Wicklow Hospital the following day for some tests but he said there's nothing else they can really do for her. She's old and her heart is giving up, that's all.'

'That's all? How can you say that? Surely there's something they can do. Maybe in Dublin . . .'

Nita put her arms around her. 'She's sick. Everyone's doing their best for her, I promise. She doesn't want anyone fussing.'

'I'm going upstairs. I have work to do.' She shrugged off her mother's arms.

'Martina. Please . . .' But it was too late. She had already left the room.

Martina leant over her cutting table and stared at the grey bag her mum had sewn. It was perfect. All it needed now was pink ribbon and sequins. She threaded the machine with pink thread, replaced the bobbin and began to sew. Her foot pulsed the machine gently and smoothly and her hands guided the bag through the needle, attaching the satin ribbon. She machined the small Kati G label to the bottom right-hand side of the bag and then hand-stitched the sequins and beads on. She stared at the finished product.

'One down, nine to go.' She placed the second bag under the foot of the sewing machine and clicked it down. She concentrated one hundred per cent on the task in hand, blocking all other thoughts from her mind.

'I'm really worried about Martina,' Nita said as she put a cup of tea on the small table beside the armchair. 'She's been out of sorts for weeks now and she won't tell me what it is. She says it's work but I'm not so sure.'

Mrs Patel looked up at her. 'She has had a fight with her boyfriend,' she said evenly.

'What? She doesn't even have a boyfriend.'

'She does, she just hasn't told us about him. I have a feeling that Martina is in love.'

'Then why won't she talk to me about it, Mum? She's my daughter, I want to help her.'

'Martina has to find her own way in the world.' She patted Nita's hand. 'It will all work out, you'll see.'

'I hope you're right. I just want her to be happy.'

Mrs Patel nodded and began to drink her tea. After a few sips her eyes began to droop. Nita took the cup out of her hands. 'Have a little nap, Mum. You need your rest.'

Walking back into the kitchen Nita could hear the whirr of the sewing machine upstairs. Whatever happened, she prayed that Martina would find the same kind of happiness that she had found with Thomas. She looked out the window. He was still kneeling in the flowerbed, weeding around the rose bushes. She smiled to herself. He was a good man – she was lucky to have him.

Anna

'Here's one,' said Conor. 'Laser 166815. White hull. Immaculate condition. Two masts, three sails, full and radial rigs, trolley and trailer. Must sell – owner going away.'

'Sounds promising,' said Anna. 'Is there a number?'

'Yes. Why don't we give them a ring? It's a Wicklow number.'

'OK. Read it out to me.'

'023 44567.'

She punched the numbers carefully into her mobile and put it to her ear.

'Hello?' A man's voice answered.

'Hi, I'm ringing about the Laser.'

'What would you like to know?'

'You say it's in immaculate condition?'

'That's right. It hasn't been sailed since the Nationals last year. I came fourth overall.'

'That's great! Well done.'

'Thanks. Is it for your son?'

'My son?' she echoed in confusion. 'No, it's for me.'

There was a brief silence on the other end of the phone. 'Would you like to see it? It's in the garage at the moment – it's been dry-stored all winter.'

'That would be great. My name's Anna, by the way.'

'I'm Stuart. Would this afternoon suit?'

'Yes, that's fine. Around three?'

He gave her the address and she jotted it down.

'Well?' Conor asked after she'd put away her mobile.

'I'm going over to see it this afternoon. Will you mind coming with me?'

'Of course not. I'd be happy to.'

'Nice house,' Conor whistled as they drove up the tree-lined drive. His jeep crunched over the generously laid new gravel.

She laughed. 'Look who's talking!'

The exterior of the large Georgian house was painted buttercup yellow and two potted bushes in the shape of dolphins stood like sentries on either side of the entrance porch. An Irish wolfhound was lounging on the gravel, his dark eyes staring directly at them.

'The dog's a bit scary-looking,' she said.

'He wouldn't hurt a flea. Look, his tail is wagging.'

As they watched the dog, a young man came bounding out of the front door. He let the dog into the house, closed the front door behind him and walked towards them smiling.

'Hi, I'm Stuart. You must be Anna.'

'That's right.' She stepped down from the jeep and shook his hand. 'And this is my friend, Conor.'

Conor nodded at Stuart who was wearing shorts and a T-shirt even though there was a distinct chill in the air.

'I'll show you *Dougal* now. Follow me.' He led them around the house to the backyard.

'*Dougal*?' Anna whispered to Conor.

He shrugged his shoulders and smiled. 'Interesting name for a boat,' he said loudly. 'Dougal from *The Magic Roundabout*?'

'Na, I'm a big *Father Ted* fan. I'm off to college in Scotland in the autumn.' He stopped outside a large shed and wiggled the bolt out of its rusting metal loops. 'Sorry, it's a bit stiff, couldn't find the WD40. We don't use this place much. It's just for the boat really.'

'Which college?' Conor asked politely.

'Edinburgh. History and English. Should be a bit of a laugh. I won't need the Laser over there – I'm hoping to do some team racing if I get onto the team. Do you sail yourself?' he asked Conor.

'Yes.'

'Conor owns a yacht called *Angie*,' said Anna, her eyes adjusting to the dim light inside the large shed. It smelt musty and the windows were decidedly dingy.

'The *Angie*?' Stuart suddenly began to pay more attention. 'The Swan that won the Round Ireland a few years back?'

Conor nodded modestly.

'Wow! I'm impressed.' He looked at the older man for a moment. 'Are you Conor *Dunlop*?'

He nodded again.

'Jeez, an honour to meet you, man. And you're buying a Laser now? Bit of a comedown, eh?'

'No,' said Anna firmly. 'I'm buying the Laser.'

'Oh, right. Are you going to sail it yourself?'

'Yes. I want to start training for the Nationals as soon as possible.'

'Really? Have you sailed a Laser before?'

Anna looked at Conor pointedly. 'Yes.' She left it at that. 'Now let's have a look at the boat, shall we? How many sails come with the boat?'

'Three. Two full-size and one radial.'

'Any new?'

'One of the full mains has only been used a few times. I bought it for the Nationals and haven't used it since.'

'Can I see?'

'Sure.'

Stuart unfurled the sail from its tube and Anna fingered it gently. 'Still nice and crisp. And the spars?'

'Two seasons old.'

Conor was examining the hull, pressing his fingers against the fibreglass in search of any weak spots. Anna glanced over at him. 'Sound as a bell,' he said.

'Are you going to sail with the full rig?' asked Stuart as they looked over the trailer and launching trolley. 'You might be better with the radial or 4.7.'

'Don't you think I can handle the full rig?'

'Ah, no. It's a very physical boat, the Laser,' he continued unabashed, 'that's all.'

Conor couldn't help himself. He'd had enough of

the condescending youngster. 'Anna won the Laser National Championships three years in a row,' he said sharply. 'First woman ever. With a bit of training she'll be right back on form.'

Stuart looked at her and began to blush. 'You're Anna *Wilson*? Daughter of Larry Wilson, the Olympic sailor?'

Anna nodded.

'Listen, I'm sorry, I didn't realize.'

'That's OK,' she said graciously.

He ran his hand through his shoulder-length hair. 'I'd be honoured if you'd consider sailing *Dougal*, really.'

'I'll think about it. I'll ring you later.'

As they drove away in the jeep she smiled to herself.

'Are you going to take the boat?' asked Conor as he turned onto the Redwood road.

'Of course I am. It's in great condition. I'm just going to let him sweat for a little while, that's all.'

'This is a side of you I've never seen. Anna Wilson – hard woman.'

She grinned. 'Actually, would you mind turning around? I've changed my mind. I'd like to collect *Dougal* now. I'll put Stuart out of his misery.'

Anna fed the sail onto the aluminium mast.

'Do you need a hand?' Conor asked. He was sorting out the main sheet, twisting the black rope into a neat coil and putting a figure-of-eight stop knot on its end.

'No, I'll manage. I'll have to get used to doing this

on my own. But thanks.' It was Tuesday evening, which meant dinghy racing at Wicklow Sailing Club, and she was taking *Dougal* out for the very first time.

Once the sail was in place, she raised the mast into the air, rested the end against her foot and took a deep breath. She then lifted the mast several feet off the ground and slotted it into the hole in the deck. 'Phew.' She panted. 'I used to be able to do that without thinking.'

'You're just out of training. You'll be fine.'

'I hope so. My drysuit is a bit tight too.' It was a one-piece – dark pink and white, she hadn't worn it for a few years and it felt a little snug around the bum. She hoped it wouldn't rip when she was sailing – she couldn't afford another one. The Laser had cost nearly three thousand euro; money she could scant afford. Her bank manager had thought she was mad taking out a loan for a sailing boat. Still, she reasoned with him, I can always sell it on at the end of the season.

'I think you look great. Always did like a woman in rubber.'

She laughed. 'Even smelly sailing gear?'

'Especially smelly sailing gear.'

She put on her favourite, white life jacket, lifted the trolley handle and began to wheel *Dougal* towards the slip. As she waited for her turn to launch she could feel interested eyes on her. What are they thinking? That I'm past it? That I shouldn't be dinghy sailing? She heard a voice to her left and turned her head to look at the water. It was Maria Doyle, the young Olympic hopeful from Wicklow.

'Anna, isn't it?' Maria was about to jump into her own boat, a Europe that was straining to sail away without her.

She nodded.

'Nice to see you on the water again. I've heard a lot about you. Are you doing the Nationals?'

'Hopefully.'

'Good luck if you are. It would be nice to see some women doing well in the class.'

'Thanks.'

After Maria had left the slip, Anna wheeled the boat down the concrete slope and launched it into the water. She could feel the cold waves lapping through her sailing boots and was glad of her drysuit, which kept the water away from her skin. Even though it was summer, the sea was still chilly. She handed Conor the launching trolley, pushed the centre board and rudder only halfway into the water – so that they wouldn't drag and get damaged on the slip – jumped onto the back of the boat, sat down and pulled the sail in. She was off.

As soon as she'd left the slip, she pushed the centreboard and rudder down fully and manoeuvred to avoid a yacht which was moored in front of her. When she pulled the tiller towards her, the boat responded beautifully. Anna sailed out of the harbour with a smile playing on her lips. The wind whipped her hair back off her face and she lowered her body over the side of the boat to keep it flat on the water in the strong breeze. The sun sparkled and tripped over the choppy waves, making the Wicklow sea look quite magical. She put a hand in the water and felt the water ripple past her fingers – she'd missed the intimacy of Laser sailing so much – it was just her and the sea, unlike big-boat sailing, where most of the time you didn't even get your face wet. For her there was nothing quite like it. She closed her eyes momentarily, said a little prayer of thanks and sailed out towards the open sea.

'I'm dying!' Anna moaned the following morning at breakfast. She was slumped over the kitchen table, her head resting on her arms.

'Hangover?' Moyra raised her eyebrows.

'I wish. It's my muscles.' She raised her head. 'I haven't been dinghy sailing for so long I've forgotten how physical it is. I'll have to start training.'

'Training? For what?'

She sighed. 'I've entered the Laser Nationals. It's being held in August. More fool me.'

Moyra smiled. 'That's great! Sure, didn't you win it four years in a row?'

'Three. But I was in my prime. I'm in bits now.'

'Your dad was nearly fifty the last time he won it,' Moyra pointed out.

'Really? There's hope for us all then. I'll have to pull out my old sailing books and make myself a hiking bench. Are they in the attic?'

'The books? I guess so. In one of the brown boxes, I suspect. But what's a hiking bench when it's at home?'

Anna smiled. 'A bizarre form of torture that the

sailing fraternity have to endure to build the muscles in their legs.'

'Sorry I asked.' Moyra laughed.

'Ollie, can you pass me the remote control, please?'

He looked up from his Gameboy and frowned. 'Mum, you made me die! Can you not get it yourself?'

'No. Please, love.'

He gave a theatrical sigh, got off the sofa and handed it to her.

'Thanks.' She changed to RTE, just catching the opening strains of the *ER* theme tune. Her legs were beginning to hurt but she was determined to suffer it out for the sake of her sailing.

The hiking bench had been surprisingly easy to make – with Conor's help that was. A long wooden frame with a solid 'step' at one end and at the other a padded strap for your feet, imitating the 'toe-strap' of her Laser. You popped your ankles under the strap, rested your lower thighs on the 'step' and took some of your body-weight on a rope that was attached to the front. This simulated the strain on your legs from hanging your body over the side of the Laser, with your feet in the 'toe-strap' – keeping it flat and level on the water in windy weather. As one of the lighter sailors in the class, Anna found herself hanging out, or 'hiking' as it was called, more often than not.

She'd already found her old weights and was going to pump iron every morning and evening until she got in shape. She was nothing if not determined. With some long-distance running thrown in to build her stamina, she'd be back in form in no time – or so she hoped.

'What are you doing, Mum? You look stupid.'

'Hiking. Practising for sailing.'

He wasn't impressed. 'Dad never did that.'

She was tempted to point out that Simon had never won any national championships either, but she thought better of it.

'He's coming over in a few weeks to take you on your cruising holiday,' she said instead. 'Won't that be nice?'

Ollie shrugged his shoulder. 'Suppose.'

'You don't sound very excited. Is everything OK?'

He said nothing.

'Ollie?'

He went quiet for a few minutes before finally asking, 'Is Conor your boyfriend?'

'Sorry?' she was taken aback. She hadn't expected that one.

'Well, is he? He's always hanging around and he brought you flowers the other day.'

'I guess he is. You like him, don't you?'

He shrugged again. 'Suppose.'

She put her hands on the floor, put her body weight on them and released her legs from the hiking bench. They felt weak and tingly. She walked a little wobbly over to Ollie and sat down beside him on the sofa.

'What's up?' she said gently. 'Tell me.'

He stared down at his Gameboy, paused on a Simpson's game. 'Is Dad coming back?'

'No, he's not.' She patted his left hand which was

still clutching the Gameboy. 'He's staying in London with Chrissie. You know that, love.'

He stood up.

'Where are you going?'

'My room,' he mumbled. 'Too noisy in here.'

She felt like running after him but stopped herself. He was obviously feeling a little displaced at the moment and nothing she could say was going to change that. She made a quick decision and picked up her mobile. 'Hi, Conor. Listen I'll have to cancel dinner this evening, something's come up. I'll ring back later, OK?'

'Ollie!' she yelled up the stairs. 'I'm going to the chipper. Will you come with me?'

'There's Geri Maye.' Anna pointed into the near distance. The attractive RTE star was standing at the top of Redwood's steps talking to Conor and Rory. 'Maybe Conor could introduce you to her later. Would you like that, Ollie?'

He nodded solemnly and patted the pocket of his denim jacket. 'I brought my autograph book just in case.'

'There's Rosie and Cass.' She pointed to the right of the crowd where Rosie was standing with two men, a woman and Cass. 'See?'

'Is the tall guy Cass's dad?' Ollie asked.

'I don't think so.' She studied the young man who seemed to be wearing a red skirt of some description. She hoped not – he looked a little strange to say the least. Still, it took all types.

Conor stood up to the microphone. 'Welcome to Redwood.' His clear voice boomed out, silencing the crowd.

Anna ruffled her son's hair affectionately. She hadn't seen Conor all week. She'd been trying to spend more time with Ollie but it was difficult to do everything. Now Conor was complaining that he never got to see her. She couldn't win.

'There's Martina, Mum.' He pointed at the doorway of Designs on Red. 'Do you want to go over?'

She hesitated. 'Yes. Hold my hand tightly, though. I don't want to lose you in the crowd.' She pulled him along behind her, mouthing 'excuse mes' along the way.

'Martina!' She smiled as she approached her. There were several people between them and her and Anna waved over eagerly.

Martina looked up. Her face showed no emotion. There were dark shadows under her eyes and her skin seemed greyer than usual. She seemed to stare straight past them.

'Martina?'

Anna watched in horror as Martina turned on her heels and walked into Designs on Red, closing the door firmly behind her and locking it.

'I don't think she saw you, Mummy.' Ollie tugged at her hand. 'Let's go back up the front. I want to see Geri Maye.'

'OK, love.' She felt sick to the stomach. Martina was never going to speak to her again, she missed her terribly and it was all her own fault for interfering.

Rosie

Rosie stood in the doorway of the gallery with Alan, Rex and Julia, watching Geri Maye officially launch Redwood.

'She's not bad,' said Alan, hands on his hips. 'Obviously did her homework.' Geri was talking about the history of Redwood, keeping it short and to the point to hold the attention of the younger members of the audience.

Rosie could see Cass with Kim on the other side of the crowd, gazing up at her favourite RTE children's presenter in awe.

Conor wanted to make Redwood a place for families to visit together so he'd made sure it was as child-friendly as possible – hence using Geri for the launch. He'd created a children's picnic area, baby-changing room and even a nursing room. He'd also invited local schoolchildren to the launch, along with their parents.

'And now I'd like to proclaim Redwood House and Wildlife Park officially open.' Geri cut the wide red ribbon, which had been stretched across the doorway of the house. Everyone cheered. Rory and Conor, both standing at the top of the steps with Geri, were beaming from ear to ear. Rosie could make out some familiar faces in the crowd – Anna and her mum; Pat Keily, the electrician, and his wife; Martina from the clothes shop; and some of the staff from the coffee shop and food hall. The others were probably frantically cooking inside.

The press had turned out in droves. Conor had hired a well-known PR man, Matty Turner, who seemed to have done his job to a T. There was no sign of Thelma Riesdale yet, but it was still early. Cameramen clicked eagerly as Geri kissed both Conor and Rory. Rosie glanced over at Martina to see if she was giving Geri dagger looks, but she had disappeared. Probably getting her voodoo doll ready, she thought to herself.

Conor stepped up to the microphone. 'And now you are all welcome to stroll in the gardens, have a browse in the Redwood Gallery or clothes shop, visit the wildlife park, or have coffee or food in the cafe. There's a bouncy castle for the children and Geri will be staying for a little while if any of the youngsters would like to meet her. So, thanks everyone for coming. And I hope you enjoy your afternoon in Redwood.'

Julia sighed deeply. 'Thank goodness for that. I'm famished. Come along, Rex. We'll have lunch now.'

'I'm staying here to help Rosie,' he said evenly.

Julia glared at him.

'I'd be honoured to accompany you.' Alan gallantly held out his arm for Julia.

She was flummoxed. Bad enough to have to stand

anywhere near this strange man in his red cotton skirt, but sitting down to lunch with him – what would everyone think?

'Splendid idea.' Rex smiled.

Julia stared at him. Her husband was clearly going mad. 'But, darling —'

'Come along, Mrs O'Grady,' Alan interrupted. 'Or may I call you Julia? I'll introduce you to Pat Kenny, he's a great friend of mine.'

Julia began to smile. 'Really?' She loved Pat Kenny with a passion. 'In that case.' She linked her arm with Alan's. 'Lead on.'

'Is Pat Kenny here?' Rosie whispered to Rex.

He shrugged his shoulders. 'I don't think so.'

She laughed. 'I don't know which of them I should feel sorry for – Mum or Alan.'

'You seem to be getting on all right,' Rex said, sitting down behind the desk in the gallery.

'With Alan or Mum?' Rosie asked.

'Your mum.'

'I guess. She's not so bad in a crowd.' They'd managed to be pleasant to each other so far all right, but the day was still young, Rosie thought wryly.

'I don't want to spoil your day, love, but Darren rang your mother earlier in a bit of a state. He wanted your new address.'

'Did she give it to him?'

'Of course not. She may not show it, but she is on your side.'

'That's nice to know.'

'You will let him see Cass though, won't you? I'm sure she misses her dad.'

She sighed. 'I know. But he's being so rude to me, I don't know if I can . . .'

Just then the first customers walked into the gallery. 'Showtime,' she said, glad for the distraction.

'Is that an original Olivia Miller?' a tall, well-dressed man asked Rosie an hour later. He was standing in front of a striking watercolour landscape in blues and greens.

She smiled. 'Yes. That one's called *Over Aran*. We have several of her pieces – would you like to see the others?'

'I certainly would.' He peered closely at the discreet price sticker on *Over Aran* and winced. 'Ouch! Are they always that expensive?'

She nodded. 'I'm afraid so. You'd pay even more in a Dublin city gallery.'

After showing the man the remainder of Olivia's pieces, she joined her dad behind the desk.

'He seems very interested in Olivia's work,' said Rex. 'Do you think he'll buy anything?'

'I hope so.'

She watched the man as he gazed at *Over Aran*. She tried not to stare as he sat down on the ash bench running down the middle of the gallery and put his head on his hands, never once taking his eyes off the painting.

'I knew the bench was a good idea,' Rex whispered to her.

She patted him on the arm and smiled.

The man rose to his feet and walked towards the desk. 'I'll take it,' he said solemnly. 'Do you accept Visa?'

'Of course,' she smiled. 'You're our very first customer.'

'It's a wonderful gallery, my dear,' he said, holding out his card. 'The best of luck with it. I'll certainly be in again.'

'Thank you. I'm afraid you won't be able to take it today, but I can arrange to have it delivered at the end of this exhibition.'

'When will that be?'

'In two weeks.'

'Perfect. I look forward to it. Here are my details – maybe you could ring me before delivery.' He handed her a business card.

'Of course.' She filed it away carefully. As she carefully placed a red sticker on *Over Aran*'s frame, her heart felt as light as a feather.

As soon as the man had left the gallery, Rex hugged her. 'Well done, Rosie. Your very first sale.'

'And you, Dad. And you.'

'Mummy!' Cass came bounding in the door, startling several women who had been loudly discussing Alan's *October Red* series. 'I met Geri, Mummy! Can we go to the wildlife park now?' She threw her arms around Rosie and hugged her tightly.

Kim came hurrying in the door, out of breath and

glaring at Cass. 'Sorry, Rosie, I couldn't stop her. She wanted to tell you about Geri. I know you're busy . . .'

'Don't be silly. This is exactly why I'm working for myself now. Dad, would you mind holding the fort for a while?'

'Not at all. It's nice and peaceful in here and it gets me away from your mother.'

Kim laughed. 'Last time I saw her Alan was introducing her to Thelma thingy from the *Irish Times* and they all seemed to be getting along famously. Thelma's sister was in school with Mum.'

'Thelma Riesdale's here?' Rosie asked her. 'Are you sure?'

'Yes. But don't worry. She's had so many glasses of complimentary champagne that she's practically floating. I'm sure she'll give your gallery a rave review.'

Rosie looked at Rex. 'Maybe I should stay. I should be here when Thelma—'

He put his hand in the air. 'Stop! Take Cass to the wildlife park. I'll be fine on my own. I've dealt with enough Thelma Riesdales in my time to know exactly how to handle them. You go off and enjoy yourselves. She's only a glorified hack, for goodness sake.'

'You're right, Dad,' Rosie said, feeling suddenly liberated. She took Cass's hand and walked out the door into the fresh air. The sun was shining down and the air was buzzing with the sound of people enjoying themselves.

Before following them, Kim kissed Rex on the cheek. 'You always know exactly the right thing to say. Thanks, Dad. You're brilliant.'

'Oh, go on,' he said, a little embarrassed. 'Now go and enjoy yourself with your sister.'

'Which way, Cass?' Kim asked. Cass was holding the wildlife park guidebook tightly and staring at the blue and green map.

Rosie looked over. 'I think she's holding it upside down,' she whispered to Kim. They were standing just inside the entrance of the park, a rolling field of green stretching out in front of them intersected by two wide paths, one to the left and one to the right.

'Most people are going right, Cass,' Kim said, watching people walking past. There were lots of young parents with buggies, in several cases three or four adults to a buggy. Like herself, they were using a friend's child as an excuse to visit the park. Kim smiled. She always thought the best kind of child was the kind you could hand back at the end of the day. She loved being Cass's godmother – it meant that she could buy cute clothes, go to the circus and the zoo whenever she wanted and she hadn't had one single sleepless night in the whole four years – perfect! Of course she wanted her own child one day, but not right now. She was a bit worried about Greg though. He had become decidedly clucky of late, since some of the lads in the football club had 'popped sprogs', as he charmingly put it.

'This way,' Cass said pointing to the left.

'Are you sure?' said Rosie. There was a large red arrow pointing clearly to the right.

'Sure, Mummy.' Cass set off determinedly in her chosen direction.

Kim laughed. 'You did tell her she could decide. And anyway, this way we're going against the traffic.'

Rosie grinned. 'It's not as if this is the last time we're going to be visiting this place. It's practically in our back garden after all.'

'Every child's dream. What I wouldn't have given at that age – she's a lucky girl. What the hell is that?' Kim jumped as a large rodent-type animal ran across the path in front of her feet.

'That, my dear sister,' she said confidently, 'is an Argentinean mara. And look –' she pointed to her left – 'I believe Cass has found the giraffes.'

Cass was watching the tall, elegant animals, which were roaming loose in a large field. Rosie and Kim stood behind her, equally transfixed.

'They're amazing creatures,' Kim said in wonderment. 'So strange-looking – if they didn't exist you couldn't make them up.'

'They're nearly extinct in parts of Africa,' Rosie said. 'They used to use giraffe skin to make water buckets. I read about it in *National Geographic* at the dentist's.'

'Quite the little naturalist.'

They walked along the high fence, following the giraffes.

'Look, Mummy. There's a baby one. And look, tigers.' She ran towards a wire fence and pressed her face up against it.

'I see she's inherited the famous O'Grady limited attention span.' Kim laughed.

243

Cass squealed, jumped back from the fence and began to cry. Rosie ran over, crouched down and wiped away her tears. 'What's wrong, love?'

Cass pointed at the fence.

'What? I don't see anything.' Suddenly two piercing orange eyes appeared behind the fence and she fell backwards on her hunkers, landing squarely on her bottom. The eyes fixed on hers, their gaze strong and unwavering.

Kim laughed. 'What are you doing, Rosie?'

'That cheetah gave me a fright.' Rosie stood up and wiped off the back of her black trousers. 'He came out of nowhere. No wonder Cass was crying. Must have scared her half to death.'

'She seems to have got over it.'

Cass was staring at the cheetah, now sitting on a grassy hillock with its mate.

'Says here they can sprint at over eighty miles an hour,' Kim said, reading the sign below the fence. 'I'm not surprised it was able to sneak up on yourself and Cass. I bet they can smell those mara things, too. Must drive them mad – dinner just waiting to be taken on the far side of the fence.'

'I'm sure it does. Come on, Cass.'

They walked on slowly, stepping over several small, baby maras who were munching grain and seeds on the path.

'Those things have no fear,' Kim said. 'I hope they don't escape and set up home in your garden. God bless your lawn if they do.'

The path veered off to the right.

'Lions, Mummy, lions.' Cass pointed at a sign.

Rosie looked at her watch. 'I'd better get back to the gallery in a few minutes. Let's check out the lions and then head back, OK?'

'No problem,' said Kim. 'We can leave the monkeys and the rest of the animals till another day. Greg has already made me promise to take him tomorrow when we're minding Cass. If he hadn't had a league match today he would have been here as quick as a flash. He's mad about animals.' She nudged Rosie. 'Hey, isn't that your man from earlier?'

Rosie looked over in surprise. Leo was sitting on the wooden fence in front of them with a lion cub in his arms, talking to an interested crowd. They stood at the back and listened.

'This is Tibo, the youngest of the Asian lions at Redwood. She's only five weeks old and is still on bottles. We're feeding her by hand as her mother has abandoned her. When she's old enough to fend for herself we'll let her join the pride. But we may still have to feed her separately as the older and larger lions may finish all the food before she has a chance to get any. Lions come mainly from Africa but there are also some in Asia. The Asian lions are a little smaller and there are only about two or three hundred left in the world, in a place called Gir Forest in India. And that's why we have the Asian lions here at Redwood and not their more common relations. They need all the help they can get.' The lion cub began to squirm in Leo's arms and he tickled her belly gently. 'Tibo likes to be around humans now, but soon she'll be too big to play with. When she's bigger she might accidentally bite my hand or knock me over. But for the next few weeks she'll still be my little friend, won't you, Tibo?' He kissed her on the head.

'Aah,' Kim said to Rosie. 'That's so sweet.'

'And now Makedde, one of the other keepers, will be feeding the bison. If you follow the path to the right you'll just catch him.'

As the crowds dispersed, Rosie walked over to Leo. 'Hello again. Big day for you.'

Leo nodded and stepped down off the barrier, Tibo still in his arms.

'Has it been busy?' she asked.

'Yes. I have to go and feed this little one, excuse me.'

'See you around. Good luck with the feeding.'

Kim nudged Rosie as he walked away. 'He's a bit unfriendly, isn't he? It wouldn't have killed him to say a few more words.'

Rosie shrugged her shoulders and watched as Cass ran after Leo.

'Stop, lion man!' Cass shouted.

Leo turned around and waited as Cass caught up with him.

'Can I say goodbye to Tibo? She lives in my garden, you know.'

Leo looked at Cass carefully. 'I guess she does.' He bent down. 'You can pet her head if you like. Stroke her gently, like a cat.'

Cass put her hand out gingerly and began to pet the tiny feline.

'Good. She likes you.' He stood up again. 'Back to your mum now.'

Leo nodded at Rosie again and walked away.

'Maybe he's not so rude after all,' said Kim. 'The strong, silent type. Cute too. What do you think?' she asked Rosie.

'I don't know really.'

'Oh, come on. Don't tell me you hadn't noticed – again.'

'Kim, up until a few months ago I was a happily married woman,' Rosie said, her eyes following Cass who had found the adult lions and was trying to climb their fence. 'Get down, Cass!'

'Being married hardly affects your eyesight. I'm mad about Greg but I still see good-looking men all over the place.'

'Let's just say I'm not interested in men at the moment, not in that way. They could look like George Clooney and I wouldn't notice.'

'So you think your man looks like George Clooney?'

'That's not what I said at all. Anyway, Leo's blonde.'

'Leo, is it? You're a dark horse. How do you know his name?'

'He told me this morning, of course,' Rosie said defensively. 'Now stop slagging me. Cass, get your hand out of that fence, it'll get stuck and one of the lions will bite it off.'

'If I didn't know better, I'd say you were blushing. My sister and Leo, the lion keeper – has a kind of ring to it.'

'I told you to stop.' Rosie was getting a little

irritated. 'It'll be a long time before I so much as look at another man.'

'You're right. Besides, he probably smells of lion dung.'

'Kim!'

'OK, OK.'

'How is everything going, Dad?' Rosie asked. Kim had taken Cass back to the cottage as she'd begun to tire. It was nearly five and the gallery was empty.

'Really well. We've sold two of the cat prints and there's a woman calling back next week with her husband to look at one of Alan's *October Red* pieces. I wasn't expecting you till later – how was the wildlife park?'

'Great. I'm just a bit wrecked today. I couldn't really sleep last night, I kept waking up.'

'I'm not surprised. You were probably nervous about the opening. I'm sure you'll fall fast asleep as soon as your head hits the pillow this evening. You've been working flat out to get this place ready, it must have taken a lot out of you. And what with Darren and everything, your poor old system's under a lot of stress.'

'I guess you're right.' She collapsed on a chair behind the desk. She sat up straighter as two women walked in and began to look around. 'Did Mum and Alan call in with you know who?'

'They certainly did.' He put his reading glasses on top of his head and began to rub his eyes gently.

'Thelma's a bit of a character, isn't she? She seemed to be getting on stormingly with your mother and Alan. They made a very colourful group. You could hear them coming a mile away – three very distinctive voices.'

Shrill more like, Rosie smiled to herself.

'Thelma said the space was "to die for, darling".' Rex imitated her distinctive voice. 'Let me see, ah yes, "Tate Modern," she said, "with a touch of the new National Gallery, and a certain Gandhi-esque air." '

'Gandhi?' Rosie wondered.

'Maybe it was Gaudi?'

She laughed. 'It probably was, Dad. I don't think Gandhi was all that well known for his architecture.'

'She loved Alan's series,' he continued unabashed, 'and the *Irish Times* photographer took loads of shots of the gallery and of Alan's and Olivia's paintings. They're all in the coffee shop now with Conor and some of the other journalists. Your mother's in her element. She can't wait to get home and ring her friends about it.'

'Did Thelma look at any of the other works?'

'Not really. I told her about Eve's prints and Ray's oils but I'm not sure if she was really listening.'

'Never mind. I hope her review's all right.'

'I'm sure it will be. Your mother has already asked her to dinner with Alan and some of her cultural-club cronies.'

She smiled. 'Not till after the review comes out, I hope. We don't want to put her off the O'Grady family for life before she writes it.'

Rex laughed. 'Why don't you go on home? I'll close up here.'

'Are you sure?'

'Yes, positive. I'll see you tomorrow at eleven.'

She kissed him on the cheek. 'See you then, Dad. And thanks for everything.'

'My pleasure.'

Rosie

'Is that all the glasses?' asked Kim. She was standing at Rosie's kitchen sink, her hands resplendent in bright yellow rubber gloves.

'I think so,' said Greg, looking at the table.

'Good, I'll do the plates now.'

He stood up and passed them to her.

'You don't have to, Kim,' Rosie protested, 'I can do them tomorrow, honestly.'

'It's fine, it'll only take me a few minutes. Just relax, you've had a big day.'

'If you're sure. And thanks for cooking, Greg. I really appreciate it.'

'The deli did most of it. And it was no trouble.' He leant against the kitchen counter and took a sip of his wine. 'I'm looking forward to seeing this wildlife park tomorrow.'

'It's great.' Kim added some more steaming hot water to the Belfast sink. 'We only saw a bit of it but I was very impressed. Nice staff too.' She caught Rosie's eye and winked.

Rosie ignored her.

Greg didn't notice. 'By the way, there was a message from Darren on the answering machine at home. He was looking for your address, Rosie. He wanted to see Cass. Sounded a bit agitated.'

'Good!' said Rosie. 'I hope you didn't ring him back.'

'No, of course I didn't.'

'Shush,' said Kim. 'I thought I heard something.' The stairs were creaking.

They looked towards the kitchen doorway. It was Cass.

'I can't sleep. I need a story.'

Rosie sighed and put down her wine glass. 'OK, love. I'll be with you in a minute. Go on up and choose one, there's a good girl.'

'I'll do it,' said Kim. 'If Greg wouldn't mind taking over the washing-up.' She looked over at him.

'Sure. I'm not wearing those gloves though – not really my colour.'

'Don't think they'd fit you anyway,' Kim teased. She patted Cass on the head and led her out of the room.

'Thanks,' Rosie said gratefully.

'No problem.'

'Good woman you have there,' she said when Kim had left the room.

'I know. I'm very lucky.'

'I don't know what I'd do without her at the moment, she's been brilliant.'

'You'd do the same for her.'

'I know, but I hope I'm not imposing too much on you both . . .'

'You're not, honestly.' He put the last of the crockery on the draining board and pulled the plug out of the sink. 'Finished!'

'Thanks.'

'Rosie.' He sat back down at the table. 'I hope you don't think I'm interfering but I think you need to talk to Darren.'

'Why?'

'I've been thinking about it and I know you don't really want to hear this, but Cass needs him. Whether you like it or not, he's still her dad. And if you don't mind me saying, she seems a little unsettled.'

Rosie was surprised. 'Actually I do. Cass is fine. She's much better off without him. She'll forget all about him in a while.'

He reached over and picked up the wine bottle. 'More wine?'

She shook her head. 'Have to work in the morning.'

He filled his own glass. 'He's still her father, whether you like it or not. He has a right to see her.'

She stared at him. 'I thought you were on my side.'

'I am. But I guess I'm also on Cass's side. Whatever he's done, he still loves her, you know that.'

'No, I don't. He left us. How can he still love us?'

'He left *you*, Rosie,' he said gently, 'not Cass. He didn't leave Cass.'

'Well thank you very much for pointing that out to me! Now I feel so much better! Jeez, you men are some piece of work. Talk about sticking together. I bet you did ring Darren back, didn't you?'

'I already told you I didn't, that's unfair. And I'm not standing up for him. What he did wasn't right. No one should just up and leave their family . . .'

'No, they shouldn't!'

'What's going on here?' Kim walked in the door. 'Are you OK, Rosie? You look a little pale.'

'No, I'm not OK. Your boyfriend here has just been telling me that I'm a bad mother for not letting Cass see Darren.'

'That's not fair! I never said you were a bad mother.' Greg glared at her.

'You implied it.'

'I did not!'

'Yes you did, you said—'

'Guys!' Kim said. 'Please stop.'

'But he—'

'Rosie, calm down. I need to talk to you.'

Greg stood up. 'I'm going to bed.' He looked at Rosie. 'If I'm still allowed to stay here that is. Maybe I should ring for a taxi and go home.'

'Don't be stupid,' said Kim. 'Go on up, I'll join you in a few minutes.'

'What did you want to talk to me about?' Rosie asked as soon as he'd left the room.

'Cass. Cass and Darren.'

'Not you as well.'

Kim ignored her. 'Cass just asked me why she can't see her dad. She thinks she's done something wrong and that he's punishing her.'

'But that's ridiculous!' Rosie insisted. 'It's got nothing to do with her.'

Kim sighed. 'Rosie, love, it has everything to do with her. Everything. I'm only saying this because I love you both. You know that. She has to be allowed to see her dad. Can't you see?'

Tears began to prick Rosie's eyes. 'But I don't want him anywhere near me. I can't see him – it upsets me too much. He's so nasty to me. It's as if he never loved me.'

Kim put her arm around her. 'He did love you. Past tense. But he still loves Cass.'

Rosie put her head in her hands and began to cry. 'It's just so damn hard. I've tried not to think about it, and not seeing him or talking to him makes everything easier.'

'I know, but you can't keep him away for ever. Maybe I could be here when he visits, that way at least he'll be civil to you. He'd better be or he'll have me to deal with. It will all get easier, I promise you.'

'I don't know.'

'I'll ring him for you tomorrow. I'll tell him that you want to talk to him but only if he's polite.'

'Would you?'

'What are sisters for?'

'Thanks.'

'And Rosie, I think Greg was only trying to help. He's mad about Cass.'

'I know. And I'm sorry I jumped down his throat. Will you tell him?'

Kim nodded. 'Yes. Now I think we should both go to bed.'

Rosie stared up at the ceiling. She was exhausted but she couldn't sleep. She knew Greg was right – Cass *was* unsettled. She was crying and throwing tantrums much more than usual and her nightly bedwetting was getting beyond a joke.

And Rosie couldn't stop thinking of Darren. One overwhelming image kept coming into her head – Tracy's mane of blonde hair whipping his chest and stomach. 'More!' he was saying. 'You're so much better than Rosie.' She shut her eyes and blinked back the tears. Kim said it would get easier in time. Let's hope she was right. She reached into the drawer of her bedside locker and pulled out a small pillbox. She opened it and popped three sleeping pills into her mouth. 'Bottoms up,' she muttered wryly as she swallowed them with a mouthful of wine.

'Rosie, are you all right?'

She heard Kim's voice cutting through her hazy sleep. She opened her eyes just as Kim started to shake her.

'There's no need to shake me,' she said groggily.

'It's after eleven. Dad was looking for you.'

She sat up gingerly. Her head was throbbing and she felt dizzy. 'Damn sleeping tablets. Shouldn't have taken them on top of the wine.'

'Rosie! You should be careful. You can't—'

'I know, I know. Listen, ring Dad and tell him I'm on my way, will you? I'm going to have a shower.'

'OK.'

'Where's Cass?' It was suspiciously quiet in the house.

'In the living room with Greg. They're playing snakes and ladders.'

Rosie winced. She remembered the conversation they'd had last night.

'It's fine,' said Kim, reading her mind, 'he's happy to forget all about it.'

'Good. I don't think I'm up to talking this morning.'

'What are you feeding them?' Greg asked the young keeper who was throwing large brown turnip-like tubers into the bison's field. As promised, he and Kim had taken Cass back to the wildlife park – not that he minded. It was fantastic and he was really enjoying himself.

'Sugar beet.'

'Where are you from?' asked Cass. 'You don't look Irish.'

'Cass!' said Kim. 'That's not polite.'

'That's OK,' he smiled. 'I'm from Kenya but I live here now with my family.'

'And you work with the animals?' Cass said, her eyes lighting up.

'Yes.'

'You're very lucky.'

'I think so.'

'What are your favourite animals?'

He laughed. 'Lions, I think.'

'Me too!'

'Have you seen Elsa yet? She's the oldest lioness we have here. She's pretty old.'

'How old?'

'Thirty.'

'Wow!' said Cass. 'Really old.'

'Old?' Greg laughed. 'Elsa's a spring chicken. Come on, Cass, according to my map it's the scimitar-horned oryx next.'

'I'm going that way myself,' said the keeper. 'Hop in and I'll give you all a ride.'

'Cool!' Cass beamed.

Kim climbed in and sat next to the keeper. Greg helped Cass, lifting her into the old green Range Rover. Once in himself, he popped her on his knee. 'I can see everything from up here,' she exclaimed in glee.

'How long have you been working here?' Kim asked the keeper as they jiggled along the bumpy path.

'Nearly a year now. I helped set up the park.' He smiled broadly. 'I'm Makedde.'

'Hi, Makedde,' she smiled back, 'I'm Kim and that's Cass and Greg. Cass lives in Rose Cottage just down the road from your entrance building.'

'Called after her mother, Rosie?'

'No,' laughed Kim. 'I believe it's been called that for years. Do you know Rosie?'

'No. My boss, Leo, said he'd met her, that's all.'

Kim was intrigued. So Leo had been talking about

Rosie – interesting. But before she had a chance to ask any more questions the jeep came to a sudden halt.

'Here we are,' said Makedde, 'the oryx.'

He jumped out of the jeep, opened the boot and pulled out some leafy branches. The others followed him.

'Can I help?' offered Greg.

'Sure. You could pass the branches to me.' He climbed over the wire fence with great agility and Greg handed him the branches. He then walked towards the centre of the large field and dropped them on the ground. He made some strange high-pitched clicking sounds, leant down and rustled the leaves with his hands.

'They're very shy,' he explained after he'd walked back to the fence, 'but if we stay quiet we'll see them soon.'

And sure enough, a few minutes later the oryx came into sight. They sniffed at the branches and began to eat, pulling the leaves off the boughs with their sharp teeth.

'Some horns!' Greg whistled softly.

Makedde smiled. 'You see why they're called scimitars. Their horns can grow up to one metre long.'

'Do the females have horns?' asked Kim.

He nodded. 'It's one of the reasons they were hunted almost to extinction. There are only about a thousand left in the world now.'

'That's terrible!'

'Yes.' He nodded. 'We run a breeding programme

here and we have already shipped some back to the Sahara where they were originally from.'

Cass was transfixed by the stunning white and brown animals. 'They look like reindeers. Reindeers with snow on them.'

'Has she ever seen a reindeer?' Makedde asked Kim in a low voice.

'No,' Kim whispered. 'Not in real life.'

'Yes, they do,' he said kindly to Cass. 'Just like reindeer.'

That evening Rosie's hands were shaking as she punched the familiar number into her mobile. 'Before you say anything, I want to apologize. I shouldn't have cut you off like that, I'm sorry.'

'Fine,' barked Darren, 'apology accepted. Now when can I see my daughter?'

'I rang you to have a conversation, not an argument. If you're going to speak to me like that I'm putting down the phone. We need to be civil to each other for Cass's sake.'

'Whatever. You're in the wrong, Rosie, not me. I've been more than civil to you.'

She took a deep breath. 'This is the last time I'm going to say this. If you can't be polite I'm not going to talk to you.'

'Sorry,' he mumbled, but she knew he didn't mean it.

'Would you like to see Cass next weekend?' she asked.

'That's a stupid question.'

'Darren!'

'Sorry. Of course I'd like to see my daughter next weekend.'

'Why don't you collect her on Saturday morning and drop her back on Sunday? Does that suit?'

'You mean she can stay overnight?'

'Yes.'

'I knew you'd see sense. I presume your lawyer's been talking to you? You know I can bring you to court—'

'Darren! This has nothing to do with my lawyer and everything to do with Cass. She misses you.'

'Really?'

'It pains me to say it but yes, she misses you a lot. I'm just trying to do what's right for her. And you're not making this any easier for me.'

'Sorry,' he said. This time he sounded sincere. 'What time will I collect her at? And can I have your new address?'

'Twelve. And the address is Rose Cottage, Redwood House.' She gave him directions.

'Great. I'll see you then.'

'See you.'

As soon as she'd stopped talking to him, she sat down. Her pulse was racing and she felt nauseous.

'Rosie?' Kim walked into the kitchen. 'You look pale. Are you OK?'

'I think so. I was just talking to Darren.'

'Darren?'

'I know you offered to ring him but I wanted to do it myself.'

261

'And?'

'He's an asshole.'

'Apart from that?'

'He's taking Cass on Saturday for the night.'

Kim smiled. 'Good!'

She looked at her. 'Why are you smiling?'

'I'm proud of you for ringing him.'

'I'm kind of proud of myself.'

Martina

'Hi, Martina, I'm Carolyn from the *Irish Times*, thanks for agreeing to talk to me. Sorry to bother you on a Saturday morning. I have another story to cover in Avoca after lunch, so I thought while I was out this way . . .' The small, blonde woman flounced in the door of Designs on Red carrying a huge flowery bag. Pink-lensed Gucci sunglasses were perched on the top of her head, and sporting a matching pink cashmere vest, flared denims and pink high-heeled sandals she looked like a life-sized Barbie doll.

'It's no problem. Thanks for coming, it's nice to meet you.' Martina held out her hand and Carolyn clasped it tightly, placing her other hand over it and giving an extra touchy-feely squeeze.

'And it's lovely to meet you too, darling,' she gushed. 'And what a palace! It's adorable!' She spun around on her heels, taking in the whole shop. 'Ooh, Sami!' She pulled a pink and red top off one of the rails. 'I love Sami. I bought tons of it when I was in

Harvey Nicks last week. I didn't know anyone stocked it over here.'

'Just us.' Martina smiled. 'Would you like to sit down?'

'Please.'

They both sat down on the sofa and Carolyn pulled out a pen and a notebook before plonking her bag on the floor at her feet. She popped the lid off the pen with her teeth and held the nib in front of Martina's nose. 'Strawberry ink, couldn't resist it.'

'Can I get either of you a tea or coffee?' Cindy smiled over from the cash desk.

'I'm fine, babe,' said Carolyn, 'but thanks. Martina?'

She shook her head. 'If you wouldn't mind looking after the phone for a while that would be great.'

'No problem,' said Cindy. 'I'll be in the stock room for a few minutes. Give me a yell if there are any customers.'

'Charming girl,' Carolyn murmured. 'Hard to get staff with experience these days. Where did you find her?'

'She found me,' said Martina. 'She used to work in Pia Bang's and she answered my ad in the local paper.'

'And how did *you* find this marvellous space, you clever thing?' Carolyn's pen was poised at the top of her notebook.

'Luck really. My family's from Wicklow and I know the Dunlop family.'

Carolyn tilted her head to one side coyly. 'Rory's your boyfriend, am I right?'

'Um, was. Not any more.' Martina stared at her

hands. She was hoping to talk about her clothes, not her personal life. This was the *Irish Times* after all, not the *Star*.

'I'm sorry, I hadn't realized. Ignore that question. It's not relevant to the piece. I'll just say you know the Dunlop family being a local yourself.' Carolyn smiled gently at her. 'Is that all right?'

She nodded gratefully. 'Thanks. I'd appreciate that.'

'I've been there myself. I'm married now, thank goodness. But I've been through enough messy break-ups in my time to know a thing or two about the whole distressing business. But hey, life goes on. But I'm not here to talk about all that, darling. Tell me more about Designs on Red. I believe the architect Kit Almquist was involved in designing the interior space.'

'Yes. I met her at a party a couple of years ago. We got on really well. She'd recently completed the Louise Kennedy re-fit in BT's and I was very impressed. I love her use of light and space. And her Scandinavian background gives her an edge on clean design, I think.'

'Quite,' Carolyn nodded, jotting frantically in her notebook. 'And the Kati G label? Can you tell me a little about the designer? I believe she's also local?'

Martina smiled. 'Yes. Kati Gallagher has a workshop just outside Wicklow Town. She went to the Grafton Academy of Design and studied under Colette Damier. Then she worked for some time in retail in Dublin city and is now designing her own clothes.'

'Excellent! And tell me a little about Spun Air. I believe she's one of the first designers in Ireland to use the fabric.'

'One of the first in the world, actually.' Martina tried not to sound too smug. 'Let's have a look at some of the Kati G range and I can explain its properties. And I'll let you into the Kati G secret.'

'A secret? Sounds fascinating – do tell. Can I use it in my piece? Who else knows this little secret?'

Martina smiled to herself. There was nothing like an exclusive to whet a journalist's appetite. She'd waited for just this kind of media moment to reveal her Kati G alter ego. The time was right – she could feel it in her bones.

Martina was exhausted. Carolyn had been charming but after two hours of intense conversation, not to mention lunch in the Redwood coffee shop when she'd heard all about the 'messy break-ups' Carolyn had alluded to earlier, she was all talked out. Or listened out.

Carolyn was also sending over a photographer on Tuesday to capture some of the Designs on Red range on film, including her Kati G label, much to her delight. She wanted enough pictures to accompany her piece – a double-page 'summer spread'. The freelance stylist they used for their fashion shoots was unfortunately on holiday, so she'd asked Martina to style the photos – which in itself wasn't a problem. But she'd also requested a 'safari' theme – complete with animals from the wildlife park. Which *was* going to be a problem as she'd have to ask Rory for permission and they hadn't spoken two civil words to each other in the last week.

Since the night he had called in, she'd been in bits – she still blamed herself for not being straight with him from the start, but she was starting to get annoyed with him for not giving her the chance to explain. The way things looked, their relationship was completely over and she was heartbroken.

'I don't think you're up to going downstairs, Mum,' said Nita. 'I'm sorry but I think you'll have to stay in bed until the doctor comes. She's on her way.'

'When will Martina be here?' Mrs Patel asked anxiously. She wasn't interested in the doctor's visit – she had more important things on her mind. 'Soon?' Her chest felt constricted and she was finding it hard to breathe normally.

'I'm not sure. She was talking to some journalist all morning so she said she's a little behind schedule. I'll go downstairs and give her a ring. You rest, OK? Dr Paul will be here soon.'

She picked up the phone and dialled Martina's mobile. 'Hi, Martina. Your gran is fretting a little. She seemed fine this morning but she's taken a turn for the worse.'

'What happened, Mum?'

'I left her for an hour to go shopping and when I got back she was really breathless. The doctor will be here any minute now but it's you she wants to see. Can you call over afterwards?'

'Doctor? Is she all right?'

'Just a little short of breath. Nothing to worry about.'

'Right. I'll be ready to leave in about an hour. I'll be as quick as I can.'

When Martina arrived two hours later, her granny was asleep. The doctor had given her some strong beta blockers and painkillers and insisted that she stayed in bed until she felt considerably better. Nita offered to wake her up but Martina wouldn't hear of it.

'Not to worry, I'll call in tomorrow. She needs her rest.'

'OK, love. Do you want a cup of coffee? I was just about to—'

'No, I have to run.'

'Are you sure? How about some dinner? You could—'

'I'm busy, Mum. I'm sorry, I can't stop.'

'Fine. But I'm worried about you, love.'

Martina sighed. 'You don't need to be, I'm up to my ears with work, that's all. I'm grand.' She opened the front door and let herself out. 'If she wakes up, will you tell her I called?'

Nita nodded silently. She closed the door behind her daughter and leant against it. Martina knew that Nita wanted to talk to her, that she was worried about her – but she wasn't having any of it. Sometimes her daughter could be impossible.

Nita woke up. She could hear something. It sounded like someone calling her name, or maybe it was the neighbour's cat. She lay still for a moment. There it was again.

'Nita! Nita!'

That was no cat. She rolled over and pushed herself slowly up so as not to wake Thomas. She needn't have worried – he was snoring gently, his bare chest rising and falling rhythmically. She tiptoed out of the room and into the hall.

'Nita! Nita!'

It was her mother. She opened her door. 'Mum, are you all right?'

Mrs Patel was sitting up in bed, her bedside light on. She turned towards her daughter and Nita noticed a strange other-worldly expression on her face. She looked almost well again. Her cheeks had returned to their normal healthy brown and her eyes had regained some of their sparkle. Nita was relieved.

'I need paper and a pen,' Mrs Patel said matter-of-factly.

Nita glanced at her watch. 'Mum, it's five in the morning. Can I get it for you later?'

She shook her head. 'Sadly, maybe not.'

Nita was confused. 'What are you talking about?'

'Nothing, my dear. But I can't sleep, I want to write a letter.'

She sighed. 'OK. But promise me you won't overtire yourself.'

She went downstairs and took a pad of writing paper and a pen out of the desk in the study. In the kitchen she found the small lap tray with its built-in cushion.

'Here you go, Mum.' She put the tray on her mother's lap and passed her the paper and pen.

'You're a good daughter. You've always been a good daughter. Sit down.' She patted the side of the bed.

Nita sat down gingerly, taking care not to touch her mother's bloated and painful legs.

'I was wrong about Thomas.' She put her hand on Nita's. 'He is a good man and he loves you very much. You made the right decision. I wanted to tell you this. I am sorry if I caused you any distress . . . I thought I was protecting . . .' She stopped for a second to catch her breath.

'Mum,' said Nita anxiously.

Mrs Patel put her hand in the air. 'Let me finish.'

Nita nodded.

'For many years now I have lived in the hope that Martina would not disappoint me in the same way that you did. She knows I want her to find a nice Indian man, have a Hindu wedding, as I had and as I wanted for you.' Her eyes misted over slightly. 'How often have I told her the story of my wedding with the garlands of flowers and the music and the dancing, shown her the photographs of the old days in Bombay. When she was a little girl I made her promise me she would marry a good Indian man – I shouldn't have done that.' She coughed gently, then continued. 'I fear I may have complicated things for her. With her young man.' She smiled. 'The look on his face when I met him this morning.'

'Whose face?' asked Nita. She was bursting with curiosity. 'What are you talking about?'

She ignored her. 'He did not know we are Indian,' Mrs Patel laughed. 'Imagine that. The poor boy nearly fainted. "Is Martina there?" he asked. "No," I said, "but I'm her grandmother, can I take a message?" The expression on his face.' She laughed again and then coughed.

'She hadn't told him that I'm Indian?' Nita was reminded vividly of the night of Martina's school debs ball.

'Mum! Put the camera away, Jimmy will be here in a minute.'

'I'm so proud of you – such a beauty.' Nita beamed. 'Just one more photo. You and your dad in front of the curtains. Please.'

'OK. One more, understand. One?' She put up one finger in emphasis.

'Yes, yes.' Nita pushed her husband into place. She stepped back and looked through the viewfinder. 'Put your arm around your daughter, Thomas. Good! Say "cheese!" Martina, you look like someone's died. Smile for goodness' sake.' Click. 'Good! Now one more.'

'Mum!' She pulled up the top of her sari which was slipping slightly. Her mother had made it for her and she was still a little unsure about wearing it. The traditional pink silk with its luxurious gold edging had been specially designed for her in her great-uncle's factory in India. Her long dark hair was piled up on top of her head, set off by a jewelled bindi nestling against the top of her forehead and glistening in the evening light. She'd kept her make-up

simple – some dark red lipgloss, tawny-gold sparkling eye shadow, mascara and a hint of bronzed blusher.

The doorbell rang.

'That must be Jimmy,' said Martina, blushing slightly. Her parents had never met her boyfriend of two months. 'Please try not to embarrass me. No more photos, Mum, OK?'

'But . . .' Nita began. Thomas put his hand on his wife's shoulder. She looked up at him. 'She's nervous,' he whispered to her. 'Go easy on her.'

Martina opened the door. Jimmy stared at her, his eyes taking in her exotic dress.

Before he could help himself he started to laugh. 'What are you wearing, Martina? It's not fancy dress you know. You look like something from The King and I.'

Martina blushed deeply. 'Do I?' she murmured. 'Come in.'

She stood back as he walked into the hallway. Closing the door behind him she made a snap decision. 'Mum just asked me to try this on for her,' she said firmly. 'She's making it for one of my cousins in India. Of course I'm not wearing it.' She faked a laughed. 'Don't be silly. I'll just go up and get ready.' With that she turned and ran upstairs in her new matching pink and gold high-heeled shoes, specially covered for the evening.

Nita followed her up and found her crying into her pillow in her bedroom. She put her hand on her daughter's head and stroked her silky hair.

'I hate being Indian! Why can't I be like everyone else?'

Nita didn't know what to say. 'Jimmy didn't mean to upset you.'

'Well he did. And now I have nothing to wear.'

'Couldn't you explain to him that saris are—'

'No, I couldn't! This is the worst day of my life! Please just leave me alone.'

Martina went to the debs in the end – in a black velvet dress that she'd bought for a Christmas party and without the bindi. But Nita had never forgotten the look on her daughter's face when Jimmy had laughed at her in the sari. He was only being a teenage boy, but he had no idea how much lasting damage he'd done to her precious daughter.

Halfway through the following morning Martina still hadn't got around to talking to Rory about the photo shoot on Monday. To be honest, she was putting it off. After their last encounter – the one on the drive with Rosie – she had no idea how he was going to react to her request. Her mother had rung her mobile several times but she'd been too busy to ring her back.

She'd put together four outfits for the photo shoot on Monday, but was having problems with a fifth. The 'safari' theme was proving to be more difficult than she'd thought to put together coherently. But Cindy was proving to be a great help. She'd already rung the best shoe shop in Wicklow – Healy's – and had managed to convince the manager to lend them several pairs of shoes and boots in various sizes for the models.

She'd also rung a friend of hers who was a hairdresser and make-up artist and enlisted her help.

'I'll never underestimate a stylist's job ever again.' Martina helped Cindy to unpack the boxes of shoes and boots from Healy's.

'How about these?' Cindy held up a pair of long, beige suede boots. She handed them over.

'Might work.' Martina placed them at the bottom of her dressed mannequin and stood back. She tilted her head. 'What do you think?'

'Definitely! They look great with the skirt.'

Martina smiled. The crisp white shirt with the heavily ruffled front set off the flamboyantly ruffled khaki Sami skirt to perfection. And Cindy was right about the boots. 'Great! One down, four to go.'

'These aren't bad.' Cindy held up a pair of very high multi-coloured wedge-heeled sandals. I'm not sure if they're very "safari" though.'

'You're probably right. But put them aside just in case we can use them.'

'What about these?' She pulled out a pair of beige leather thong sandals.

'Perfect! Put those over by the white trouser suit. And these would be great with the snakeskin print chiffon dress. What do you think?'

Cindy nodded at the black chunky sandals with thin leather ties that laced up the leg. 'Very Roman slave.'

'You're supposed to say "very safari"!'

'Oops, sorry.'

'And we have to use these!' She pulled out a pair of high-heeled animal print boots. 'They're amazing!'

'Are you sure you're paying me for this?' Cindy grinned. 'I haven't had so much fun in ages.'

'You won't say that on Saturday when we find the size eight clothes are all too big for the models and we have to pin them into them.'

'Really?'

Martina nodded. 'Let's hope they send up some girls with a sense of humour. I'm not sure being mauled by lion cubs is everyone's idea of a good time. Which reminds me . . . would you hold the fort for a while? I have to go and talk to Rory about the animals. And if you could find one more pair of shoes to go with the Kati G denim-look skirt I'd be very grateful. And maybe have a look for a shirt to go with the outfit.'

'No problem, boss.'

As Martina walked out of the shop her mobile rang. She pulled it out of her pocket and looked at the screen. It was her mum again. She couldn't talk to her now, she had far too much to do. She'd ring her back later. She put the phone back in her pocket and crunched up the gravel drive towards Redwood House.

'Hi, Rosie, do you have a minute?'

Rosie looked up. Rory was standing in front of the desk, his hands buried in the pockets of his jeans.

She smiled at him. 'Sure. Fire ahead.'

'We're going to hold a charity auction and ball in aid of the World Wildlife Fund. And we're setting up an "Adopt an Endangered Animal" programme in

Redwood and the ball would be a good place to launch it.'

'So you thought you'd do a bit of fund-raising and PR all rolled into one?'

'Exactly.' Rory nodded. 'Would you be interested in donating some paintings for the auction?'

'I could certainly fund one piece of work, but maybe some of my artists would like to donate as well. I'll have a ring around and ask them.'

'Thanks. I have a brochure all about the endangered species programme up in the house if you're interested. They're the part of the organization who manage the breeding of the endangered animals, like the lemurs.'

'Sounds interesting. We're pretty quiet this morning. Why don't I pop up to the house with you? I could do with a break. Give me one second, I'll just put a note on the door.' She scribbled 'Back in 10 minutes' on a sheet of paper and Sellotaped it to the wooden door, checking in her pockets for her keys before closing it behind her.

Coming out of Redwood House together a few minutes later, Rory gave Rosie a kiss on the cheek. 'I really appreciate this. Thanks for your support.'

'Don't mention it.' She smiled. 'It'll be fun. And the ball is a great idea. I can't wait to get into my glad rags.'

As she walked down the steps Rosie saw Martina staring up at them.

'Hi, Martina,' Rosie called over. She waved at her but Martina ignored her and walked back towards

Designs on Red. 'Is she all right, do you think?' Rosie asked Rory.

'That's debatable,' he muttered. 'Sorry, yes, I'm sure she is.'

That was all she needed. Rory was flirting with Rosie again. Martina thought about going back up to the house to tell him exactly what she thought of him. Maybe she would. Just then Cindy came running out of the shop.

'There you are. Your mum is on the phone. She says it's urgent. Something about your gran.'

The blood drained from Martina's face. 'Gran? Is she OK?'

'I'm not sure. You'd better come in and talk to your mum.'

Anna

'What do you think?' Conor asked Anna. 'Will anyone come?'

'I think it's a fantastic idea! Just what Redwood needs. It will put us on the map with a bang and raise money for a good cause into the bargain. Have you talked to anyone else about it?'

'Only Rory. He seemed to think that Rosie might donate some pictures and we could have a charity art auction on the night.'

'The Redwood Wildlife Ball and Charity Art Auction. Very grand.'

'Wildlife Ball?'

'Of course. A ball has to have a theme. How about a masked ball? We could invite everyone to wear animal masks. That would be fun.'

'Do you think?' He wasn't entirely convinced. He'd never been into masked balls personally – his face was broad and he could never get a decent mask to fit him. He usually ended up looking ridiculous – the mask's elastic digging into the sides of his cheekbones and leaving thin red welts for the whole evening.

'Maybe,' she said.

'It's up to you, I guess.'

'Sorry? I don't understand.'

Conor grinned. 'You're organizing it.'

She looked at him incredulously. 'I am most certainly not. I wouldn't have a notion. You need someone who knows all the local bigwigs. Philly Thorburn and Cha Cha Shine-Thompson. Those types.' Philly and Cha Cha regularly appeared in the pages of *Social and Personal* and *Image* magazines and were Wicklow's own version of the glitterati.

'How about we organize it together then? I'll deal with the "bigwig" end of things, publicity, tickets and that sort of thing, and you deal with the more practical side.'

'Like the food and the music?'

'Exactly.'

Anna thought for a second. 'I wouldn't mind that. And I could do the flowers and the decorations, I suppose.'

'Do you think Martina and Rosie might give you a hand?'

'They might.' She refrained from adding 'if Martina ever speaks to me again.' She'd called into the shop earlier to see her, but Martina had been out to lunch with some woman from the *Irish Times*, according to Cindy. She was obviously moving in different circles now and didn't need Anna any more.

'Excellent!' He took her by the arm. 'Now let's have

a look at the ballroom and the drawing room. I'm not sure where to hold the auction and the dancing. Maybe they should be in separate rooms.'

'Oh, what a dilemma!' She laughed. 'Which huge and ornate room will I use? You know your problem, Conor Dunlop? You have too much choice. It's not always a good idea to give a man options.'

He smiled at her. 'Perhaps you're right, my dear.'

Anna's mobile rang. She took it out of the back pocket of her jeans and looked at the number on the screen. She was surprised but delighted.

'It's Martina. Do you mind if I take it?' she asked Conor. 'I'll be quick.'

He shook his head and smiled. 'Go on.'

She clicked on the phone. 'Martina?'

'Anna, thank goodness. Anna.'

Martina didn't sound herself. Her voice sounded high-pitched yet weak.

'Martina? What is it? Are you all right?'

'It's Granny. She's . . . she's gone.'

'Hello, Martina, Martina?'

There was no answer.

'I'll be there as soon as I can. I have to call home and then I'll be right over, OK? Where are you?' There was still silence on the other end of the phone. 'Martina? Are you still there?'

'Yes,' she managed. 'I'm at Mum and Dad's.'

'What's up?' Conor asked as soon as she clicked off the phone.

'Martina's granny died. They were very close.'

'Poor girl. I understand she and Rory are having

some sort of argument. He won't talk to me about it but I hope they sort things out soon. She's a lovely girl.'

'I hope so too.' Anna had been far too embarrassed to tell Conor about her own attempt at reconciling Martina and Rory, or about the incident with Martina in the coffee shop. She was still ashamed that she'd tried to interfere and she didn't want Conor to think badly of her. Rory was his son after all and it was just a little too close to the bone sometimes. They'd never discussed Rory and Martina's relationship – it was a kind of unwritten rule between them – and she wasn't about to change things now. Still, it was a pity she couldn't talk to him about it.

'I'm sorry, but I'm going to have to go now. She sounds in bits and I promised I'd call over.'

'Of course, I understand. Give her my love.' He leant over and gave her a gentle kiss on the lips. 'Ring me later.'

As she walked out the door, Anna could feel the muscles in her forehead pulling the skin into a deep frown. She was extremely worried – and she had every reason to be. Worried because only yesterday she'd interfered in Martina's life again in a major way – and this time she had no idea what the repercussions might be.

'Listen, I'm so sorry, Rosie,' Anna said into the phone, 'I'm not going to be able to make dinner this evening. Martina's granny died this morning and I'm going over to see her. I might be there all evening. They were pretty close. But I'd love to go out another night – maybe next weekend?'

'Don't worry about it. I'll talk to Kim and we'll arrange something at a later date. Poor Martina. When's the funeral?'

'Martina didn't say. Sometime this week, I presume. I'm not sure if they'll be having a conventional funeral though. Mrs Patel was Hindu.'

'Oh, right.'

'Anyway, I'd better go. I have to settle Ollie for Mum before I go anywhere.'

Anna put down the phone and sat massaging her temples.

'Mum?' Ollie was standing in the hall staring at her. He'd been out playing in the garden with the boy from two houses up and his face was covered in mud. He'd torn the knees out of his jeans again, too.

She looked up and wiped away the tears that had started spilling from her eyes.

'Are you all right, Mum?' He put his little arms around her and hugged her tight, which really set her off.

'I'm fine. You remember Martina's granny? Well, she died.'

She could feel her son's body go taut. 'She was very old,' Anna explained carefully, 'much older than your granny. Mrs Patel was sick too. Your gran's still flying around the place, isn't she? She's not sick.'

'What were you saying about me?' Moyra asked, walking through the living-room door.

'Mrs Patel died and I was just explaining to Ollie that you weren't going anywhere.'

'Too right! I've years in me yet. So don't worry, young man. Now, let go of your mother and we'll get you into your pyjamas.'

'Thanks, Mum. I'm going to call over to Martina instead of going out for dinner. So I shouldn't be too late.'

'Give the family my regards. Tell them that she'll be missed. She was one of a kind.'

Anna smiled. 'She sure was.'

'I liked her too,' Ollie piped in. 'Can I do a drawing for her? To put on her coffin.'

Anna looked at her mother. Moyra shrugged her shoulders.

'I guess so. I'll ask Nita, but I'm sure she wouldn't mind. What kind of picture were you thinking about?'

'One of India, I think. When I was over at the house with you and Martina one day she told me all about being a little girl in India. She said she'd like to go back there one day before she died.'

Anna started to cry again. Moyra patted her hand. 'Let's go upstairs, Ollie. I think there are some copies of *National Geographic* in the study and if I remember correctly there are photos of India in one of the more recent ones.'

'Thanks,' Anna mouthed. She went into the kitchen, tore off some kitchen roll and wiped her eyes. Opening the fridge she took out some salmon pâté and a small tub of potato salad. She knew she should eat something before she went out.

*

Anna stood on the doorstep of Martina's family home. She took a deep breath and rang the doorbell. A few seconds later Nita opened the door. Her eyes were bloodshot and she looked pale. Anna gave her a hug.

'Thank you for coming,' said Nita. 'Martina's very upset but she won't really talk about it. Maybe you could get her to open up.'

Anna followed her into the hall. 'I can certainly try. Although, to be honest, she's not really talking to me at the moment, I'm afraid.'

Nita sighed. 'Not you as well. She's barely talked to me the past week or so either. I don't know what's got into her. Mum said she was in love but . . .' She began to cry. 'Sorry, I'm a little . . .'

'You don't have to explain. When Dad died I found it very hard. I know it's a bit of a cliché, but it does get better, honestly.'

Nita nodded. 'Martina's upstairs, in the workroom.'

'I'll go on up if that's OK.'

'Please. I'm sorry, I've been very rude. Would you like tea or coffee? Or something to eat?'

'Not at all. I'm fine, I've just eaten. But thank you.'

Climbing up the steep steps to the attic, Anna's heart was thumping. She had no idea how Martina would react to seeing her and she was extremely nervous. Maybe visiting wasn't such a good idea. Maybe she should have waited till after the funeral. But it was too late now. As she reached the top of the ladder and popped her head into the attic space she found it difficult to see. There were no lights on and the evening light had begun to fade, leaving the attic in murky half-darkness.

'Martina? Are you up here?'

She heard a rustling in the corner and she looked over. Martina was curled up on the small sofa, her head resting on one of the arms.

'Martina?' Still no answer. 'Is it OK to come up?' She couldn't stay perched on the top of the ladder for much longer without going either up or back down again. 'Please. I'd really like to talk to you. I'm so sorry about your gran. I want to help you.' She gave it one more try. 'I miss you, love. Let me help you, please.'

She heard what sounded like a sob. 'I'm coming up,' she stated determinedly. She carefully stepped onto the wooden floor and walked slowly towards the sofa, making sure she didn't tread on anything. Reaching the sofa, she sat down beside Martina. She wasn't sure what to do. After a few seconds she decided she'd do what any real friend would do and leant over and put her arms around her friend's shaking body.

'It'll be OK, love.' She stroked her head gently. 'Get it all out.'

Martina sobbed deeply.

'That's right. I'm here now. Just let go.'

Anna felt her own eyes fill with tears, warm drops began to fall down her cheeks and she brushed them back with her sleeve. 'She was a great women. She deserves your tears.'

'I never called in to her,' Martina gulped. 'I was too damn busy for my own gran. And now I'll never see her again.' She began to sob again.

'She knew how much you loved her.' Anna pulled a crumpled tissue out of her bag. It had been used to clean chocolate from around Ollie's mouth, but in the circumstances Anna didn't think Martina would mind. 'Here.'

'Thanks.' Martina stabbed at her eyes, rubbing them until the tissue had almost disintegrated. She looked at Anna. 'I'm so sorry for everything. Thank you for coming.' She began to cry again.

'It's all forgotten. Don't worry about it. It would take a lot more than that to get rid of me, believe me. And you were right, I shouldn't have interfered. I only did it because I love you.'

Martina was overwhelmed. She wanted to tell Anna she loved her too, but she couldn't speak. She turned her face towards Anna, her eyes flooded with tears.

Anna hugged her again. 'I know. I know.' And then she knew she couldn't tell Martina about yesterday morning. She'd had enough shocks for one day – her poor system wouldn't take it. She would tell Martina – she'd have to now that Mrs Patel was gone – but not this evening.

'Now, are you sure you've packed everything?' Moyra asked Anna the following morning. 'Sun cream, a hat, insect repellent . . .'

'Mum! Stop fussing. Ollie's going to the British Virgin Islands, not the depths of Africa. He'll be fine.'

'But the sun will be very strong, and I hear there are big bugs in the sand in hot countries that jump up and bite you, leaving red welts all over your legs and feet.'

'What? Where did you hear that?'

'On *Gerry Ryan*.'

Anna laughed. 'Oh, then it must be true.'

Moyra sniffed. 'He's only young. I'm just saying—'

'I know, Mum. To be honest, I'm not exactly thrilled at the prospect of Ollie going cruising either. Not with Simon and Chrissie anyway. But I'm trying not to think about it. You're not making it any easier.'

'Sorry. I didn't think.' Moyra sat down on Ollie's bed. 'What are you worried about exactly?'

Anna sighed. 'Nothing. Everything.' To be honest she was tired to the bone after visiting Martina last night. Her whole body ached and she had a throbbing headache. She leant over the large black sailing bag they had just finished packing and began to zip it up. This proved to be a little more difficult than she'd imagined, the zip reached halfway before stubbornly refusing to go any further. She pulled out a beach towel and tried again. This time the zip closed easily. 'I hope Simon has packed an extra towel.'

'It'll be hot,' Moyra pointed out. 'He probably won't even need one.'

The doorbell rang. They heard Ollie's footsteps running along the hall from the kitchen where he'd been sitting playing his Gameboy.

'Daddy!' they heard. 'Daddy!'

'I suppose we'd better go down,' said Anna.

'You go.' Moyra stood up. 'I still can't look that man in the face without feeling the urge to spit on it.'

'Mum!'

'He's as selfish as they come. And he's getting worse as he gets older. And as for that little troll—'

'Leave it, Mum. Please.'

'Sorry. You're right. Go on. I'll follow you down in a few minutes. I want to say goodbye to Ollie.'

Anna walked down the stairs. She could feel her heart beating a little more quickly than normal and her palms had begun to sweat. Simon always had this effect on her now and she hated it.

'Anna, darling!' Simon beamed up at her. He was standing in the hall with Ollie by his side. 'Great to see you. Looking fab.' He moved towards her to give her a kiss. She stood tensely upright as he air-kissed her on both cheeks, barely making contact but with audible London 'wuh wuh' kissing noises issuing from his full lips.

'And you.'

He looked her up and down. 'Lost some weight, I see. Suits you.'

She was speechless. He was so rude.

'Mum's been running,' Ollie piped up, 'and watching telly on a hiking bench and lifting weights.'

Her heart sank.

Simon raised his eyebrows. 'Really? Toning up? Hard hitting forty for a woman, old thing. Chrissie's dreading it. Still, she's only twenty-three. Bit of a way to go yet.' He smiled broadly at Anna.

'Where is Chrissie anyway?' she asked, trying not to let her annoyance show. How dare he? She was in much better shape than he was. His jowls were gravitating towards his chest, giving him an unattractive no-neck look. His stomach had been treated to too many corporate lunches and dinners and was looking decidedly flabby and un-toned. But she was damned if she was going to belittle him in front of Ollie.

'In London. We're meeting her in JFK this evening.'

'And you're flying directly from Dublin to New York with Ollie?'

Simon nodded. 'Then on to St Thomas. Staying there overnight and flying to Tortola first thing to collect the boat.'

'And where will you be cruising?' she asked, trying not to sound too anxious. Ollie was only eight after all.

'Along the St Francis Drake Channel. Stopping at Virgin Gorda for a week or so. I've booked us all in to a top-notch snorkelling course.'

'Ollie's not as sallow as you. He burns quite easily, so please if you're out in the sun for the day . . .'

Simon put his hands up. 'I know, I know. Remember the suncream. It'll be fine, Anna, stop worrying.'

'I can spray it on myself,' Ollie said proudly. 'Granny showed me how. You spray it onto your skin and it turns you green. And a few minutes later you're normal colour again. Granny says it's special "Incredible Hulk" suncream.'

Anna smiled. 'Good lad. And don't forget to wear your hat.' She patted him on the head.

'I won't. And a T-shirt with my swimming trunks, I know. It's a pity you can't go with us. But I know you have to train for the Laser Nationals. I hope you win.'

Simon stared at her. 'Laser Nationals? You can't be

serious? You're not sailing dinghies again, Anna. Not at your age. You're hardly fit enough. You'll make a fool of yourself.'

'But Mummy's been winning races in Dun Laoire and in Wicklow,' Ollie said before Anna could retort. 'I watched one last week with Conor. She's really good, you know.'

Anna could have hugged him.

'Who's Conor?' Simon asked suspiciously.

'Mummy's boyfriend,' Ollie said innocently.

Anna groaned inwardly.

Simon looked at her. 'Is this true? You've been leaving my son with your boyfriend while you go off gallivanting—'

'Hello, Simon,' Moyra interrupted from the top of the stairs. She'd been standing on the landing listening to the conservation and she didn't like the turn it had just taken. 'Ollie, why don't you go upstairs and get your bag? Be careful though. It's pretty heavy.'

'OK, Gran.' Ollie bounded up the stairs, past Moyra and into his bedroom.

'Have you packed extra games for your Gameboy?' She shouted after him.

'No, good idea, Gran,' he yelled from his room.

Moyra walked down the stairs. As she reached the bottom she stood in front of Simon, her face as close to his as possible. She had an irrational urge to stick her tongue out at him.

'Conor Dunlop is a good man. He is kind and respectful and he is very fond of Ollie.'

'But—' Simon began.

Moyra put her hand up to stop him. 'Let me finish. You live in London. You see Ollie a few times a year. Anna is doing a terrific job with that boy and I won't see her belittled or trivialized in front of him. Do you hear?'

Simon took a step backwards. He'd always been very nervous of Moyra. She was a formidable woman.

'Do you understand?'

He nodded. 'But—'

'If Anna trusts Conor with Ollie, then you should trust Conor with Ollie. Anyway, it's good for the boy to have a male role model. Someone decent he can look up to.'

'But he has me,' Simon protested.

Moyra looked him straight in the eye. 'Exactly.'

Simon could feel the blood rush to his face. 'What are you saying?'

'Here's Ollie,' Anna said trying to keep the conversation from getting nasty. 'Careful down the stairs, love.'

The bag was slung carelessly over one of Ollie's shoulders and it banged against his legs as he descended.

'We'll have to shorten the straps, young man.' Moyra smiled. 'Did you find some games?'

'Yes, Gran.'

'And you're all set?'

He nodded eagerly.

'Can I have a hug?' asked Anna.

'Course.' Ollie dumped the bag on the floor and threw his arms around her. She tried to hold back the tears. She'd miss him. Still, she reasoned with herself, it's only two weeks.

'I love you, Mum. And don't forget Mrs Patel's picture, OK?'

'I won't – it's on the hall table, I'll bring it over to Martina's later, I promise.' She hugged him tightly. 'Love you too.'

After they'd gone Anna looked at her mother. 'Thanks.'

'For what?'

'For sticking up for me. I always feel such a loser when Simon's around.'

'You're a fine, strong woman. He's just a bully. He always liked to control you, he's bloody power mad. Now you're living your own life and he doesn't like it one little bit.'

'I suppose.' Anna seemed doubtful.

Moyra put her arm around her daughter. 'Let's have a cup of tea and you can tell me all about this great ball that yourself and Conor are running. I might even go myself.'

Anna smiled. 'Mr Shine-Thompson will be there. He's always had a bit of a thing for you.'

'You know, I might even dance with the old bugger just to annoy Cha Cha. Never could stand the woman.'

Anna laughed. 'You're such a troublemaker, Mum!'

Rosie

It was Saturday evening and Rosie was sitting alone on the squashy blue and white sofa in the living room. She thoughtfully rubbed the pale, embossed skin where her wedding ring used to live. First thing that morning she'd wiggled her ring off and nestled it into the blue velvet of the jewellery box, beside her engagement and eternity rings. Darren hadn't said anything about it when he'd called that morning to collect Cass and keep her overnight as arranged. She knew he'd noticed though, as she'd caught him looking at her ring finger intently a couple of times.

Her hand felt funny – lighter – and she figured it would take a while to get used to going ring-less. But as she no longer felt married it felt wrong to be still wearing it out of habit. Or was it her gold safety net? A 'sorry I'm not available'. Not that she was available. Not really. Cass and the gallery were her life now, thanks to her darling ex-husband. Still, at least he hadn't brought Tracy with him in the car to collect

Cass; Rosie didn't think she could have coped with that.

Cass had been really excited about seeing her dad. All morning she'd asked, 'What time is it, Mummy? . . . What time is it now, Mummy?' At bang on eleven o'clock she'd toddled into the hall clutching her Barbie overnight bag against her little chest and sat down on the big hall chair, her short legs dangling over the edge swinging backwards and forwards impatiently. Luckily Darren had been only ten minutes late and his daughter didn't have too long to wait.

Rosie hadn't known what to do with herself all day – it was so quiet without Cass. It was the first time in as long as she could remember that she'd spent a weekend without her. She'd had lunch in Wicklow after browsing in the Bridge Street Bookshop and Healy's shoe shop. She'd had a gander in some of the clothes shops for a dress for the Redwood Ball but, after scouring them all, decided that she'd have to go into Dublin city to find something suitable. Driving home from Wicklow, the thought crossed her mind to have a look in Designs on Red, but Martina might be there. Much as she hated to admit it, she was more than a little afraid of the woman.

Rosie heard something outside and looked out the window. She could have sworn she saw a flash of grey in amongst the leafy trees at the back of the garden. She stood up, walked over to the glass and peered out. It was a clear evening and the sun had just begun to set behind the trees, a delicate shade of pinky red. 'Red sky at night, sailor's delight,' she murmured to herself. Seeing nothing out of the ordinary she sat back down on the sofa and went back to reading her copy of the *Irish Art Review*. There was an interview with Olivia Miller in it and the artist had mentioned the Redwood Gallery. Rosie continued the piece where she'd left off. 'I suppose if I had to choose a favourite new gallery,' Olivia said in her interview with Thelma Riesdale, 'it would have to be Redwood, although I can't stand that Conor Dunlop man. More money than sense. The girl who runs the gallery, Rosie O'Grady, isn't bad. I think she actually likes art – which is something at least. She's lucky to have me of course . . .' She wondered what Conor would say to that. Might be prudent not to show it to him, although someone was bound to, Wicklow being Wicklow.

She put the magazine down, punched a nail through the taut foil stretched across the top of the salt-and-vinegar Pringles tube and smiled as it gave a familiar 'pop'. She thrust a handful of the thin rounds into her mouth and munched away, washing them down with a slurp of red wine. It was eerily quiet, but she could certainly get used to it. She hadn't felt so relaxed in a long time.

'What the hell is that?' Rosie woke to a loud chattering noise outside early the following morning. It sounded like some sort of bird or wild animal. She sat up in bed. There it was again. She got up and padded over to the window, rubbing her eyes. Pulling back the curtains, she jumped back in fright and hid from sight, pressing her body firmly against the cool wall beside the window. Two beady yellow eyes stared at her from the tree overhanging her bedroom window. What the hell? She braced herself, took a deep breath and looked again. The eyes had disappeared but she could now see a black-and-white tail hanging from one of the branches and swinging jauntily from side to side. She rapped loudly on the window, hoping to scare away whatever was in the tree. The tail disappeared immediately and she spied two grey flashes making their way to the top of the tree, causing the leafy branches to sway precariously. There were monkeys in her garden, no less. Monkeys! She smiled to herself. If only Cass were here, she would have loved this. She looked at her watch. It was just gone nine. She picked up her mobile from the bedside table and dialled the wildlife park, her eyes glued to the window.

'Hello?' she heard a gruff voice answer. 'Hello?'

'Hi, this is Rosie O'Grady from Rose Cottage on the grounds. I think you may want to call over here. I have something in my garden belonging to you.'

Twenty minutes later Rosie was standing in her garden staring up at the offending primates with Leo.

'Ring-tailed lemurs,' he said matter-of-factly. 'It's not the first time they've escaped and I'm sure it won't be the last. They're playful little devils. I think there's two of them up there, from what I can see.'

Rosie folded her arms over her chest protectively. 'They're not dangerous, are they?'

'No, not at all. Now if there was a group of mandrills in your tree I'd be a bit worried, but these guys . . .'

'Mandrills? Do you have them in Redwood?'

'Na. They do in Fota in Cork though. The dominant males can get quite aggressive sometimes, you wouldn't want to mess with them – they bite.'

She was more interested in her own newly acquired 'pets'. 'How are you going to catch the lemurs then?'

'With a net. But hang on a second.' They heard something move in the bushes towards the back of the garden. 'I think we may have more company. Maybe you should move inside, if you wouldn't mind.'

She didn't have to be asked twice. 'Sure. I'll be in the kitchen.' She spun around in her red wellies and went inside *tout de suite*.

He followed her in after a few minutes. 'One of the cheetahs escaped from the vet's enclosure yesterday, I think she may be hiding in your shrubbery.'

She nearly dropped her cup of coffee. She was speechless. 'Um, right,' she managed eventually. 'I see.'

'I'll have to go back up to the park and get a tranquillizer gun,' he said calmly. 'Don't worry, cheetahs don't tend to attack people, especially not if they've been fed recently. Stay inside. It's highly unlikely she'd go near you, but just in case.'

'I'm not going anywhere. How long will you be?'

'Ten minutes, maybe fifteen. I'll need to fetch Makedde to help with the net.'

'OK.' Rosie let him out the front door. Friendly primates in her tree were one thing, but a cheetah in her shrubbery. No one would believe her. It was like something out of *Born Free*. She sat down at the kitchen table. She'd love to ring Kim but it was too early on a weekend morning to bother her. Her sister loved her

Sunday lie-ins. She sat back down at her kitchen table and flicked through yesterday's *Irish Times* while she waited for Leo's return.

He was as good as his word. Rosie watched out the window as he lined up his gun and shot several times at the bushes. After a few minutes he walked cautiously towards the shrubbery and called to his assistant. Together they lifted and manoeuvered the large cat's body onto a canvas stretcher, swinging the poor animal deftly by its legs, and carried it out of the garden.

They came back carrying a large net and dumped it on the grass under the tree. Rosie knocked on the window and opened it a crack. 'Is it safe to come out now?'

Leo nodded and almost smiled. 'The cheetah's fast asleep in the jeep. She won't be going anywhere for a few hours. Come on out.'

She took him at his word, although she still felt decidedly nervous. What if the monkeys took a liking to her hair or something? Maybe they could get caught up in it – like bats. She ran upstairs and took a white fleece hat out of her chest of drawers and pulled it firmly onto her head. She wasn't taking any chances. But she didn't want to miss out on any of the action. She toyed with the idea of taking her camera but decided against it – what would Leo think?

'We need your help,' Leo said as soon as he saw her. 'We'll put the net over one side of the tree. Then Makedde and I will make sure that the lemurs are safely in it before we pull the drawstrings and trap them.'

'They won't be hurt will they?'

Leo looked at her for a few seconds. 'No. We'll be gentle, I promise.' There was a wisp of a smile on his lips. 'And we'll need you to encourage them into the net. Do you have a broom?'

She stared at him. 'I'm not hitting any monkeys with a broom. They haven't done me any harm.'

Makedde, who was standing behind Leo, began to laugh.

'What's so funny?' she demanded.

'You'll be hitting the branches of the tree, not the monkeys.' He grinned.

'Oh.' She could feel a blush beginning to touch the tips of her ears and spread its hot little tongues of embarrassment across her cheeks. 'I'll go and get a broom.' She turned on her heels and rushed inside. Leo followed her. 'Are you OK?' he asked. 'It's good of you to help. We could probably manage on our own if you have things to do.'

'I'd like to help.' She opened the long cupboard in the kitchen and took out the brush. 'It's not every day you get to see monkeys, after all. I'm a city girl at heart. Even cows are interesting to me. It's a pity Cass isn't here, she would have loved all this excitement.'

'Cass is your little girl?' he asked as they walked outside. 'I met her in the park – she petted Tibo.'

Rosie nodded. 'She's at her dad's at the moment.' She hesitated for a second, feeling the need to explain further. 'We're separated.'

'I understand,' he said quietly.

They caught the lemurs as planned without a hitch

and placed them carefully in the back of the jeep beside the heavily sleeping cheetah. Makedde slammed the jeep boot shut and smiled at Rosie. 'Thanks for your help.' He shook her hand, turned around and climbed into the driver's seat. He stuck his head out of the open window. 'Better get back to the enclosure or the cheetah might wake up and eat the lemurs.'

Leo looked at Rosie. She had a startled expression on her face. 'He's only joking.' He thumped the side of the jeep. 'You go on, Makedde. Rory will give you a hand with the animals – he's in the office. I'll follow you up in a few minutes.'

'OK, boss!' He stuck his head back in and turned the key in the ignition. The jeep sped off, leaving gravel jumping from the wheels in its wake.

'Sorry about all that,' said Leo. 'You've been great. Not everyone would be so easy going.'

She smiled. 'Living on the grounds has its moments. Can I offer you a cup of coffee?'

He looked at his watch. 'Maybe just a quick one.'

She led him into the kitchen and clicked on the kettle. 'Sit down.' She gestured at the kitchen table. 'Can I get you something to eat?'

'No, I'm fine. Just the coffee. I was up early and I could do with some caffeine in my system.'

'What time do you start working?' she asked as she poured coffee granules into the cafetière.

'Eight normally. But I'm still feeding Tibo at the moment and she has some appetite. She's like a baby – up every few hours for a bottle.'

'A bottle? How old is she?'

300

'Six weeks now.'

'And she's still on bottles?'

'Lion cubs are usually milk-fed by their mum until they're about eight months old. Then their adult teeth start to kick in and they can eat meat.'

'So she'll be on bottles for ages?'

'Yeah. At about twelve weeks I'll add cod-liver oil, glucose and some bone meal to her diet – build her up a little.'

'That's fascinating.' Rosie poured boiling water from the kettle into the cafetière and pushed the plunger. She poured the steaming coffee into two large mugs. 'Do you take milk and sugar?'

'Just milk, thanks. Lots of it.'

She joined him at the table. 'Have you always worked with animals?'

'Pretty much. I studied zoology at Trinity and then worked in Africa for a few years. Near where Makedde's from in Kenya. Then I got a job in the zoo, met Conor and here I am.' He drained half his coffee cup and pushed back his chair from the table. 'I'd better be going. Tibo will be getting hungry again. I don't suppose . . . No.'

'You don't suppose what?' she asked with interest.

'That you'd like to feed her?'

'Really? Are you sure?'

He shrugged. 'If you like. If you're not busy in the gallery, that is.'

'No, my dad's covering for me today. Are you being serious?'

He nodded.

'Then, I'd love to!' She jumped up. 'I'll just run upstairs for a second. Don't go without me now.'

Leo sat in the kitchen and waited. He ran his finger down the still warm mug. This was a turn-up for the books. Makedde said he was sick of Leo going around all day with a long face and what his boss needed was a good woman like his own Cindy. But he feared there wasn't anything even an exceptionally good woman could do to relieve the heavy sadness he felt in his heart. Not now, not ever.

'Where were you earlier?' Darren asked. 'I was trying to ring you. You weren't at the house or answering your mobile.'

None of your beeswax, Rosie felt like saying, but she held her tongue. 'I was up at the wildlife park,' she said nonchalantly, 'bottle-feeding a lion cub. Sorry, I forgot to take my mobile with me.'

'Feeding a lion cub!' Cass squealed. 'Really, Mummy?'

'Really. Tibo – you met her in the park before, remember?'

'Yes! You're so lucky. We only went shopping. Tracy made me take them off and leave them at her house before I came home. She said they'd get dirty in Wicklow.'

'Sorry? What do you mean she made you take them off? Take what off? What's Cass talking about, Darren?'

He looked sheepish. 'Tracy wanted to buy Cass some new clothes – you know – trendy stuff in BT2's.'

'Go on,' she said sternly.

'I got pink Doc Marten's with flowers on them,' Cass smiled, 'and Tommy Hil-something jeans and a Goo-Goo T-shirt.'

'A what?'

'Gucci,' Darren explained.

Rosie patted her daughter gently on the behind. 'Go inside, there's a good girl, and put on your *Clifford* video. Say goodbye to your dad first.'

Cass reached up and threw her arms around Darren who lifted her up and kissed her on the top of her head. 'See you soon, love.'

He put her down and Cass ran inside without a second glance.

'She seems happy,' he said.

As soon as Cass was safely inside Rosie glared at him. 'What were you doing buying her expensive designer clothes? She has loads of clothes.'

'I know. Tracy just thought—'

'I don't care what Tracy thought, Cass is my daughter not hers. And I expect her to be dressed in clothes I've bought her, do you understand? She's not some sort of doll to be dressed up and played with – she's a little girl.'

'Fine. I don't know why you're so bothered. Cass adored being dressed up. She was parading up and down the shop in her new gear without any encouragement.'

'She's not bloody Cindy Crawford!' Rosie was losing all patience with him. 'Please, no more clothes, OK?'

'Whatever. When can I see her again?' He jiggled his car keys in his hands nervously.

'Next weekend, I suppose. Same time. Does that suit?'

'Sure.'

'Thanks.' He opened the car door. 'I really appreciate it.'

'I'm doing it for Cass, not for you,' she said, trying not to snap at him.

'Fine. And Rosie?'

'Yes?'

'You look really well. Country life obviously suits you.'

Before she had a chance to reply, he'd stepped into the car and turned on the engine. She watched as he drove away, not knowing how to feel. Unfortunately he also looked well – too damn well for her liking.

'How did everything go yesterday, Dad?' asked Rosie.

'It was quiet enough,' said Rex, 'but I sold one of Alan's paintings. To the man who bought one of Olivia's pieces on the opening day, remember?'

'I remember. Nice guy. He did say he'd be back. I have to ring Alan about the charity auction. Nice to have a sale to tell him about – he'll be thrilled.'

'Just to warn you, your mother's on her way in. She wants to show her cultural cronies the gallery one morning, followed by lunch in the coffee shop. Apparently Alan promised to talk to them about his work. I told her she'd have to run it by you first.'

Rosie sighed. 'I can hardly say no, can I?'

'I suppose not. Still, look on the bright side – maybe you'll sell some paintings. Give her lot enough wine and flattery and they're bound to think they're the new Medicis and buy something. And the more expensive the better.'

'And I'll give them ten per cent off,' she said. 'They may be rich, but they're suckers for a bargain.'

He laughed. 'Great idea!'

'Speak of the devil,' she murmured.

'Darling!' Julia breezed in the door, her hand-painted red and white scarf fluttering behind her. She kissed Rosie on both cheeks. 'Lovely to see you,' she cooed.

'No need to over-compensate, Mother,' Rosie said archly.

'Don't be like that, chicken. I know I gave you a hard time about moving to the sticks but now I can see I was wrong. Wicklow is the new Dublin. No one wants to go into the city any more, not in the summer any-way.'

'I see. Dad says your cultural gang are interested in visiting – is that right?'

Julia threw a look at Rex. She'd wanted to tell Rosie herself. 'Yes. Alan has kindly agreed to give a lecture on his work and I thought we could have lunch in the coffee shop.'

'And check out Designs on Red?' Rosie suggested. 'They've got some lovely autumn clothes in already.'

'Darling, it's a cultural club, not a shopping club. I hardly think so.'

'What are you talking about?' Rex said. 'Last time you went to the Tate you came back with a second suitcase full of new clothes.'

'That was different.' Julia sniffed. 'Quite different.'

'And when you were in Rome . . .' Rex continued.

'Yes, yes.' Julia was getting a little irritated. She hated it when her husband and her daughter started ganging up on her. At least Kim wasn't there to add to the opposition. 'So what do you think, Rosie? When would suit?'

'Any morning during the week is fine by me,' she said magnanimously. 'Just give me a week or so's notice. And I'll give you all ten per cent discount on any piece you buy.'

Julia cocked her head. 'Ten per cent? Surely twenty per cent would be more appropriate – I am your mother, after all.'

Rex put his hand on his daughter's arm. He could see she was about to say something stinging to Julia. 'Let's settle on fifteen per cent, OK?'

'Perfect.' Julia smiled. 'The ladies will be delighted. Now I must dash. I've been invited to Cha Cha's for coffee.'

He walked over to the door and opened it for her. 'Give my regards to Cha Cha.'

Julia kissed Rosie goodbye. 'And I'm so looking forward to the ball next month. What excitement! I've told all the ladies about your charity art auction – they think you're simply wonderful. I'm so proud of you, darling.'

'Thanks, Mum.'

'Pity it's only in aid of monkeys and things, though. African children would have been better. Still.'

'Goodbye, Julia,' Rex said firmly, practically pushing her out the door.

As soon as she'd gone Rosie sat down behind the desk. 'That woman will be the death of me. Only monkeys indeed. And I can't believe you said you'd give her cronies fifteen per cent. She has some bloody nerve. I've a good mind to charge them all double.'

Rex put his hand on hers. 'At least you're not married to her.'

She laughed. 'You don't mean that, Dad.'

'No, I don't. She may be annoying, but her heart's in the right place.'

'Not again.' Rosie grimaced. Julia was walking through the doorway.

'Rex, darling, there's something wrong with the car. It's making a funny noise – can you have a look, please?'

'Sure. But what kind of noise?'

'A kind of clicking noise.' She waved her hands in the air. 'Oh, I don't know.'

He winked at Rosie and walked outside. Julia's lack of mechanical know-how was no secret.

Julia turned towards Rosie. 'So, darling, Rex tells me that Cass stayed with Darren last weekend. Isn't that nice?'

'Yes, Mother, it's just lovely.'

'Don't be so sarky, dear. He is her father, you know.'

'How can I forget? Everyone keeps pointing it out to me.'

'How is he? Darren, I mean.'

'Fine. Why?'

'No reason. I saw him in town the other day, that's all.'

'I don't really want to talk about Darren if you don't mind, Mum.'

'I understand, darling. It must hurt still. But I'm sure he misses you and maybe in a few weeks time when his little blonde infatuation is over—'

'Just stop it, Mum. He's with Tracy now. I don't want to hear this, it's over.'

'But Cass needs her father, poor pet. I'm sure he'll come around.'

'*Mum! I said stop, OK?*'

'What's going on here?' Rex asked with concern. 'I could hear you from outside, Rosie.'

'Mum was just leaving. Weren't you?'

'Fine.' Julia sniffed. 'I was only trying to help.'

'Help? If that's what you call it I can do without your "help", thank you very much.'

Julia flounced towards the door. 'I'm going to Cha Cha's now. I know when I'm not wanted.'

'I'll see you out,' Rex interjected before Rosie could say anything else. He walked Julia to her car. 'The rear windscreen wipers were on. That's what the noise was.'

'Stupid things. Must have turned themselves on.'

'Must have. And what were you upsetting Rosie for?'

'As I said, I was only trying to help. I just think this nonsense between her and Darren has been going on long enough. It's time they made up. For Cass's sake, if not for their own.'

He looked at her carefully. 'And you honestly think that that's the best thing for Rosie?'

'Of course, darling, don't you?' She smiled a little too brightly at him.

'I'll see you later.' He kissed her on the cheek.

He stood and watched her drive away. 'Silly, silly woman,' he muttered.

Rosie

'I have news for you, Alan,' said Rosie on the phone. 'Are you sitting down?'

'News? What kind of news? Good or bad? You're getting rid of me, aren't you? No more Alan in your dotey gallery. Oh, Rosie, if you'd just—'

'Alan! I'm not getting rid of you. Quite the opposite.'

He sighed theatrically. 'I know it's something terrible. Tell me quickly, I can't bear the suspense.'

'You're not listening. I said good news. I've sold *October Red: Study Two*. Well, Dad has to be precise.' There was silence. 'Alan, Alan, are you still there?'

'Oh, Rosebud, darling. I'm so happy. I thought you were going to dump me. Wouldn't be the first time either. Unlucky in love, that's me. Did I ever tell you about Ricardo, my little Italian stallion—'

'Alan, I'll send a cheque over to you this morning,' she interrupted. Alan was quite capable of spending all morning talking to her about his lost loves and she had to ring all her other artists about the charity art auction.

'A cheque?'

She could hear his eyes light up with euro symbols – ping!

'Yes. For two thousand euro, no less. I've deducted the gallery's percentage, of course.'

'Of course. I'm speechless, darling. Speechless.'

Great, she thought to herself. 'And Alan?'

'Yes, honey child?'

'I've been asked to run a charity art auction on the twenty-sixth of July in Redwood in aid of the World Wildlife Fund, followed by a ball – a wildlife ball. Would you like to donate a painting to be auctioned? It would be good publicity and—'

'Darling, I'd be happy to. How about *October Red: Study Three*? Would that do?'

'Alan, that's worth a thousand euro, you can't donate that! Why don't you give me one of your sketches or a smaller oil?'

'Rosie, I can afford to be generous. I've just sold a painting, haven't I? It would be good karma for me to give something back.'

'But . . .'

'Please, do as I say, ducky. Include it in your auction. And I presume I'll be invited to the ball as a guest?'

Rosie had to hold back her laughter. She could just see Alan dancing with Cha Cha and all her minions; he'd have them wrapped around his little finger. 'Of course. You'll be one of the guests of honour.'

'Excellent! I must go now and design a costume. Ciao, darling!'

'But it's not . . .' – the phone went dead – 'fancy

dress, Alan.' She smiled to herself. She'd ring him back later. One artist down, seven to go. She had to ring Olivia next, before her nerve failed her.

'Hi, Olivia, it's Rosie O'Grady, from the Redwood Gallery, are you there?' She said tentatively into the answering machine. 'Can you pick up if you are? Um, well you're obviously out so—'

'Out?' Olivia's voice shrilled down the phone. 'I'm not out, silly girl. Where would I be, for goodness sake? I can hardly move with my bloody hips. And it's raining. Land sakes, girl, of course I'm not out.'

Rosie gulped and took a deep breath.

'Are you still there?' Olivia asked. 'Speak up, girl, I can't hear you.'

'Sorry. I was wondering if you'd be interested in donating a painting to a charity art auction in aid of the World Wildlife Fund,' she said quickly.

'What fund? You're gabbling, girl. Repeat.'

'The World Wildlife Fund.'

'They look after Asian lions, you know,' Olivia said after a few seconds.

'And other big cats,' Rosie added. This was looking hopeful. She kept on the 'cat' theme. 'Rory Dunlop told me all about their work in Namibia with the cheetahs.'

'Namibia? The cheetah sanctuary is there. I give them a donation every year.'

'So you'll consider it?'

'Consider what?'

'Donating a painting.'

'Yes, yes, of course. I'll send something over in a

taxi this morning. Now did you read my interview in the *Irish Arts Review*?'

'Yes.'

'And?'

'I was flattered. I'm delighted that you like my gallery and . . .'

'Good! You're not a bad sort as girls go. You'll learn. Must dash.'

The phone went dead. All my artists are completely bonkers, Rosie thought to herself. She dialled Eve Marley's number. Eve, a gentle soul, would be nice and 'normal' after Alan and Olivia.

An hour later she'd been promised two prints from Eve, a painting from Ray Davy and a watercolour from Robert McCarthy. She was delighted with herself. Plus she'd sold two of Robert's exotic flower prints to a local hotelier, who'd promised to be back for more prints the following week. All in all, a very good morning indeed.

'Hello again, how's tricks?'

Rosie lifted her head. She'd been weeding the small front garden of the cottage while Cass was playing with her Barbie on the doorstep. It was Leo.

'Hi. Good, thanks. Nice evening, isn't it?'

He wiped his brow. 'I guess it is. I've been chasing maras, bloody things have got out again. What's new?'

She stood up and wiped her earthy hands on her

old jeans. 'How's Tibo getting on? Cass was gutted that she missed all the monkey and cheetah excitement.'

'Tibo's great. And thanks for the help on Sunday, you were great with her, really gentle.'

'It was a pleasure. She's adorable. Any time.'

'Can I feed Tibo too?' Cass ran over. 'Please?'

Leo looked at Rosie and shrugged his shoulders. 'We'll see what your mother says.'

'It's OK by me. Are you sure?'

He nodded. 'As long as we're both there to supervise it should be fine. How about tomorrow evening around six? Would that suit?'

'Yes!' Cass said decidedly.

Rosie smiled. 'Great. Listen, what are you doing this evening?' she said, surprised by her own spontaneity. 'Would you like some dinner, it'll be ready in a few minutes? It's only lasagne and salad I'm afraid, nothing too exciting, but it should be edible.'

He looked down at the ground. 'Um, thanks, but I don't think so. I have to get going. I'm expecting a phone call.'

She'd asked innocently enough – it was only dinner after all – but he seemed embarrassed. He didn't think, oh no . . . 'Of course,' she faltered, 'I understand. Maybe some other time. We'll see you tomorrow.'

'Sure.' He walked away quickly.

'Why did he not want dinner?' Cass asked.

'He's a vegetarian. He doesn't eat meat. Now let's get you ready for dinner, young lady.' She patted Cass gently on her bottom, ushering her inside.

Leo looked back towards Rose Cottage with regret.

He would have loved to have had dinner with Rosie but he couldn't. Not this evening.

'I'm sure I went scarlet,' Rosie said to Kim on the phone that evening. 'I was completely mortified. He must have thought I – you know.'

'Fancied him?'

'Yes!'

'And you don't?'

'Of course not. He's a nice guy but I'm not interested, you know that.'

'Um.' Kim sounded unconvinced.

'I'm serious. I've too much on my plate at the moment without a man to worry about. The art auction for one thing – Rory has organized a photographer to come over on Friday morning to take snaps of all the pictures to be auctioned for a catalogue. I don't have half of them yet and I have to chase up all the artists, which I'm not exactly thrilled about as they've all given their work free and—'

'Hold it right there! Take a deep breath and slow down. You'll send yourself into an early grave. I thought the whole idea of moving to Wicklow was to spend more time with Cass and to have a life for a change. It sounds to me as if you're busier than ever.'

'I know, I know. But this is me we're talking about. I like being busy, remember? But don't worry, I'm happy, honestly. Just a little overwhelmed today, that's all. It'll calm down later.'

'I *do* worry about you. I can't help it. Part of the

sister territory, I'm afraid. Listen, Greg's not mad about going to the ball – it's not really his kind of thing. He offered to babysit for Cass instead. But I'd love to go. Will you get me a ticket – I hear they're rarer than hen's teeth, according to Gerry Ryan's radio show.'

'Wasn't that a scream? I can't believe Gerry and Conor got on so well. I was expecting him to write Conor off as some sort of posh git with more money than sense. But the interview went brilliantly for Conor.'

'He's a bit of a natural, all right. And he made the ball sound like the event of the century. But who the hell is Cha Cha thingy when she's at home? The one who rang in and said she was Conor's best friend and what a wonderful man he was. Talk about batty.'

'I'll get Conor to introduce you at the ball,' she laughed. 'You'll love her – she's completely for the birds.'

'So you'll get me a ticket?'

Rosie laughed. 'Kim, we've only sold fourteen so far! Of course I'll get you one, you can have as many as you like.'

'The power of radio. And here was me thinking they were almost sold out.'

'Good! If you thought that we're on the way to making it a success, it can't do the gallery any harm to be associated. Right, I'd better go. I can hear Cass upstairs and she should have been asleep hours ago. And thank Greg for me – if he's sure, I'll happily take him up on the babysitting offer.'

'Anything from Darren this week?'

'He rang yesterday. He's calling into the gallery tomorrow to talk to me.'

'Sounds ominous.'

'He was actually being pretty nice, to tell the truth. So fingers crossed. I hope he has some good news on the house sale.'

'Is that still going on?'

'Yes, he had a buyer but they pulled out apparently. Maybe he's found another interested party.'

'Maybe.' Kim wasn't convinced. She'd been following the property pages carefully and from the way houses in Glenageary were selling, by rights Rosie's place should have been snapped up ages ago. She didn't trust Darren one little bit and she wouldn't put anything past him at this stage. 'I hope it goes OK. If you want to talk afterwards I'll be in the office.'

'Thanks, I appreciate it. But I'm sure it'll be fine.'

'I'm sure it will.' Kim put down the phone and stared into space. Darren was up to something, she could sense it. But what?

'Hi, Rex, is Rosie here?' Darren asked, walking into the gallery.

'She's just popped out. She'll be back in a minute.'

'I'll just have a look around, I guess, if that's OK by you.'

Rex looked at the young man in front of him. He wanted to punch his lights out, but that wouldn't be appropriate. Anyway, he wasn't that kind of man. Violence had never been his way. Maybe he should try to talk to Darren instead, tell him just how much he'd hurt his daughter and what a selfish and inconsiderate man he was. But would it do any good? Probably not. He held his tongue. 'Fine. How was your weekend with Cass?'

'Great! I've really missed her. That's why I'm here today really – to try and sort things out.'

'I see.' But Rex didn't see at all. Sort what out? The whole messy business? Him and Cass, him and Rosie? What arrogance. As if he could undo months of hurt with a few minutes of 'sorting out'.

'Hi, Darren.' Rosie walked in the door. Rex noted that she'd tied her hair back and had put some sort of shiny substance on her lips. 'Would you mind holding the fort for a while, Dad? We're going for a walk.'

'Sure. Take as long as you want. I'll need your help later with the books though.'

'No problem, I won't be long.' She walked outside, followed by Darren.

'I don't think he's too thrilled with me,' said Darren as they crunched across the gravel in front of Redwood House.

'I wonder why?' Rosie said archly.

'Don't be like that.'

'Like what?'

'You know.'

'No, I don't. But I'm sure you're going to tell me.'

He grabbed her elbow and made her stop walking. 'Rosie. Please.' He looked into her eyes and smiled gently. 'Please.'

She could feel her resolve melting. How could she

be strong and tough with him when he was being so damn nice? 'Sorry,' she murmured.

'I just want to talk to you. Is there somewhere we can sit down?'

She nodded and led him towards a wooden bench to the far side of the coffee shop. It overlooked the rose garden and delicious, delicate scents of tea roses wafted over, soothing and calming.

'It's lovely here,' he said after they'd sat down. 'I can see why you like it. And it seems to be suiting you – you look amazing. Your cheeks are all pink and healthy-looking. A real country girl.' He put his hand on hers but she pulled it away quickly.

'Don't!' she said.

'Don't what?'

'I know what you're trying to do and it won't work.'

'What am I trying to do?'

'Wangle your way into my good books so that you can see Cass more. Well, you don't need to. You can see her as often as you want to. So just stop, OK?'

'That's not what I'm trying to do.'

'No?' Rosie could feel her heart beating faster in her chest and she began to feel a little nauseous. She was afraid of what he was going to say. She stood up abruptly. 'I have to go now. Dad—'

'Said to take as long as you needed,' Darren finished smoothly. 'And I have something to say. Please sit down.' He gazed at her unwaveringly.

She did as he requested, sitting down and staring at her hands, which where clasped in her lap. 'What?'

'I think we're being a little hasty,' he began. 'I don't

think we should rush into any major decisions, like separation or selling the house. It seems wrong until we're both sure that's what we want.'

'I thought you *were* sure. I don't understand.'

'I've been doing a lot of thinking since the weekend. I miss you both – Cass and you – that's the truth.'

'You can't say that! Not now.' She stood up again and turned towards him. 'I'm fine now, everything's fine.'

'Rosie!' he followed her. 'Please come back. I love you.'

She stared at him. 'You don't love me. How dare you! If you loved me you wouldn't have left us like that. What about Tracy?'

'I made a mistake.'

'Mistake! It was a lot more than a mistake, Darren. You broke my heart. I don't know if I'll ever trust anyone again the way I trusted you. Mistake! You're an arrogant pig and I don't want anything more to do with you. Leave me alone.' She walked quickly towards the gallery. She could hear his footsteps behind her and she swung around. 'Did you hear what I said? Go away!'

'I can't! I love you. Please believe me. I'm sorry, I really am. I need you.' He held her by the arm. 'Look me in the eyes and tell me you don't love me. Go on. You can't, can you?'

'Let go of my arm.'

'Think about Cass. Think how happy she'd be to have her dad back. And you're calling *me* selfish.'

'If you don't let go of my arm I'm going to scream.

Then I'm going to ring the guards and press charges for assault. Do you understand?'

'Fine.' He let go. 'You've changed, Rosie. I don't know what's got into you. But I know you still love me and I'll be waiting. I'm not going to go away. I'll wear you down, you'll see.'

She ran in the doors of the gallery.

'Rosie?' her dad asked with concern. 'What's happened? Are you all right?'

'Don't let him in, Dad. Promise me.'

Rex looked towards the doorway. Darren had almost reached it. Rex stepped outside and faced him, blocking his entrance.

'I need to see Rosie,' Darren said. His eyes were icy cold.

'You're not going in.' Rex wasn't budging.

'Don't be ridiculous.'

'I mean it. You've upset her enough. Just go.'

Darren muttered something under his breath, which sounded suspiciously like 'Fuck you, Grampa'.

'Sorry?' asked Rex. 'I didn't quite catch that.'

Darren ignored him, turned on his heels and strode away.

Rex breathed a sigh of relief and went back inside. Rosie was slumped over the desk, her head resting on her arms. Luckily there were no customers.

He stroked her hair. 'What happened?'

'I hate him!' She managed between sobs.

'Why don't you go home?' he suggested kindly. 'Come back after lunch when you're feeling better.'

'He might be waiting for me at the house. I don't want to see him.'

'Did he hurt you, love?'

'No, not physically anyway. He said he still loves me.'

'Ah. I see.'

He watched as large tears dropped onto the open stock book, smudging some of the ink. 'Let me move that,' he said gently. 'We won't be able to read it soon.'

'Sorry.'

'Don't worry about it. The only thing that's important right now is that you're OK.'

A customer walked in the door, a tall elegantly dressed woman, and looked over at the desk.

'Are you open?' she asked.

'Yes,' said Rex. 'We've just lost one of our artists. Very sad state of affairs.'

'Oh, I'm sorry. Not Olivia Miller, I hope.'

'No, she's very much alive and kicking.'

'Good. I was hoping to pick up one of her pieces this morning as a wedding present.'

'If she died, the value of her paintings would go ballistic,' said Rosie, wiping her tears on her sleeve.

Rex looked at her with alarm.

'You're right you know,' the woman said. 'Morbid, but right. But let's hope that doesn't happen.'

'If you need any help, just ask.' Rex smiled.

'Thanks.'

As the woman wandered around the gallery Rex turned towards Rosie. 'Are you sure you don't want to go home?'

She nodded. 'I'm better off here. I'll only worry myself into an early grave in the cottage. But thanks all the same.'

'If you're positive . . .'

'Stop fussing. I'm fine, honestly. I just got a bit of a fright, I guess. Please, don't tell anyone about . . . about Darren and what he said. Promise me.'

'But you should talk to Kim about it. She knows Darren all too well and—'

'Please, Dad. This is something I need to deal with on my own.' She put her hand on his.

'If you're sure . . .'

'Yes.'

'OK then. I'll keep stum. But don't let him manipulate you, love. Stick to your guns. You've built a life for yourself here and Cass seems to love it. It would be a pity to throw it all in for . . .'

'For what? For my husband?'

Rex looked at her carefully. 'Rosie, he stopped being your husband when he betrayed you. I know it's hard but . . .'

'Is this one for sale?' the woman interrupted. She pointed at one of Olivia's paintings that were propped up against the side wall, waiting to be hung.

'Not at the moment,' Rex explained. 'Olivia donated it to the charity art auction in aid of the World Wildlife Fund.'

'When's the auction?'

'Before the Redwood Ball on the twenty-sixth of July.'

'I heard about that on the radio. Sounded great.' She

stood back and looked at the painting once more. 'I may just have to attend. Where do I get tickets?'

'You can buy them here,' said Rosie. 'And if you give me your name and address I can send you out the art auction catalogue. We haven't printed them up yet but they should be ready by the end of next week.'

'Perfect,' the woman said. 'I look forward to it. How much are the ball tickets – I presume you take Visa.'

As Darren drove away from Redwood House along the N11 he cursed Rosie's dad. If Rex hadn't got involved everything would have gone swimmingly. Rosie wanted him back, he knew it. If he'd just had a little more time with her to smooth things over, things would have been back to normal. Tracy was becoming increasingly demanding and clingy. She was far worse than Rosie had ever been. So he'd decided he may as well take Rosie back. Better the devil you know. At least he understood Rosie. She might be getting on a bit – her breasts weren't as pert as Tracy's, or her buttocks for that matter – but she wasn't a bad sort underneath it all.

As he approached Sandycove he decided to call into Fitzgerald's pub for a quick pint. He'd promised to take Tracy out to dinner tonight in La Stampa. Stupid girl had read in *VIP* that former model and Dublin socialite Karla Wilton had had her birthday bash there and now Tracy was obsessed with the place. 'It's really trendy,' she kept saying. 'Karla goes there all the time. We might see her, Darren, imagine that.' He wasn't in the least bit interested in star spotting but he'd decided to humour her. After all, it was the least he could do. Maybe if he were nice enough to her she wouldn't kick up too much of a fuss when he got back with Rosie.

Julia looked over at the table again. It was definitely Darren. And the blonde girl he was feeding with his fork must be Tracy. She watched in disgust as he reached over and wiped his dinner companion's mouth with his napkin. The girl simpered and giggled. Julia lowered her gaze to the floor and noticed that one of the girl's feet was nowhere to be seen. One gold sandal lay forlornly under the table. Julia didn't like to think where her other foot was – but from the lustful expression on Darren's face she could imagine. He was some piece of work. Well, she wasn't going to be party to this blatant display of adultery and disrespect. It made her feel ill just thinking about it. She stood up.

'I'm sorry, girls, I can't stay. I've just remembered Rex is expecting me home.'

'But we've just sat down,' one of the cultural club exclaimed. 'You can't go, Julia, you promised to give us all the inside gossip about the lovely Conor Dunlop.'

'Another time. Ciao, darlings.' She kissed her hand and waved it in the air. As she rushed out the door she breathed a sigh of relief. Darren hadn't seen her. And he obviously hadn't got over his blonde infatuation. Suddenly something clicked into place. Rex was right.

Sarah Webb

Maybe Rosie *was* better off without a man like Darren. She'd been far too hard on her daughter.

'Darren, do you love me?'

'Of course I do, Tracy. You know that.'

'As much as you loved Rosie?'

'More, baby, much, much more.'

She giggled as he moved his hands up and down her inner thighs, grazing the skin with the tips of his fingers. 'That tickles.'

'What about this?' He licked the index finger of his left hand and began to move it in tiny circles around and around her nipples – one and then the other.

She moaned. 'Don't stop.'

He watched her carefully. Her eyes were screwed shut and her mouth hung open, her breath coming in short pants. He was in complete control – exactly as he liked it. He moved his right hand towards her most intimate area and began to stroke it gently with the tip of his finger.

A dark pink blush began to spread over Tracy's chest and up her neck. He removed both his hands and stared down at her. She opened her eyes and looked at him beseechingly.

'Do you want more?'

She nodded.

'What do you say?'

'Please.'

'And?'

She turned over obediently and presented her pert pink rear to him.

He moved his body behind hers and entered her in one swift, sudden movement. She gasped, her head and upper body forced onto the bed by his weight.

'Don't move,' he commanded. 'Stay completely still.'

She did as he requested and several minutes later he rolled off her and collapsed on the bed beside her. 'Good girl,' he said slapping her on the bottom. 'Good girl.'

Martina

As soon as Martina woke up on Monday morning she knew that something had changed, but it took her a few seconds to realize what it was. When she remembered, feelings washed over her like a wave of icy cold water – her granny had gone and she hadn't had the chance to say goodbye. Her head was throbbing as if she'd been on the tiles the previous night, even though she hadn't touched a drop, and the skin around her eyes felt tight and itchy. She sat up slowly and rubbed her eye sockets with her knuckles. Bright sun shone through her blinds, throwing skinny slats of light onto her bedroom wall. She got up gingerly, keeping her head low, as she felt decidedly faint. Did I eat anything yesterday? she wondered as her stomach growled angrily. Probably not, she surmised. She couldn't remember eating, anyway.

She stood up, slid her feet into her slippers and wrapped her towelling robe around her body, tying it tightly at her waist. She opened her bedroom door and padded through the hall into the kitchen. She looked out the kitchen window – it was a beautiful day. The sky was a clear, intense and cloudless blue. The flashing orange digital clock on the cooker said it was ten past eight. Martina flicked the switch up on the kettle, sat down at the kitchen table and waited for the water to boil.

Cindy had kindly offered to open the shop for her this morning and Hattie had offered to cover lunchtimes and afternoons the whole week. Martina was extremely grateful to them both – without them she'd have had to close the shop for a few days. Her mum needed her help in organizing the funeral, which was being held on Wednesday. Her dad had offered of course, but, being Catholic not Hindu, he wouldn't be able to help with the actual service.

Martina hadn't thought about religion at all in the last few years, to tell the truth. She'd been too busy building her own career, relationships and friendships to have much time for anything else. She'd been brought up Hindu and as a child had prayed with her mother and grandmother on a daily basis at the family shrine to Lakshmi and Vishnu, two Hindu gods, offering up sweets, flowers and fruit on holy days. Although she hadn't practised her religion for many years she still felt strongly about family traditions and she knew her granny had wanted a traditional Hindu funeral. And she and her mum had decided the previous evening to do everything in their power to make this happen. They were meeting the local undertaker, Pol Reilly, that morning. He'd taken the body away the previous evening and seemed like a decent man. He'd already warned them that traditional Hindu cremations – where the body was burned on an open pyre – were not catered for in Ireland but assured them that Glasnevin Crematorium was the next best thing.

Cremation. Martina rubbed her eyes again. What a thing to be thinking about at this hour of the morning. Hearing the kettle click she stood up, fetched a cup from the draining board and dumped a large spoon of instant coffee into it. She hadn't the energy to make real coffee. She added some milk from the fridge and shook her cup slightly, swirling the milk through the brown liquid. She popped a piece of bread into the toaster and sat back down to wait for it. Everything seemed to be taking longer than usual – the kettle, the toaster, her brain.

After finishing her coffee she began to feel a little better. The toast had stuck in her throat; its yeasty pulp just wouldn't go down, much as she tried to swallow it. She gave up after a few aborted attempts, emptying the masticated lumps onto her hand and dumping them disgustedly onto her side plate.

At nine o'clock she was still sitting at her kitchen table, numbly flicking through a fashion magazine when she heard her intercom buzz once – short and sharp. She walked over to it and pressed the button.

'Yes?'

'Martina, it's me, Anna. Can I come up?'

'Of course.' She pressed the red button and a few seconds later could hear her friend climbing the stairs. She opened her front door expectantly.

'Hi,' said Anna, puffing slightly from her speedy ascent. She smiled at Martina gently. 'How are you this morning?'

'Been better,' Martina admitted. She stood back from the doorway. 'Come in.'

'I know it's early but I thought you might like some company.'

'You were right. I didn't sleep all that well – I was tossing and turning all night.'

'I'm not surprised.'

'Would you like some coffee?'

'Please.'

Martina flicked the kettle on again and fetched another cup. 'I have to go over to Mum and Dad's soon. To arrange the funeral.'

'I'll drive you over if you like. Ollie's away with Simon for the next two weeks so I'm free all day. And I'm on holiday from the crèche for the whole month. It feels really strange, to tell the truth. I don't know what to do with myself.'

'Thanks, I'd appreciate that. And, Anna?'

'Yes?'

'Thanks for last night.'

'That's what friends are for.'

On the way over to the Storeys' Anna let Martina stare out the window silently. She knew that her friend had a difficult few days ahead of her and could do with some peace and quiet, for however short a time.

Martina kissed her on the cheek as they pulled up outside her family home. 'I'll ring you later,' she promised. 'Thanks for the lift.'

'Any time. And ring me if you need me, you hear.'

'Thanks,' Martina said again. She fished her keys out of her bag and let herself in. Usually she rang the doorbell out of courtesy but today was different. If her mother was resting she didn't want to wake her up. As she opened the front door she heard Nita's voice in the hall. Martina waved at Anna and shut the door behind her gently. From what her mother was saying and the language she was saying it in Martina knew she was talking to one of their relations in Bombay.

He mother looked up and put her hand over the mouthpiece. 'Uncle Kishan,' she whispered.

Martina nodded and walked into the living room, where her father was sitting.

'Hi, Dad.' She kissed him on the top of his slightly balding head.

'Hi, love. Sit down and join me. Your mother's been on the phone for the last half an hour to India. Heaven knows how much it's going to cost.'

She frowned at him.

'Not that it matters, of course,' he added quickly. 'Kishan's distraught. He wants to come over for the funeral but apparently he's been pretty ill himself. The nursing home won't let him go, from what I can make out. Your mother's tried talking to the matron but it doesn't seem to have done any good.'

'Poor Kishan.'

Nita walked into the room. 'He's very upset.' She collapsed onto the sofa beside Martina. 'He really wants to come over and I don't know what to do. The matron said that there's no way he can travel at the moment.' She sighed deeply.

'There's nothing you can do in that case,' said Martina. 'It's out of your hands.'

'But there'll be no one at the funeral from her family. No one from India. There's not enough time for the cousins to arrange flights apparently. Ria and Varun said they'd try, but they'd have to get someone to mind little Aliya.'

'We'll all be there. And her friends from Redwood will too, I'm sure,' said Thomas. 'She'll have a good send-off, you'll see.'

'I know, I know, it's just . . .' Nita began to cry.

'Dad's right,' said Martina. 'Even if none of the Indian relations can make it, her Irish friends and family will be there.'

'But who will do the readings? And organize the music? I doubt they have any Indian music in Glasnevin. I'm not sure I like the idea of having the service in the crematorium, anyway.'

'Well, don't then,' Thomas said evenly. 'Have it here.'

'It's not big enough.' Nita wiped her eyes with the edge of her sleeve. 'Where would we put everyone?'

'We could hire a marquee,' Martina suggested. 'Have some prayers in the crematorium and have the proper send-off in the garden. Gran would like that – she loves the garden. Then we can send her ashes back to Kishan and ask him to arrange for them to be scattered in the Ganges.'

'He might even be able to do that himself,' Thomas added, 'if he's up to it. That way he'd feel involved.'

Nita smiled at them both through her tears. 'That's a good plan. But where will we get a marquee at such notice?'

'Leave it to me,' said Martina. 'I'll organize the food, the drink and the marquee. You concentrate on the cremation and the service, OK?'

'We can't leave everything up to you,' Nita protested, 'you're too busy. Don't you have a photo shoot tomorrow?'

Martina's heart jumped in her chest. She'd completely forgotten about that. 'I want to, Mum, please let me. I need to do this.'

Nita nodded. 'If you're sure.'

'Yes, positive.'

Martina left her parents in the living room discussing the ceremony while she used the phone in the hall.

'Anna?'

'Yes?'

'Are you still free today?'

'Yes, why?'

'I really need you. Can you call over?'

'I'm on my way.'

By that afternoon Martina and Anna had nearly everything sorted. Moyra had offered to do the flowers, Conor had come up trumps with a marquee company who were willing to provide not only a marquee but also fold-out chairs; and lasagne, quiche, salads and brown bread had been ordered from the local deli to be delivered on Wednesday morning. Thomas had insisted on dealing with the drinks himself – he said it was the least he could do. And he and Nita spent several hours with Pol, the undertaker, going over funeral details and were now both more than satisfied with the arrangements for Wednesday morning.

Which left the remainder of the day to arrange the fashion shoot.

When Martina and Anna walked into Designs on Red later that day they found Cindy looking ashen-faced.

'What's up?' asked Martina.

'There's a strike at Accent Model Agency,' gulped Cindy. 'The photographer rang me an hour ago.'

'A strike?' Martina sat down on the sofa beside the door. 'Are you serious?'

Cindy nodded. 'I'm afraid so. Something to do with working conditions, apparently. I've tried some of the other agencies but none of them can do it on such short notice. I was offered two nineteen-year-olds by the Morgan agency but they weren't suitable.'

'Why not?'

'They were men.'

'Ah. What the hell are we going to do? Did you ring Carolyn?'

'Yes, she said unless we can come up with some models ourselves she'd have to scrap the Designs on Red piece and do a feature on the Brown Thomas fashion show instead.'

'Over my dead body!' said Martina, regretting the

expression as soon as the words had left her lips. Suddenly overwhelmed with emotion, she leant forward and put her head in her hands. 'I can't deal with this today,' she murmured. 'I'm too tired. Ring Carolyn, tell her to go ahead with the Brown Thomas piece.'

Cindy picked up the phone and started to dial.

'Put down the phone,' said Anna. 'I have an idea.'

Cindy looked at her. Anna seemed serious so she did as requested.

'Cindy,' she asked, 'what needs to be done for the shoot? In order of importance.'

The young woman thought for a few seconds. 'First of all we need to talk to Rory about using some of the animals in the shoot.'

'You haven't done that yet?'

'Um, no. Martina was going to but . . .' Cindy broke off.

Anna turned her head towards Martina, who was still slumped in a heap on the sofa.

'And?'

'Models – we need at least three models, if not four or five.'

'But three would do?'

'I suppose so, at a pinch.'

'And?'

'That's it really. Hattie said she'd mind the shop and I have the make-up and hair organized. The clothes and accessories are all ready to go – each set of clothes in three different sizes just in case.'

Martina raised her head. 'Three sets of each outfit?'

'I figured that the new models might come in

slightly larger, more normal sizes than eights and tens; and Hattie helped while I rang all the agencies. She came in for a couple of hours this morning, bless her.'

'Cindy you're a genius. Why didn't I think of that?' Martina sat up.

'What?'

'We can use normal women to model the clothes, Redwood women.' She looked at Anna hopefully.

'Don't look at me like that!' Anna protested. 'I've never modelled in my life and I don't intend to start now, thank you very much.'

Martina stood up. 'But this is an emergency. Please.' She raised her eyebrows expectantly. 'Pretty please?'

'All right then, but you'd better put me in something decent. I'm not wearing anything skimpy, mind.'

'How about Rosie from the gallery?' Cindy suggested. 'She has a nice figure.'

'Good idea. She just might be persuaded. And what about yourself?' asked Anna. 'If I have to, Cindy, I don't see why you can't.'

'I look too young in photographs,' Cindy said rationally, 'and anyway I need to help Martina with the styling.'

Just then a customer walked in the door. It was Cha Cha Shine-Thompson. Her long red hair hung down her back, swaying attractively over the orange lacy-edged Lainey Keogh cardigan. She was barefaced for a change, her lightly freckled skin glowing with health, which was surprising considering the amount of partying the woman did.

Cindy glanced at Martina and nodded slyly. Martina

sat up, took a deep breath and smiled broadly. Things were looking up – maybe the fashion shoot could be saved after all. 'Hello, Cha Cha. How's our favourite customer?'

'Good, thanks. I was looking for a little something for the Redwood Ball. A bustier top I think, in velvet perhaps.'

'We have just the thing,' said Martina leading her towards the rails at the back of the shop which held the evening wear. 'And what are you doing tomorrow, Cha Cha, if you don't mind me asking? I might have something else that's right up your street.'

While showing her the velvet Luna bustiers Martina filled her in on the fashion shoot.

'Are you serious, darling? I'd love to do it. And it will get me out of going to Philly's little tea party thing. Wait till she hears – she'll be so jealous.'

'Excellent. We're meeting outside the main house at two o'clock, is that OK, Cha Cha?'

'Perfect.'

'And if you don't mind me asking, what size are you?'

Cha Cha swatted her on the arm. 'As long as you don't tell anyone, darling.'

'Of course not,' Martina promised.

'In that case, I'm something between a twelve and a fourteen. Better say fourteen just to be on the safe side.'

'We'll see you at two then.'

Cha Cha smiled. 'And I think I'll take this and a few of those velvet Luna scarves as well – the red and the purple.' She handed Martina a dark red bustier and pointed at the scarf display on the wall.

Martina removed the two scarves and brought them to the desk. 'I'll give you a ten per cent discount on everything, Cha Cha.'

'Very kind. But how about fifteen? They give me fifteen at Lian's in Wicklow, you know.'

Cindy and Anna who were listening to every word tried not to laugh.

'Um, fine.' Martina stepped behind the cash desk. In the circumstances she was hardly in a position to argue. 'Fifteen it is.' She swiped Cha Cha's card, wrapped the purchases in pink tissue paper and placed them carefully in a Designs on Red bag.

As soon as Cha Cha was out of hearing Anna asked, 'Are they always that scabby?'

'Who?'

'People like her.'

'Rich people with more money than sense, you mean,' said Cindy.

'Exactly.'

'Always,' Cindy smiled. 'The richer they are the more they expect.'

'Rosie was saying her mother asked for a special discount in the gallery. She's bringing all her friends in to visit the place apparently,' Anna said. 'I don't think she's quite in Cha Cha's league money-wise though.'

'God love her if she has a mother anything like Cha Cha.' Martina laughed. 'I'll call in to her now and ask her about modelling. Will you talk to Rory, Anna, about the animals?'

'Me! Why me? Surely it would be better coming from you?'

'Please.'

Anna sighed. 'OK, I'll do it. But what will I ask him exactly? What animals do you want? No dangerous ones, surely?'

Martina shrugged her shoulders. 'Don't know really. What do you think, Cindy?'

'Don't ask me,' Cindy smiled. 'I have no idea. But I suppose I could ask Makedde, he might know. Then you might not sound so clueless about the animals when you talk to Rory.'

'Great idea!' Anna smiled. 'You leave it to us, Martina. Go and harass Rosie.'

'Are you sure?'

'Yes! Go on, get going.'

As soon as she stepped outside the shop Martina rang her mother on her mobile. 'Hi, Mum, how's everything?'

'Hi, love. Fine, I think. Kishan was able to fax me some readings from the holy books that he'd like read at the ceremony and your dad's recording some of Mum's favourite music onto one tape to play, too. And Ria and Varun can make it after all. They're leaving Aliya with her granny for a few days. I think it's all coming together. Oh, and Pol said he found two envelopes in her dressing-gown pocket. He's calling over later to drop them round.'

'Envelopes?'

'Yes, one of them's addressed to you apparently. And, this is the weird thing the other one's addressed to— Listen, I have to go, your father's calling me. I'll talk to you later. Love you.'

'Love you too, Mum.' She clicked off her phone and stared into space. Envelopes? What was that all about? And who was the other one for? She walked towards the gallery, thoughts racing through her head. She wouldn't have time to call over to her parents' till this evening, what with the fashion shoot and everything. Still, maybe it was for the best. It would stop her thinking about her gran too much.

She took a deep breath just before she pushed open the glass door to the gallery. She hadn't exactly been all that welcoming to Rosie. Anna was very fond of her, so she must be all right, even if, as Martina suspected, there was something going on between Rosie and Rory. But desperate times called for desperate measures after all. Besides, Cindy was right, she did have a nice figure and the Kati G clothes would fit her perfectly.

Martina

Martina breathed a sigh of relief as a shiny black jeep pulled up beside her motley crew who were all sitting on the ornate steps at the back of Redwood House. The public had no access to this particular garden area, so Rory and Conor had allowed them to use it. The steps swept down to the once ornate gardens, which were now in need of some tender loving care. The cameraman was twenty minutes late, but as the weather was bright and reasonably warm no one seemed to mind. Hattie was holding the fort in the shop and Cindy was in the stock room, putting the final touches to the heaving clothes rail, home to all the clothes for the afternoon's shoot. Her friend Ella, a freelance make-up artist, had arrived and was champing at the bit to get started.

A tall blond man jumped out of the vehicle and walked towards them, followed by a smaller woman with long curly dark hair tied back with a jaunty red scarf. He was wearing denims and a creased white linen shirt, and owned rather a fine set of glistening white teeth, Martina noticed as he smiled widely at them all. The woman was his almost identical twin, in denims and a tight-fitting white T-shirt.

Cha Cha had come fully made-up, her hair piled on top of her head in an elaborate chignon. Wearing a pink flamenco-style dress, her lips blood red and dripping wet with lipgloss, she looked as fabulous as her outfit. Rosie and Anna were still in their civvies and getting a little paranoid about sitting beside the fully pumped-up other 'model'.

'Hi, I'm Martina.' She stood up and smiled at the man.

'Hi, Martina.' The man shook her hand warmly. 'Owen Frost, the *Irish Times*.' He didn't introduce his sidekick. 'Lovely day, isn't it?' He continued before Martina had had a chance to answer. 'Great setting. Might shoot exactly where everyone's sitting if that suits. Give me one second.' He clicked his finger at the woman, who scuttled back to the jeep and opened the boot. She pulled out a large camera and handed it to him. He held it up to his right eye, pointed it at the women on the steps and began to squeeze the shutter. The camera whirred into action. Stopping for a brief moment and taking the camera away from his eye, he handed the woman a black rectangle which he'd extracted from the back of the camera, making a ripping sound not unlike a wax strip leaving a leg or bikini line, Martina thought.

'Just banging off some test shots,' he explained.

The woman waved the black rectangle in the air.

'He's testing the light,' she leant over and whispered to Martina, who was looking on in bewilderment, along with Anna and Rosie. Cha Cha who was well used to photographers was ignoring him, smoking a More cigarette which she'd jammed into a long tortoiseshell holder, whose smoke lingered all around her face in dramatic grey puffs. 'I'm Jane, by the way, Owen's assistant.'

'Nice to meet you,' said Martina. 'What happens next?'

Before Jane had a chance to answer, Owen spun around and grabbed the test shot from his assistant's hands. 'Good! Great light. Nice relaxed poses on the steps, I think. Draped over animals. Where are the animals? Dogs are they? Great Danes? Irish wolf-hounds?' he asked Martina nonchalantly. 'Carolyn didn't say.'

'Not exactly.' Martina smiled broadly. 'Will I get the models dressed and ready first? Makedde, the keeper, said it was better not to leave the animals hanging around if possible.'

'Keeper?'

'Yes, keeper. Redwood has its own wildlife park, didn't Carolyn tell you? It's a safari-themed shoot.' She winced. 'Excuse the pun. The manager of the park, Rory Dunlop, is letting us use a young snow leopard, some of the ring-tailed lemurs and a baby lion. It'll be good publicity for the park. Is that OK?'

Owen's face drained. 'Um, I suppose.' He'd never worked with wild cats before and to be honest he'd had a bad experience with a monkey a few years previously who'd stolen one of his lenses and nipped him on the finger when he'd attempted to retrieve it. 'If you could get everyone ready, Martina, that would be great,' he said a little nervously. 'I'll start setting up the equipment.' Jane gave a little cough. 'With Jane's help, of course. And then we'll get started.'

'So no animals till later then?' Martina asked wickedly.

'No, no animals till later.'

Jane threw Martina a smile as she began to unload the jeep. Owen busied himself fiddling with the camera.

'Can I get someone to help you?' Martina asked her kindly. 'That looks awkward.' Jane was struggling with a large silver-coloured object which had become wedged in the boot of the jeep.

'No, I'm well used to it. Thanks.' Jane glanced over at Owen who was sitting on the steps, polishing a lens. 'I know what you're thinking but he's not so bad. One of the best in the business, too. Takes a bit of getting used to though. It's great experience for me even if he is a bit lazy when it comes to unloading the stuff. Snappers are all a little strange, to tell the truth.'

Martina smiled at her. 'If you're sure.'

Jane nodded.

'In that case, I'd better go inside and help dress the girls. Excuse me. But please do ask if you need anything.'

'I will. And thanks.'

Inside the shop, things were getting a little heated.

'I'm not wearing that!' Cha Cha stated, pointing

345

at the white trouser suit. 'It'll make my bottom look enormous.'

'No, it won't,' said Cindy. This was the third outfit she'd offered the exasperating woman and she was getting a little tired of her. 'And anyway, the shots will all be taken from the front. Your bum will be well hidden.'

'Are you saying it *is* big?'

'No! Of course not. Please, just try it on.' She handed the suit to her again. 'Please?'

'Fine. But if it doesn't look good—'

'We'll find you something else, OK?'

Martina was having an easier time of it with Rosie. Ella had already pinned Rosie's hair back into a sleek ponytail, leaving wispy tendrils on either side of her heart-shaped face. Rosie's skin already had a healthy tan, so Ella had simply livened up her cheeks with some gold-sheen bronzer, added some dramatic dark brown eyeshadow and eyeliner and dosed her lips liberally with dusky rose-pink Mac gloss. Dressed in a white ruffled shirt, khaki skirt and floppy beige suede boots, with a thick brown leather belt slung low around her hips, she looked fantastic.

'Weird.' Rosie stood in front of the full-length mirror.

Martina looked at her quizzically.

'It's not me, but I kind of like it.'

'Good.' Martina breathed a sigh of relief. 'Would you mind if I left you for a second – I need to check Anna's clothes.'

'Fire ahead. I'll just talk to the strange woman in the mirror.'

Martina laughed. 'You do that.' She walked towards Ella and Anna. 'How are you getting on?' she asked Ella.

'Great. Anna's got fantastic bone structure – she's easy.'

'That's what they all say,' quipped Martina.

'Here, I'm doing you a favour,' Anna complained. 'Less of that. I might refuse to wear some of your clothes.'

'Cha Cha's beaten you to it,' Martina said in a low voice. 'She's already in her third outfit.'

'You mean I'm getting one of her cast-offs?' asked Anna.

'You've got a much better figure,' Martina whispered. 'The Luna dress looked terrible on her – it hugged all the wrong places.'

'Done!' Ella stepped back and smiled at her handy work. And she had every right to be proud – Anna had been transformed. Her blonde hair had been teased into a bouffant 'mane', framing her almost perfectly oval face. The heavy eyeshadow accentuated her eyes dramatically and Ella had made her lips appear full and bee-stung.

'Wow!' Martina said. 'You look amazing!'

Ella passed Anna a hand mirror. 'What do you think?'

'I'm not sure. Is it really me? Is my hair supposed to look like I've been dragged backwards through a bush?'

'That's exactly what Rosie said.' Martina laughed.

'Well, almost. And your hair looks great – very lion-ish. Now are you ready to get dressed?'

'I suppose so.'

Ten minutes later Martina and Cindy led out the three 'models', Ella following closely behind – hairbrush, hairspray and powder puff at the ready in case she needed to do any last minute de-shines or rearrangements.

'Ladies!' Owen grinned. 'Looking good. Can I have all three of you first on the steps, please? Lion lady—'

'It's Anna,' said Cindy helpfully.

'I told you,' Anna hissed to Martina.

'Shush!' Martina scolded. She was trying not to laugh.

'Anna lying on the balustrade with her arms behind her, propping her up. Can you demonstrate, Jane?'

'Sure.' Jane jumped up and positioned herself on the pale grey cut stone like a pro.

Anna watched carefully.

'See?' Owen asked.

Anna nodded and moved towards the balustrade. Jane shimmied down and Anna gamely climbed up, trying to copy where the woman's body had been without damaging the silk dress she was wearing.

'Good, good,' said Owen, 'but a little more relaxed. Try crossing your ankles over each other. Excellent! But while I'm shooting you'll all need to smoulder, OK?'

Rosie snorted.

Martina looked at her and smiled. 'You'll be great,' she assured her. 'I'm sure you're a great smoulderer.'

'Are you sure that's a word – "smoulderer"?' Rosie grinned.

'Cha Cha, could you stand with your back to Anna? Put your hands behind your body and lean back slightly towards her, great. You're a natural.'

Cha Cha beamed. 'Thank you, darling.' She blew him a kiss.

'And . . .'

'Rosie,' said Martina.

'Rosie, I want you in front of Anna.'

Rosie moved towards the other two women.

'To the left a little, more. Stop! Perfect. Now everyone freeze while I have a look.'

He took his position behind the camera, which was supported by a tripod stand. Jane stood directly beside him. He stared through the viewfinder and then raised his head.

'Cha Cha, move your right hip slightly forward . . . perfect. Try putting your right hand on your hip . . . that's it. Anna, loosen the shoulders, you're still a little stiff. Rosie, lean back more . . . that's it.' He stepped behind the camera again, pressed the shutter and handed another black triangle to Jane. 'I need you to stay exactly as you all are until this test shot has developed.'

'My bum's going numb,' Anna complained good-humouredly.

'Darling, I'm not surprised – you have no padding, you're all muscle,' said Cha Cha. 'You should count yourself lucky.'

'Cha Cha, that suit is stunning on you. You look amazing,' Rosie said admiringly.

'Thank you, babe.'

Ella crunched towards them on the gravel and powdered their noses. 'Just getting a little shiny, girls. Have to keep you matt.'

As she stepped back Owen clapped his hands. 'Great, the poses are perfect. We'll try a few without the animals, how's that? But maybe you could get them ready, Martina?'

'Of course, I'll be back in a few minutes. Cindy's staying here and, Ella, would you mind helping Owen and Jane? Hattie's in the shop, if you need anything.'

'Sure, no problem.' Ella smiled. 'I don't think I'd be much use with the animals anyway.'

Martina heard the clicking and whirring of the camera as she walked quickly towards the office of the wildlife park. Her heart gave a little leap when she realized that Rory was standing outside – she'd been expecting Makedde. As she approached him she couldn't help but stare at his face. He was wearing dark glasses and his features weren't displaying any emotion at all.

'Hi, Martina, I've been waiting for you.'

'Sorry, I hope I haven't inconvenienced you.'

'Not at all. Any excuse to skive off work for a little while. And I do believe the sun's staying out.'

He was right. She could feel the heat on the back of her head.

'I wanted to catch you on your own,' he said.

'Oh?' To have a go at me, no doubt, Martina thought.

'I'm so sorry about your gran. She was a lovely woman. I only met her once, but I know how much you loved her. And she adored you – you were her pride and joy.' He took off his glasses. His eyes radiated kindness and sympathy.

Martina's heart melted. How could she have thought the worst about Rory? 'Thank you,' she whispered. 'I appreciate it.' But did he just say that he'd met her gran?

'And I met your mum this morning,' he continued, 'stunning woman. I can see where you get your looks.'

Again Martina was taken aback. 'What was Mum doing here? I don't understand.'

'She was delivering a letter. Didn't she tell you?'

Martina shook her head dumbly.

Rory sighed. 'I wish you'd introduced me to your family earlier, Martina. I know you said that you wanted to keep your relationships private, that it wasn't up for discussion, but I should never have accepted that. I was a fool. I see that now. I was too scared of losing you to demand anything. Anyway, your gran was a lovely woman and I'll be at the funeral tomorrow. If there's anything you need in the meantime, anything . . .'

Martina felt faint. She could feel the blood rushing to her head and her heart began to pound in her chest.

'Are you all right?' he asked with concern. He put his arm around her. 'You've gone very pale, maybe you should sit down. Come in, I'll get you a glass of water.'

He sat her down in the small hallway and fetched

some water from the cooler in the corner. 'Here.' He handed her the plastic cup and knelt down beside her.

'Thanks.' She breathed deeply. 'I thought I was going to keel over there.' There were so many things reeling around in her head that she was rendered speechless. She wanted to ask him when he'd met Gran but words failed her.

'It's my fault, I shouldn't have brought up your mum and your gran. I know you have a busy afternoon. But I really wanted to talk to you alone. I'm sorry. Can we meet up later?'

She looked at him.

He smiled warmly at her. 'Please?'

She didn't want to cry but she didn't know how to stop herself. 'Yes,' she said finally. 'I'd like that.'

'Don't cry, you'll ruin your make-up. And what would the *Irish Times* people think?'

She smiled wanly. At this precise moment she didn't much care, to tell the truth. She'd much rather talk to Rory, but she knew that everyone was waiting for her – numb-bum Anna most of all.

'You're right, I'd better get moving. Are you bringing the animals over?'

He nodded. 'With Makedde. He's around the side with the snow leopard and Tibo, the lion cub. I'll be along with the lemur and her baby in a few minutes.'

'Her baby?'

'Did Anna and Cindy not tell you? We have several lemur babies at the moment. Wait till you see them.' He held out his hand and helped Martina up. 'We'd better get going. Makedde's waiting.'

'Rory?'

'Yes?'

'Before we go, can I have a hug?'

'I thought you'd never ask.' He put his arms around her and held her tightly. Martina breathed in his familiar musky smell.

'Thanks,' she whispered into his neck, 'I needed that.'

'Hi, boss,' Makedde said as they approached him. 'All set?'

'Yes. Martina will give you a hand if you like.'

'Great.' He handed her two bottles full of milk. 'Can you take these? I'll get the cats.'

'Baby bottles?'

Rory nodded and smiled. 'I'll see you in a few minutes on the back steps, OK?'

'Fine.' She felt as if a heavy weight had been lifted from her shoulders. Rory wanted to talk to her. She'd forgotten how much she missed him. Was there a possibility that this time they could get it right? She knew at that moment that if there was any chance of Rory wanting to give it another go that she'd put her heart and soul into making things right. She loved him. It was as simple as that.

'Martina?' Makedde interrupted her thoughts. 'Are you ready?'

He was carrying two wild cats in his arms – a lion cub and a snow leopard with the most amazing white and fawn dappled fur.

'Look at those two, they're adorable! Can I touch them?'

'Pet them, you mean?'

She smiled. 'Sorry, I know they're wild animals. I'm sure I can't pet them.'

He laughed. 'You can pet them. They like it just as much as domestic cats. Try rubbing gently behind their ears . . . that's it.'

She put her hand down and did as instructed. 'Yuck!' Martina squealed, drawing her hand back as Tibo licked her. 'That lion cub has a really rough tongue.'

'Tibo,' he said. 'How do you think they get all that raw meat off the bones?'

'Never thought about it really. But it makes sense. Here's the gang.'

'Hi, Cindy.' He smiled at his girlfriend as they walked towards the tableau.

Owen was staring at the cats in his arms. He began to smile widely. Maybe this wasn't going to be so bad. 'What beautiful animals. Can we put them in the next shot?' asked Owen.

'Sure. Tibo's used to Rosie, maybe she could hold him. And Lola could sit at the lion lady's feet.'

Martina laughed. 'I'm afraid that's going to be your new nickname, Anna – "lion lady".'

Anna smiled. 'It's marginally better than dragon lady, I suppose.'

'I kind of like it,' said Rosie.

'Can we get the shot set up?' Owen said loudly, interrupting their banter. 'Jane and . . .' He looked at Makedde.

'Makedde.'

'Jane and Makedde, can you place the animals?'

'I hope the clothes will be OK,' said Cindy. 'It wouldn't take much to tear that silk dress on Anna. Martina?'

'Sorry, I was miles away.' Martina was watching the pathway, waiting for Rory. 'What were you saying?'

'Anna's dress. I hope Lola doesn't take a shine to it, that's all.'

'I'm sure it'll be fine.'

The cats were behaving remarkably well and Owen was very impressed. Tibo was quite happy sitting in Rosie's arms and Lola was basking in the sun at Anna's feet.

'I have no animal,' Cha Cha complained.

'I'll give you one to hold in the next shot,' Owen promised. 'There's another one coming, Martina, isn't there?'

'Yes, a lemur with her baby.'

Cha Cha was satisfied. 'That's like a puma, right? A black cat.'

Before Martina had a chance to answer Owen was off again. 'Places, everyone. Cha Cha move to the left a tiny bit . . . that's it. Anna, lean back, loosen those shoulders again. Smiles this time. Enjoying the animals, people. Rosie, look up. Lola . . . Lola . . . Is there any way you can attract her attention, Makedde?'

'Sure.' He stood behind Owen and began to whistle softly. Lola raised her head and gazed at him.

'Perfect,' Owen murmured. He kept his finger on the shutter, capturing the magnificent scene in front of him. They were going to be stunning pictures, he just knew it. The sun was splitting the heavens, the women looked exotic and the animals – what beauties. He took one last shot and then stood up, raising his arms over his head and stretching his back. 'Excellent! We'll take a break now. Are there other outfits, Martina?'

'Yes, I'll take Rosie and Anna off to change. Cha Cha's staying as she is. We're just going to give her some fresh accessories and a different jacket.'

'Good.' He glanced at his watch. 'Ten minutes. Is that all right?'

'We'll give it a go.'

'Great.' Owen sat down on the steps and pulled out a box of cigarettes. Jane sat down beside him.

'I'll stay here with Cha Cha,' Cindy offered.

'I'll do that,' said Martina. 'You go in and help Anna and Rosie.'

'Are you sure?'

'Yes.'

'OK, then. The extra accessories are there.' She pointed at a large wicker basket. 'And the Kati G top is there too.'

'Perfect. See you in a few minutes.'

Anna, Rosie, Cindy and Ella made their way towards Designs on Red to change outfits.

Martina stayed outside with Cha Cha, trying not to inhale too much of the woman's billowing smoke. 'Are you enjoying yourself, Cha Cha?'

'Very much.'

'When you've finished the cigarette we'll get you changed.'

She'd just finished rearranging Cha Cha's outfit,

giving her a dark green Kati G wrap-around cardigan, set off by a dramatic single conch shell choker around her elegant neck, when she heard the gravel crunch behind her.

It was Rory, followed by Leo who was carrying a heavy plastic box with bars in the front and a handle on top. He lowered it gently to the ground, wiped his hands on his navy work trousers and held out his hand.

Rory turned towards Leo. 'Are you staying? I know you're mad busy.'

Just then Rosie appeared. Leo seemed to stand up straighter. 'I'll just say hello to Rosie,' he said, spotting her over by the steps. 'That is her, isn't it?' he asked Martina.

Martina laughed. 'Hard to believe, isn't it? She looks so glamorous with all that heavy eye make-up on.'

'Didn't know she was a model,' said Leo.

'She's not. She kindly stepped in at the last minute when the models we'd booked went on strike.'

'I'll bring the lemurs back afterwards,' Leo said to Rory. 'I know you have a mountain of paperwork to finish.'

'The invoices.' Rory winced. 'I'd almost forgotten. I'll get back to it in a minute.'

'Hi, Leo,' Rosie said as he walked towards her. 'How are you? I was giving Tibo his bottle before Makedde took him back to the park. He's getting bigger by the day.'

Leo nodded and coughed. 'You look nice.'

'Thanks, I feel a bit stupid. I wouldn't usually wear this kind of thing.'

'No, you look lovely.'

Just then Owen clapped his hands together. 'Places, everyone.' He explained how he wanted them all to pose.

'And can we have the animals now?' he asked.

Leo walked towards the women with the box. 'Where do you want them?' he asked Owen.

'As close as possible to their feet,' Owen said.

'I'll throw down some food,' said Leo. 'Otherwise they're unlikely to stay in the same place for very long.'

'Good idea. They're not dangerous, are they?'

Leo looked at him. 'Not at all. As long as you don't try to touch the baby they'll be fine.'

'Good.' Owen was still a little nervous – they were monkeys after all. 'You can fire ahead, so.'

Leo reached into his rucksack, pulled out a plastic bag and began to scatter orange segments and apple quarters on the gravel. Then he opened the boxes. A grey monkey with a black and white striped tail rushed out and began to eat the fruit. She was the size of a domestic cat and had a tiny baby monkey clinging to her back.

'They're just perfect,' Martina sighed. 'Thank you so much, Rory.'

'It's him you should be thanking, really.' He nodded at Leo, who was moving the boxes out of the camera shot. 'I didn't think he'd agree, he's very protective about the animals, but he's mellowed a bit in the last few weeks. Even had Rosie and her daughter in feeding Tibo. Think he has a bit of a soft spot for her.'

'Oh, right.' Martina felt stupid. Of course there was

nothing going on between Rory and Rosie – that was quite obvious from the easy way he spoke of her. Martina's green-eyed monster had taken hold every time she'd seen them together, making a flirtation out of a simple friendship. She'd never really given Rosie a chance. She'd have to make up for it now, especially after Rosie had so kindly agreed to model for her and was really getting into the spirit of the day. Anna was right – Rosie was really nice and great company.

'It looks like the photographer's finished.' Rory looked at his watch and frowned. 'I'd better get going. Can I call over later, say six-ish?'

Martina looked at her watch. It was nearly five, it didn't give her much time to have a shower or get changed. 'Seven would suit me better. But I have to go over to Mum and Dad's at eight, so I won't have much time, I'm afraid.'

'Maybe we should leave it then.'

Martina's heart sank. 'No. Call over at half six. OK? I'd really like to see you.'

'OK.' He nodded. 'See you then.'

Martina grabbed a towel and wrapped it around her soaking wet body. She stepped out of the shower and ran towards the intercom, swearing. She pressed the button down.

'Who is it?'

'Me, Rory.'

'What time is it?'

'Twenty to seven.'

'I only got in a few minutes ago, I was in the shower. Sorry. Have you been there long?'

'No. Can I come in?'

'Of course.' She buzzed him in, dashed into the bathroom and grabbed a hand towel. She wrapped it around her dripping hair. There was a gentle knock on the front door.

'Just a second.' Damn, she muttered, where's my bathrobe? She couldn't find it.

She padded to the front door in her towel and opened it. Rory was almost hidden behind a huge bouquet of white stargazer lilies.

'Come in.' She stood back into the hall.

'These are for you.' He handed her the flowers and as she reached out to take them, her towel fell away from her body. She bent down and retrieved it, mortified at her frank exhibition.

'I'm just out of the shower,' she murmured, her cheeks blushing bright pink. 'Sorry, it's been quite a day.'

'Here, let me help you.' Rory took the flowers back off her and put them on the hall table. 'Anyway, it's nothing I haven't seen before, remember?'

Martina looked at him. He was smiling broadly. He moved towards her. 'It's nice to see you,' he said. 'All of you.'

She laughed. 'I'll just go and get dressed.'

'Really? And why would you do that?'

'Rory!' He put his arms around her, his cool hands resting on her back. 'I thought we were going to talk.'

'Were we?' He raised his eyebrows. 'OK, then. Martina, will you marry me? Just say yes or no.'

'What? Marry you?' she faltered. 'But we have so many things to sort out. We can't just . . .'

'Do you love me?' he asked.

'You know I do.'

He kissed her gently on the forehead. 'Then we have nothing else to talk about, not now anyway. So I'll ask you again, will you marry me?'

'I'll tell you tomorrow.'

'Is that a yes?'

'Yes, almost.' She put her finger on his lips. 'Don't ask.'

'OK. I'll wait, but only one day mind.' This time he understood why she was procrastinating.

'I promise. One day. Tomorrow evening, OK?' Tears began to well up in her eyes.

'Yes, but don't cry, you're supposed to be happy.'

'But I am.' Martina smiled through her tears. 'Very, very happy. Now can I go and get dressed please?'

'No. Certainly not.' He moved his hands over her bare back and kissed her shoulder tenderly. 'I've missed you so much, Martina.'

'I've missed you too.' She closed her eyes as he kissed her gently on the lips. They had a lot of talking to do but it could wait. Right at this moment all she wanted was to be held and to be loved.

Martina

Martina sat on the sofa in the attic of her parents' house holding the envelope in her hand. She stared at the writing on the front – her granny's spidery letters spelling out her name. She took a deep breath, slipped a finger under the gummed-down flap and gently ripped the thin blue paper. Pulling a single folded sheet from the envelope and opening it she started to cry. Brushing back her tears with the sleeve of her shirt she began to read.

My dearest Martina,
  I don't have long on this earth. Please don't be sad, I know we will meet again in some other life. I am not afraid, Martina. Everyone dies in the end and I've had many, many years of happiness in India and in Ireland. My only regret is that I will not see my beautiful grandchild on her wedding day.
  Martina, Rory Dunlop is a good man. A man not unlike your own father. Strong but kind. Above all

kind. He loves you, my dear. I met him only once but I was most impressed. It would make me very happy if you took him as your husband. I know I haven't made things easy for you. I know I asked you when you were only a little girl to find a nice Indian man, a Hindu, but I should not have. Thomas has been a delightful son-in-law and I could wish no better for my Nita. I see that now and I've made peace with your mother.

Marry Rory. He will make you happy. I give you my blessing. I love you my darling.

Always,

Granny Patel.

'Martina!'

'Up here.'

She could hear her mother at the foot of the attic steps.

'Don't come up, Mum. I'll be down in two minutes. I'm just tidying up.'

'OK.' Nita was worried. Martina had been in the attic for nearly an hour. 'We need to leave in ten minutes.'

'I'll be ready, I promise.' She folded up the letter, put it back into the envelope and kissed the paper. 'Thank you, Gran,' she whispered. She wiped her eyes one more time and climbed down the steep steps.

'Just as man discards old clothes and buys new ones, the soul discards worn-out bodies and enters new ones,' Nita read. 'We meditate upon the brilliance and glory of the God of the sun which lights up the heavens and the earth. May he inspire us and may he bless us and may he keep Mira Patel, my mother, in his safe and loving care. We will all miss you, Mum.'

Nita nodded at the undertaker, who closed the short red curtains.

Martina could no longer see her gran's coffin and she began to cry. Her dad held her hand tightly. Ria and Varun were standing on the other side of Nita. They had arrived late the previous evening and were staying with the Storeys.

'This is a lovely ceremony,' Ria whispered to Martina. 'She'll always be with you, remember that.'

Martina nodded. 'I know. Thank you. Is it me now?' She looked over at her mum, who nodded. She began to read. 'The soul is born many times on earth. The body may grow old and die but the soul lives on, reborn. Gran, I'll never forget you. I... I...' She brushed away her tears.

'Go on,' Nita said gently.

'I was just going to say that I love her, that's all. I should have told her more. And that I'll miss her.'

'She knew,' Nita soothed. 'She always knew, you didn't have to say it. She knew.' Nita also began to cry. 'Mum,' she sobbed softly. 'Mum.' Thomas put his left arm around his wife and his right around Martina. They stood together and listened as sitar music poured out of the speakers.

'Ravi Shankar.' Martina smiled, wiping away her tears. 'She loved him, didn't she?'

'She sure did,' said Thomas. 'Used to drive me mad at first, but I kind of like it now.'

'She was one of a kind.' Nita smiled through her own tears.

'That she was.' Thomas nodded. 'That she was.'

'How did it go?' Rory asked as he walked into the house later that morning. 'Sorry, I didn't mean that to sound flippant, I just . . .'

'That's OK,' said Martina. 'It went well. Mum read some of the Rigveda.'

'The what?'

'Indian holy poems. Then we each said goodbye and listened to some music. Gran would have liked it.'

'I'm glad. And are you all right?'

'Kind of. We've been rushing around for the last hour getting the food and drink ready so I haven't really had time to think about it.'

'That's no bad thing. Do you need me to do anything?'

'No, it's all under control. Come outside and see the marquee. Your dad arranged it for us.'

'So he told me. He'll be along later with Anna.'

Martina took his hand and led him outside. The sky was patchy – blue in places, grey in others. The sun was hidden but it was only a matter of time before it burst free of its cloud shackles and shone brightly down.

They walked into the marquee. It looked fantastic – layers of sheer white silk-like material covered the walls and were draped from beam to beam, decorating the 'ceiling'. There was a table to one side groaning with buffet food and another laden with drink. The round tables were decorated with vases of tall white lilies.

'It's beautiful,' said Rory. 'Looks more like a wedding than a funeral, if you don't mind me saying.'

Martina smiled. 'We decided to have a kind of Irish-Indian funeral. In India white is the funeral colour. And Gran always liked the idea of an Irish wake. She wanted her life to be celebrated, not mourned. So it's a party for her life, I guess.'

'Sounds great. It might take a little time for people to get used to the idea but I'm sure they'll get into the spirit of the day soon enough.'

'I hope so. Speaking of spirits, can I get you a drink?'

'I'd love a glass of wine if you have one. But let me get it. In fact, I can be barman for the day, how about that?'

'Dad's hoping to do it, I think. He said it would get him out of having to have any long conversations with anyone. I think he's rather exhausted, to tell the truth. He's been looking after me and Mum all morning so he deserves a break.'

'I'm here to look after you now.' Rory raised her hand to his lips and kissed it gently. 'Don't forget that.'

'And who is this kissing my lovely daughter?' Thomas asked, walking into the marquee.

Rory held out his hand. 'I'm Rory Dunlop, sir.'

Thomas smiled. 'Thomas is just fine. And I'm very glad to meet you. Any friend of Martina's is a friend of mine.'

Martina looked at Rory and back at her father. Rory

was right – she should have introduced him to her family a long time ago. If only her own stubbornness hadn't got in the way. Well, it was never too late to change. 'Actually, Dad, Rory's my boyfriend and we've got something to tell you.'

'Wonderful, wonderful.' Thomas shook Rory's hand warmly. 'I'm delighted to meet you. But I think your news may have to wait. I just heard the doorbell and your mother's still getting dressed. It's probably Ria and Varun. I'm afraid I'll have to leave you both for a moment.'

'That's OK. We'll tell you later.'

As Thomas strode away Rory turned towards her and smiled.

'What?' she asked.

'Nothing. You look beautiful, that's all. That dress . . . um . . . sari, really suits you.'

'Thanks,' she said. 'I got it for my debs but I've never worn it.'

'Your gran told me about your debs and what happened with that boy,' Rory began cautiously. 'We talked for a good while, to tell the truth, sadly only the morning before she died. It was most enlightening and I feel most privileged to have met her. I have Anna to thank for arranging the meeting. I want you to know . . .'

She drew away from him. She didn't want to remember that particularly painful part of her teenage life, and certainly not now.

'Martina! Listen to me, please. Your gran said you might not want to talk about this.'

'What?' He had her attention now.

'I love you. I always have – from the first time I met you. Your background and your family are an important part of you and they will also be an important part of our life together. Since talking to your gran, I've been thinking about it and I'd like us to have a traditional Indian wedding.'

'What?' she said again.

'In her letter to me your gran said that however we wanted to get married she'd be OK with it – bungy jumping, on the top of a mountain, underwater, even Catholic Mass – she just wanted you to be happy.'

'She really said that?'

He nodded.

'Even Catholic Mass?'

He smiled. 'Even Catholic Mass.'

Martina began to cry. 'Rory, I'd love a Hindu wedding, but are you sure? Have you any idea what it involves?'

'No idea whatsoever.' He grinned. 'But if it means wearing a Kermit the Frog suit and singing "Lady in Red" while standing on one leg, I'll do it.'

Martina smiled. 'It's not quite that bad.'

Rory hugged her. 'Whatever you want, I'll do it.'

'Thank you,' she said into his shoulder. 'I don't deserve you.'

'Yes, you do,' he said simply. 'You're my princess.'

'Hello, you two.' Martina turned her head around. Anna and Conor were standing just behind them.

'Hi, both of you.' Martina let go of Rory and kissed them both firmly on the cheeks. 'Thanks for coming.'

'How are you bearing up?' asked Conor.

'I'm OK.'

'And your mum?' asked Anna.

'She's OK too, I think. She's putting a brave face on things. This morning was hard on her but at least we both had a chance to say goodbye. Thank Ollie for the picture, will you, when he gets back? Gran would have liked it very much. She loved elephants and tigers. We put it in her hands in the . . . you know.'

Anna nodded and put her arm around Martina's waist. 'I'll tell him. It looks beautiful in here.' Anna looked around the marquee. 'You've done your gran proud. And those lilies are only gorgeous.'

'She always liked lilies. They're my favourites too.' She squeezed Rory's hand. 'My apartment is full of them. Rory arrived last night with a huge bunch of them.'

Anna looked at Rory and raised her eyebrows. 'Less of that, you. And before you ask, yes, we're back together again. Can I tell them, love?' he asked Martina.

She nodded and smiled.

'Martina's agreed to marry me. You're the first to know.'

'Excellent, Rory. I couldn't be more pleased,' Conor said. 'Welcome to the family, Martina, and congratulations.'

'Thanks,' she replied.

Anna grinned from ear to ear. 'That's wonderful news. Your gran would have been thrilled, Martina. And I'm sure wherever she is she knows and is smiling down on you both.' She hugged her friend warmly.

'Well done,' she whispered in Martina's ear. 'He's a keeper.'

'Thanks,' Martina murmured, overcome by emotion.

'And you're not annoyed with me, are you?' she said quietly as Rory and Conor discussed the marquee.

Martina raised her eyebrows. 'About what?'

'About bringing Rory over to visit your gran. Your dad thought it was just me, but I snuck Rory in while he was in the back garden.'

'I should be. But no, I'm not. I know you did it for all the right reasons. And how could I be annoyed with my best friend in the world?' She gave Anna a huge hug. 'Thanks for being there for me. I know I don't say it often, but I do appreciate it.'

'I know.' Anna hugged her back.

The tent began to fill up with friends from the village. The Redwood active retirement group arrived en masse in a minibus organized by the local priest, Father Jacks, and the vicar, Reverend Simmons, was also there to pay his respects. Soon the tent was thronged with people.

'Popular woman, your gran,' Conor said to Martina. 'Mr Simmons was just telling me how he used to have heated theological debates in the supermarket about reincarnation.'

Martina laughed. 'That would be Gran, all right.'

'You must miss her,' he said kindly.

'I do and I will. But she had a good life.'

'I'm delighted to see yourself and Rory getting on

so well. He hasn't been himself recently and I know he was missing you.'

Martina smiled. It was about time everyone shared in their good news. She located her mum in the crowd and made her way over. Nita excused herself to Father Jacks and followed Martina out of the tent.

'Mum,' Martina began, 'I want to say something to everyone when I say my few words about Gran. It's kind of an announcement. Where's Dad? I wanted to tell you both first.'

'He's in the kitchen getting more glasses. Wait here and I'll fetch him.'

Martina stood nervously waiting for her parents' return. She listened to the animated chatter coming from the tent and smiled. No doubt many of them were talking about her Gran – Mrs Patel loved being the centre of attention and she would have enjoyed this gathering.

'Here we are, love. Now what have you got to tell us?'

A few minutes later Martina made her way to the back of the tent, took a deep breath and tapped a wine glass with a fork to attract attention. Rory was standing in front of her smiling supportively, with Anna and Conor by his side.

'Hello, everyone,' said Martina. 'I've been asked by the family to say a few words about Gran. Where do I start? She moved to Redwood many years ago from Bombay to live with my mum and dad. When she first came over she joined the active retirement group, which she enjoyed very much, and I must thank them all for coming here today to celebrate her life. She made many, many friends there and always spoke especially highly of Father Jacks.'

The priest raised his glass. 'She was quite a woman.'

Martina continued. 'As you know, Gran was Hindu, and believed that the soul never dies, it just passes through a series of lives in different bodies until it reaches salvation. So we haven't seen the last of her by a long stretch.' Everyone laughed. 'Gran's ashes will be taken back to India by our relations Ria and Varun to be scattered in the river Ganges by her brother, Kishan – this is what she wanted. Before she died she had one last request and I want to honour that today.' She looked at Rory who nodded. 'Before she died she met Rory Dunlop and was quite taken by him. And her dying wish was that I marry him. So I'd like to formally accept his proposal. Rory, if you'll have me, I'd love to marry you.'

He looked up at her, tears in his eyes. 'Yes, of course I'll have you.'

'And now I ask you to raise your glasses to Gran – Mrs Patel.'

'Mrs Patel,' everyone chorused and clinked their glasses together.

'Now please help yourselves to food and drink. And in case you're wondering, the music coming on now is Gran's favourite, Ravi Shankar. Tom Jones and Elton John will be next and we even have some wee Daniel O'Donnell – you've been warned. I hope you enjoy the day. It's a pity Gran can't be here, she would have loved it!'

As Martina walked towards Rory and threw her arms around him the crowd clapped and cheered.

'Well done, love,' said Anna, patting her back. 'You did her proud.'

'How do you feel now, Mrs Dunlop?' Rory had been massaging Martina's tense shoulders for several minutes.

'Better, thanks. But who says I'll be taking your name?'

'I'd be honoured if you would, but either way, I'm happy.

'You could always take my name.'

'Rory Storey? I don't think so.'

'It has a nice ring to it – tell us a Storey, Rory – don't you think?'

'No! I don't think so.' He reached over and put his arms around her. She squealed. 'I'm trying to make a list, Rory. We have masses of things to do if we're going to get married in September, you have no idea.'

'Put the pen down and come here, woman. We have loads of time for that. And I'm sure your mum and Anna would be only too pleased to help.'

She smiled at him. 'You're right. I just like being organized, that's all.'

'You've had quite a day. Give yourself a break.'

'You're right. It can wait till tomorrow.'

Rory smiled.

'What?' demanded Martina.

'Nothing. I'm just glad to have you back, that's all.'

'Really?'

'Really!' He looked up at the ceiling. 'Thanks, Mrs Patel!'

'Yes, thanks, Gran.'

Anna

'Here they are, and only three weeks late!' Moyra said as she picked up a large brown padded envelope from the hall floor. Ollie was at summer camp in the local GAA club and he'd been waiting for the promised package of holiday photographs from his father for weeks.

'How do you know that package is from Simon?' asked Anna.

Moyra sniffed. 'His handwriting is quite distinct. I'm no expert but I'm sure the small, thin letters must say something about a person's generosity and kindness. Give me big, generous handwriting any day.'

'Mum! You're being ridiculous. Hand it over.'

Anna looked at the envelope and studied the writing. 'However, you're right, it is from Simon.'

Her mother looked smug. 'Let's go into the kitchen and have a look. I'll put the kettle on.'

Anna followed her, opening the envelope as she walked. She sat down at the kitchen table and read the postcard which was enclosed with the photographs. 'Hope all is well,' she read out loud. 'Enjoyed holiday. Chrissie and Ollie got on like house on fire. Talk soon, Simon.'

'He's so insensitive,' said Moyra. She took two mugs out of the cupboard and slammed them down on the kitchen counter. 'Mentioning Chrissie like that. What is he like?'

Anna sighed. 'Mum, he's not going to change. We may as well just get used to it. I think he may be thinking about marrying her too and we all have to tolerate each other, for Ollie's sake.'

'Marrying her? She's only a child.'

'She's nearly twenty-four.'

'Like I said – a child.'

'Ollie seems to like her.'

'I don't know how you can be so damn gracious about the whole thing.'

Anna looked at Moyra. 'Mum, I left him, remember?'

'And he hasn't given you a cent since?'

She shrugged her shoulders. 'I guess. It wasn't the most friendly of partings. But he does send money sometimes.'

'He should be paying you proper maintenance, it's only right. Ollie is his son.'

'We've been over this before. Just drop it, OK?'

'You need to toughen up, my girl. That man always bullied you and he's still doing it now.'

Anna ignored her. 'Look! Here's one of Ollie in his snorkelling gear. Doesn't he look darling?' She held up a photograph. He was dressed from head to toe in black neoprene and the goggles looked impossibly big on his neat little face. 'And he's in the water in this one.'

Moyra sat down beside her and leant over her shoulder. 'He looks like he's having fun. Is that their boat?' She pointed at the large white yacht.

'I guess so.' She looked at the side of the vessel and squinted her eyes to read the letters. 'Yes. *Spirit of Gorda.*'

'It's looks amazing. Look at that sea – it's so blue. No wonder Ollie talks about it all the time.'

Anna stood up. 'I'll ring Simon and tell him they've arrived, get it over with.'

'You shouldn't bother,' Moyra said to her daughter's departing back. 'But if you have to, ask him for some money while you're at it.'

Anna smiled to herself as she dialled Simon's number. Her mum was incorrigible.

'Hi, Simon, it's Anna, can you talk?'

'Briefly,' he said, 'what's up?'

'I was just ringing to say we got the photographs this morning. Thanks. Ollie will love them. The boat looks amazing – is it a Swann?'

'A Swann 60,' he said, a little too smugly for her liking. 'Listen, I was going to ring you later. A friend of Chrissie's is getting married the weekend after next. Needs a stand-in pageboy apparently. Her own one broke his arm at some soccer camp or other.'

'Might be OK, let me check my diary and get back to you.' She heard her mother exclaim loudly. 'I'll ring you back in a few minutes.' She put down the receiver and walked back into the kitchen. 'What's up, Mum?'

Moyra handed her a photograph. 'This!'

Anna looked at the snap in her hand. It was of Ollie and Chrissie – a topless Chrissie.

'I can't believe that woman was gallivanting practically naked in front of my grandson. Has she no shame?'

Anna wasn't sure what to say. She agreed with her mother in some respects but didn't want to be a prude.

'What are you going to do about it?' Moyra demanded.

'Not much I can do now,' Anna said levelly. She spied her bag on the fridge and pulled her diary out. 'Of course.' She flicked through the pages. 'How could I have forgotten?' She put her diary back in the bag. 'I have to ring Simon again. I'll be back in a minute.'

'Tell him you're not happy with Chrissie flashing at Ollie,' Moyra said to her back. 'Don't forget.'

Anna dialled again.

'Well?' Simon said without giving her a chance to say hello.

'How did you know it was me, or do you greet all your clients that way too?'

'Number recognition,' he explained. 'Your name flashes up on the screen. Ollie's actually.'

Charming, she thought to herself. She wasn't even a name on his telephone any more.

'Can he make it?' he asked.

'Actually, no. I'd completely forgotten. It's the final

day of the Laser Nationals and the prize-giving and dinner are on that evening. I'd like him to go.'

Simon snorted. 'You're hardly going to win anything, are you?'

She stiffened but said nothing.

'As I've said before, your dinghy days are over. Now Chrissie—'

'Simon!' Anna interrupted a little more sharply than she'd intended. 'I've been training hard for this event. And whether I do well or not, I'd still like Ollie to be there with me.'

'A sort of consolation prize?' Simon said in an ugly manner. 'Lost the boyfriend, have you? Gone off with some younger bird no doubt. Man like that with lots of money. Girl magnet.'

She'd had enough – how dare he be so rude to her? 'Simon, Ollie won't be joining you at the wedding or at any wedding until you pay me the maintenance that is due to me, not the pittance you send when you remember. Ask your lawyer, he has all the letters from my solicitor. And I'd like that backdated, please, as requested.'

'What? I thought we'd discussed this. I send you money when I can, as we agreed.'

'No, as *you* agreed. You bullied me into it. I wanted Ollie to know his father, I wanted you to be involved in his life. I thought that was the best thing for him, for all of us. But I was wrong. He needs a kind, decent man in his life, not just someone who happens to be his biological father.'

'Are you saying I'm not a good father?'

'That's exactly what I'm saying.' She was on a roll now and nothing was going to stop her. 'You see him twice a year, when it suits you. You never ring him or write to him and last year you forgot his birthday because you were in Thailand with Chrissie.'

'But—'

'No buts. Unless there's a marked improvement in your commitment to him I won't let him have anything to do with you. And he certainly won't be going on holiday with you again.'

'But—'

'Sort out the maintenance, set up regular telephone calls, make more of an effort to come over and see him. Do you understand?'

'Um, yes, but—'

'And one last thing: if I ever see Chrissie's tits again it will be too soon. Tell her they're much too saggy for a twenty-four-year-old.' With that she slammed down the phone.

Moyra clapped her hands. 'Bravo,' she said. 'I didn't know you had in it you.'

'Neither did I.' The phone rang almost immediately. She picked it up and put the receiver sharply back down.

'Take it off the hook,' Moyra suggested. 'And come in and drink your coffee. We can stick pins in Miss Saggy-Tits' photograph.'

'Good idea,' Anna agreed, grinning.

Anna was standing barefoot on the refreshingly cold

tiles in the hall at Redwood House taking a minute's break. She heard the gravel outside crunch. 'Not already,' she muttered to herself. The ball was on this evening and she'd spent all day troubleshooting – sending the bar staff back to base to collect cocktail glasses they'd forgotten, moving the huge vases of flowers into place, checking the fires were primed and ready to be lit later in the evening if it got a little chilly – the list was endless. The last thing she needed was any very early guests.

At least the caterers seemed to be well prepared. She'd hired a local chef, Joe Mooney, who'd just gone out on his own, was enthusiastic and horror of horrors seemed to really want the work. The other caterers she'd tried were all very laissez-faire about the pro-posed job – 'late supper for three hundred revellers, no problem,' they'd yawned, 'what sort of food do you want?' Joe had immediately suggested several delicious-sounding hors d'oeuvres – salmon pâté on melba toast, crab toes with seafood dip, Thai chicken kebabs – for early in the evening, followed by a buffet fit for a king or queen to be served at ten o'clock. He'd arrived earlier that day with his assistants and had got stuck into preparing the food in Conor and Rory's rather old-fashioned kitchen.

She looked up. It was Rosie and Martina. She waved at them and smiled. 'Thank goodness,' she said. 'Here come the cavalry.' She was delighted that her two friends had been getting on so well. Ever since the funeral Martina had made a real effort to get to know her new work neighbour, taking Rosie for lunch, and meeting and playing with Cass, who adored her mother's glamorous new young friend.

'You go home and get changed,' Martina commanded. 'We'll take over now. What's left to do?'

Anna glanced at her watch. It was almost five o'clock. 'Would you mind? I have to be back at half six to talk to the jazz band.'

"Course not,' Rosie said.

'Right, most things are done. You just need to put some more water in the vases in the ballroom and the drawing room,' said Anna. 'They're huge and I only put enough water in them to cover the stems of the flowers. I couldn't have moved them if they'd been full.'

'The Waterford crystal vases?' asked Martina.

Anna nodded.

'I'm not surprised you couldn't move them. They weigh a ton. So – water in the vases, anything else?'

She shook her head. 'No, that's it really. Joe the caterer is in the kitchen, he might need a hand finding something, I guess. Oh, and the barmen should be back any minute with cocktail glasses. Could you check they have some decent ones? Otherwise send them back to the off-license.'

'Fine,' said Martina. 'Now scoot or you won't have time to make yourself beautiful.'

After Anna had left, Martina and Rosie sat on the steps of the house for a few minutes catching some rays. It was a beautiful evening and they bathed in the glow of the late-afternoon sun.

'I suppose we'd better water the flowers.' Rosie

sighed and climbed to her feet. She held out her hand to Martina. 'Come on you. Time to get up.'

The two women walked inside. The hall table was covered in huge vases of plain white roses.

Martina leaned over and smelt one. 'These are from the rose garden. They have a really delicate scent, not like the ones you buy.'

'The ones that don't smell of anything?'

'Quite.'

'Hi, girls.'

They looked up. Rory was walking down the stairs. 'Where's Anna?' he asked.

'Gone to get changed,' said Martina. 'You should do the same.' She wrinkled her nose at his dirty work trousers and sweaty T-shirt. 'What were you doing? Chasing maras again? You're filthy.'

'Myself and Leo were moving the oryx in the side paddock. The giraffe babies have got so big that the oryx have been feeling a little claustrophobic.'

Rosie smiled. 'Can't have that, can we?'

'Is it OK if I borrow Martina for a few minutes?' he asked Rosie. 'We have a few wedding details to go over.'

'No problem,' said Rosie. 'Just show me where I'll find a jug to fill the vases if you wouldn't mind.'

Walking back upstairs Martina slapped Rory on the bum. 'What wedding details were you talking about?'

'In here,' he said shoving her gently into his bedroom, his hand on her shoulders, and closing the door firmly behind him.

'Rory . . .' she began.

He put his arms around her.

'Rory, I have to—'

He kissed her on the lips, silencing her protests. 'Rosie will be fine on her own for a few minutes.'

'But you're all sweaty.'

He laughed. 'Since when has that bothered you?' He stood back and pulled his T-shirt off in one swift movement. 'Is that better?'

'You're incorrigible.'

'I know, that's why you love me.'

'Be quick then – I have to go home and change.'

He snorted. 'Be quick? Would you listen to yourself?'

She put her hands on her hips. 'That's all that's on offer, I'm afraid.'

He put his arms around her again and manoeuvered her toward the bed, pushing her down on it. 'In that case . . .'

'Rory!'

'Stop the complaining, woman.' He grinned. 'You love it really.'

Ten minutes later Martina found Rosie having a debate with one of the barmen on the steps.

'Martina will be able to tell you,' Rosie said to the young man. 'I'm sure she knows exactly what a vodka-martini glass looks like.'

Martina collected her wits. 'Show me what you've got. I'm an expert on cocktails.'

*

Anna stood in front of her full-length mirror and studied herself critically. Why had she let Martina talk her into this one? The heavy silk chestnut brown evening dress was slashed to the waist, showing a large expanse of cleavage. She had to admit that the fake tan had worked a treat, but she was still nervous about the dress gaping open at inopportune moments. Maybe she should wear the thick brown leather belt as Martina had suggested. Leather and silk seemed a strange combination to her, but she'd try it and see. She clasped the belt around her waist and looked in the mirror again. It stopped the dress gaping quite so much and accentuated her slim waist – toned from all the sit-ups she'd done in the past months. The Laser Nationals were next week and she was in the best physical shape she'd been in for years. It meant no alcohol this evening and a reasonably early night, but it was a small price to pay for a place in the Nationals that she could be proud of.

She'd left her blonde hair down, tumbling over one shoulder in a wave of pure gold. Her make-up was subtle, a smattering of gold powder on her neck, face and chest, gold eyeshadow, coral lipstick and a touch of mascara and blusher. She was pleased with the effect. Gold high-heeled sandals completed the outfit. She took one final look in the mirror, grabbed her pale gold pashmina and her beaded black handbag and headed into the hall.

As she reached the bottom of the stairs she realized that Ollie and her mum were waiting for her.

'You look lovely, dear.' Moyra smiled. 'Really lovely.'

Ollie was impressed. 'Are you not doing your lion hair?' he asked. 'Like in the newspaper?'

'No, love,' she said. The *Irish Times* had a lot to answer for. The newspaper's editor had liked the Redwood photographs so much that one of Owen's prints had appeared on the front page of the weekend magazine, much to Anna's horror and Martina's delight. Anna's 'lion hair' had become a talking point in the village, and she couldn't walk down the street without being 'roared' at. At least she wasn't being referred to as the 'monkey woman'. Cha Cha was not amused. Still, she reasoned, it had put Martina's shop and her Kati G range firmly on the map.

'You look lovely too, Mum,' said Anna. Moyra was wearing a fuchsia-coloured raw silk dress with shoe-string straps.

'Martina found the boa for me.' Moyra flung the matching boa over her shoulder ostentatiously. 'What do you think?'

'Fantastic!' Anna smiled. 'Now are we all ready? Ollie, have you got your overnight bag?' Kim's boyfriend, Greg, had kindly offered to look after both Cass and Ollie at Rosie's.

Ollie nodded.

'Then we're all set. We just have to wait for the taxi.'

'The taxi's already outside, Mum,' Ollie said. 'He's been waiting for you for ages.'

Anna laughed. 'Why didn't you tell me? Let's go then.'

*

Conor met Anna and Moyra on the steps. 'You both look beautiful.' He kissed them both on the cheek.

'And you scrub up well,' Moyra remarked. 'Nice tux.' Conor was wearing a black velvet dinner jacket with a white shirt and black bow tie. A gold handkerchief peeped jauntily from the jacket pocket.

'Very dapper,' Anna agreed. 'Is the jazz band here yet?'

Conor nodded. 'Everything's under control, don't worry. Martina and Rosie only left a few minutes ago. They said to say the glasses are perfect and they've already tested a few Bellinis and vodka martinis just to make sure. They said they'd be back at seven to try some more.'

Anna laughed. 'We'll have to roll them home later at this rate.'

'The band is just setting up. Would you like to go in and have a word?'

'Sure.'

Moyra smiled. 'The calm before the storm. I think I'll relax out here and enjoy the sun if you don't mind.'

'We'll be back in a few minutes, Mum. I'll just check the band. I'll send someone out with a drink for you, what will you have?'

'A vodka martini sounds good,' Moyra said. 'In for Flynn.'

Anna shook her head. 'Not you as well, Mum.'

'Sorry, love. Yes, me as well. You can roll us all home – how about that?'

'Great.' Anna rolled her eyes heavenward. 'Just great.'

At eight o'clock most of the guests had arrived and those who were not outside enjoying the evening sun were milling around the drawing room, studying the paintings Rosie and Rex had hung on the walls earlier, apart from Alan's huge oil, which was propped against the back wall. They had put together a catalogue and Rory had offered to be auctioneer for the evening, leaving Anna and Conor free to enjoy some sun while the auction was taking place. They had retired to the private rose garden for a few minutes' peace.

'Can we get the auction started?' They heard Rory's voice ringing through the open drawing-room windows.

'I guess we should go back inside.' Anna sighed. They were sitting on a garden bench in the walled garden.

'Why?' Conor smiled and raised her hand to his lips.

'They'll be waiting for us.'

'No they won't. I told Rory to start. He and Rosie are well able to hold the auction without us. Martina's there too, and Rex. They can all help.'

'I suppose.' Anna was still a little tense.

'Are you all right?' Conor asked. 'You seem a little preoccupied.'

'I'm fine. Just thinking about what could go wrong,

you know. And I'm off alcohol, remember? You've all had a few drinks to relax you.'

'You can have one glass of wine. It's not going to make much difference.'

'I guess not.'

Conor stood up. 'I'll go in and get you one. Red or white?'

'White. Thanks.' As she watched him walk away she tried to still her mind and to relax. It wasn't the ball she was thinking about at all. Try as hard as she could, she just couldn't stop worrying about Ollie. Simon still hadn't phoned after their last 'words'. Maybe she shouldn't have been so hard on him. Simon wasn't all that bad – was he? Surely she could put up with it for the sake of her son? She was a bad mother and Ollie deserved . . .

'Penny for them.' Conor handed her a large glass of white wine. It felt deliciously cold to the touch, the glass frosting up with condensation. She took a sip. 'What's this? It's lovely.'

'Cloudy Bay Sauvignon Blanc, from New Zealand. I have a couple of bottles in the fridge for special guests.'

'Am I a special guest?'

'A very special guest.' He kissed the top of her head gently. 'Now tell me what's bothering you.'

Anna sighed. 'It's Simon.' She explained what had happened the previous day and how guilty she felt about driving her son's father away.

'Guilty!' Conor exclaimed. 'You're a saint, Anna. I don't know how you ever married the man, but he didn't deserve you. You were quite right to give him an ultimatum. Ollie is a brilliant little boy and he also deserves better.'

She squeezed his arm. 'Thanks.'

'Would you like to talk to my solicitor? Would that help? Or maybe *I* could talk some sense into Simon.'

'I don't think so,' Anna said quickly. She couldn't think of anything worse. That would really get Simon's hackles up.

'Stick to your guns,' he said gently. 'It'll all work out in the end, you'll see. I know it's hard, but give it a few weeks. He'll come around. And if he doesn't you can reassess the situation, talk to him again. Or write to him. Nothing is as bad as it seems.' He patted her arm.

Anna finally began to relax. Conor had such a calm, soothing manner and he knew exactly how to make her feel better. They were great together. She put her head on his shoulder and closed her eyes.

They sat in silence for a few minutes, breathing in the relaxing fragrance of the mixed rose bushes.

'I'm a lucky woman,' she murmured eventually, raising her head and smiling at him.

'Sorry?' Conor asked.

'I feel lucky to have met you. You're one of the good guys, Conor. I'm just sorry it took me so long to realize it.' She stroked his hand. 'I wish I'd taken you up on your dinner invite earlier, but—'

'There's no need to explain, I understand. And we're together now, that's all that matters,' he said, smiling.

'But I feel like I've wasted precious months of our time together.'

He laughed. 'Anna, I may be a few years older than you but I'm not dead yet.'

'I didn't mean it that way,' she said. 'Sorry. I think what I'm trying to say is, thank you.'

'For what?'

'For having the patience to wait. For always being there for me. For loving me, I guess. You make me happy.'

'I'm glad.' He raised her hand to his lips and kissed it. 'You make me happy too. In fact, there was something I wanted to ask you. I was going to wait but . . .'

'Yes?' Anna turned and looked at him.

He smiled at her, looked down and shook his head. 'Well?' she asked.

'Doesn't matter.'

'Conor! You can't do that, what were you going to say?'

He gazed into space. 'I was going to ask you to marry me.'

'What?' Anna was genuinely shocked. She hadn't expected this.

He looked at her, his blue eyes radiating warmth and kindness. 'I love you, Anna. And I love Ollie. I want us to be a family.'

'Yes, but . . .' Thoughts started to race around her head. She'd just begun to get her life back together after Simon, to be her own person. She didn't think she was ready to be someone's wife again. And how would Ollie take to having a 'new' father?

'But what?'

'Nothing.' She didn't know what to say.

'I take it that's a no, then.'

'No, it's not. It's a maybe. I need to think about it.'

'I'm not Simon. I won't take over your life, I won't try to change you or bully you. I love *you*, Anna, the real you. All of you.'

But who am I? Anna felt like asking. Who am I really? A wife, a mother?

'When you're ready you can give me your answer,' he added. 'There's no rush. I'm not going anywhere.'

'Thanks.' She looked down at her hands.

'But please, don't leave it too long. Promise me?'

'I promise.' She raised her head. 'I'm sorry I can't be more . . .'

'Shush,' he said. 'Let's just enjoy the rest of the evening, OK? Have a think about it and get back to me. I'm fine, honestly.'

She smiled gently. 'Thanks. Can I have the first dance?'

'Of course.'

They heard the sound of loud clapping from the drawing room.

'How do you think it's going?' asked Anna.

'Good, from the sound of things. We can go inside if you like.'

'No, it's lovely and peaceful out here. Let's just stay for a few more minutes.'

She kissed him on the lips. 'I do love you, Conor Dunlop. You know that, don't you?'

'I do now,' he said, kissing her back firmly. He put

his arms around her and drew her close. 'And you look absolutely edible. Like a chocolate goddess.'

'Darling, you looked fantastic on the cover of the *Irish Times Magazine*,' Nick Shine-Thompson said to Anna. 'I was just telling Moyra how beautiful you look this evening.'

'Thank you.' Anna smiled graciously. She'd wondered how long it would take Nick to monopolize her mother. Cha Cha was sitting on the stairs drinking Bellinis with two men who looked young enough to be her sons. The catering staff had finished clearing away the plates and cutlery and everything was going very smoothly.

'Your mother has kindly agreed to dance with me later,' Nick continued. 'When's the rock-and-roll band starting?'

'In a few minutes. Hope you have your dancing shoes on, they're fantastic.'

'What are they called?'

'Johnnie Be Goode. They're playing at my friend Martina's wedding and I've been listening to their demo tape all the time.'

'Martina's the girl in the red?'

'That's right, Rory Dunlop's fiancée.'

'Stunning creature. Might have to borrow her later for a little spin.'

Poor Martina, Anna thought. She smiled at her mother. 'Martina would love that, wouldn't she, Mum?'

Moyra smiled back. 'Yes, definitely. There's Philly under the feathers, I must go over and say hello.'

'I'll come too,' Nick said, following quickly at her heels like a prize Labrador at a dog show.

'Your man really does have a thing for your mother, doesn't he?' Martina grinned as she, Rosie and Kim joined Anna; dark pink drinks in their collective hands.

'What are you all drinking?' asked Anna.

'Raspberry martinis,' Kim explained. She licked her lips. 'Delicious.'

'Are you all having a good time?'

'The best!' Kim enthused. 'The food was fantastic. Lovely men too. Who's that?' She pointed at a tall, dark-haired man who was slouching against a wall and slugging back his drink.

'René Montgomery, bit of a wild child. He's Philly's nephew.'

'He's only gorgeous.' René looked over and caught the four women staring unashamedly at him. He raised his glass to them and gave them a smouldering look.

'Oops, he's caught us.' Rosie giggled.

'You're the only single one among us,' Martina cajoled. 'Go over and talk to him.'

'I'll do no such thing,' she said primly. 'He's only a young one.'

'Exactly!' Kim winked at her. 'If it wasn't for Greg, I'd be straight in there. That Cha Cha's got the right idea. Where is she anyway? I saw her on the stairs with two delectable cuties a while ago.'

Anna groaned. 'Not already.' She looked at her watch. 'It's not even eleven.'

'She's gone home?' Rosie asked innocently.

'Home?' Anna raised her eyebrows. 'Upstairs more like. Find the locked bedroom door and you'll find Cha Cha.'

'No!' Kim's eyes widened in astonishment. 'With the two of them? What about her husband.'

'He doesn't seem to mind. Probably glad of the rest. She's years younger than him. Rumour has it she likes women too, so I'd watch out.'

'To think I stripped practically naked with her beside me.' Rosie wrinkled her nose.

'You're safe then,' Kim said. 'That will have put her off.'

'Thanks a lot.' Rosie laughed. 'Sisters – don't you just love them?' The band took to the stage and began to play the opening strains of 'Hard Day's Night'.

Kim nudged her in the side. 'Lover boy's coming over to you.' René was striding towards them.

'He's not coming over to *me*,' she protested. But it was too late. Anna, Martina and Kim had already moved behind her, abandoning her to her fate.

'Would you care to dance?' he asked her, holding out his arm.

'Um.'

'Yes!' Kim gave her a gentle push. 'She'd love to.'

They watched as René smoothly led Rosie away and into the middle of the room. He began to throw her around the dance floor, his strong arms spinning her with great strength and agility.

'Good on you, Rosie!' Kim called.

'Go, girl!' Martina added.

Anna felt a tap on her shoulder. 'May I?' Conor smiled at her and held out his hand.

'Of course. But be gentle with me.'

Conor leant down and whispered in her ear. 'I could say something very rude but I won't.'

She smiled at him. 'Later. Let's dance.'

'Are you sure this is OK?' Anna asked nervously. 'Should we not stay downstairs and say goodbye to the guests?'

Conor waved the suggestion away with his hand. 'They'll be fine. Come this way, young lady. The four-poster awaits you.' He pushed her along the wide corridor.

'Conor!'

He stopped outside his bedroom and put his finger to his lips theatrically. 'Shush, can you hear something?'

Anna listened for a moment. There were noises coming from the room.

'I think there's someone in there.'

'It's probably Cha Cha,' Anna said.

'No, she's in the blue guest room.' Conor smiled. 'She sent one of her boys downstairs for some ice a little while ago. I found him in the kitchen and followed him up.'

'You're terrible!'

'It was one of the Montgomery boys,' he said. 'René, I think.'

'René? The one who was with Rosie earlier? I haven't seen her for ages. I presumed they'd disappeared off together somewhere.'

He shrugged his shoulders. 'Dunno. Should I open the door? Maybe I should leave them be.'

'Go on. It's your room, you have every right to evict them.'

He turned the ornate crystal knob and pushed the door open. He walked in, followed by Anna, and they both squinted in the semi-darkness. A man lay naked face down on the bed, a woman by his side.

Anna gasped as the woman looked towards the open door. At first she couldn't place her, but with a flash of recognition Anna realized she looked very like – 'Rosie!'

Rosie

'Rosie, are you ready to start the auction?' Rory asked anxiously. 'I think Philly's going to eat us alive if we don't get going soon. She's chomping at the bit to get her hands on Alan's *October Red* painting.'

Rosie scanned the crowd in the room. She couldn't see her dad anywhere and she was reluctant to start without him. Kim was sitting near the back beside Cha Cha. Rosie waved and smiled and Kim waved back. 'Give me one minute.' She walked towards the door and out into the hallway. 'There you are,' she said to Rex. 'I was beginning to worry.'

Rex smiled. 'I was just talking to your mother on the mobile. She's been held up but she wants me to bid for her on Olivia's *Wicklow Harbour* watercolour.'

Rosie wrinkled her nose. 'I'm not sure if that's strictly ethical, Dad. We're supposed to be helping Rory auction the paintings, not buying them ourselves.'

'She'll be very disappointed,' warned Rex. 'She has her heart set on hanging it over the hall table.'

Just then Martina walked towards them, a cocktail in her hand. 'Hello,' she said smiling broadly. 'I haven't missed anything, have I? Has the auction started yet?'

'No, but it will right now if you can do us one little favour,' said Rosie. She explained their dilemma.

'Course I'll bid on the painting for you,' said Martina. 'How high will I go?'

'Three thousand euro,' Rex said firmly.

Rosie gasped. 'Are you sure, Dad? It's only worth two, you know.'

Rex winked at her. 'It's for a good cause. Besides, your mother can afford it. She's just sold some of her Data Electric shares.'

Rosie shrugged her shoulders. 'In that case . . .'

'OK then,' said Martina. 'I'd be delighted to spend your mother's money for you.' She stuck her head around the door of the drawing room which was buzzing with the sound of people and had a quick look. 'I'll be sitting towards the back, beside Kim if there's a seat. See you both later.'

'Have fun,' said Rosie. She turned to Rex. 'I suppose we'd better get the ball rolling. What do you think?'

Rex nodded and held out his arm. 'Come on, young lady. We have art to sell.' They walked in together and made their way towards the top of the room where Rory was waiting patiently.

Rory smiled widely. 'Thank goodness. The crowd's getting very restless. I'll give a brief introduction and then hand over to you, Rex. Does that suit?'

Rex turned to Rosie. 'Are you sure you want *me* to speak? I really think you should . . .'

She patted his arm. 'Please, Dad. You know how much I hate public speaking.'

'OK then. If you insist.' He nodded at Rory, who rapped his small wooden gavel firmly on its wooden plinth. The chatter began to subside and all eyes were fixed on him.

'Ladies and gentlemen, I'm Rory Dunlop and I'd like to welcome you all to the inaugural Redwood charity art auction in aid of the World Wildlife Fund. As you all know, Redwood Wildlife Park's mission is to contribute to the conservation of endangered wildlife, and help ensure a future for all kinds of threatened animals. Every hour of every day one species of animal or plant life disappears from our earth, never to return. By buying art here this evening and by attending the ball you are all helping to make a real contribution to saving world wildlife. At present, we at Redwood are involved in conservation projects in Kenya, Namibia, and Central and South America. In ten years' time we hope to be a leading contributor to world wildlife conservation. Thank you for making this dream possible. And now I'll hand you over to Rex O'Grady who will talk to you about Redwood Gallery and the paintings here tonight.' The crowd clapped loudly and Martina whistled, joined by Cha Cha and Kim.

'As Rory has said, I'm Rex O'Grady and I help my daughter Rosie run the Redwood Gallery.' He smiled at Rosie. She could feel herself blushing and she looked down quickly, studying the auction's catalogue in her hand. Rex continued. 'Our artists have kindly donated their works completely free of charge to be auctioned here tonight in aid of the World Wildlife Fund and I'd like to start off by thanking them for their generosity – Olivia Miller, Alan de Markham, Eve Marley, Ray Davy and Robert McCarthy.' Everyone clapped warmly. Just then the door to the drawing room flew open.

'Tell me I haven't missed the auction!' a familiar voice said loudly. Alan was wearing a blue and green silk kaftan, with a dramatic feather headdress made from what looked like real peacock feathers perched precariously on his head.

'Rosie, darling, there you are. I'll come and sit at the front.' He squeezed past the seat.' 'Excuse me, excuse me. *Pardonnez-moi.* Excuse me.'

Rex, temporarily thrown, regained his composure. 'And this, ladies and gentlemen, is one of our leading young Irish talents – the artist of the *October Red* series that is causing quite a stir – Alan de Markham.' Rex brought his hands together and began to clap, swiftly followed by the rest of the room.

Alan, by now at the top of the room, turned towards his audience, brought his fingers together at his lips and blew kisses to the bemused crowd. 'Too kind. Thank you, all.'

Rosie smiled at him. 'Good to see you. Thought you weren't going to make it.'

'And miss my moment of glory? *Mais non*, my little cabbage.'

Rex cleared his throat and looked over at Rory. 'I think it's only appropriate to start the action with Alan's work. So, ladies and gentlemen, if you'll just turn to page two of your catalogue, thank you. So let's start the bidding on *October Red: Study Three* by Alan de Markham. As you can see from the catalogue it's a large piece, ten feet by twelve feet, oil on canvas. I hope you've all had a chance to look at it, as I won't even attempt to hold it up!' A ripple of laughter spread through the room. 'And I'm sure Alan will tell the lucky new owner all about the series and how he painted it.'

'Try stopping me, ducky!' Alan grinned.

'And now I'll hand you over to Rory to start the bidding.' He sat down beside Rosie.

'Well done, Dad,' she whispered. 'You were great.'

'You think?'

'Yes, definitely.'

'Who would like to start the bidding at five hundred euro . . . anyone?' Rory looked around the room expectantly.

A man in the middle of the crowd raised his catalogue in the air.

'Thank you, sir. I have five hundred euro. Who will give me six?'

Philly raised her hand.

'Excellent, six. Seven, anyone?'

'Eight!' said a voice from the back of the room. It was Cha Cha. Herself and Philly were ostensibly the best of friends but everyone knew they were highly competitive. Whatever Philly had, Cha Cha wanted two.

'Nine!' Philly said loudly.

'Ten!' Cha Cha countered. 'I mean, one thousand.'

'One thousand two hundred.'

'Three hundred.'

'Four hundred.'

'Five hundred.'

'Six hundred.'

'Seven hundred.'

The two women were firing bids at each other like bullets. Rory could see Cha Cha's husband putting a hand on her arm. She ignored him.

'Two thousand!'

Rory looked at Philly. She shook her head. He brought the hammer down on the gavel.

'Sold to Cha Cha Shine-Thompson for two thousand euro.' Cha Cha beamed.

'Well done, you!' Alan stood up and clapped his hands together. 'Cha Cha Cha, everybody go Cha Cha Cha.' He began to sing and sway his hips dangerously.

Rex stood up swiftly. 'Next up we have two water-colours from one of Ireland's greatest living artists, Olivia Miller. First we have *Dreaming of Cats*, a delightful study of some of the artist's pets.' He held it up for everyone to see.

Rosie prayed that Cha Cha and Philly didn't take a shine to her mother's chosen harbour piece. Rory sold *Dreaming of Cats* for fifteen hundred euro to a blond man in dark glasses in the middle of the room.

'And now we have the second watercolour by Olivia Miller, *Wicklow Harbour*. Can I start the bidding at—'

He was interrupted by Martina. 'Three thousand euro,' she said excitedly. There were gasps in the crowd. It was a lot of money for a small watercolour. No one had any intention of topping her bid.

Rory looked at her. 'Um, I don't think I can accept

that bid.' Had she gone mad? Where was she going to get that kind of money? And besides, as far as he knew, she wasn't interested in art. He looked at Rex. 'I'll just have a little chat with my colleague.' Rex quickly explained the situation.

Rory smiled. 'It seems I can.' He brought the hammer down. 'Sold to Martina Storey for three thousand euro.'

'That was close,' Rex said to Rosie. 'Poor Rory nearly had a heart attack.'

The remainder of the paintings and prints sold equally well, Eve's prints for three and four hundred euro respectively, Ray's landscape for five hundred and Robert's print for two.

After the hammer had come down for the final time, Rory breathed a sigh of relief. 'Thank goodness. That was really stressful. I don't know how those house auctioneers do it. You need nerves of steel.'

'Balls of steel more like,' Rosie said cryptically.

Rex stayed quiet. He wondered whether Rory knew that Rosie's ex was in the business.

'You were brilliant,' she said, 'both of you. I'll start wrapping the paintings in case any of the new owners want to take them home this evening. I'll leave the others in the gallery till Monday. They can collect them during the week.'

Cha Cha strode towards them, her heavy red taffeta skirt rustling like tissue paper. 'Where is my wonderful painting? I must see it immediately.'

Rosie pointed towards the back wall. 'Just there. I'll

get it delivered for you Cha Cha. It's too big to fit in your jeep, I think.'

Cha Cha's face paled under the make-up. 'That one?' She nodded at the painting. 'But it's enormous. Where will I put it?'

'Did you not read the catalogue, Cha Cha?' Rosie asked nervously. 'And I'm sure Dad said—'

'No matter.' Cha Cha moved closer and began to study the oil painting intently.

Alan appeared by her side. 'What do you think?' he asked. 'Fan-bloody-tastic, isn't it? If I say so myself.'

Rosie held her breath.

'Yes, I think it is, my dear,' Cha Cha said finally. 'You are a very talented young man.'

'Oh, *merci, merci*,' he cooed. 'Let me tell you all about it. You see there was this Italian stallion, Eugio, what a heartbreaker, anyway last October ...' He was launched.

'They make a right pair,' Rex whispered to Rosie.

After Rory had received all the cheques for the paintings and prints and had safely tucked them into his breast pocket he told them all the good news. 'We made seven thousand nine hundred euro.'

'That's amazing!' said Rosie.

'Thank you both so much.' Rory flung his arms around Rosie and gave her a warm hug.

'Hey, less of that,' said Martina, appearing from behind Rex. 'I've been watching you two and I won't have it, do you hear?'

'I'm so sorry ...' Rosie began and then looked at Martina. Martina had a huge smile on her face. A few weeks ago Martina would probably have scratched her eyes out for touching her beloved Rory, but things had obviously changed. In fact, she and Martina shared many lunches together and were becoming good friends.

'I'm only joking,' Martina insisted. 'You don't need to worry. I know he only has eyes for me.'

'I'd better even things up, just in case,' Rory said. He put his arms around Martina and drew her closely to his side.

'That went well,' Kim said joining them. 'Talk about starting with a bang – Cha Cha and Philly were out for blood – each other's!'

'No kidding.' Rosie laughed.

Just then they heard Philly's voice ringing out from the hall. 'Didn't even want the damn picture. Just had the house redone – it's all blue and gold. Wouldn't fit in with the colour scheme.'

'Sore loser!' Cha Cha shouted through the door.

'Tough titties!' Alan added. Cha Cha and Alan erupted into fits of giggles.

'And the night's only just begun.' Rory smiled.

'I think it's going to be a good one,' said Kim.

'Hi, Rosie.'

Rosie spun around. At first she didn't recognize the man standing in front of her. He was wearing a well-cut dark suit with a dark pink silk shirt and orange tie. It was a brave combination but it worked.

'Leo! You scrub up well.' As soon as the words were out of her mouth she regretted them. She berated herself for drinking too many cocktails with the girls earlier.

'Charming.' He smiled, the skin around his eyes crinkling attractively.

Blue, Rosie thought to herself, what lovely dark blue eyes. She snapped herself out of it. 'Sorry. But you look so different out of your work gear.'

'I know. Like you dressed up for the photo shoot?'

'Exactly.' She smiled. 'So what are you doing here?'

'I bought a picture, remember – *Dreaming of Cats*.'

It hit her. 'The first Olivia Miller watercolour, that was you?'

The keeper nodded. 'I can't believe you didn't recognize me.'

'I didn't know you were interested in art.'

'There's a lot about me you don't know. I have to go now, I'm afraid. I'm expecting a phone call.'

'You're not staying for the ball?' Rosie felt strangely disappointed. Why was a mere phone call so important? He was always running off to take phone calls.

'I might be back later on. I gave Rory a cheque for the picture. Is it OK if I take it now?'

'Sure, I'll just put some extra bubble wrap around the edges to stop the frame getting chipped.'

He watched as she secured the bubble wrap with some Sellotape.

'In case I don't make it later, maybe you'd like to grab some dinner this week if you're around,' he asked when she'd finished.

She was caught off guard. Was he asking her out? Surely not.

'To say thank you for helping with Tibo,' he continued. 'She's really thriving. She loves your daily visits.'

'Hey, it's cheaper than getting a dog,' she quipped. 'And anyway, I'm getting quite fond of the little mite, but she won't be small for long.'

'You can still visit her. You won't be able to play with her but she'll still know who you are. They don't forget.'

'Really? Like elephants?'

Leo laughed. 'Like elephants.' He glanced at his watch and tucked the painting under his arm. 'Have to fly. Don't forget about dinner.'

'I won't. I look forward to it.'

Kim dug her in the side. 'What was that all about?'

Rosie tapped her nose. 'For me to know and you to find out.'

'Don't be so childish. Go on, tell me.'

'Later,' Rosie promised. 'I think I can hear Mum in the hallway.'

They listened.

'Yes, I'm so proud of Rosie. She's my eldest, you know. And my other daughter Kim's very high up in the bank. Has a lovely chap called Greg. He's babysitting for Rosie's little girl, Cass, this evening – darling man. He'll make a wonderful father.'

Kim grimaced at Rosie.

'They're super girls. Rosie's got brains to burn, and such a good mother. You should see her playing with Cass, they're more like best friends than mother and daughter.'

Kim squeezed Rosie's arm. 'Not a bad word about either of us. Wonders will never cease.'

'Let's go outside,' René suggested to Rosie after they'd finished their explosive dancing session together, 'just you and me.' He draped his arm around her shoulders and swung her around to face the door.

'Um, I don't think so . . .' Rosie began. She was still a little dizzy and light-headed from being twirled around the dance floor.

'May I cut in?' a familiar voice asked. It was Leo.

'Sure,' René said, most disgruntled. He had been hoping to make some moves on this most attractive older lady. Still, there was always Cha Cha, he reasoned. He removed his arm. 'She's all yours.'

As René walked away Rosie turned towards Leo. 'Thanks,' she said. 'He wasn't really my type.'

'My pleasure. Would you like to dance?'

'To be honest, I'm all danced out for the moment. I need to catch my breath.' She fanned her face with her hand.

'Would you like some water?' he asked kindly.

She nodded gratefully. 'Please. And a vodka and cranberry juice, if you wouldn't mind.'

'I'll be back in one minute. Don't move.'

As she waited for Leo to return, she hoped that René wouldn't spot her and come over again, but he seemed to have disappeared, much to her relief.

'Here you go.' Leo handed her a large chilled plastic bottle of water and a full cocktail glass.

'Very posh,' she said, taking the bottle from him.

'Thought you could do with it. Would you like to get some air?'

'Yes, why not?' With Leo, she realized, she wouldn't mind one little bit.

He put his free arm around her and gently led her towards the double doors at the end of the ballroom, leading to the garden. It was a beautifully clear night, stars twinkling in the clear sky. Rosie shivered. The lack of cloud cover made it a little nippy.

'Here.' Leo put his glass down on the white metal table in front of them with a clink and whipped off his jacket. He threw it around her shoulders.

How gallant, she thought. She smiled at him. 'Thanks.'

In the cool air she began to feel the effect of all the alcohol in her system. In fact, she was starting to feel quite drunk.

'What are you thinking about?' Leo asked. 'You look miles away.' He pulled out a chair for her, the legs scraping on the patio with a sharp metallic ring, and sat down beside her, leaning over towards her. They were facing the ballroom and watched the dancing through the windows. He was so close that Rosie could feel his warm breath caressing her face.

'Nothing really. I'm just enjoying the evening. I haven't been out dancing for so long – I've missed it.'

'I know what you mean.'

'You like dancing?' Rosie asked.

'Don't sound so surprised.'

She smiled. 'Sorry. I'm glad you made it. How was

your phone call?' she asked before she could stop herself.

Leo looked at her, his gaze lingering on her face for a long second as if trying to decide how to answer her. 'Good,' he said finally. 'Very good.' He took a sip of his drink. 'So where would you like to go to dinner next week? How about Bruno's in Wicklow?'

'Sounds good. Will I bring Cass?'

'Sorry?'

'Cass. Will I bring her?'

'Um, if you want to.'

'Do you want me to?'

'Honestly?'

She nodded.

'Not really. I thought we could talk, you know. Get to know each other properly.'

'Ah.' She grinned at him.

'Ah what?' He was a little confused. Rosie wasn't making much sense.

'I was just trying to work out what sort of dinner it was, that's all.'

'And what sort of dinner is it?' he asked with a smile. 'Or have you decided?'

'A date kind of dinner.'

'Is that right?'

'Yes.' She nodded firmly, her head lazily flopping backwards and forwards, making her head spin. She took a large gulp of water and held the cool bottle to her cheek.

'Are you OK?' he asked kindly.

'Never better,' she said. 'Just a little drunk, to tell the truth.'

'I see.'

'Do you like me, Leo?' she asked.

'Excuse me?'

'Do you like me?'

'Of course I do.'

'No, I mean *really* like me.'

'Let's talk about this some other time,' he said gently.

'No, I want to talk about it now,' she said firmly. 'Kiss me.'

'Rosie, I don't think . . .'

'You said you liked me.'

'I know but . . .'

She turned her head towards him. 'Kiss me. Please?'

He smiled and stroked the side of her face with his hand. 'If you insist.' He leant over and placed a tender but firm kiss on her lips.

Rosie felt a tingling sensation on her lips. She hadn't been kissed in so long – it was heavenly. She smiled. 'Kiss me again.'

But as Leo moved towards her a figure stepped out of the darkness behind them.

'Hello, Rosie.' It was Darren.

Rosie

'What the hell are you doing here?' Rosie demanded.

'Is that any way to talk to your husband?'

'Ex-husband, remember? Or have you conveniently forgotten? I seem to remember you leaving me for Pamela Anderson. Oh no, sorry, Tracy Mullen. How could I have confused the two?'

Darren ignored the jibe. 'Have you been drinking?'

'What do you think? It's a ball, I'm here to enjoy myself. Of course I've been bloody drinking.'

'There's no need to keep swearing at me, thank you.'

'Oh, really? Just feck off then.'

Leo stood up. 'I think I'd better—'

'Sit down!' said Rosie. 'Darren was just leaving.'

'I'm not going anywhere,' Darren said firmly.

'Then please excuse me. I'll see you later, Rosie,' said Leo politely.

'Wait!' Rosie stood up and handed him his jacket. 'You don't have to go.'

'Yes, I do. You should talk to him, Rosie.' He kissed her on the cheek. 'I'll see you later.' He walked away.

'Leo!' she called to his retreating back. 'I'll join you in a few minutes.'

He swung around, raised one hand and waved at her. She waved back and then turned towards Darren.

'You've some nerve,' she said, glaring at Darren. 'What are you doing here?'

'Have a wild guess.'

She shook her head. 'No. Actually I don't give a damn why you're here, I just want you to leave. This is *my* ball, not yours.'

He smiled. 'Would you listen to yourself?' He picked up her glass. 'What's this?' He sniffed it. 'Vodka?'

'Vodka and cranberry juice, if you must know.'

'And who was the guy?'

'It's none of your business.' She picked up her glass and gulped down half the cocktail.

He laughed. 'Rosie O'Grady, you wild woman, you! I haven't seen you so drunk since Cass's christening. Remember that night? When you put on that pink baby-doll set I got you in Ann Summers, remember?'

Rosie ignored him. 'I thought I'd asked you to leave.'

'You did, but I'm not going anywhere. Would you like to dance?'

'Dance!' she spat. 'With you? Are you joking?'

'You know how I feel about you, Rosie. I've been leaving messages on your mobile every day. I know you've been getting them. And did you like the flowers?'

She stared into space, trying to block out what he

was saying. He'd sent her several deliveries of roses – pink tea roses, yellow roses, red roses – dozens of them in huge, elaborate bouquets. She was on first-name terms with the driver from Lizzie's Blooms by this stage.

'Please, don't be like that. I'm not going to give up. I love you, I've never stopped loving you. From the first time I saw you I knew . . .'

She stood up, wobbling a little and steadying herself with a hand on the table. 'If you won't leave then I will. And please don't follow me. Understand?' She began to walk towards the wooden bench in the middle of the rose garden, drawn by the heady scent of the flowers. She couldn't bear to go back inside yet, she felt flushed and in need of the cool air and the peace. She sat down on the bench, rested her arms behind her along the edge of cool wood and closed her eyes. Images swam through her mind – images she'd tried to suppress all this time, images of her and Darren in the good days. She tried not to cry but it was no use. The alcohol in her system wasn't helping, intensifying her emotions to an almost unbearable level. Fat tears began to sting her eyes and stream down her cheeks in hot rivulets.

Darren sat for several minutes before following her into the rose garden. Here he found her sobbing her little heart out. He smiled to himself.

'Don't cry, love. I'm here now. Let me look after you.'

'No!' she protested. 'Please go away.'

'As I keep telling you, I'm not going anywhere.'

He handed her a large freshly laundered handkerchief. 'Wipe your eyes,' he said gently, stroking her hair. He planted a kiss on the top of her head.

She didn't have the strength or the energy to push him away. She dabbed her tears and flinched as he put his arm around her shoulders.

'Don't fight it,' he said. 'Let me take care of you.'

She allowed him to leave his hand there. She knew it was dangerous, but something in his voice captivated and soothed her. Right at this moment she needed someone's arm around her, she felt so at sea and so confused.

'You're home now, Rosie,' he crooned. 'You have no need to cry any more.' He traced his finger along the edge of her jawbone, sending delicious shivers up and down her spine. 'Don't fight it,' he said again. He leant forward slowly and kissed her, his lips warm and firm against hers. She could feel her own lips respond automatically. He had always been a masterful kisser and she couldn't help herself. She knew she should push him away but . . . she kissed him back.

'That's right, babe,' he whispered as he nuzzled the nape of her neck. 'You know it's right.'

They kissed for what seemed like forever before he stood up and held out his hand. 'Come with me, I have something to show you.'

'No, Darren, I'm staying here.' Even in her intoxicated state, she knew being with him was wrong – very wrong. And she shouldn't have kissed him – that was really stupid. What was she thinking of? Leo was waiting for her inside.

He looked at her, smiling. 'Please, come with me. It's getting cold out here.'

After he'd said the word 'cold' she shivered involuntarily. Darren, unlike Leo, hadn't offered her his jacket and her shoulders had began to develop goosebumps, the hairs on her arms standing to attention like little blonde soldiers. He was right about the cold, they should go inside. She stood up and followed him wordlessly. He led her in the back door, through the kitchen and up the back stairs to the first floor. He'd been studying the house all evening, locating the bedrooms and the back stairs just in case. There were always lots of different entrances and exits in a big old house like this – he'd seen so many of them in his line of work he was an expert by now. If Rosie hadn't acquiesced, he'd been sure there would have been someone else who was on for it.

'Where are we going?' she asked a little nervously.

'You'll see.' He pushed open a door and stepped inside, pulling her in behind him. The curtains were open and moonlight spilled in the tall, mullioned window. There was a huge four-poster bed in the middle of the room.

'Amazing bed, isn't it?' he said. 'Come on. You need to warm up before you go back downstairs.'

'We can't go in here!' she protested. 'This could be Rory or Conor's room.'

'It's the guest room.'

'Are you sure?'

He nodded. 'Of course. Don't you trust me?' Realizing what he'd said, he continued quickly. 'We'll just

417

have a little lie down on it, OK? Then we'll go back downstairs.'

'Lie down? No way!' She pulled against his arm.

'Rosie,' he said soothingly. 'Aren't you tired?' He yawned, stretching his arms over his head. 'Just a little rest. It'll do us both good, believe me.'

'I don't know . . .' Rosie stifled a yawn. She'd kill for a little nap right about now. She felt decidedly woozy.

'You see. You're tired too. We'll just stay here five minutes, OK?'

'Promise?'

'Promise.' He put his arms around her and lifted her onto the bed. He kicked off his shoes and joined her, pinning her down on the luxurious feather-filled duvet with one practised move.

'Darren!'

He kissed her firmly, his tongue powerful and insistent. Rosie felt herself kissing him back. Her head spun a little when she closed her eyes, the vodka soaring through her veins. She knew she shouldn't be here with Darren but all her willpower had abandoned her. It had been so long since she'd felt the warm glow of physical attraction spread through her body and this evening it felt like a drug, intoxicating and mesmerizing her until she couldn't think straight.

She gasped as he snaked his hand up her silk dress and toyed with her lacy thong.

'Let's get rid of that, shall we?' he whispered.

Rosie was about to tell him to stop when he pressed his fingers firmly against the front of the slip of lace.

Warmth flooded her lower body, spreading up towards her chest. She sighed and gave in completely to the sensations.

'You want more?' he murmured. He knelt in front of her, inched her thong along her thighs and threw it behind him. She felt powerless to resist. He raised the skirt of her dress to her waist and began to kiss the inside of her thighs, making his way up her body towards her stomach and back again, his fingers exploring her creases and folds with the touch of a master.

'No, Darren, this isn't . . .'

She could bear it no more, her body exploded in a huge orgasmic rush, her head swimming with pleasure. She arched her back like a cat, rising off the bed and collapsing back again. She groaned. Damn, she'd missed this.

Darren looked up at her, a strange expression on his face. He supported his weight on his hands and feet, he crawled his body up towards her face and started to kiss her with studied intensity, making her gasp for breath. He undid the front of his trousers with one hand and whipped out his hardness. Within seconds he had entered her in one sharp, managed thrust.

She gasped in surprise, too shocked to protest. Using both arms he lifted her legs up, rested them over his shoulders and placed a pillow under her buttocks.

'But Darren . . .'

'You know you want me, Rosie. Don't fight it.' He kissed her again, hard, silencing her.

'Come to Daddy,' he said, drawing up and smiling

wickedly. After a few more thrusts his head dipped back and the veins in his neck stood out. He moaned and collapsed on top of her. 'Good girl,' he murmured. 'Good girl.'

Rosie, hearing something, raised her head. There were two figures standing in the doorway, their bodies silhouetted against the hall light.

'Rosie!' a woman's voice rang out. The blood drained from Rosie's face as she realized who it was – Anna and Conor. She sobered up instantly. Anna closed the door almost immediately, her and Conor outside.

Rosie sat up. Darren looked at her. 'What was that?' he asked.

'Not what, who? Anna and Conor. We have to get out of here. I'm so embarrassed.' She started to feel a lot more sober. What had she done?

'Conor Dunlop?' asked Darren.

She nodded. 'The owner of the house.'

He began to laugh.

'It's not funny,' she insisted. 'How am I going to look him in the face again? And as for Anna.' She put her hands to her cheeks. 'I'm mortified.'

'It's no big deal.' He jumped off the bed and began to re-fasten his trousers. 'Forget about it.'

'I'll have to go outside and talk to them.' She scrambled to the end of the bed and grabbed her thong.

'What?'

'If I leave it till later I'll bottle out. It has to be now.'

'But Rosie . . .'

'Wait here.' She looked around the room frantically. 'Where's the bathroom?'

'Try over there.' He pointed to a doorway to the side of the room. 'I'm going back downstairs to get a drink. I need one.'

A few minutes later, she'd tidied herself up and was having second thoughts about going back downstairs. What if she bumped into Leo – how could she face him now? And she didn't really want to talk to Darren either – she was so ashamed at her behaviour. She heard a knock on the door.

'Rosie, are you decent?' asked Anna.

Rosie felt her cheeks burn once more. She took a deep breath and opened the door.

'I'm so sorry,' she gabbled. 'I don't know what came over me. It must have been the drink. I feel terrible.'

Anna smiled at her. 'It's OK. Come and talk to me.' She gestured at the table and chairs in front of the window. They both sat down. 'You gave us both a bit of a fright but it's no big deal. But tell me, who's the guy? You dark horse, you. We thought you were with Leo. I saw you go outside with him earlier.'

'It's Darren.'

Anna stared at her. 'Your ex-husband?'

Rosie nodded.

'Oh.' Anna didn't know what to say. 'Are you back together?'

Rosie shrugged. 'Not exactly.'

'I don't understand.'

'He just turned up this evening out of the blue and one thing led to another.'

'I see.'

'Please don't tell anyone. After everything he's done,

I feel so stupid. And there's no way I'm taking him back.'

'Does he want to try again? Is that why he came to the ball?' Anna asked gently.

'Yes, or so he says.'

'And what about you? Would you take him back?'

'No! Certainly not.' Rosie was confused. She'd thought that her and Darren were completely over, banished to the history books. But now, after tonight, she wasn't so sure. How could she still have such strong physical feelings for someone if she didn't . . .

'Do you still love him?'

'I don't know. I thought I hated him, but obviously not.'

'Do you trust him?'

'No! But sometimes he does seem to genuinely want me back.'

'Seems?'

'You never quite know with Darren.'

'Do you trust him enough to give him the benefit of the doubt?'

'No. At least I don't think so. Oh, Anna, everything's such a mess.'

Anna smiled gently. 'You owe it to yourself to find out for sure. Living with regret is crippling, but so is living with the wrong man. But if there's a chance your marriage could be saved . . . who knows? Maybe you should think about it. But don't rush into anything. He'll need to prove himself one hundred per cent to you, remember that. You have to be able to trust him.'

'Thanks. I will think about it. And Anna?'

'Yes?'

'Tell Conor I'm sorry. I didn't mean to show any disrespect.'

'You can tell him yourself, he's right outside.' Anna opened the door. 'You can come in now, Conor.'

He smiled at Rosie.

'Please, don't say anything,' she pleaded. 'I'm mortified.'

'It's forgotten,' Conor said putting his arm around Anna's back. 'It's just between us, OK? But who was the man?'

'I'll tell you later,' Anna promised. 'Now let's all go downstairs and dance.'

'Good idea.' Conor smiled.

As they reached the bottom of the stairs, Darren was waiting. He jumped up and held out his hand to Conor. 'Sorry about that.'

Conor patted him on the back. 'Not a problem . . . um . . .'

'Darren, Darren O'Grady, Rosie's husband.'

Conor looked at Rosie, who nodded, and back at Darren. 'Pleased to meet you.' He held out his hand. 'Any friend of Rosie's is a friend of mine,' he said without displaying any emotion.

'Thanks,' Rosie said gratefully.

'I'm afraid I'm leaving now,' said Darren. 'But I'm sure we'll meet again.'

Anna looked at Rosie. 'You're leaving? So early? It's only one.'

'*I'm* leaving, not Rosie,' Darren explained. 'I want

her to have some fun with her friends. I've monopolized her for too long already this evening.'

'Will we order you a taxi?' asked Anna.

'Not at all, I've already ordered one on my mobile. Thanks for the offer.'

'We'll see you in a few minutes then, Rosie. Nice to meet you, Darren.'

'And you.' As Anna and Conor made their way diplomatically into the ballroom, Rosie felt unsettled. 'You're going?'

'Yes.' He kissed the top of her head. 'It's better this way.' He was nervous of bumping into Rex or Julia. He'd already seen Kim but hoped she hadn't spotted him. Rosie was one thing, her family was another. 'I'll give you a ring tomorrow from Blackrock.'

'Blackrock?'

'My new apartment. Surely I told you?'

'Told me what?' She was confused.

'Tracy and I have broken up. I've moved into an apartment in Blackrock.'

'What? No, you didn't tell me.' She was almost lost for words. She'd had a lot to take in this evening. 'When did this happen? What did Tracy say?'

Darren kissed her on the cheek. 'We'll talk tomorrow, I promise. Bye, my love.'

'But, Darren, this doesn't change anything. I'm still—'

He put his finger on her lips to silence her.

She watched as he walked down the front steps to where a taxi was waiting.

'Mr Leeson?' the taxi man leaned over and asked out the window.

Darren nodded. Rosie looked down at him in surprise.

He smiled up at her. 'He can have mine.'

'Where to?' the man asked.

'Blackrock.' He stepped into the back of the cab.

Rosie stood and watched as the car drove away. She was dumbfounded. He'd left Tracy. She kept going over and over it in her head. He'd left Tracy.

'Actually it's Sandycove,' Darren said as the taxi drove away, 'if you don't mind.'

The taxi man shrugged. 'All the same to me, mate.'

Darren sat back and relaxed. Mission accomplished. Now he just had to sort out the last piece of business with Tracy and things would be perfect.

'Hi, Rosie, it's me,' said Darren. 'Can you talk?'

'No, I'll ring you back later.'

'Before you go, can I call over this afternoon?'

'We'll see. As I said, I'll ring you back, OK?' Rosie clicked off her mobile sharply. She was in a total state this morning. Racing through her mind was everything that had happened last night at the ball. Sex with Darren. His announcement about leaving Tracy.

'Who was that?' Kim asked, stirring whipped cream into her coffee.

'Anna. I'll ring her back later.' Rosie hated lying to Kim but she was much too embarrassed to tell her sister about last night and her encounter with Darren.

She just wanted to forget about the entire sordid encounter. It had been a mistake. A big mistake.

'Anna looked fantastic last night,' Kim said. 'That brown dress really suited her. Are there any more strawberries?'

Rosie forced herself to smile. 'You've already eaten the bones of a whole punnet.'

'I'm a growing girl.'

'You'll only grow one way by eating the way you do and that is most certainly not up.'

Kim flicked some cream at her sister. 'Spoilsport! Well, are there?'

Rosie squealed and wiped the cream from her arm where it had landed. 'Are there what?'

Kim sighed theatrically. 'Honestly? Where's your brain this morning? Strawberries!'

Rosie looked at her watch. It was well after twelve. 'Afternoon. And, yes, in the fridge. You'll need to wash them though.'

Kim stood up and fetched the second punnet. Cass screamed in the living room. 'Is she OK, do you think?'

Rosie nodded. 'I'd say Greg's tickling her from the sounds of things. I can't believe he hasn't had enough after babysitting last night.'

'You know Greg and children. And don't say what I think you're going to say.'

'Would I?'

'Yes!' Kim placed the bright red berries in the sink, ran the cold tap and began to wash and de-stalk them. 'Do you want some?'

'No, I'm fine, thanks.' Rosie was thinking about

Darren again. She'd made a complete fool of herself. Sleeping with Darren, and on Conor's bed too. She'd been drunk, very drunk, but that was no excuse. Not really. She'd just got carried away in the heat of the moment. How was she ever going to face Conor again? Although he'd been so decent about it. And as for Leo – how could she go out for dinner with him now? Hopefully Darren would act as if nothing had happened when he called over this afternoon and everything could go back to normal, with him at least. If you could call anything normal. It was probably best if he did call over – it would get it all out of the way and finished with.

'Earth calling Rosie? I asked you a question.'

'Sorry, I was miles away. What did you say?'

'I asked how your head was now.'

Rosie had had a stinker of a headache earlier that morning and had swiftly downed some painkillers, donated by Kim. 'Not bad. I'm not going to do anything too strenuous today though, just in case.'

'Good idea. We have to go to a barbeque this evening in Greg's sister's house. But we're around till then. How about a walk or something this afternoon?'

'Sorry, no can do. Darren's due to visit.'

'Really? I thought he wasn't going to take Cass till next weekend.'

'He changed his mind. He left a message on my mobile last night.'

'That reminds me, I thought I saw Darren at the ball last night. But it can't have been. It must have been someone who looked like him.'

The blood drained from Rosie's face.

'Are you all right?' Kim asked with concern.

'Yes, sorry, I just feel a little nauseous. I'm not used to drinking spirits, that's all. I think I'd better just rest this afternoon.'

'No problem. In that case I'm going to drag Greg up the mountains, it'll be good for him.' Kim popped the damp strawberries into a bowl, topped them with a dollop of cream, sprinkled some sugar over the top and began to tuck in with relish. 'What are you up to next weekend?' she asked, a few berries later.

'I'm not sure.'

'I'll give you a ring during the week and we'll arrange something. I haven't spent a day with Cass for ages. We could go to Brittas Bay or something.'

'That sounds good.'

'Are you OK, Rosie? You seem a little preoccupied.'

'Sorry.' She smiled quickly. 'I'm fine. It's just my head.'

Kim smiled back. 'I understand.' She polished off the last of the strawberries, a large chunk of cheddar cheese and some green grapes, sat back and sighed. 'That's better.'

'Quite finished?'

'Nearly. Do you have any ice cream?'

Rosie snorted. 'You're unbelievable!'

'Hi, Rosie.' Darren handed Rosie a huge bouquet of tea roses, the delicate cream buds tied up with a huge matching cream ribbon.

'Thanks.' She took them off him and led him into the kitchen. 'Shut the front door behind you, will you? I'll put these in the kitchen with the others.' She leant over and smelt them. They had absolutely no scent whatsoever. 'They're lovely, but as I keep telling you – you shouldn't have. Would you like a cup of coffee? Or tea?' she gabbled. 'The kettle's just boiled so it's no trouble. Cass is outside playing in the garden, but I'll call her in. She's dying to—'

'Stop!' he said, putting his hand on her arm. 'Look at me.'

She put the flowers down on the kitchen counter and did as he requested. As his eyes hit hers she began to blush and looked down at the floor.

'Last night meant everything to me,' he began earnestly. 'I floated the whole way home. To Blackrock,' he added pointedly. 'Please say it meant something to you. I know I haven't been the ideal husband over the last while . . .'

Rosie snorted.

He ignored her. 'But I love you with all my heart and I want to make it up to you more than anything else in the world. Please say you'll consider taking me back. Please?'

She stared at him, her blush faded and her head spun. She felt quite faint. 'I can't believe you have the nerve to come in here like this and—'

'Rosie, you have every right to be angry with me. I've behaved despicably. I know that. But you were always the one with the big heart. You kept our

family together. You were and are everything to n
and to Cass – the earth mother, the lover, the artis
the—'

'Darren!' If she wasn't feeling so overwhelmed wi
emotion she'd laugh. 'What are you talking about? Yo
were the one who said I didn't spend enough time wi
Cass. You accused me of being a bad mother.'

'You can't honestly think I meant that?' He looke
at her calmly, his eyes dripping with sincerity. 'It w
said in the heat of the moment. Please forgive m
You're a fantastic mother, you must know that. I'm n
going to give up, you know. I've changed, I'm not tl
person I used to be. I miss you both so much. I mi
the life we all had together. I want us to be a fami
again. I love Cass and I love you. I know I've hurt yo
and I don't deserve to be happy ever again, but
you could find it in your heart to give me one mo
chance I'd never let you down again. I promise.'

As if on cue, Cass came running into the kitche
'Daddy!' she squealed and threw her arms around h
waist. 'I've missed you. Have you got anything f
me?'

'Cass!' Rosie scolded.

'That's OK,' he said. 'As a matter of fact I do, you
lady. It's in the car. Will we go and get it?'

Cass nodded and grinned.

He led her out by the hand. Looking back towar
Rosie he smiled. 'Happy families again.'

As soon as they'd left the room Rosie slumped on
a kitchen chair and put her head in her hands. Did sl

ave any right to deprive Cass of a happy family life? erhaps Darren *had* changed. But could she ever trust im again? Maybe Anna was right – Rosie had to know ne hundred per cent one way or the other.

Anna

'Mum, have you seen my life jacket?' Anna pulled open the cupboard under the stairs. 'Ow! Damn!' she swor as Ollie's fishing net hit her on the head. She scrambl among the sailing clothes, roller blades, old plast shopping bags and discarded toys, throwing everythin onto the hall floor in her haste.

'Is this what you're looking for?' Myra asked. Sh handed Anna a yellow life jacket.

'No, that's my spare, but it'll do.' It was a little tigl on her but beggars couldn't be choosers. She hoped wouldn't prove too uncomfortable during the lor races. Anna started to put everything back into th cupboard.

'Leave it,' said Moyra. 'I'll do it when you've gon You'll be late otherwise.'

'Thanks, Mum.' Anna stood up. One of her kne cracked loudly. 'Did you hear that? I'm falling apar My leg will probably seize up while I'm sailing and I' have to be rescued.'

432

'Has that ever happened to you before?'

'No.'

'Then it's hardly likely to happen today.' They heard a car horn beep outside. 'That's Conor.' Anna flung her sailing bag over her shoulder and opened the hall door.

'Good luck, love.' Moyra gave her a firm hug. 'Ollie! Your mum's leaving.'

Ollie rushed into the hall from the sitting room where he'd been playing his Gameboy. 'Good luck, Mum. I hope you win.'

'Thanks, pet. I'll see you later.' She ruffled his hair. 'Be good for your gran.'

'I will,' he promised.

As she closed the door behind her Anna could feel butterflies storming around in her stomach, bouncing off the walls and flittering up and down her throat. Conor jumped out of the jeep and opened the boot for her. 'Let me take that.' He lifted the bag off her shoulder and swung it into the large boot. 'What have you got in there? It's very heavy.'

'Spares for the boat,' she explained. 'Duct tape, batons, a leatherman – bits and pieces. In case I break anything.'

'Expecting heavy weather?' Conor asked, trying not to smile. There wasn't a breath of wind and the forecast was good.

'You never know.'

Conor opened the passenger door for her.

'Thanks,' she mouthed.

As they drove past Redwood House on the way to the sailing club Anna gazed out of the window, trying

to calm herself down. She hadn't been this nervou
since the first Laser Nationals she'd ever sailed in Sligo
She'd been all of fifteen then, a mere slip of a thing
but tall for her age. Her dad had taken the whole weel
off work to be with her and they'd shared a caravan
parked conveniently beside the sailing club. It was thei
first time away together without Moyra, and Anna had
loved having her dad all to herself for the whole week
She'd come seventeenth in the end, quite an achieve
ment for a young sailor. She'd been placed second
woman and best newcomer and her dad had been
thrilled. As the final results had been read out he'd pu
his arm around her and whispered, 'You've made m
very proud.' She'd never forgotten it. In all her year
sailing it had been the one moment that stood out in
her memory more than any other.

'Penny for them,' Conor said as they drove into
Wicklow town.

'I was thinking about my dad.'

'Do you miss him?'

'Very much, he was a lovely man.'

'He'd be proud of you today.'

'Proud? I haven't done anything yet.'

'Yes, you have. It's not every thirty-eight-year-ol
mum who takes up dinghy sailing again. I think it'
pretty brave.'

'Pretty stupid, you mean. I can't believe I'm goin
through with this.'

Conor said nothing for a few minutes. After he'
parked down the quay from the sailing club he turne
towards her. 'Anna, you're ready for this. You've bee

training really hard and doing really well in the local events.'

'But this is the Nationals!'

'So what? It's the same thing, just with more boats.'

'Seventy-three boats. I'm used to fleets of twenty.'

'And how many were there at the Worlds in Cowes?'

'A hundred and fifty.'

'And at Barcelona?'

'Nearly two hundred.'

Conor smiled. 'And you're worried about a mere seventy-three? Anna, you have more experience in big fleets than most of the other sailors put together. And you also have another huge advantage over them. Actually, you have two.'

'And they would be?'

'One, everyone thinks you're out of contention. No one expects you to win, they won't cover you and if you take a flyer they are unlikely to follow you, especially if you really bang the corners.'

'I guess you're right. And two?'

He smiled again. 'You have me as your coach.'

She laughed. 'You're right, how can I lose? Now I'd better get moving or I'll miss the briefing.'

After the briefing Conor slotted Anna's sail onto her mast as she changed. When she came back out he was rigging her main sheet. 'Missing anything?' he asked.

'Sorry?'

He held up her white life jacket.

'I was wondering where that was.' She took off the yellow one. 'Could you hang onto this one for me?'

'Sure. It's always good to have spares.'

'Are you teasing me?'

'Would I?'

She smiled. 'Is the racing running to schedule, do you know?'

'I'm not sure. I presume so. Several people have launched already. Maybe you should get going. Have I mounted the compass correctly?'

She checked it over. 'Yes, thanks. The wind seems to be picking up. I hope it stays light though. I've no chance against some of these guys if it gets heavy.' She gestured with her head towards the top of the slip where several large men were waiting to launch their boats.

'But they'll sink their Lasers in this wind.' Conor smiled. 'And you can always use your radial sail if the full sail gets too much for you.'

'I suppose. Hopefully I won't need to.'

'Ready to launch?' an official in a Laser National T-shirt asked.

'Yes,' said Anna.

'If you could make your way to the top of the slip over there and join the queue. We're trying to get everyone on the water as soon as possible.'

'No problem.' She picked up the trolley handle and began to wheel it over to where the woman had pointed.

Conor waited with her for a few minutes. 'You have your protest flag? And your water?'

She nodded. 'I'm all set.'

'I'll leave you be, in that case. I'll go and find Oscar.

If you need anything while you're on the water just wave over at us in the rib.' His friend Oscar was taking him out in his large white inflatable rubber speedboat to watch the racing.

'See you later,' she said. As Conor walked away she mentally ran through her last minute checklist – outhaul, kicker, extra cord just in case. Satisfied that everything was in order she tried to clear her mind of all other thoughts and prepare herself for the race ahead. As she wheeled her boat down the slip and slid it into the sea, she could feel icy cold water spearing her feet and lower legs through the thin rubber of her dry suit. Thank goodness for modern sailing gear, she thought. Her trolley was taken for her by an official, leaving her free to launch the boat. She stepped into it carefully, put down the dagger board and rudder and sat in position. Pulling in the main sheet and getting underway she heard a voice from the slip.

'Hi, Anna.' It was Maria Doyle.

Anna waved and smiled. She'd seen Maria many times in the sailing club since they'd first met – they had chatted in the bar after sailing and she liked the young woman very much. Although she was only nineteen, Maria had already become one of Ireland's top female sailors and Anna enjoyed talking to her about her training and race tactics.

'I didn't know you were sailing,' Anna said, shielding her eyes from the sun.

'Didn't know myself until the night before last. I was supposed to be going to France to train but that fell through. So I thought I might as well sail this event, it's always good fun. It'll be strange sailing a Laser though.'

'I'm sure you'll do well.'

'Hope so. Looks like we'll finally be racing against each other. Should be interesting.'

'Should be,' said Anna. 'Listen, I'm holding everyone up, better go. See you on the water.'

'Wait for me and we'll sail out together.'

'Sure.' Anna let go of the slip and sailed around in circles for a few minutes until Maria joined her.

'Ready?' Maria asked, powering away from her. 'Come on, slowcoach.'

'Last time I wait for you,' Anna said, catching up with her.

'Let's do some pacing,' Maria suggested.

'We could beat up to the mark boat over there.'

'Fine by me.'

Anna pulled in her main sail and headed towards the mark. Maria was quick, but her lack of experience in the Laser showed. Her roll tacks weren't as polished as Anna's and it cost her dearly. Anna reached the mark well ahead of her opponent and put the boat head to wind, stalling it.

'You're going really well,' Maria said as she slowed her own boat beside Anna's. 'You've a good chance of winning today if the wind stays light.'

'Thanks,' Anna said. 'But I don't know about that. Would you like to work on some roll tacks? I could do with some practice myself.'

'That would be brilliant,' Maria said gratefully, 'if you wouldn't mind.'

'Not at all.'

Before the first start Anna sailed up and down the line, looking for a slot. At least fifty boats were sitting on the line, sails flapping, waiting for the starting gun.

'Feck this, I'm not getting caught in everyone's dirty air,' she muttered. She sailed towards the port end of the line. I'll start on port and tack onto starboard, she thought. And hopefully get ahead of the fleet. It was risky, as boats sailing on port, or the left tack, had to give way to boats sailing on starboard. A couple of other brave souls, Maria included, had had the same idea. Anna looked at her watch which was counting down the time. Twenty seconds, ten seconds, five, four . . .

'Starboard!' a male voice called.

Anna had to give way, changing course slightly and gliding behind the transom of his Laser expertly.

Bang! The starting gun was fired and seventy-three boats began to sail through the line. Anna concentrated. She kept *Dougal* heeled ever so slightly and focused her attention on getting her moving. The wind had dropped even further and some of the heavier sailors were at a disadvantage, their boats sitting lower in the water than Anna's. As she passed the leading starboard boat she realized that she'd practically been holding her breath. Relief overwhelmed her. She'd crossed the whole fleet on port. If she could sail a good beat she'd reach the mark first at this rate. She studied the surface of the water and the clouds overhead. There was wind filling in from the left side of the course, she was sure of it. She checked her compass bearing and then checked again several minutes later. The wind was definitely shifting. She looked around her, executed a perfect roll tack and headed towards the wind.

As she rounded the top mark several boat lengths ahead of the next competitor she heard clapping from a nearby rib.

'Way to go, Anna!' Conor shouted over. 'Keep it up.' She allowed herself a smile before focusing her attention again. If she lost concentration for even one more moment the race might be lost. She fixed her eyes on the next mark, an orange buoy in the far distance.

Three hours later she crossed the finishing line in first place. As she was given her gun she waved at the officials on the committee boat to thank them and they all congratulated her.

'Well done!'

'Stunning race.'

'Excellent race, Anna.'

'Thanks,' she said, overwhelmed with emotion. She'd forgotten what it felt like to win an important race like this.

Conor was waiting for her to the right of the finish line. She sailed over and came alongside the rib. He leaned over and gave her an awkward half-hug. 'Get in here so I can hug you properly, woman. What a race!'

Anna laughed. 'I think I need to lie down. I'm exhausted.'

'And it wasn't even windy,' said Oscar. 'You women, no stamina,' he joked. 'You played a blinder, Anna. Congratulations. Why don't we tow you in?'

'That's very kind of you but it's not great for *Dougal*. I'll just have a bit of a rest and then sail in myself. I'd like to see the other boats finish.' As soon as she'd climbed into the rib the gun went again.

'Who's that?' asked Anna.

Conor stared at the dark-haired man. 'James Kenny. He weighs nothing – must have been a huge advantage today.' Another gun sounded. 'Followed closely by Anto Hamilton. Anto's the national Laser champion, isn't he?'

'That's right,' said Anna.

'Hey, Anna.' Conor smiled. 'You beat the national champion. How does it feel to be a contender?'

'Great,' she said, grinning. 'Really great.'

Sunday was the last day of the Nationals and Anna was lying fourth. After her win on Thursday the wind had picked up and she'd been disappointed with a fourteenth and a sixth on Friday. Saturday went a little better with a fifth and a seventh. As she launched her boat on Sunday morning she was feeling hopeful. Although it was bucketing down, the rain bouncing off the sea, it wasn't at all windy. It fact, there was only a slight breeze, with only just enough puff to move the boats along the water.

She sailed out towards the racecourse, trying to psych herself up for the race ahead. There was only one race today, as many of the sailors had travelled from all over the country and needed to leave Wicklow in reasonable time to drive home.

Moyra had promised to bring Ollie down to the prize giving. Anna hoped they'd all have something to celebrate. She had a good chance of coming third if she could keep her head today. Anto had already clocked up enough good races to win overall, as each competitor had a 'discard', which meant they only had to count their best five races. And if James came in the top three in this race he would be second overall. If Anna sailed well today she could drop her sixteenth place which was dragging her overall rating down. But if she sailed badly . . . she tried to block it out of her mind. However I finish up today, I'm proud of myself. Like Conor says, I'm a contender. Robert de Niro's *Raging Bull* character rang in her ears. 'I useta be a contender.' She smiled to herself. Whatever happened, she'd had a great few days.

'Hey, Anna, it's your weather,' Anto shouted over from his boat. 'Shitty wind. I'm barely moving.'

'I know. Are you scared?'

'Terrified!'

'You should be!' She laughed.

'It's James you need to watch today, not me. I sink in this weather.'

'What are you saying about me, gorilla features?' James shouted over.

'I was telling Anna she'd need to watch you today, that's all.'

'Too right!' James grinned. 'Bring it on, girl. I'm ready for you.'

Anna laughed again. After her win on Thursday, the younger sailors who hadn't known her before started treating her with a new respect. And everyone knew she was Larry Wilson's daughter, an unbeatable pedigree if ever there was one. She felt like one of the guys now and enjoyed this pre-race banter.

'Hey, it's ladies' day. I can feel it in my bones,' Maria said, joining in.

'Where are you lying, Maria?' asked Anna.

'I'm tubed. I had trouble with the tiller extension yesterday – I had to retire from the first race and missed the second.'

'Bummer!' said James.

'No kidding. So I'm out of the medals this time.'

'The Waterford crystal, you mean? Do you not have enough glasses to open a pub at this stage?'

Maria laughed. 'Almost.' As they all reached the committee boat they dispersed except for Anna and Maria.

'Best of luck today,' said Maria. 'I'll be looking out for you. You can still come second, you know.'

Anna sighed. 'It's unlikely unless James capsizes on a roll tack or something.'

'Have some faith, girl. You can do it.'

'Thanks.'

Before the start Anna decided to play it safe and go for a starboard start on the pin end of the line. She couldn't afford to mess up. As she lined herself up Maria sailed past her.

'Follow me,' said Maria firmly. 'You're not starting with the pack. You're going to win this one, girl. I keep telling you.'

'But . . .'

'Trust me. Tack, Anna!'

Anna did as told and tailed Maria's boat to the far end of the line.

'The wind's shifting,' said Maria. 'We can't make the line from here right now, but wait a few minutes and you'll see. I recognize the wind pattern.'

'Thanks,' said Anna gratefully.

'May the best woman win.' Maria smiled.

Anna looked around her. No one was up this end. Absolutely no one. She checked her compass. The wind hadn't changed yet. She said a quick prayer and checked again. Bingo! Only a small shift, but enough to allow them to sail over this end of the line. Maria was right. She looked at her watch. Only one minute to go. Too late for anyone else to join them. She concentrated on getting *Dougal* moving. As the gun went she glided smoothly over the line. She was going to have a good race, she could feel it in her bones.

As she rounded the last mark in first place, James was hot on her heels, held back only by Maria who was lying second. The wind had started to pick up halfway through the race and the ten leading boats were very close together. She had two choices: she could cover

James the whole way up the last beat and hold him off, risking losing places to the other boats, or she could take the other tack, away from him, risking losing her place to him. Damn, she muttered.

Maria sailed by just under her sail.

'Tack,' she said softly. 'Go up the middle and play the shifts. James looks like he's banging the right corner. I'll cover him. Go!'

'Are you sure?'

'Yes, just go!'

Anna tacked away from James and Maria tacked directly on top of him.

'Feck!' he swore under his breath.

Anna stared at her compass. Another shift. She sailed on for a moment and then tacked, her foot catching in the toe strap and jerking the boat slightly. Damn, she muttered. Concentrate, Anna, concentrate. You can do this. She shifted her weight out over the side of the boat a little more and pulled in her sail as hard as she could. The wind was picking up and she was having trouble keeping the boat flat.

'Starboard!'

Anna looked under her sail. It was Anto. She dipped him, coming so close to his transom that she nearly clipped him. If she didn't put more effort into keeping the boat flat he was going to be through her in no time at all. She pulled her thighs and calves bolt tight, braced her stomach muscles and pulled against the boat with all her might, keeping it flat on the water. As each wave hit the front of *Dougal* she pitched her weight against it, pushing the dinghy through. She focused her attention on the finishing line, willing her body to stay functioning. Her muscles felt as if they were going to snap and her back ached like it had never ached before. As each fresh gust hit the sail she pulled against it, as every wave hit the bow she shifted her weight forward. Keep going, she said to herself. Don't give up, you're almost there. Don't give up. There were only a few yards left until the finishing line.

She tacked onto starboard. As soon as she'd tacked she could see Anto under her sail.

'Starboard!' she yelled. 'Starboard!'

He was forced to tack and just as he did so she crossed the line. Bang! The gun was fired followed by another a split second later for Anto.

'Yes!' Anna screamed, dropping the tiller extension and collapsing into the boat. She heard the put-putting of an engine beside her. It was Conor. He pulled *Dougal* alongside the rib and smiled down at her.

'You did it! You won. You're second overall.'

'But James . . .'

'Finished fourth after Anto and Maria. You beat him, Anna.'

She started crying.

'Anna?' Oscar asked. 'Are you not pleased?'

She nodded. 'If I didn't hurt so much I'd be over the moon!'

'We're towing you in immediately,' said Oscar. 'Hand us the painter.' He and Conor lifted Anna into the rib, removed her kicking strap and main sheet and pulled the mast and the sail in also. As they bounced towards the sailing club over the choppy waves Conor put his arm around her. 'I'm so proud of you.'

She smiled through her tears. 'Thanks.'

Anna stood in the shower, hot needles of water massaging her aching shoulders and back. She closed her eyes and stood directly under the head, allowing the water to fall over her hair and down her face. As she brushed her dripping hair back off her face she heard her name being called.

'Anna, is that you in the shower?' It was Maria.

'Yes, I'll be out in a minute.'

'They're starting the prize-giving in ten minutes. I thought I'd better warn you.'

'OK.' Anna reluctantly turned off the shower, grabbed her towel off the rail and dried her face and body. She squeezed her hair out and tied it back with a large clip. Wrapping the damp towel around her torso she stepped into the changing room, immediately hit by the cool, sharp air. She shivered.

'Are you all right?' asked Maria, who was standing in front of the mirror outlining her lips with rose pink lipliner. There were two other women sitting on the benches exchanging views on the day's racing.

'Fine.' She smiled at Maria. 'You're all changed and ready.'

Maria laughed. 'You've been in that shower for hours.'

'I needed it, my poor old body is in bits.'

'Old, my ass! If I look as good as you do in a few years I'll be delighted.'

'Thanks.' Anna coiled a second towel around her head and dried her lower legs and feet. She pulled on her pants and jeans, wincing as something caught in her left shoulder. She was getting straight into the bath as soon as she got home to soak away some of the aches.

'That was some race you sailed today, girl,' a woman getting changed said in a thick Cork accent.

'Thanks,' said Anna. She looked over at Maria. Maria smiled at her.

As soon as the other women had left the room Anna joined Maria at the mirror. She put her fingers to her face, lifting the lines under her eyes and groaned. 'It's Botox for me soon, I fear. Look at these lines.'

'What are you talking about?' Maria laughed. She studied Anna's face. 'Can't see a thing.'

Anna took her hands away and began to root in her make-up bag for some concealer. Her cheeks were bright red with windburn and she felt like a clown.

'I'm so glad you won today,' Maria said. She leant in towards the mirror to examine a spot. 'I love seeing women doing well.'

'So do I.' Anna smiled. 'When I first started sailing Lasers there were very few women in the class. But now with the 4.7 and radial sails there are a lot more. But you know I couldn't have done it without you. Helping me get a decent start today. And as for tacking on James like that and covering him up that last beat – I don't know how to thank you.'

'You helped me, remember – the pacing every day

before the start and the tips on tacking and sailing downwind. I was only returning the favour.'

'Have you spoken to James yet?' Anna asked.

'Yes. He wasn't impressed,' Maria admitted. 'I was talking to him in the dinghy park while I was de-rigging.'

'What did he say?'

'He was complaining about women and how they always stuck together.'

'I see.'

'But I told him not to be so stupid, that it was only a race. And that you deserved to win.'

'And what did he say to that?'

'Actually he agreed with me.'

'What?'

Maria grinned. 'I shouldn't tell you. He'll kill me.'

'Go on.'

'He said he was into the whole "Mrs Robinson" thing and that you were fine. He wondered if you'd be into having a toy boy.'

'No!'

'I'm serious.'

'I won't be able to look him in the face now. What age is he?'

'Twenty.'

Anna laughed. 'Now that really has made my day.'

'And in second place and the winner of the Master's Trophy is Anna Wilson in *Dougal*. Congratulations, Anna!'

As she walked towards the top of the room to collect her prize the clapping and cheering was unbelievable. She could hear Ollie shouting, 'Well done, Mum,' and Conor whistling. Maria patted her on the back as she walked past her and James, who was standing beside Maria, winked.

'Would you like to say a few words, Anna?'

She nodded and stepped up to the microphone. She looked at the sea of faces in front of her and smiled, her face lighting up with delight as Ollie and Conor both blew her kisses.

'First of all, I'd like to thank Wicklow Sailing Club for hosting this event. I think you'll all agree that they've done a great job.' Everyone clapped. 'And I'd also like to thank my coach, Conor, my son, Ollie, and my mum, Moyra, for their support. They've been behind me all the way. And finally, I'd like to wish Maria every success in the next Olympics.'

As she walked back through the crowds she felt as high as a kite.

'Well done, love,' said Moyra. She squeezed Anna's arm gently. 'I knew you could do it.'

'Thanks, Mum.'

And at that moment Anna felt perfectly complete.

The following day, as Anna had feared, she ached all over. Her legs were covered in bruises and she could hardly lift her arms. It was just as well Little Daisies was closed for the whole of August, there was no way she would be able to cope with children today. Moyra had kindly offered to take Ollie to the aquarium this morning as he was full of energy and careering around the house like a mad thing. So Anna was catching up – trying to sort out Ollie's school clothes and find the textbooks she'd bought in June and carefully stored away. She wanted to cover them with sticky-back plastic but she was damned if she could find them. She jumped up as soon as the phone rang, happy for the distraction.

'Hello?' she answered.

'Hi, it's me, Simon.'

'Hi, Simon. How can I help you?' She tried to keep her voice level. She hadn't spoken to her ex-husband for ages, not since their rather heated phone call several weeks ago.

'I rang to apologize.'

Anna nearly dropped the phone. 'What?'

'Don't sound so amazed. I have done a lot of thinking over the past few weeks and you're right.'

'I'm right?'

'Yes. I should try to be a proper father to Ollie. I'll pay regular maintenance and I'll ring him every week. I'll have more time now, anyway.'

'You haven't lost your job, have you?'

'No! Nothing like that. Chrissie left me, that's all.'

Anna gasped. Much as she disliked Simon at times, she wouldn't wish that on anyone. 'I'm sorry. Are you all right?'

'Yes and no. It was all a bit messy. I thought if I took her to the British Virgin Islands that she might fall in love with me again and stop seeing him.'

'Seeing who?'

'Her accountant. He's twenty-five.'

'Ah.'

'I'm sorry I had such a go at you about the sailing and about . . .'

'Conor.'

'Yes, Conor. You didn't deserve it.'

'I know.'

'What can I say? I'm sorry.'

'That's OK.'

'Really?'

'Yes.'

'You've always had such a big heart, Anna.' The line went quiet for a few seconds.

'Simon? Simon?'

'Sorry.' He sounded like he was crying. 'I'm OK, honestly. At least I have Ollie. You will let me see him, won't you?'

'Of course, you're his dad. Why wouldn't I?'

'Thank you.'

'And Simon?'

'Yes?'

'I know things are hard at the moment, but you'll meet someone else. London's teeming with beautiful women. You could try choosing someone a little nearer your own age this time.'

'That's not a bad idea. Actually I have a date this evening. A girl from work's sister. Bit of a looker too.'

Anna laughed. 'Then what are you worrying about? You'll be fine.'

'Thanks for listening, Anna. Maybe we could talk

again, even be friends. You could tell me about Conor. He sounds like a good bloke. Ollie really likes him. He asked me would I mind if he had two dads. I wasn't quite sure what to say but I told him it was OK. I hope that was the right thing to do. Are the two of you thinking about marriage?'

'Conor would like to but I'm not so sure, to tell the truth. Marriage is a big step.'

Simon sighed. 'I know we had our problems but don't let that put you off. Marriage is a good thing. Look at my parents. They've been together for years. And yours were happy too. You deserve to be happy, Anna. You of all people. And I hate to say it, but it might be good for Ollie to have another man about the house.'

'Thank you. You've certainly given me something to think about. Listen, I'll get Ollie to ring you later. And good luck on your date. You can ring and tell me about it next week if you like.' As she put down the phone she smiled to herself. Ollie liked Conor – that was good to know.

She'd forgotten to tell Simon about her sailing success over the weekend. She'd ring him back later. She'd been looking forward to breaking the news after all that he'd said about her fitness levels – but now proving herself to him somehow didn't seem all that important. Were she and Simon finally becoming friends? Wonders would never cease.

*

Sarah Webb

Less than an hour later Anna and Conor were sitting in the Redwood rose garden.

'Are you sure?' asked Conor. 'What made you change your mind?'

'Truthfully?'

'Yes.'

Anna smiled. 'My ex-husband. He said I deserved to be happy. And you make me happy. And I know you won't smother me or try to change me.'

He kissed her on the forehead. 'Good. And Ollie?'

'He adores you. I adore you. That's all that matters.'

'Come here and kiss me, Anna.' He pulled her gently towards him.

Rosie

It was Wednesday evening and Rosie was completely exhausted after an exceptionally busy day at the gallery. Luckily Cass had been worn out too. She'd gone to sleep blissfully early, leaving Rosie a few hours to relax on the sofa before bed. Rosie had taken the phone off the hook and turned off her mobile to get some peace. She was just settling into her new Anne Tyler novel (kindly donated by Kim) when she heard a knock on the door. She groaned. 'Typical,' she muttered. She put the book down and dragged herself off the sofa and into the hall.

'Coming!' she shouted.

She opened the door to find Darren smiling broadly at her. He handed her a bottle of champagne and a punnet of strawberries. 'For you, my love.' He leant over to kiss her on the cheek but she drew away. He pretended not to notice.

'I can't stay long,' Darren said, walking straight past her and into the hall. 'I'm on my way to Cork. I have to look at an estate first thing in the morning, so I thought I'd call in to you on the way. Look what I brought.' He thrust the bottle at her. 'Let's open the bubbly immediately and celebrate.'

'Celebrate what?'

'Us, of course.'

Rosie knew she had to say something. The man was mad! 'Darren, as I keep telling you, there is no us, we're just friends. Nothing else. Do you understand?'

'Whatever makes you happy,' he said evenly. If things kept going according to plan, he thought, he'd have Rosie back in no time at all. After the scene at the ball he knew she wanted him. And then the whole messy business with Tracy Mullen would be a distant memory. He'd be the good guy again, happily ensconced with his wife and daughter. Hell, he might even let Rosie have another baby if things went well. That would keep her happy. They'd have to get a nanny of course – he was damned if he was going to help, he was much too busy for that. But maybe a nice Swedish or Italian nanny wouldn't be too bad – or even one of each. That definitely had possibilities. He smiled to himself – roll on the easy life.

'What are you smiling about?' she asked suspiciously.

'Nothing, my love,' he said smoothly. He walked into the kitchen. 'Got any champagne glasses?'

She followed him. 'I'm not really in the mood for drinking to tell the truth. Why don't you keep the bottle for a special occasion?'

'You were certainly in the mood for drinking at the

ball.' He grinned. 'Knocking those cocktails back like there was no tomorrow.'

Rosie winced. She wished he'd stop going on about the ball. She could feel a hot blush spreading up her neck and onto her cheeks.

'Yes, well, that was different,' she countered. 'It was just a moment of weakness on my part. I'd appreciate it if you'd put the entire evening out of your mind. Listen, Cass is asleep. I'm tired. Can we just leave it at that, please?'

'I suppose so,' he said, more than a little disgruntled. Rosie couldn't hold her champagne and he was hoping she'd get tipsy so he could get a little physical with her this evening. Tracy had gone completely off sex in the last few weeks and it was driving him crazy. He had his needs after all. Although the new girl in the office had distinct possibilities.

'Maybe I should go,' he said.

'Yes, maybe you should.'

He looked at her carefully. She had a stony expression on her face and her arms were crossed in front of her chest.

'You're no fun this evening,' he said, stroking her cheek with the palm of his hand.

'Please don't.' She drew away.

He grinned. 'That's not what you said—'

'I've already told you – that was a mistake,' she interrupted. 'It shouldn't have happened – I was very drunk and I didn't know what I was doing. I'd appreciate it if you'd stop talking about it, OK?'

He laughed. 'Are you saying it really didn't mean anything to you?'

She nodded. 'As I said, I'm sorry. Now let's just forget all about it.'

He stared at her. 'I refuse to believe that. But if it makes you happy, I'll go now. I'll call in later in the week. We can talk then.'

'Darren, I'd prefer if you didn't. We have nothing to talk about. Please – leave it.'

He ignored her. He wasn't giving up that easily. 'I'll see myself out.'

Rosie stood in the kitchen and listened as he strode down the hall and banged the front door behind him. She sighed deeply. Why was life so complicated? The worst thing was she had only herself to blame this time.

A little later Rosie looked up from her book. She could have sworn she heard a knock at the front door. She glanced at her watch. It was just after eleven. Who the hell was it this time? She hoped to goodness it wasn't Darren again.

There was another knock, louder this time. She placed the book face down on the sofa and went to open the door, flicking on the light as she walked into the hall. She'd settled down to read her novel over two hours ago, just after Darren had left, when there was still some daylight outside, and she'd been in another world ever since.

She opened the door. It took her a few seconds to recognize the woman standing on the doorstep as her blonde hair was tied back severely and she was devoid of her usual caked-on make-up. She looked pale and there was some sort of pink rash on one side of her face, her neck and around her eyes. She was wearing a light blue tracksuit which was hanging off her gaunt frame. But it was still Tracy Mullen.

'What the hell are *you* doing here?' Rosie said with a sinking feeling of déjà vu. She felt sick. She could feel an angry blush spreading up her neck and into her cheeks.

'I'm sorry,' said Tracy, her eyes fixed on the ground. 'It was a bad idea. I'd better go.' She looked up and Rosie could see that she was crying.

'Why are you here?' Rosie asked again, this time a little more kindly.

'I just needed someone to talk to and I thought . . . it was stupid, I know. My family won't have anything to do with me since I moved in with Darren . . .'

Rosie's heart jumped. How dare this woman of all people talk to her about her husband?

' . . . and I've lost contact with my friends,' Tracy continued, oblivious. 'I thought you might understand. Darren says—'

'Let's get this clear, Tracy. I have no intention of discussing Darren with you. Not now, not ever. Understand? I can't believe you had the nerve to come knocking on my door. What possessed you? Don't you think you've done enough damage?'

'I'm sorry,' Tracy sobbed. 'I never meant to. He said it was all over between the pair of you. I never meant to . . .'

'Mummy?' Cass walked into the hall rubbing her eyes. 'Who's here? Is it Daddy?'

'No, love,' Rosie said, closing the front door to and blocking Cass's view of Tracy. 'Go back up to bed and I'll be up in a minute. OK?'

'OK, Mummy.' Cass toddled back up the stairs, her nappy padding her little bottom like an eighteenth-century woman's bustle.

Rosie opened the door again. She hoped that Tracy would have disappeared but she was still there and still crying. She looked so young and vulnerable that Rosie felt a little sorry for her.

'You'd better come in or you'll disturb Cass again.' She stood back and allowed her in. 'This way.' She led her into the sitting room and gestured towards the sofa. 'Sit down.'

'Thanks.' Tracy wiped her eyes on the sleeve of her tracksuit and sniffed. 'I'm so sorry . . .'

'Stop saying you're sorry,' Rosie snapped. 'I don't want to hear it.'

Tracy sniffed again.

'Look, this is ridiculous. Does Darren know you're here?'

Tracy began to cry again.

Rosie sighed. 'I'll get you a tissue.' She couldn't find any in the kitchen so she grabbed some kitchen roll instead. It would be a bit rough on Tracy's eyes but at this precise moment she didn't care.

'If you want to talk I suppose you'd better get on with it,' Rosie said handing her the kitchen roll and sitting down in the armchair. 'I must be mad though.'

Tracy mopped the tears from her face. 'Darren's way on business in Cork. He thinks I'm at home in ed. I rang him before I left.'

'Home? At your parent's?' Rosie asked in confusion.

'No – home. Our home. In Sandycove.'

The penny dropped with a resounding clunk. arren hadn't left Tracy at all – he was lying through is teeth. Rosie could feel her face drain and her head vim. She hoped she wasn't going to faint.

'Rosie? Rosie?'

'Sorry, what were you saying?'

'He'll go ape shit if he finds out I've been here. But had to know . . . to find out for myself. I get the feeling is mind is elsewhere half the time. Is he, Rosie? What o you think? You know him better than anyone.'

'Is he what?'

'Seeing someone else?'

'How would I know? I can't believe you're asking ie this. I think you should leave.'

'But I have to know! I have to!' Tracy began to cry ;ain.

Rosie sighed. She was completely exhausted and is whole scene was like something out of a bad ountry-and-western song. Dolly Parton had a lot to iswer for. She stood up. 'I'm sorry, I can't help you. ou'll have to go.'

Tracy looked up, her eyes full of tears. 'Rosie, I'm regnant and I'm scared. What if Darren leaves me? m not like you – I'm not strong. I can't go through is on my own. He won't talk about it. He says it'll l be fine, but if he leaves me for someone else . . .'

'Darren knows you're having his baby?'

'Yes.' Tracy nodded.

Rosie sat down again, put her head in her han
and tried to blink back the tears that were gathering
her own eyes. What a mess, she thought to herse
What a fucking mess.

'Rosie? Are you all right?'

'I don't know,' she answered honestly.

'I didn't mean—'

'Tracy, you don't bloody mean anything and frank
it's annoying. Stop saying it, OK. Just shut up!'

'OK,' she whispered.

'I'm sorry, I shouldn't have shouted at you.'

'I should go.'

'Yes, you should.'

'I didn't mean to upset you.'

'What did you mean then?' Rosie demanded. 'W!
are you here?'

Tracy looked her in the eye. 'I know he still lov
you. I'm not completely stupid. I know he's be
seeing you. I've heard him talking to you on the phor
I wanted to know if you still loved him, that's all.'

Rosie steeled her gaze. 'We were married for yea
we have a child – what do *you* think?'

Tracy blanched. 'I . . . I didn't . . .'

'And don't say you didn't mean to break up o
marriage, or you didn't mean to hurt me or to hu
Cass. You have. I'm sure he said that our marria
was over, our sex life was non-existent and that v
argued all the time. But it's the oldest lie in t

ook and I can't believe you were stupid enough to fall
or it.'

Tracy winced. 'But—'

'But nothing! You came here to tell me you're preg-
ant in the hope that I'd keep away from him. You
hought that because I'm a decent person and family
neans something to me that I might let him go. You
vere right there – family means everything to me. But
ou know something, to answer your question, no, I
lon't love him any more. Not after all the lies. I really
lon't. You should never have got involved with him in
he first place. He's not worth it, Tracy, you're more
han welcome to him. He's not good enough for me.
Vou deserve each other. Good riddance to the both of
ou.' She stood up.

'But—'

'I'd like you to leave my house now. And don't
vorry, I won't say anything to Darren about you
oming here.'

'But—'

Rosie pushed her out of the sitting room and into
he hall, both her hands on the woman's shoulders.
Tracy turned towards her.

'I never meant—'

'I hope you and Darren will be very happy – as I
aid, you deserve each other. Now goodbye.'

Tracy glared at her and walked out the door towards
ter car. Only when Rosie heard the car drive away did
he allow herself to move. She took a deep breath. How
ould she have been taken in by Darren for so long?

He was a lying, cheating bastard. And she intended t
tell him exactly what she thought of him. She felt angr
upset yet strangely empowered. If Tracy wasn't suc
an idiot she might even feel sorry for her.

Rosie

The following day Rosie nipped into Anna's for lunch while Rex minded the gallery. As they drank their coffee Anna dropped a bombshell. 'Rosie, you never told me the good news about the house.'

'Excuse me?'

'You know – about selling your old house. I can't believe Cha Cha's daughter will be living there – what a coincidence. Conor told me. He was talking to Cha Cha yesterday.'

Rosie looked blankly at her friend. 'I'm sorry but I have no idea what you're talking about.'

Realization dawned on Anna. 'But they bought it several weeks ago. Did Darren not tell you?'

'No. I'm confused. Are you talking about our house in Glenageary?'

'Yes. At least I think so. The four-bedroom one beside Rathdown School?'

'That's it, all right. And you're saying Darren sold it?'

Anna nodded. 'To Cha Cha's daughter Cleo and he
husband. It was a private sale apparently. They paid
tidy sum for it too – a cool one million euro. Did h
not discuss it with you?'

'No.'

'I'm sorry, love, I didn't mean to give you such
shock. I presumed Darren . . .'

'Are you sure they've bought it? Maybe they're jus
in negotiations with Darren at the moment.'

'No, apparently Cha Cha's daughter has sold he
own house and they are moving to Glenageary in tw
weeks. I'm sorry, I don't know what to say.'

'It's not your fault. I'm glad you told me.' Rosi
thought for a minute. 'I need to check the ban
accounts. If Darren has sold the house the proceed
should be in our joint savings account. I haven't see
a recent statement. Maybe he just forgot to tell me.'

'Maybe,' Anna said doubtfully. 'You never know.'

Rosie sighed. 'It's unlikely, isn't it? Listen, I have t
go.'

'I understand. I'll ring you later to see what's hap
pened. I'm here if you need me, remember that.'

'Thanks.' Rosie gulped down the last of her coffe
and stood up. Anna saw her out. As soon as Rosie g
back to Rose Cottage she picked up the phone an
dialled Ulster Bank in Dun Laoire. 'This is Rosi
O'Grady and I'd like to speak to Eoin O'Neill pleas
It's urgent.'

The manager came on the line almost immediatel

'Eoin, it's Rosie O'Grady.'

'How are you, Rosie?'

'Fine. I need you to check our bank accounts – mine ɪd Darren's.'

'I can certainly check yours, but I'm not sure I ɪn . . .'

She cut to the chase. 'Eoin, Darren has sold our ɪouse without telling me and I'm worried. I have no ɪea what he's done with the money. I need your help please.'

The line was silent for a few seconds. 'I can check see if he's made a large deposit in his own account ɪt I can't give you any details.'

'I understand. Thank you.'

'Hold the line and I'll be back to you in one minute. ɪ be as quick as I can.'

She scribbled on the cover of a Viking Direct ɪtionery catalogue as she waited nervously. Eoin was ɪe to his word.

'There have been no large deposits in any of the ʳcounts, Rosie – your joint account and Darren's ɪrrent and deposit accounts included. I'm sorry.'

'Thank you for checking,' she whispered.

'I'd suggest you ring your lawyer,' he said kindly. ɪnd sooner rather than later.'

Rosie put down the receiver and stared into space. ʰat the hell had Darren done with one million euro? ɪe was now starting to worry. She'd throttle him for ɪtting her through this. Her heart was thumping in ʳr chest and her palms felt cold and clammy. Darren ɪd taken advantage of her again, but this time she ɪasn't going to let him get away with it. She'd had ɪough, it was time for her to take control.

'Hi, Polly, is Darren there?' Rosie asked the rece
tionist at Diffney's Estate Agents.

'No, he's out of the office.'

'Can you tell me where he is, please? He's n
answering his mobile.'

There was a brief pause.

'Please. It's important.'

Polly was torn. Darren had specifically asked h
never to give his whereabouts to either his ex-wife
his girlfriend, Tracy. She'd always thought this w
slightly iffy, especially as it was common knowled;
that he'd had affairs with at least three colleagues
the office. He'd even tried it on with her more th;
once – not that she'd go near him, smarmy bastard.

'He's holding an auction at the office in Ballsbridg
she said finally.

'For which property?'

'Fern Glen on Killiney Hill. Eddie Irvine's place. I
due to start at twelve.'

'Thanks, Polly.'

She put down the phone and sat thinking. After
while a plan began to form in her head. She smiled
herself – it was perfect, just perfect. She was goir
to fight back – to hit him where it really hurt.

She picked up the receiver again. 'Are you OK
your own this afternoon, Dad? There's something
have to do in town.'

Rosie slipped into the back of the Ballsbridge auctic
room and stood against the wall. The place was pack(

to the gills. Fern Glen was a huge Victorian house perched on the side of Killiney Hill, on five acres of prime real estate. It had stunning views of Killiney Bay and with such a glamorous owner had attracted some serious attention from the media and the punters alike. She'd read all about it in the *Irish Times* Property Supplement and knew that this would be the most important auction of the year for Diffney's. She adjusted her dark glasses, which were pinching the bridge of her nose. She was just in time. Darren was about to step onto the platform. She watched nervously as he scanned the room.

Good, she said to herself. He hasn't noticed me. In dark glasses and a dark pink beret, borrowed from Cass's room, he was unlikely to. Besides, he'd never been the most perceptive of men.

Rosie felt excited and terrified simultaneously. She had no idea whether she'd have the guts to go through with her plan.

Darren cleared his throat and began. 'Welcome, ladies and gentlemen, to the auction of Fern Glen, one of the most spectacular properties to come onto our books in recent years. At the back of the room is my colleague Tom Stevens, and to my right is Rita Connors – both will be assisting me. My name is Darren O'Grady and I'll be your auctioneer today. And now I'm going to start the bidding at one million euro. Do I have any offers at one million euro?'

A tall man in a three-piece suit who was sitting in the back row raised his hand.

'Someone's solicitor,' the woman beside Rosie whispered to her.

Rosie smiled at her and nodded.

'Do I have one million and two hundred thousand euro, anyone?'

A woman in a red suit sitting in the middle of the crowd nodded her head.

'Another solicitor,' said Rosie's new friend.

'One million four hundred thousand euro?' asked Darren.

Another hand was raised.

Rosie watched and listened carefully to the heated bidding, which was proving difficult as the women beside her was keeping up a running commentary.

'Three million.' The woman whistled softly. 'A builder, no, an artist, definitely an artist. He has some sort of paint or plaster on his hands. But even a builder wouldn't have that sort of money.'

'Do I have any more bids?'

Darren studied the room carefully.

'Three million euro ... going once ... going twice ...' – he raised the gravel – 'Going—'

'Three million two hundred thousand euro,' Rosie said distinctly.

The woman beside her gasped audibly.

All eyes were on her. Rosie felt sure Darren would recognize her now. But his eyes lingered on her for only a few split seconds. He was seeing euro signs, she decided, not people.

'Three million and two hundred thousand euro from the lady at the back. Do I have any more bids, ladies and gentlemen?' He looked at the man in the front. The man shook his head. 'Selling Fern Glen at three million two hundred thousand euro. Going once . . .'

Rosie held her breath.

'Going twice . . .'

She raised her hand to her head and whipped off the beret.

'Going three times. Sold!' As Darren brought down the hammer she removed her dark glasses.

'It's for my husband,' she said loudly. 'He'll be paying for it from his offshore account.'

Darren stared at her and his face drained instantly. 'Rosie! What are you doing?'

She ignored him and strode towards the door. The room went deathly quiet.

Darren's colleague Tom was standing by the door and recognized her instantly. He was flabbergasted. 'Rosie, you can't just walk out. You have to—'

'I don't *have* to do anything any more.' She smiled. 'Bye, Tom.'

'Rosie! Rosie!' she could hear Tom's voice joined by Darren's and she smiled to herself. 'Come back. You can't do this!' She ran out the door, into the hall, past the astonished receptionist and towards the front door.

'I bet that's one of Eddie Irvine's ex-girlfriends getting her revenge on him,' the woman who'd been standing beside Rosie said loudly. 'Poor girl.'

'Shouldn't we try and stop her?' a man asked.

'Na!' the woman said. 'He probably deserves it.'

Once outside she jumped in her car, cunningly parked in the managing director's slot, facing outwards for a quick getaway, started the engine and beeped the horn at the pedestrians on the pavement in front of her. She could see Tom and Darren running into the hall in her rear-view mirror.

'Come on, come on,' she muttered, willing the traffic to stop and let her pull out.

As Darren sprinted out the door and towards her she spotted a gap, slammed her foot down on the accelerator and sped off, leaving him staring after her, his face like thunder.

As she drove down the N11, once she ascertained that she wasn't being followed, she started to laugh. Darren's face when he realized who he'd sold the property to. She was dying to tell Kim all about it. Her sister wouldn't believe her ears. She half expected to be stopped by the Garda, alerted by Darren, but by Donnybrook she began to relax. She'd got away with it. And now Darren would have to pick up the pieces – for a change.

'You did what?' asked Kim. Rosie hadn't been able to wait to tell her. She'd pulled into the side of the dual carriageway after Foxrock and rung her on her mobile. 'I don't believe you! Darren's going to kill you.'

'I know.' Her mobile bleeped. 'He's trying to get through to me now.'

'Are you going to talk to him?'

'Not bloody likely.'

'What will happen to the house?'

'It'll get sold to the underbidder. If they still want it.'

'Will you get arrested or fined or something?'

'No. Darren will have a lot of questions to answer though. He didn't even recognize his own wife.'

'I bet it'll be on the news.'

'No it won't!' Rosie laughed. 'They have better things to be reporting on than house auctions.'

'I'm not so sure.'

Kim was right. Today FM picked up on it almost immediately, followed by RTE and 98 FM. That evening and the following day it was all over the newspapers. 'A leading Dublin auctioneer failed to recognize his own wife at the sale of the exclusive Fern Glen house in Killiney' (*Irish Times*). 'Revenge is Sweet Says Scorned Wife Rosie' (*Irish Mirror*). 'Wife Says Husband Will Pay for Affair – Over Three Million Euro' (*Irish Independent*).

Unbeknownst to Rosie, several journalists had been at the auction hoping to catch Eddie Irvine. In the absence of the infamous racing driver, they'd settled on this bit of scandal instead. Scorned wives always made good copy. Especially when they were as pretty as this Rosie O'Grady. Of course, the snappers had all been asleep when she'd made her swift exit and the best they could do were photos of the irate ex-husband. And he was pretty irate. He was calling her all sorts of unpublishable names. The receptionist, Hilda, had been most helpful though. The *Irish Mirror* ran an exclusive interview with her – My Affair with Love-Rat Auctioneer – with lots of cleavage shots. Hilda rather fancied a new career as a glamour model.

Darren had been quiet after his barrage of phone

calls to Rosie's mobile directly following the auction. She'd expected him to camp outside her house that night and yell at her at the very least, but it was all ominously still.

She couldn't sleep all night for thinking about it and rang Polly first thing in the morning.

'Hi, Polly, is Darren there?'

She figured ringing him at work was probably safer than ringing his mobile. He couldn't swear as much at work, she hoped.

'He's in a meeting with the partners,' said Polly. 'I'd say he'll be there all morning. They weren't exactly thrilled with the press coverage of the auction.'

'Will he be fired?'

'I wouldn't think so. Having affairs left, right and centre is hardly a sackable offence.' Polly drew in her breath. 'Oh, shit, Rosie, I'm sorry. I shouldn't have said that.'

'It's all right.' Rosie leant against the wall. She'd read all about his torrid extra-curricular love life in the papers so it was no longer news to her. 'What happened with Fern Glen? Did they sell it in the end?'

'Yes, to the underbidder.'

'Good. I hoped that would happen.'

'Rosie?'

'Yes?'

'Well done. I really admire you. We all do. He didn't deserve you.'

'Thanks.'

'And did you see the *Irish Mirror* this morning?'

'No, why?'

'They'll have forgotten all about the auction by this afternoon, you'll see. Hilda's been busy. She only had an affair with Dick Bailey, the minister. They gave her twenty thousand euro for the story apparently. Everyone's up in arms. You should have heard *Morning Ireland*. We were all glued to it in here. Who would have thought – Hilda was so quiet.'

'You have to watch the quiet ones,' Rosie said. 'They're the worst.' Like Tracy Mullen, she thought to herself.

Polly was right. By the following day Dick Bailey had been embroiled in a storm of controversy as his wife threw him out of the family house and spilled the rest of the beans – that her darling husband had four separate offshore accounts bolstered by 'donations' from several leading Irish builders and businessmen. This news hadn't made his party very happy and he'd been forced to resign with immediate effect. The 'love-rat auctioneer' story paled into insignificance beside this new revelation for which Rosie was eternally grateful. She felt like sending flowers to Hilda but decided it would be a little OTT. Polly had kept her up to date with the goings-on in the Diffney's office. Darren had been taken off residential sales in Dun Laoire and had been made letting agent in the Rathmines/Rathgar office instead – notorious flat land for students. Polly said he was devastated by the decision and was thinking about leaving the company. And to cap it all, several officials from the tax office had grilled him for several hours about his offshore account. All in all, it wasn't looking good for Darren.

Rosie had had a barrage of phone calls after the story had appeared in the papers – everyone from Cha Cha to Philly had rung to give her their good wishes and to say 'Well done.'

Kim had been staying with her since the day after the auction and Rose was glad of the company. Luckily Cass was too young to understand any of the snippets she overheard. True to form, Kim had arrived with a huge bag of goodies for her niece, new Disney videos, a new Barbie and a pair of pink glitter shoes that she'd found in the Avoca Handweaver's shop. Cass was in seventh heaven.

Anna, Martina, Conor and Rory had all rung to give her their support, and Rex and Julia had called in too. But the most surprising phone call of all had come from Leo.

'Hi, Rosie. It's Leo.'

'Leo? How are you?'

'Fine, how are you? I've been reading all about you in the papers. I just wanted to check that you're all right.'

'That's really kind of you. I was in shock for a while I think, but I'm getting back to normal now.'

'That was a brave thing you did – bidding at the auction like that. It can't have been easy.'

'No, it wasn't. But I was so angry with him I had to

do something. Some people cut up clothes, I bid at auctions, I guess.'

'I know how it feels to be betrayed like that.'

'Really?' Rosie was taken aback.

'My wife left me for another man a few years ago. I did nothing, except feel sorry for myself. I felt so angry and upset – I didn't know what to do.'

She wasn't sure what to say. 'I didn't know you'd been married. You never said.'

'I know. We broke up badly and she refused to let me see my daughter. They live in Paris now.'

'I'm sorry, I had no idea.'

'That's OK. I've come to terms with it, although it still hurts sometimes. But things are looking up. I've been talking to my ex-wife, Chantal, on the phone over the last few weeks. It hasn't been easy but we've managed to sort a few things out. My daughter, Fleur, is coming over in a few weeks to visit for the first time. She's about Cass's age. Maybe they can play together.'

'How long will she be here for?'

'Only four days. Chantal is staying with a friend of hers in Dublin.'

'You must be excited.'

'I am. But nervous too.'

'Nervous. Why?'

'I haven't seen Fleur for three years. She probably won't even recognize me.'

'Maybe not. But hopefully she'll have seen photographs and might remember something. Anyway, you're still her dad, whatever's happened. Cass still adores her dad, regardless. She always will.'

'Are you going to let him see her after all the trouble he's caused?'

Rosie sighed. 'I'd love to completely cut him out of both our lives. But that wouldn't be fair on Cass. He's still her father, whatever he's done.'

'You've got a big heart. Not everyone would be as generous.'

'Thanks.'

'We have even more in common now and if you want to talk about Darren I'm a good listener . . . I was wondering . . .'

'Yes?'

'Would you like to meet up? It doesn't have to be for dinner or anything.'

'Leo, I'd love to have dinner with you. And I'm so sorry about the way things have happened. About the ball and everything. When Darren arrived . . .'

Leo stopped her. 'Rosie, that's all in the past now. There's no need to explain. Why don't we both start all over again? How about dinner tomorrow night?'

'Are you sure?'

'Yes! Positive. What do you think?'

'I could do with a night out and my sister, Kim, is staying with us at the moment. I'm sure she'd babysit. I'll agree on one condition.'

'Name it.'

'That we don't talk about Darren. Not even for one nanosecond.'

Leo laughed. 'Agreed. I'll collect you at eight. I'll book somewhere local.'

'Great, see you then.'

'Who was that?' asked Kim, walking into the sitting room.

'Leo.' Rosie smiled. 'Can you look after Cass tomorrow night? He asked me out for dinner.'

'Of course I can.' Kim looked at her sister carefully. 'Are you sure you're ready?'

'For what?'

'You know.'

'I don't. What?'

'For another relationship.'

'Kim, I'm going out to dinner with the guy, not marrying him. It's just a bit of fun.'

'Sorry, ignore me. I'm being overprotective. Anyway, he seems nice.'

Rosie put her arm around Kim and gave her a hug. 'He is nice and I'm glad you care, it means a lot to me.'

'Mum, how are you?' Rosie leant over and kissed her on the cheek. 'Where's Dad?'

'He decided not to come. Conor invited him to play golf this evening. You'll see him in the gallery tomorrow anyway, won't you?'

'Yes. Come in. Would you like some coffee?'

'No, dear. Otherwise I'll never sleep.'

'How about a glass of wine?'

'I shouldn't.'

'Go on,' Rosie cajoled, leading her into the kitchen. 'There's a bottle of white open in the fridge.'

'Well, in that case.'

Rosie opened the fridge and took out the chilled

Sarah Webb

bottle. She took two glasses out of the cupboard, placed them on the table and began to pour.

'That's enough for me!' said Julia, putting her hand over the glass. 'I have to drive.'

'OK, Mum.'

'Where's Kim?'

'She went home this evening. Greg was missing her.'

'And Cass?'

'In bed. She's wiped out from her summer camp. I tried to keep her up but she was exhausted.'

'Not to worry. I'll call in and see her over the weekend if that suits.'

'That would be nice.' Rosie, who had been hovering at the kitchen counter, sat down.

'There's something I wanted to say to you, Rosie.'

'Yes?'

'I know this has been one hell of a year for you but you've come through with flying colours. I know I haven't always made things easy for you but I want to try and help more. I'd like to mind Cass after school in the afternoons if you'll let me.'

'But what about your cultural club and your lunches?'

'Culture, smulture! I've had enough of those damn women to last me a lifetime. All they talk about is money and clothes.'

'Not art and culture?'

'No. More's the pity. Much as I tried to deny it, we spent most of our time shopping and gossiping.'

Rosie smiled. Rex had been right.

'I'm bored with it all,' continued Julia. 'Besides, I

want to spend some real time with my granddaughter before she's all grown up. I want to do something real. Looking after Cass will be real.'

'Very real,' Rosie agreed. 'If you're sure, I'll let Anna know. She was holding a place for her in afternoon care.'

'Yes, absolutely.'

'Thanks.' Rosie put her hand on her mum's. 'She'll love it.'

'And I will too,' Julia said. 'Thank *you*.'

Martina
Three months later

Rosie gazed out the Redwood House window, deep in thought. In the past three months, she had become firm friends with Anna and Martina. She and Martina had lunch at least once a week in the Redwood coffee shop and Martina had even babysat for Cass several times when Rosie had been out with Leo. Martina had asked Rosie and Anna to be bridesmaids at her wedding and Rosie had agreed instantly, delighted and flattered to be included in the wedding party.

'Are you both ready?' Nita asked Anna and Rosie.

Rosie came back down to earth. 'Yes.' She smiled at Nita.

'I think so,' said Anna. 'But this back bit seems a little loose. Can you pin it for me?'

'Of course.' Nita opened a safety pin and attached Anna's sari to the little gold top she was wearing underneath. 'That should hold.'

Anna moved her shoulders gently. 'That feels more secure. Thanks.'

'You both look beautiful,' Nita said. 'Martina will be so pleased. And I'm looking forward to introducing you both to the rest of the Patel and Dubey families from Bombay. You met some of them last night.'

'They were great fun,' said Rosie as she pulled at the front of her own dark pink and silver sari. 'They really enjoy their dancing, don't they?'

Nita nodded. 'We all love a good party. It's a pity Mum couldn't be here, she would have loved to have see Martina getting married.'

'She's here in spirit,' said Anna. 'I can feel it.'

Nita squeezed Anna's shoulder gently. 'Thank you, my dear. Now we'd better go and find your escorts. Are they still next door?'

'I think so,' said Anna. 'Let me just check.' She walked out of Conor's room and knocked on Rory's door. The wedding party were all getting changed in Redwood, even Martina, who was currently in Conor's en-suite bathroom. Cindy's friend Ella, who had done such a good job for the photo shoot, had made the bride look like an exotic Eastern princess, all sultry gold and chocolate-brown eyes, dark red lips and a dusting of gold powder on her shoulders and chest.

Conor opened the door.

'Hey! It's Laurence of Arabia,' Anna said, grinning. 'You look great, Conor.' He was wearing white trousers and a matching white mandarin-collared jacket with delicate black embroidery along the cuffs and collar. She kissed him. 'Oops, lipstick.' She wiped his cheek with her fingers.

'And you look stunning. That sari really suits you. You should wear them more often.'

She laughed. 'I don't think they're quite the thing for work. Besides, I don't know how Indian women cope. The bit on my shoulder keeps falling down. I had to get Nita to pin it for me 'cause it was driving me mad.'

'Is Martina nearly ready?'

She nodded. 'Almost. Ten more minutes or so.'

'I guess we'd better get moving then.' He called into the room. 'Gentlemen, are you ready?'

'One second,' Rory shouted back.

'I'll come and get you and Rosie when we're ready.'

As Anna walked back into the room where the other women were, she smiled.

'Anna!' squealed Martina. She was sitting on the side of the bed in a light blue basque, suspenders and stockings. 'Close the door. Someone will see.'

'You'd better get dressed, the boys are nearly ready,' warned Anna.

'Scat, so.' Martina jumped off the bed. 'I don't want either of you to see me in my dress before I come down those stairs. Mum can help me get ready.'

'Are you sure you don't need us?' Rosie asked in disappointment. She was dying to see the dress.

'Yes! Now get going.'

There was a knock at the door. 'That's Conor,' Anna explained.

'Shit!' Martina said. 'Wait!' She ran into the en-suite and closed the door firmly behind her.

'Ready, girls?' asked Conor as Anna opened the door. Anna nodded and she and Rosie walked out.

Rory whistled. 'You both look beautiful.'

'You don't look too bad yourself,' Rosie said, admiring the black silk Indian suit with cream embroidery. 'The suit is only fabulous.'

'Martina's uncle Kishan had it made for me in India,' said Rory.

Leo put out his arm for Rosie. 'May I escort you down the stairs?'

'Please do.' They'd got on swimmingly over the last few months and although she wasn't ready for another serious relationship yet, Leo would certainly be the main contender when she was. He was wearing a white suit similar to Conor's and it really suited his tall, slim frame.

'How's Martina?' asked Rory as they all walked down the stairs.

'That would be telling,' Anna said. She patted his arm. 'Nervous but fine,' she whispered.

'Thanks,' he said.

As Anna, Rory, Conor, Rosie and Leo approached the ballroom they could hear the sounds of people enjoying themselves. Martina and Rory had had the 'legal' wedding in a registry office in Wicklow the previous week but this was the real wedding celebration. All their local friends were there, and family members from both sides had travelled from as far off as New Zealand to be with them on this special day. The extended Patel family, including Granny Patel's brother Kishan, who had made a remarkable recovery and had insisted on travelling, were all present, the women in bright and colourful saris, the men in all manner of Indian and Western suits. The room was decorated with huge vases filled to bursting with stargazer lilies, Martina's favourite flowers. Every flat surface was covered with white tulle and topped with simple arrangements of flowers and white candles. Lengths of silk in all colours of the rainbow hung from the ceiling in elaborate swags. Smartly dressed waiting staff mingled among the guests, topping up champagne glasses. The atmosphere was electric. At the far end of the large room there was a cream silk canopy covering the area where the wedding ceremony would be conducted. Gold chairs stood stiffly facing the canopy, waiting patiently for their occupants.

Upstairs, Martina was sitting on the bed again.

'I feel sick, Mum. What am I doing?'

Nita smiled. 'You'll be fine. Every bride feels like this on her wedding day.'

'Did you?'

Nita nodded. 'Of course. It was even more difficult for me as your granny wasn't exactly thrilled with Thomas.'

'Only because he wasn't Indian.'

'Yes. But it was a great disappointment for her.'

'She got over it.'

'I guess she did. It's a pity she's not here today. She would have been so proud of you.'

'She's here, Mum. I can feel it.'

'That's what Anna said.' Nita smiled. 'And I think

you're right.' She looked up at the ceiling. 'Hello, Mum. I love you.'

Martina laughed. 'You're losing it.'

'Just trying to make you smile. And it worked.' She looked at her watch. 'It's quarter past four. Time to go downstairs, I think. I told Conor to have everyone waiting in the hall for ten past. Your father is probably outside this door, waiting.' Just as she said this she heard a discreet knock.

'Tell him I'm not even dressed yet,' said Martina.

'We'll be ten minutes,' Nita explained to Thomas.

'Take your time. I'll wait out here,' Thomas said, smiling at his wife.

'You'd better hurry.' Nita came back in, quickly opened the large mahogany wardrobe and took out the light blue silk dress. She removed the protective plastic sheath. 'Here you are.' She handed Martina the dress.

Martina stepped into it carefully and Nita fastened the tiny buttons. She then draped the matching light blue 'veil' over her daughter's head. When her mother had finished arranging the veil, Martina slipped her feet into the kitten-heeled slippers.

'Stand back and let me have a look at you.' Nita had tears in her eyes. Her daughter looked magnificent. The dress was perfect. Martina had designed it herself – a mix of traditional Indian and modern Western wedding dress, with a sweeping full skirt and a divine little fitted top with sari over-the-shoulder detail. The matching veil in the same material edged with silver embroidery completed the outfit. All Nita could do was nod and smile.

'Thanks, Mum,' Martina said, close to tears hersel
She put her hand on the handle and opened the doo
'Ready, Dad.' She stepped out and took his arm. Sh
gave her other arm to her mother. It wasn't traditiona
in the West or in the East but it was how Martin
wanted it. As they walked down the wide marbl
stairway together there was a collective gasp from th
crowd below. Suddenly someone began to clap and
within seconds the whole hall resounded with the nois
of over a hundred hands. At the bottom of the stair
Rory was waiting with Conor and Leo. He gazed uj
at his bride-to-be and smiled. He felt as if his hear
would break – she looked so beautiful.

'That was an amazing service,' said Rosie wiping awa
yet another tear. 'I've never seen anything like it.'
Leo patted her hand. 'I know. Let's join the others
There's drinks in the drawing room now while they se
this room up for the meal.'
'Hi, Rosie.' Cindy and Makedde waved over from
the window as they walked into the drawing room
'Wasn't that a great service? You look great. Love th
sari.'
'Thanks.'
'Do you know she asked me to be manager of th
shop?'
Rosie nodded. 'And what have you decided? '
'To say yes. She needs me. It will be a lot of worl
but I'm ready for it. Since the *Irish Times* piece Martina'
been so inundated with requests for Kati G clothes tha

her mind hasn't really been on the shop. Even Brown Thomas want her clothes. She's going to go into designing full-time. She's had several offers for backing too.'

'That's brilliant for both of you. Congratulations.'

'Thanks.'

'And how are you, Makedde?'

'Good. I've started my veterinary studies in UCD and I'm also working part-time for Leo in the wildlife park.'

'You must be very busy.'

'Busy but happy.' He put his arm around Cindy. 'I have everything I could ever want.'

Rosie smiled. 'That's lovely. And you both deserve it. Well done.'

Just then Cass ran over. 'Mum!' she threw her arms around Rosie. Kim followed behind looking a little sheepish. 'She wanted to see you in your sari. I'm sorry, I'm a pushover. We won't stay long.'

'That's fine,' Rosie said. 'Don't worry about it. I'm sure Martina won't mind. Ollie's here with Moyra somewhere too.'

Within minutes Cass had found another girl to play with, leaving Kim to talk to Rosie. Leo had gone to fetch drinks from the bar area in the hall.

'Are you enjoying the day?' asked Kim.

'Very much.'

'And how's your lovely escort?'

'Fine, thank you very much. And please take that filthy grin off your face.'

'Only asking. There's Anna. Let's go over and say hi.'

'Hi, Kim.' Anna kissed her on the cheek. 'Nice to see you.'

'And you. Love the sari.'

'Thanks. I've been getting nothing but compliments all day, I may have to buy one at this rate. Did you bring your boyfriend?'

'Greg? No, he's got some sort of match on today.'

'I haven't seen you for ages. We must arrange dinner some evening and catch up properly.'

Kim smiled. 'That would be nice. I think Conor and Greg would get on well. And maybe Rosie and Leo could come too.'

Rosie threw Kim a look.

'And Martina and Rory.' Anna laughed. 'That would be quite an event! We'd need to have it here to fit everyone – my table at home isn't big enough. I'm sure Conor wouldn't mind, as long as I did the cooking.'

'Sounds great.'

'As soon as Martina and Rory are back from their honeymoon I'll give you a ring.'

'Excellent!' Kim beamed. 'And I believe that is Leo looking for me and Rosie at the far end of the room. We'd better put him out of his misery. If I don't see you later, have a great evening.'

'We will. See you soon.'

'There you are, girls,' Leo handed them their drinks. 'I thought I'd lost you both.'

'We were talking to Anna,' said Rosie.

'I'll check on Cass,' Kim said after glancing out the

window. 'She was playing on the steps outside with Aliya Patel but I'll just make sure.'

'I can go,' Rosie offered.

Kim put her hand up. 'No, you stay. I'm not even supposed to be here. As soon as I've found her we'll go. I'm sure your dinner is soon and I don't want to get in the way. I'll say my goodbyes.' She kissed her sister and Leo on the cheeks. 'Behave yourself,' she whispered in Rosie's ear.

'No intention of it,' Rosie whispered back.

Later that evening Anna and Conor were dancing to the band, arms draped around each other, bodies moving to the gentle strains of 'Moon River'.

'I wish this wedding could go on for ever,' said Anna. 'Everyone's enjoying themselves so much.'

'Are you?'

'Enjoying myself?'

'Yes.'

'Very much. I have a fantastic dance partner – what more could I ask for?'

'A wedding of your own. We should really set a date and pick a venue.'

Anna was silent for a few seconds. She'd been stalling a little but Conor was right. 'Yes. We should. How about New Year's Eve? I can't think of a better way to celebrate the new year. A quiet ceremony followed by dinner and dancing for close friends and family.'

'At Davey's Boathouse? The owner owes me a favour, I'm sure I could persuade him.'

'Exactly. At Davey's Boathouse.'

'Where I first fell in love with you,' said Conor. 'My beautiful Anna.'

She was speechless. She pulled him closer and swayed against him to the music. 'Thank you,' she whispered.

'For what?'

'For being so wonderful.'

'It's nothing,' he kissed her tenderly, 'really.'

'We saw that,' Rory shouted over from the other side of the dance floor.

Martina smiled at him. 'Leave them be. It's nice to see them getting on so well.'

'You're right.'

'Not to mention that you should be giving me your total, undivided attention.'

'You're right again.' He kissed her passionately.

'And you're giving out about your father, Rory Storey?' Martina said as she came up for breath.

He kissed her again. 'Yes, I am, Mrs Dunlop.'

Rosie

don't believe you!' Kim grinned. 'Tracy's pregnant ith twins?'

Rosie nodded and shifted her bottom on the wooden arden bench. They were sitting in her garden, enjoying he last few rays of late-September sun while Cass layed in the sandpit under the oak tree. 'Polly in iffney's told me. She rings me whenever there's any ossip. Tracy has known for ages apparently but only ld Darren this week.'

'I don't believe you. That's hysterical. Darren must livid.'

'No kidding. He hates babies. And twins will be ouble trouble.'

'Really?'

Rosie nodded. 'He wouldn't have anything to do ith Cass until she was six months old. He wouldn't ld her or give her bottles or bath her. I did all the ght feeds and nappy changes myself.'

'No! You never told me.'

'I was too embarrassed. I didn't want you to thi
badly of him.' She grinned. 'Stupid, I know. He t
me he'd had a bad experience with his little broth
when he was two – he dropped him or something
think. Anyway, Darren said he'd had a baby pho
ever since.'

'And you believed him?'

'Have to admit I did. What a fool.'

'It wasn't your fault, he was a good liar.'

'He was all right. And he's still at it apparen
According to Polly he's having a fling with some g
from accounts and she's only nineteen.'

Kim snorted. 'Yuck! You're well rid of him.'

'Aren't I just? And my lawyer, Brian, said that
separation agreement is ready to be signed. Appare
Darren has agreed to most of our terms. Once he's p
back all the tax he owes to the government and I
given me my share of the house proceeds he wo
have a cent to call his own.'

'Serves him right, I have no sympathy for that slea
ball. Anyway, enough about him. How are things w
you and Leo?'

Rosie smiled. 'Wonderful, couldn't be better. We
still taking it one day at a time, which suits us bo
Actually he's coming over later with Fleur.'

'Fleur?'

'His daughter. The one who lives in Pa
remember?'

'Sorry, you did tell me. What age is she again?'

'Five – a little older than Cass but I'm sure the
get on.'

'I'm glad everything's working out for you.'

'Thanks. What about yourself and Greg? Mum said you had some news and that you wanted to tell me yourself. You're not getting married, are you?'

'No! Nothing like that. We've just put down a deposit on a new house in Greystones.'

'That's brilliant! I didn't know you were thinking about moving.'

'We weren't really to tell the truth. But we were visiting some friends of Greg's and the house down the road from them was for sale – this beautiful cottage with a little stream running through the back garden. You'll love it, Rosie. So we decided to view it and I guess we both fell in love with it instantly. I think we'll be happy there.'

'How big is it?'

'Big enough – three bedrooms.'

'Three!' Rosie grinned. 'Now what would you and Greg be wanting with three bedrooms. You're not thinking of having—'

'No! Not at the moment anyway.'

'But you are thinking about—'

'Rosie! Would you stop? Yes, we're thinking of getting married and starting a family. Will you please drop it?'

'That's all I wanted to know. I'll gladly leave you alone now.' Rosie looked around the garden. It had all but stopped flowering but she spotted one lone pink rose braving it out forlornly. 'Everything's coming up roses,' she murmured softly to herself. Cass looked over, waved at her and smiled. She waved back.

'Did you say something?' asked Kim.

'No.' Rosie said, putting her head on her sister's shoulder. 'Nothing at all.'